Praise for Fiona

Bet Against Me

"Riley writes with purpose and ease, which makes for a compelling reading experience. She adds enough details to the settings to make them come to life without getting lost in the details. Her use of humor brings another dimension to the story, adding bonus points for sharp dialogue…This is a super sexy and fun read that hits all the right notes."—*Lesbian Review*

A Christmas Miracle (in *All I Want for Christmas*)

"I enjoyed all three stories and I love how they fit together. They're very different, both in tone and level of heat (Fiona Riley has not been dubbed Queen of Steam by accident) and balance each other really well…*A Christmas Miracle* is light and sexy and the perfect way to conclude this anthology."— *Lez Review Books*

"Fiona Riley knows how to get me every damn time! Talk about sexy, and honestly, she writes the best dialogue without a doubt. I weirdly get her characters and feel like between the sass and the sarcastic sexy banter, I'd get on with them exceptionally well. What a book to finish on!"—*Les Rêveur*

Not Since You

"Riley strikes an impressive balance between steamy sex scenes and sweeping romance in this tender second-chance-at-love story…Riley endearingly captures the growth of Charlotte and Lexi's relationship from when they were in high school to when they are reunited as adults. Readers will root for this well-matched couple."—*Publishers Weekly*

Not Since You "is well written and hot. So hot."—*Jude in the Stars*

"This book has all the elements of a perfect romance—beautiful characters seeking to rekindle a lost love with heat and passion under sunny skies and starry nights on a cruise ship traveling to a tropical paradise."—*The Lesbian Book Blog*

"[A]n entertaining story with a lot of sexy scenes. Not surprisingly, this would be a good beach vacation read. I recommend to those who are interested in romance, second chances, vacationing, cruises, bartending, friends who collude, dirty talk, sexual tension, and packing (not luggage)."—*Bookvark*

"This book is exceptional lesbian fiction, and the characters (especially Charlotte) were swoon-worthy…honestly, I think I hugged my Kindle at one point…This is to date the sexiest book Fiona Riley has ever written and let me tell you, she has written some of the sexiest lesbian fiction scenes to date."—*Les Rêveur*

Media Darling

"A great mix of characters, some great laughs, and a good romance. A great well written read that was emotional and fun."—*Kat Adams, Bookseller (QBD Books, Australia)*

"{A] sweet romance with the addition of a critique of the media role in their portrayal of celebrities. Both main characters are multi-layered with their personalities well defined. Their chemistry is absolutely off the charts…an entertaining, poignant and romantic story with a side of social critique to celebrity culture and the media. Five stars."
—*Lez Review Books*

"I really dig the way Fiona Riley writes contemporary romances because they're sexy and flirty with a whole lot of feelings, and *Media Darling* is no exception."—*The Lesbian Review*

Media Darling "was well-executed and the sex was well-written. I liked both of the characters and the plot held my interest."—*Katie Pierce, Librarian, Hennepin County Library (Minnesota)*

Room Service

"The sexual tension between Olivia and Savannah is combustible and I was hoping with every flirtious moment they would jump each other… [A] sexy summer read."—*Les Rêveur*

"*Room Service* by Fiona Riley is a steamy workplace romance that is all kinds of fabulous…Fiona Riley is so good at writing characters who are extremely likeable, even as they have issues to work through. I was happy to see that the leading ladies in *Room Service* are no exception! They're both fun, sweet, funny, and smart, which is a brilliant combo. They also have chemistry that sizzles almost from the get-go, making it especially fun to watch them grow in ways that are good for them as individuals and as a couple."—*The Lesbian Review*

"*Room Service* is a slow-burn romance written from the point of view of both main characters. Ms. Riley excels at building their chemistry that slowly grows to sizzling hot."—*Lez Review Books*

"Riley is a natural when it comes to delivering the heat between characters and undeniable chemistry."—*Book-A-Mania*

Strike a Match

"Riley balances romance, wit, and story complexity in this contemporary charmer…Readers of all stripes will enjoy this lyrically phrased, deftly plotted work about opposites attracting."—*Publishers Weekly*

"[A] quick-burning romance, with plenty of sex scenes hot enough to set off the alarms."—*RT Book Reviews*

"*Strike a Match* is probably one of the hottest and sexiest books I've read this year…Fiona Riley is one to watch and I will continue to get extremely excited every time I get one of her books to read."
—*Les Rêveur*

"While I recommend all of the books in the Perfect Match series, I especially recommend *Strike a Match*, and definitely in audio if you're at all inclined towards listening to books. Fans of the other two installments will be happy to see their leads again, but you don't have to have read them to pick this one up. It's sweet, hot, and funny, making it a great way to spend a day when you just want to hide away from the world and immerse yourself in a lovely story."—*Smart Bitches, Trashy Books*

"*Strike a Match* is Fiona Riley's best book yet. Whether you're a fan of the other books in the series or you've never read anything by her before, I recommend checking this one out. It's the perfect remedy to a bad day and a great way to relax on a weekend!"—*The Lesbian Review*

"I love this series and Sasha is by far my favourite character yet. I absolutely loved the gritty firefighter details. The romance between Abby and Sasha is perfectly paced and full of wonderful grand gestures, magical dates, and tender, intimate moments."—*Wicked Reads*

"Fiona Riley does a nice job of creating thorny internal and external conflicts for each heroine…I was rooting for Abby and Sasha, not only to be together, but also that both of them would grow and change enough to find a true HEA. The supporting cast of family members, friends, and colleagues is charming and well-portrayed. I'm looking forward to more from Fiona Riley."—*TBQ's Book Palace*

Unlikely Match

"The leads have great chemistry and the author's writing style is very engaging."—*Melina Bickard, Librarian, Waterloo Library (UK)*

"Two strong women that make their way towards each other with a tiny little nudge from some friends, what's not to like?"—*The Reading Penguin's Reviews*

"*Unlikely Match* is super easy to read with its great pacing, character work, and dialogue that's fun and engaging…Whether you've read *Miss Match* or not, *Unlikely Match* is worth picking up. It was the perfect romance to balance out a tough week at work and I'm looking forward to seeing what Fiona Riley has in store for us next."—*The Lesbian Review*

Miss Match

"In this sweet, sensual debut, Riley brings together likable characters, setting them against a colorful supporting cast and exploring their relationship through charming interactions and red-hot erotic scenes… Rich in characterization and emotional appeal, this one is sure to please."—*Publishers Weekly*

"*Miss Match* by Fiona Riley is an adorable romance with a lot of amazing chemistry, steamy sex scenes, and fun dialogue. I can't believe it's the author's first book, even though she assured me on Twitter that it is."—*The Lesbian Review*

"This was a beautiful love story, chock full of love and emotion, and I felt I had a big grin on my face the whole time I was reading it. I adored both main characters as they were strong, independent women with good hearts and were just waiting for the right person to come along and make them whole. I felt I smiled for days after reading this wonderful book."—*Inked Rainbow Reads*

By the Author

Miss Match

Unlikely Match

Strike a Match

Room Service

Media Darling

Not Since You

A Christmas Miracle (In *All I Want for Christmas*)

High Stakes Romances

Bet Against Me

Bet the Farm

Visit us at www.boldstrokesbooks.com

BET THE FARM

by
Fiona Riley

2021

Credits
Editor: Ruth Sternglantz
Production Design: Stacia Seaman
Cover Design by Tammy Seidick

Acknowledgments

Thank you to all the readers and the BSB family out there who supported my decision to venture into this new series. I'm having a blast writing these stories, and if not for your encouragement (and enablement), I'm not sure I would have successfully completed this book during a pandemic. It's been rough for everyone, but I've had the gift of escaping into a HEA or two. Writing relationships and worlds full of love has never felt more important than now. I hope you enjoy this brief escape.

To Ruth Sternglantz: You have the patience of a saint, the gentleness of an angel, and the brain of RBG and Maya Angelou combined. You are strong and sincere and resilient, and you share freely and without expectation of anything in return. You have been a light during these difficult months, and you made writing this book far too easy considering the challenges around us at all times. You are one of my closest friends and greatest confidantes and I know that will never change. You're my favorite (don't tell the others). ;)

To Kris Bryant: I could write all about the ways you help me storyboard or meet my writing goals for the day, but I'll save that for the next book when I can't come up with something more creative to say. For now, I'll say this: Meeting you during this journey has been one of the greatest and most cherished gifts of my life. You're a gift, wrapped in rainbows and unicorn paper. And probably full of donuts.

To Georgia Beers: Thank you for your Polos, your surprise treats, and listening to me vent when life gets so heavy. I'm grateful for you.

To my littles: You bring me so much joy. You're both so magical and lovely and hysterical and beyond sweet. My brilliant, fierce little gingers, I love you so. Thank you for napping midday so I could finish this book.

For Jenn.

There's nothing like writing a series and raising two littles
while living through a pandemic to remind me
that marrying you was still the best decision I ever made.
Thank you for this wonderful family
and for always having my back.

You are my whole world.

CHAPTER ONE

L auren Calloway cheered as another round of champagne bottles emerged, each one opening with a satisfying *pop.*

"To finally winning Realtor of the Year," her best friend Trina Lee said with a raised glass. "I couldn't have done it without all of you."

Lauren looked around The Mirage, the hottest bar in town, at all her closest friends and felt the most at home she'd felt in a long time.

She watched Trina kiss her girlfriend and ex-rival Realtor, Kendall Yates, and she sighed a happy sigh. She was glad her friend had found love in the most unlikely of places. And success in finally achieving her Realtor of the Year title. Trina had worked damn hard for everything she had, and Lauren was happy for her. Even if she was a little jealous she had a girlfriend while Lauren remained woefully single. But they were a fantastic match, and she was excited things were working out between them. Even if that meant she had less alone time with her bestie. Having Kendall join their girls' nights on the couch never felt weird. It was just a little different, that's all. But this week she could really have used some of those old one-on-one times with Trina. She missed that.

"Uh-oh. That's a very serious look, Miss Calloway. Do you have serious things on the mind? Because this is a celebration, and there is no serious allowed at this party. I know because I made the guest list." Trina placed a delicate kiss on her cheek.

"Hmm?" Lauren was still grappling with the major misstep she'd made earlier in the week that cost her what would have been the largest solo deal of her career. Trina had been busy with her own clients and was nervous about the awards ceremony tonight, so Lauren hadn't mentioned her own setback. She didn't want to bring her friend down then, and especially not now on her big night. She'd shelve it for later.

Tonight was Trina's night. "Nothing serious, just thinking about what a wild ride this year has been."

"You're telling me. Never in a million years did I think I'd be here one year ago today." Trina shook her head. "That feels like a lifetime ago."

"I'll say," Lauren agreed. This time last year she was consoling Trina after she lost out on the coveted Realtor of the Year title to no one other than Kendall. That night their boss Ellison Gamble made a bet with Kendall's boss that Trina could outsell Kendall in a high-stakes sales challenge. The sales race had been intense, and somewhere along the way Trina and Kendall had fallen into bed and in love in the process. But not without plenty of drama and tears.

"I know I've told you this a thousand times before, but I would be nowhere without you," Trina said, her expression sincere. "I never would have survived that bet or sorting through my feelings for Kendall without our dish sessions on the couch and your incredible way with curse words."

"Damn right," Lauren said with a smile.

"And that amazing brain of yours." Trina tapped her forehead. "You are so incredible in so many ways, Lau. I never would have sold that penthouse if it wasn't for your fast thinking and outside-of-the-box approach. That country club idea was genius, and I owe that to you."

"Perhaps"—Lauren shrugged—"but you sold that other one all on your own."

Trina grinned. "I did, didn't I?"

"And to Hollywood's new lesbian royalty, no less." Lauren pretended to bow down to her.

Trina laughed, pulling her up into a tight embrace. "Who would have thought this incredible adventure would have ended with us casually meeting newlywed Hollywood supernova Emerson Sterling and her award-winning screenwriter wife, Hayley Carpenter, on Newbury Street when we begged out of a staff meeting—"

"Only to end up with you convincing her to see the still unsold Harborside super unit." Lauren laughed as they swayed side to side. They'd had no idea at the time that Emerson was opening her own production company, one she'd hoped would be based in New England. It had been a serendipitous meeting in every way imaginable. But Trina's never-absent boldness was what got the ball rolling. "The ovaries on you, T. I mean, *huge*."

"Huge." Trina leaned back and gave her a high five. "You gotta seize the day, bitches."

"What's all this cheering without Jax?" Jax Pearson, her other best friend and coworker asked as they strolled over. Jax had a particularly contagious twinkle in their eye tonight, and Lauren was sure it was because this bar held an important place in all their hearts. They'd hosted Jax's very successful top surgery fundraiser here last year. Jax seemed to glow in this moment, so many months post-surgery later. They were finally living their best life as their true self. Lauren was so glad to be a part of that life.

"We were just talking about how much of a boss Trina is," Lauren said as she accepted one of the full champagne flutes Jax was handing out.

"Such a boss." Jax raised their glass in agreement.

"Who's a boss?" Ellison Gamble—their actual boss—asked as she walked over.

"You are," Lauren said as she saluted her, and everyone laughed. Ellison had that effortless grace that Lauren never quite understood. She seemed to glide into every space, almost like she was floating. Her boss was a smooth operator in every sense of the word. Nothing rattled her. Not a hair was ever out of place. But she was honest and compassionate and supportive in a way that people wouldn't expect. And she was the best employer Lauren had ever had.

"Well then, carry on," Ellison said with a wink. "Oh, Trina, by the way, this dress looks killer on you. Is this a Talia special?"

"It is—she's the best. Thank you for letting me borrow her," Trina said, and Lauren had to agree—Trina's red dress tonight was amazing. But pretty much everything that Ellison's personal stylist Talia French recommended was. Including the gown Lauren had on tonight. She was a phenom, that one.

"Anytime," Ellison said before stifling a yawn. "I'm heading out, but I just wanted to congratulate you, Trina"—she placed her hand on Trina's shoulder before addressing Lauren and Jax—"and you two for making this night possible. I know Trina would agree with me when I say this was a team effort in every sense of the word. You guys killed it to make sure Trina was successful, and she should pay for every drink you consume over the next year to show her appreciation."

Trina winced. "Fair."

"Best. Boss. Ever," Lauren said.

"That's my cue." Ellison waved. "See you all at the office on Monday. Enjoy your night. Make good decisions. Get home safe."

"Well, you heard the boss." Trina held up her glass. "To my best friends, who will not spend one single dime on a drink until a new Realtor champion is named—I love you. I need you. Drink bottom shelf liquor only."

Lauren burst out laughing as Jax snorted their drink and started coughing next to her.

Trina patted them on the back as she wiped tears from her eyes. "Jax, the point is to swallow, not gag."

That caused Jax to choke mid-recovery sip, and Trina cackled. Her friends were idiots.

"I freaking love you two," Lauren said as she shook her head. "Let's do shots."

"Shots?" Kendall stepped up behind Trina and wrapped her arms around her waist, kissing her neck until Trina turned and joined their lips. They were so cute together that it was almost too much to handle. Lauren decided she needed to get laid soon, or she was going to start getting resentful of her bestie. Of course, if she could find someone to date, that would certainly help in that department.

She looked over at Jax, who still had not recuperated from the snorting and choking. It appeared she'd be making this mission solo. She glanced over to judge how busy the bartenders were, but instead she got distracted by the attractive brunette in a leather jacket sitting at the bar. When did she get here?

"I'll grab them," Lauren volunteered. She wanted to get a closer look at the mystery woman. "You in for shots too, Kendall?"

"Sure." Kendall was gazing moon-eyed at Trina. Lauren wasn't sure Kendall even knew what she was agreeing to.

Yeah, she needed to get laid. It was decided.

"Awesome, top shelf shit it is," she said.

"Bottom!" Trina called out, and Lauren smiled. She had a good life even if she was in the middle of a romantic and sexual dry spell.

CHAPTER TWO

"H ey." Teagan nudged her hand from across the bar. "You there?"

"Hmm?" Thea Boudreaux was staring at the melting ice in the bottom of her cup, wondering how she'd ended up here.

"I asked if you'd like another," Teagan said, motioning toward her glass.

"Uh…" Thea wasn't so sure about that. She wasn't so sure about anything right now.

"Yes," Avni Patel supplied from beside her. "Make it a double."

Teagan reached for the glass but hesitated, waiting for Thea's approval. Thea and her coworkers came to The Mirage often, and Teagan was one of her favorite bartenders. She wasn't pushy, which Thea liked.

Thea nodded. "With a lime, please."

"Thatta girl." Avni slapped her on the shoulder as she sidled up next to her at the bar.

"You're a terrible influence," Thea said, surveying her best friend. They'd become fast friends when Thea started working at Boston Bio five years ago even though they couldn't be more different. Avni was the lead developer at the tech start-up and was barely half Thea's height, but she had double the personality to make up for any vertical deficits. She'd been in a committed relationship with her boyfriend Raj for ten years, and she was stable. Reliable. Solid. And brilliant. She was brilliant in every sense of the word, especially with work stuff. But outside of their small friend group, she was shy. Almost insecure. Thea knew she could start her own firm and be twice as successful as she was at Boston Bio, but she doubted herself too much. Thea was working on that with her.

Not that Thea was exactly excelling at life. She *was* recently promoted to administrative manager at work, but she wasn't curing cancer or anything. And though she had no trouble finding a bedroom partner, she'd never managed to maintain a relationship more than a few months. But she knew she was charming like her dad. And loyal. Though not always punctual. But she tried. There was credit in trying, right?

"You love me," Avni said with a shrug. She was watching Teagan work, which was nothing new. Though Avni and Raj had been together since college, Avni had a super crush on Teagan. Thea secretly loved it, even though she felt a little sorry for Raj.

"Just ask her out." Thea elbowed her.

"I have a boyfriend," Avni repeated like she had so many times before.

"Just ask for a weekend pass, and get on with it," Thea said with a teasing smile. "You know you want to."

Avni rested her head on her hand and sighed. "We both know that this crush works because it's never going to happen. It's like a forbidden fruit kinda thing. I'm curious, but—"

"A total coward." Avni punched her in the arm. "Ouch."

"That's a lot of talk coming from someone who's been holed up for the last week like a freaking hermit, afraid to call her mom back."

Thea dropped her head. *Shit.*

"I'm sorry. That was a little harsh, huh?" Avni rubbed her back. "I'm in love with Teagan's ass in those jeans. Fine. I admit it. I'm lashing out because I'll never know if those buns are as firm as they look."

Thea laughed. "I bet if you asked her if you could squeeze her booty, she'd let you."

Avni looked scandalized. "And take away all the fun of torturing myself? I could never."

Thea watched as Teagan bent over. She did have a nice ass. But she wasn't her type. Though clearly, she was Avni's.

A loud cheer came from the back of the bar, and a group of well-dressed people danced and sang in a small circle. They all looked so happy. Thea felt envious.

"What do you think their deal is?" Avni asked, nodding toward them.

"A coworker celebration thing. One of them just got a big award," Teagan said as she placed a drink in front of Thea. She took Avni's empty martini glass and pointed to it. "Refill?"

"S-sure," Avni stuttered, and Thea laughed.

That earned her another arm punch.

"That's gonna bruise," Thea said as she rubbed her arm.

"Don't embarrass me in front of my soul mate," Avni hissed.

Thea rolled her eyes. "Did you trip over your tongue when you met Raj? Or is this just a Teagan thing?" she asked, but she already knew the answer. Avni got so nervous around Teagan it was comical.

"I hate you," Avni whispered as Teagan placed a bright red cosmo in front of her.

"I added a cherry. Just the way you like it." Teagan gave her a wink before moving on to another order.

Avni held her hand over her heart and pretended to die on the bar top when Teagan walked away.

"You're so dramatic," Thea said.

"She knows how I like my cosmo," Avni said, like that was some big deal.

"We come here all the time. She's our regular bartender. And all you drink is cosmos. That's, like, her job," Thea replied.

"You're ruining this for me."

Thea frowned. "Sorry. I know I'm not much company. I shoulda stayed home."

"Ugh. No. Wrong." Avni pointed to the drink in front of her. "Take a big swig and tell me what's up. And I know something is up, so let's not dance around it."

Thea sighed and obliged, letting the cool liquid and the tangy lime taste coat her mouth before taking a hearty swallow. The gentle burn on the way down was satisfying in the most delightful way.

"My mom called me the other day and told me she has to sell the farm." Saying it out loud made it hurt all over again.

"What?" Avni's drink was suspended in midair. "Your dad's farm?"

"Yes." That fact hurt doubly hard.

"Whoa." Avni placed her glass down and reached for her hand. "That's a big deal."

"I know." Thea sighed, feeling lost all over again. "I can't help but feel like it's my fault in some way."

"What do you mean?"

"I don't know. Maybe if I hadn't left. Maybe if I'd helped more…" Thea had never regretted leaving the family dairy farm until that call. And now she hated herself for it.

"Hey." Avni squeezed her hand. "Don't do that. I know how hard it was for you after your dad died. The farm was his life, not yours. You told me that a hundred times when I asked you to wear plaid and overalls to casual Friday. You don't own overalls. You're a terrible farmer."

Thea laughed. "This is true. I'm literally the worst."

"What happened?" Avni asked.

Thea wasn't totally clear on the details, but from what she gleaned from her mom's call and her texts with her brother Carl, the farm was deeply in debt, and her mother had been keeping it a secret until it was too late. Until now.

"The farm got to be too much for Mom and Carl, and they started getting behind on mortgage payments. They've had to lay off a bunch of staff and are trying to downsize, but it's not working fast enough. Mom thinks we have to sell by the end of the summer." Thea took another sip and swallowed hard. She couldn't imagine her life without the farm she grew up on being just a few hours away. There were so many memories there, even though some of them were painful. That farm had been her whole life.

"Thea, I'm so sorry," Avni said. "I had no idea."

"Me neither." At first Thea had been mad at the revelation. She was angry her mother hadn't told her sooner, so she could try to help. But she realized she wasn't mad at her mother. She was mad about the life she left behind, and that pained her even more. She'd left them. And this was all her fault.

"What are you going to do?" Avni asked. Thea hadn't quite figured that out yet.

"Call my mother back. Then head up there and see what I can do to help, I guess." Not that she was sure there was anything she could do, but she'd certainly try.

Avni nodded. "Well, that's a plan, at least. If I can help, let me know."

"Thanks." Thea sipped her drink, glad to have gotten that secret off her chest. As much as it sucked to talk about, she felt better having Avni in the know.

"I know what will make you feel better," Avni said with a mischievous grin.

"What's that?" This should be good.

"Getting laid."

Thea laughed. "Oh yeah?" She didn't doubt that rationale, but she'd like to hear more.

"Yeah, you need some really great sex to forget about your worries. In fact"—Avni sat up a little straighter and looked around—"I bet there's a lucky lady here in this bar that could be that distraction for you."

"Aren't you always trying to stifle my—what do you call them— *player ways*? Something about getting me to settle down and be unhappy like you?" Thea teased.

"Well, yes. Though I resent you saying I'm unhappy." Avni shot her a look. "But in this instance, hot sex is exactly what the best friend ordered."

"I certainly wouldn't say no to that. As long as she's not a stage-five clinger or anything," Thea mused. It had been quite a while since she'd scratched that itch. Avni's suggestion was intriguing.

"See? I'm always right. Remember that." Avni looked down at her buzzing phone and sighed. "Goddamn it, Raj. I swear to God, I'm dating a child."

"What?"

Avni grabbed her coat off the back of the chair as she motioned to the text on her phone screen. "I have to go because my darling boyfriend was watching YouTube videos while he took the trash out in his boxers and got locked out of the apartment building. And now he's near-naked, hiding behind the back dumpster, afraid that Old Lady Creedon will see him in his state of undress and call the police."

"She totally would," Thea said. The way Avni told it, Mrs. Creedon was the apartment building's self-proclaimed neighborhood watch, and she took joy in reporting everyone for anything. Supposedly she hated Raj because she said he never closed the trash bins and was inviting critters to take up residence out there.

"Of course she would. And she should. Because he's in his underwear outside her windows hiding behind a trash bag of empty take-out containers while watching *Call of Duty* walk-throughs in the dark and shivering in his skivvies." She pulled on her jacket with a huff. "I would call the cops on him, too. Moron."

"You know"—Thea picked a piece of lint off Avni's jacket—"I bet Teagan has never gotten locked outside in her underwear because she was distractedly doing chores while also watching videogame tutorials on her phone."

"You're probably right." Avni frowned. "But maybe? I mean, it's possible, right? She can't be *that* perfect, can she?"

Teagan was walking past, so Thea decided to ask.

"Hey, Teagan, have you ever gotten locked outside in your underwear and had to call your girlfriend home from her best friend drink date because of it?"

Teagan laughed and flashed her crooked smile. "I don't wear underwear. So…no."

"I hate you even more now." Avni groaned as Teagan moved on to take another patron's order.

"Why? Because now you know she doesn't wear underwear?" Thea teased.

"Yes. No." Avni looked flustered. "I stand by my original statement—I hate you."

"You don't mean that." Thea blew her a kiss as Avni flipped her off before disappearing out the door of the bar.

"Bad first date?"

Thea turned to find an attractive woman surveying her curiously. Her long dirty-blond hair was up in a stylish twist, and a perfectly penciled eyebrow was raised in Thea's direction.

"No. What makes you ask that?" Thea turned to face her, appreciating the sexy black dress she was wearing and the green necklace that complemented her hazel eyes.

"Well, she left in a hurry, with her drink still half full next to you," sexy mystery woman said as she pointed to Avni's forgotten drink. "That's alcohol abuse. Or bad manners. Or you just *really* offended her. Because even on a bad date, I've never left a half-full glass."

"What makes you think I offended her?" Thea asked, charmed by this woman's forwardness.

"The well-manicured middle finger in your direction," she said with a shrug.

Thea laughed. "She's my work bestie, and her boyfriend had an embarrassing emergency, so she had to split. But I appreciate the narrative you concocted. It's quite imaginative."

"I've been known to have a vivid imagination," she said. "I'm glad to hear you weren't just dumped on the spot. I was feeling bad for you."

"Well, she did leave me with a full drink and no company," Thea reasoned, in no rush to stop talking to this woman. "I'd be interested in hearing more about this imagination of yours if you'd like to join me."

She seemed to consider this. She glanced over her shoulder, and Thea realized she must be with the coworker group Teagan mentioned.

"You're with the fancily dressed people in the back, right? They probably wouldn't miss you for a few minutes." Thea motioned for Teagan to come over. "Can I buy you a drink?"

"Sure." She smiled.

"Great." Thea pulled out the chair next to her, pushing Avni's abandoned cocktail toward the back of the bar.

Teagan stopped in front of them, and Thea was about to ask her new acquaintance what she'd like when she realized she didn't know her name. "So, uh…?"

"Lauren," she supplied.

"Hi, Lauren. I'm Thea." She smiled. "What can I get you?"

"A lemon drop with a sugar rim, please."

Teagan nodded and disappeared.

"You're into sweet things?" Thea asked.

"Not necessarily," Lauren replied, and Thea knew she'd met someone special already.

"But you are into women?" Thea didn't feel like wasting her time on a beautiful straight girl. She'd bedded plenty of those, and she hadn't found them worth the trouble afterward. Not that she had any afterward in mind. But still.

"Not necessarily," Lauren repeated as Teagan dropped off her drink and walked away.

"Really? See, I was hoping you spoke to me originally about feeling bad that I'd just gotten dumped on my first date because you wanted to join me for a drink. Because you're into women." Thea feigned sadness. "But I'm wrong, huh?"

"I didn't say that," Lauren said as she sipped her drink.

Thea took that as a green light to continue flirting. "Well then, in that case, I *was* just dumped on a first date."

"Seriously?" Lauren asked, shocked.

"No, Avni's boyfriend got locked outside in his boxer briefs," Thea replied. "Though I'm sad she had to leave, I'm glad to have met you—Lauren, of the fancily dressed people."

"Oh, this old thing?" Lauren motioned toward that amazing dress, and Thea let her eyes linger on the way the fabric hugged Lauren's curves just so.

"If this is one of your old things, I'd be happy to watch you model some of your newer articles of clothing," Thea said. When Lauren didn't flinch at that comment, she dialed up her flirtation a few notches. "Or less clothing."

"That could be arranged." Lauren smiled before licking at the sugar on the rim of her glass. All of Thea's worries from before disappeared at the quick flick of that pink tongue. Lauren had all her attention. And suddenly Avni's playful prediction from before felt a whole lot more likely.

Chapter Three

Lauren wasn't quite sure what had come over her, but she was thoroughly enjoying this exchange with Thea. Maybe it was the champagne, or maybe it was those steely blue eyes and the way Thea's long dark hair framed her face in the sexiest way. Or maybe it was because she hadn't been flirted with like this in a long time. But something about their easy banter was getting her hot. And making her move faster than she usually would.

"I'm starting to think my friend leaving me alone at the bar was the best thing that could have happened to me." Thea's lips were full and inviting. There was something about the way she purred those words that made Lauren want to jump her on the spot. Which was ridiculous since she'd just met her. But Lauren could feel the chemistry between them like an electrical current. And she wanted to know if Thea's touch would feel the same way.

"The best thing?" Lauren asked. She could think of a few things that were more enjoyable.

"Well, not the best thing, I suppose." Thea dropped her hand from the bar to tug at the short hem of Lauren's dress. The touch was innocent enough, but Lauren felt her excitement build, nonetheless.

"I'm sure we could find a few suitable alternatives," Lauren said as she stilled Thea's hand on her thigh, holding it in place. "If you're over being left, that is."

"So over it." Thea licked her lips as she gently squeezed Lauren's thigh. Lauren bit her bottom lip in response. Thea's touch was gentle but firm. She wondered what else her touch could make her feel.

"Good. Then I'm glad she's gone." Lauren slid Thea's hand a little farther up her thigh.

"Me, too." Thea leaned in, cupping Lauren's jaw with her free hand. Her touch was cool. Lauren could feel the droplets of condensation transferred from Thea's glass along her jaw. One slow droplet tickled along her neck as it plunged toward her chest. "Has anyone ever told you that you have a gorgeous mouth?"

Lauren exhaled as Thea stroked her thumb along her jaw. "You should see what it's capable of."

Thea moaned. "Show me."

Lauren closed the distance between them, pressing her hand against the one on her thigh to ground her as Thea guided their lips together. The kiss was soft at first, almost curious. But that changed when Lauren opened her mouth, letting Thea's tongue sweep along her lower lip, pulling a pleased sigh from her lips in the process. Thea cradled her cheek as she alternated between kissing her slowly and deeply to playfully teasing her lips along Lauren's mouth. Lauren let herself get lost in the talented tongue that was taking her breath away. Thea was a first-class kisser.

"Whoa." Jax's unmistakable voice jarred her from her make-out session.

Jax. Shit. Her friends.

She pulled back from Thea's lips, her eyes scrunching in embarrassment as Trina said, "Don't stop on our account."

She winced before looking to her right to find Trina and Kendall wrapped up in each other, looking amused. "Uh, hi."

"Hi," Trina said with a delighted expression on her face. She looked at Thea, who Lauren noticed seemed a darker shade of red than before. "Who are you?"

"Thea," she replied, wiping Lauren's lipstick off her mouth.

"Thea. Hi, I'm Trina. Nice to meet you. This is my best friend Lauren. Don't do anything you don't want me to have to kill you over, okay?" Trina displayed all her teeth with the smile that accompanied that threat.

"Save those teeth for later," Kendall said as she nipped at Trina's ear. "Lauren's a big girl. Right, Lauren? You good?"

"Great," Lauren said with her brightest, most convincing grin.

Trina gave Thea a once-over before continuing. "Jax has hit their limit. So we're taking them home. Would you like a ride to your place on the way?"

"I can make sure she gets home okay," Thea said but seemed to regret it when Trina hissed.

"We're not friends yet, Thea. Let's not forget what I just said to you. Uber will take her home, and she'll send me the route confirmation," Trina bit back.

Lauren laughed because Trina was all talk. Mostly. "I'll be fine. Thank you for tonight. Sorry I never made it back with those shots."

"Shots?" Jax said as they swayed. Kendall reached out to steady them.

"No shots for you tonight, Jaxy." Kendall placed a kiss on their cheek, and Lauren was grateful that she fit so seamlessly into their friend group.

Kendall wrapped her arm around Jax to keep them from wandering and wrapped her free arm around Trina to pull her back. She spoke directly to Lauren. "Let us know when you get home safe. We love you. Have fun. I'll manage these two."

Jax was oblivious to being handled, but Trina looked like she wanted to bristle about it. Kendall leaned forward and whispered something in her ear, and Trina sighed, her demeanor changing a bit as she nodded.

"What's the square root of forty-nine?" Trina asked.

"Seven. You're not even trying," Lauren scoffed.

"I don't have a calculator to check on your Lauren-brain. I have to pick the ones I know the answer to," Trina said with a sly smile. "Just making sure you are of sound mind before we leave you with a stranger."

"And testing my math skills is your litmus test for that?" Lauren teased, and Trina rolled her eyes.

"Just don't forget to text us," Trina said as she slipped out of Kendall's grasp to give Lauren a quick hug. She looked at the hand Thea still had on Lauren's thigh before she motioned between their eyes. "I have eyes everywhere. Just keep that in mind."

"Good-bye, my darlings," Lauren said as she slipped out from under Thea's touch to hug and kiss her friends before she ushered them toward the door. "I'll talk to you later."

Lauren watched them leave before she hazarded a glance back at Thea. "They mean well, I promise."

"What's with the math stuff?" Thea, though still a little red, didn't seem fazed by the friend interruption.

"I'm good at math. Sometimes my friends try to test my skills. It's like a party trick to them." She shrugged.

"Which one is the award winner?"

Lauren raised her eyebrow at that.

Thea backtracked. "Teagan mentioned you guys were coworkers and that one of you won a big award."

"Oh, the little one with the threats," Lauren supplied with a laugh.

"Something tells me she's not the type that would like it if she knew you called her *little*," Thea said. And she was right.

"Well, if you said it, it wouldn't go well. But I get a best friend's pass," Lauren said as she resumed her seat next to Thea at the bar.

"Special privileges, huh?" Thea said, and the flirtation from before their interruption was back. Lauren was more than happy about that.

"So many," Lauren said as she brought Thea's hand back to her thigh. She liked the feeling of it there. "But I'm worth them, I promise."

"I bet you are," Thea said, and Lauren loved the darkness in her eyes.

She thought about something that Trina had said earlier—*Seize the day.* "Hey, do you want to get out of here?"

"Yes." Thea didn't hesitate, and that made Lauren feel drunk with want.

"Good." Lauren finished her cocktail and eased out of the chair Thea pulled back for her.

❖

In a matter of minutes, they were outside waiting on Lauren's Uber, and Thea was making sure she stayed plenty warm in that tiny dress by holding her close and kissing her often. It was quite chivalrous of her, in Lauren's opinion.

The car ride to her place was a blur, but Lauren was acutely aware of how badly she wanted it to be over once Thea's lips found her earlobe. She'd always been a sucker for that. It was a surefire way to get her trembling with desire. There was just something so sexy about the closeness of a lover's mouth and the breathy exchange that felt so loud and so hot along the side of her face.

She clutched at Thea's thigh as Thea whispered naughty things to her that Lauren could see her driver was desperately trying to hear. She dug her fingers into the firm, muscular flesh when Thea licked the shell of her ear, and her lower abdomen tightened with every word Thea uttered.

"I know you are so wet for me," she said, and Lauren had to stifle a moan. "I can tell because you can't sit still, and I like that."

She wasn't wrong. Lauren was ready to be out of this car and out of these clothes, like ten minutes ago.

She turned her face to catch Thea's lips and purred at the enthusiasm that met her.

A cough broke them apart. Lauren gave the driver an embarrassed nod before crawling out of the car and dragging Thea with her. She needed to get upstairs. Now.

Thea's hands were at her hips as she struggled through the apartment door. Once inside Thea spun her on the spot, walking her backward against the wall of her foyer. Lauren hadn't been with a woman this confident in a very long time. It was refreshing in so many ways, and they were just getting started.

"You've got a great place," Thea said as she kissed along her neck.

"You haven't even seen it," Lauren said as Thea sucked at her pulse point.

"You're here. That's enough for me." She was charming, so charming.

Lauren let her hands wander under Thea's leather jacket, shifting it off her shoulders and discarding it in a heap to the floor. She slipped her hands under Thea's Henley shirt and palmed at her breasts over her bra as Thea reclaimed her mouth. Lauren loved the fullness in her palms—Thea's chest was the perfect size to grip and toy with. Not too much to hold comfortably but full and supple to her touch. Thea's hips bucked forward at the contact, and Lauren relished the feeling of her weight against her, pressing her more firmly to the wall behind her.

"You like that?" she asked, but Thea's breathy noises told her the answer already.

Thea deepened their kiss, and Lauren massaged the flesh in her hands, stroking and teasing at Thea's aroused nipples until Thea ground her hips forward again, finally breaking from their kiss with a curse.

"Lauren," Thea said as she pulled back, surveying her. "I need you out of that dress now."

Lauren couldn't agree more. She stopped fondling Thea's chest, but not before stripping her of her shirt. She took in the sight before her with a pleased smile. Thea was strong—her shoulders well defined and muscular, much like the thigh Lauren had gripped during the car ride. She had an athletic build with narrow hips and a long torso. Her perky breasts were framed in a soft black sports bra that Lauren wanted out of the way.

She reached for it, but Thea stopped her, intertwining their fingers with a subtle head shake. "You first," she commanded as she pulled at the fabric of Lauren's dress, and Lauren felt her knees weaken.

"I'll soon be underdressed," Lauren warned, knowing that she was certainly wearing fewer undergarments than Thea was. A bra didn't exactly go with this dress. Or anything more modest than a thong, for that matter.

"I can deal with that," Thea said as she guided her away from the wall and into her embrace.

Lauren looked up at Thea and smiled at the intensity she saw there. Thea was completely dialed in to her. Good.

"Give me a moment to freshen up, and I'm all yours," Lauren said as she stepped out of Thea's grasp.

"All mine?" Thea asked, pulling her back for a quick kiss.

"Within reason," Lauren replied, and Thea laughed.

"Don't forget to text your friends," Thea said, and Lauren thought that was adorable.

"I will. Make yourself at home. I'll be right back."

"Hurry," Thea said, and Lauren intended to.

She slipped into her bedroom and let out a shaky exhale. She'd had plenty of trysts with women, but never had one escalated this quickly to the sex stage. In fact, she'd never had a one-night stand before. Which she supposed this might very well be. It's not like she knew Thea or anything. But if she fucked as good as she kissed, then Lauren figured that was enough to know for right now. And she was eager to find out.

She sent a text to Trina to let her know she'd gotten home safe before she freshened up and headed back out to the kitchen, smiling at what she found there. Thea was still shirtless, but her hips were moving to a silent rhythm as she dried her hands by Lauren's sink. Two tall glasses of ice water sat on Lauren's kitchen island, and one of the peaches from Lauren's fruit bowl was sliced and waiting on a plate.

"You certainly made yourself at home," Lauren teased.

"I am great at following directions," Thea said as she turned, leaning against the sink, looking edible with Lauren's dish towel draped casually over her shoulder.

Lauren moved toward the island. "We're drinking water now?"

"Gotta stay hydrated," Thea said as she handed her a glass.

"Am I in danger of getting dehydrated?" Lauren asked. She sipped the water and closed her eyes at the refreshing coolness.

"Most definitely," Thea said, her voice closer than it was before.

Lauren opened her eyes to find Thea standing right in front of her,

her hands on either side of Lauren's hips, resting on the counter behind her.

"And the peach?" Lauren asked as Thea leaned into her.

"Sustenance," Thea replied as she took the glass from Lauren's hand.

Lauren reached out to cup her jaw as Thea's hands settled at her hips. "Am I in danger of getting hungry?"

"Well, I'm starving," Thea said as she gave her a once-over. "But the peach is more than just food. It's foreplay."

"Oh." Lauren's breath caught at the mention of foreplay. But Thea's lips on hers distracted her from overthinking what that might mean.

After a few heated moments, Thea pulled back and brought a sliver of peach to Lauren's mouth. She dragged it along her bottom lip until Lauren opened her mouth, accepting the fruit. She hummed at the juicy sweetness on her tongue as Thea watched her in amusement.

"Mmm." Lauren made a show of licking her lips, and Thea rewarded her with another slice. Lauren caught her hand and sucked on Thea's fingers for a moment before chewing the new piece.

"You are incredible," Thea said as she ran her hands up and down Lauren's sides, settling at the zipper on her dress. "But also incredibly overdressed."

"Take it off," Lauren said after she swallowed.

Thea worked the zipper down slowly, caressing each exposed inch of skin with a delicate touch. She stripped her deliberately and sensually, and by the time the dress slipped off Lauren's hips, she was practically clutching at Thea to get her closer again.

Thea appeased her with a kiss before pulling back and taking in Lauren's topless, thong-clad form. "*Incredible* doesn't really do you justice."

Lauren smiled at the compliment. "There's a lot of talking and not enough kissing."

"We're done kissing for a bit," Thea replied, and Lauren frowned. "We are?"

Thea nodded as she reached for a peach slice, teasing it across Lauren's lips before pulling it out of reach of her mouth. "Yes. We've moved into the licking and sucking territory."

Lauren felt her mouth drop open as Thea brought the peach slice down her sternum and teased as she moved across her chest. Thea squeezed the slice, and Lauren felt the sticky juice drip onto her now erect nipple. She shivered at the sensation initially, but when Thea's mouth quickly descended upon the wetness, she moaned in ecstasy.

She ran her fingers through Thea's hair, holding her tightly to her chest as Thea sucked and licked at the peach juice on her nipple. She groaned in frustration when Thea pulled back, but her objections were stifled when Thea moved to her other nipple. Thea massaged her breast and pleasured the skin until Lauren's hips bucked forward involuntarily.

Thea looked up at her and popped the slice into her mouth, licking her bottom lip as she motioned for Lauren to pass her another. "We're not done yet."

Lauren's clit was thrumming, and her heart was racing as she handed Thea another slice, eager to see what she had in mind.

Thea dragged the sliver between her breasts and down toward her navel, circling the area before kneeling in front of her. Lauren's hands found her hair again as she threw her head back at the sensation of Thea's lips kissing the skin just above her underwear.

"You still with me?" Thea asked against the waistband of her thong, and Lauren nodded, resisting the urge to press her sex into Thea's face.

"Barely," she breathed out. The teasing was killing her. She looked down to find Thea looking up at her.

"Good," Thea said before eating the peach slice and reaching out for another. "Hand me a real juicy one. The messier the better."

"Fuck," Lauren said as she searched blindly. She settled on a softer, stickier piece at the edge of the plate.

Thea accepted it with a smile. "Perfect."

"Perfect for what?" Lauren was afraid to ask but at the same time desperate to know.

"This," Thea said as she nudged Lauren's legs apart, tracing a wet trail of peach juice up the inside of her thigh and down the other side, skipping over where Lauren wanted her to touch the most. She chased the dripping nectar with her tongue, and within seconds Lauren was trembling.

"I'm not sure how much more of this I can take," she admitted as she combed through Thea's hair, scratching at her scalp when Thea's nose bumped against her still clothed clit.

Thea nodded, nudging her again, and Lauren pulled her hair gently to get Thea to look up at her.

"I promise you—I'm plenty turned on."

Thea smiled and Lauren inched her pussy forward. Thea used her free hand to guide the fabric of the thong away from the front of her sex, sighing contentedly at what she found there. Without breaking eye contact with her cunt, Thea asked, "Fingers or mouth?"

"Yes," Lauren answered.

Thea's sexy laugh did nothing to temper Lauren's arousal. "Deal."

Lauren pushed down at the offending fabric, and Thea helped her out of it, tossing the thong to the side. Thea used the flat of her tongue to lick along Lauren's lower lips once, pulling a whimper from Lauren's mouth when she stopped.

"I won't make you wait anymore, I promise."

Thea rose from her knees, and Lauren grabbed her by the waist of her pants, pulling her against her as she helped Thea out of the rest of her clothes. She wrapped her arms around Thea's strong shoulders to bring her closer as her body ached for contact.

Thea delicately held the last piece of peach between her lips, leaning in to bring it to Lauren. Lauren accepted her portion, chewing briefly before Thea joined their mouths again. She kissed her deeply, her tongue wet and sweet and strong, winding Lauren up even higher than before.

Lauren gripped at Thea's ass and back, spreading her legs as Thea reached between them, touching her for the first time. Lauren nearly climaxed at the contact, pulling her hips back to slow her ascent. She kissed Thea hard, running her hands over her body, claiming what she could where she could.

Thea touched her again, and she trembled as Thea's fingers teased over her lips before dipping inside tentatively. She needed more. She reached down and guided her inside, gasping as her body enveloped Thea's strong, confident fingers.

"Damn," Thea breathed out against her mouth as Lauren ground down against her hand, seeing stars with each roll of her hips. Thea spread her fingers, and Lauren felt herself start to release.

She gripped Thea's wrist hard, slowing her movements because they had an agreement. "Fingers *and* mouth."

Thea nodded, kissing her briefly before dropping to her knees. She licked at her clit while she continued her slow thrusts, and Lauren came harder and faster than she had ever done before. With anyone. Ever.

She braced herself against the counter to keep her knees from buckling, and Thea placed gentle kisses along the skin just above her sex.

Lauren pulled her up into a hug, desperately trying to catch her breath in the process. Thea held her, and she was comforted by the contact even though Thea was still very much a stranger. A stranger who was incredible at pleasuring her, but still a stranger. Lauren leaned in to connect their lips, and Thea smiled against them.

"There's that gorgeous mouth I like so much," Thea said playfully.

Lauren reached between Thea's legs, pleased at the amount of wetness she found there. "It doesn't seem like you need the fruit seduction, huh?"

Thea bit her lip as Lauren stroked along the heated flesh. "Touching you was plenty of foreplay for me."

"Good," Lauren said as she stepped out of Thea's embrace to take her hand. "Now get your fine, naked ass in my bed, so I can return the favor."

"Lead the way."

Lauren intended to do a whole lot more than just lead.

CHAPTER FOUR

Thea was barely paying attention, and she knew that was a dangerous game to play while on the highway. She slowed her car and shifted into the center lane to force herself to be more attentive. That lasted for a few minutes, but her mind quickly wandered back to Saturday night.

Thea hadn't wanted to socialize, even with Avni. But she was damn glad she'd agreed. And that had everything to do with meeting Lauren. Wow, just, *wow*. That woman blew her mind and broke her clit. Thea couldn't remember another time when she'd found such a compatible sexual partner. Everything just seemed to click between them. So much so that Thea found herself interested in a hell of a lot more than just a one-night rendezvous. Which was also out of the ordinary for her, but Lauren was too intriguing to spend only one night with. And too damn talented.

Thea had left the next morning, but not before she'd enjoyed Lauren a little more. They'd exchanged numbers, and Thea had promised to call, a promise she intended to make good on. But she had to face her fears before diving headfirst into this new adventure with Lauren. It was time to handle the mess back home.

She pulled off the exit she'd taken so many times before and made the familiar drive along the slow country back roads toward her family farm. She was confident she could make this commute with her eyes closed, and though that should bring her comfort, she felt a growing sense of dread instead.

A bit of that dread faded when she drove up to find her younger brother Carl adding a fresh coat of paint to the decades-old wooden sign announcing her arrival to the Boudreaux Family Dairy Farm.

"Looks good, little bro. But I think you missed a spot," she called out as she exited her car, kicking up dust as she walked toward him.

"Do my eyes deceive me?" Carl shielded the sun with his paintbrush, nearly painting his forehead in the process. "Is that Thea? From the big city? Home to help with some chores?"

Thea stopped short. "If you think I'm here for chores, then yes, I'm a mirage."

Carl laughed. "Well, I hope you're here to do something more than critique my painting skills."

Thea took the brush from him and fixed his edging along the hand-carved sign her grandfather had made. Once satisfied with her adjustment, she handed it back to him. "See? I helped."

He gave her a look. "You'd better be ready to do a lot more than that if you plan to actually help around here."

She frowned. "How bad is it, Carl?"

"Bad," he said, and for the first time she noticed how much older he looked than his twenty-four years. He looked tired and wearied. The sandy-blond hair sticking out from under his baseball cap was sweat slicked and shaggy looking. His clothes were covered in paint droplets and grease marks, and the steel of his right steel-toed boot was exposed with the leather pulling back in a deep, jagged slice.

"Carl," she said, and her heart ached. Those boots were familiar. They were her daddy's.

He frowned and covered the damaged boot with his opposite heel. "I was hoping maybe if I wore his boots, some of his magic might find its way into me. We need Dad's magic to save the farm, Thea. But all I managed to do was ruin his favorite boots in the process." He hung his head.

"Come here," she said as she reached for him. And though they had never been overly affectionate, he slipped easily into her embrace with a near inaudible sniffle. She held him tightly and kissed the side of his sweaty head. "I'm so sorry, Carl."

"This never would have happened if Dad was still around." He sniffled again as he pulled away, wiping his eyes with the back of his hand.

Thea wiped away her own tears as she nodded. He was right. All the good memories she had of this place died with her father on that fateful summer night nine years ago. And as she looked at the farm beyond them, she saw how much it had changed. It looked as run-down and tired as her brother. There was no magic here anymore. That had left with her father, too, it seemed.

Carl followed her gaze. "I'm doing my best, but Mom thinks

I should save my energy. I had to fix the sign. I couldn't look at it anymore. But the barn is next. Even if we can't save the farm, I won't let the barn rot like that. I can't."

The once beautiful, bright red barn now looked dull and lackluster. Paint was peeling along the most sun-drenched wall, and she could see a few of the eaves were barely hanging on. That barn had been on every printed label and advertising material they had ever made. It was as much a staple of this farm as the Boudreaux family name. Her grandfather had built that barn by hand, and he had been so proud of it. Just like her daddy had been.

Thea sighed. "I'll help—we'll fix it," Thea said, not knowing what that meant.

"How? You gonna quit your job in Boston and start breaking your back like me and Hector?" Carl's question had an edge to it.

She looked at him and saw anger when before she'd only noticed sadness. "Carl."

"You left, Thea. You left and only came back when it was convenient for you. And now we're going to lose everything." Carl shook his head. "You can't just come in at the end with promises of helping while this whole time our world crumbled, and you weren't here to even notice."

"It's my home, too," she bit back. She was embarrassed and ashamed. Her brother was right again.

"You have a real funny way of treating a *home*." Carl tossed his paintbrush into the nearby tray. "I'd hate to see the kind of home you keep back in Boston."

That hurt. Thea had invited her brother to her place dozens of times, but he'd never come to visit. She only ever saw him and her mother if she came back here. They'd told her they were always too busy with work. She got the feeling that maybe it wasn't just an excuse. Her brother seemed exhausted on top of angry.

"Wait." She caught his elbow as he stormed past. "I'm sorry. You're right. I wasn't around."

"You weren't." He was taller than her now. The light stubble along his chin was the same faint red as her father's. He had their mother's brown eyes, but his jawline was her dad's. She was struck by how much he looked like him now, all grown up and no longer her kid brother anymore. He'd aged so much these past few months.

Thea didn't argue with him. There was no point.

"Thea," Hector called out, his voice full of joy. "Welcome home!"

Carl shrugged out of her grasp and grabbed the paint supplies as he walked silently past the farm's key employee.

Hector Alverez had worked with her father nearly thirty years. He'd started as a teenager helping with milk and dairy deliveries, but he'd quickly climbed the ranks to be her dad's closest and most trusted employee. Hector managed the farm—he made sure all the machines ran, the cows were healthy and happy, and the deliveries made it to their destinations on time. He was a carpenter, a mechanic, a plumber, and a ranch hand. If it needed to be done, Hector was your man.

"Hector," she said with a smile as she ran to him. "I missed you."

"You too, Dee," he said, and the nickname her father used to use for her nearly caught her breath.

"It's been years since someone called me that," Thea said sadly.

"Would you prefer something else?" Hector asked, looking sincere.

"No, it's a nice reminder." Hector and her father had used that name for her since she was a little girl—asking him to change that felt wrong.

"Your father was a good man." Hector took off his hat and held it over his heart.

"He was," she agreed. That's when she noticed the glove on Hector's left hand. "What's with the glove?"

He looked embarrassed. "Oh, I thought your mom or Carl would have mentioned it."

"Mentioned what?"

Hector put his hat back on before gently removing the glove. His left hand was frail and thin. "I had a stroke a few months back. I wasn't watching my blood pressure like I should have been. Got lazy with the pills." He shrugged. "I haven't had as much use of the hand as I used to, but I'm working on it."

She watched as he struggled to make a fist. "I had no idea." That made her angry. Why hadn't anyone told her?

"I'm told it was a small one and there's a chance I'll get full use of my hand again. The arm is moving much better than it was, so that's a good sign." He lifted his arm and swung it around a bit. "But it's certainly slowed me down around here."

A loud clanging noise in the distance drew her attention. Carl had tossed open one of the barn doors.

"I know he's moody, but he's trying his best. He really stepped up around here. Without him, we'd be much worse off." Hector scratched his head and sighed. "If not for him, I'm not sure I would even be here today."

"What do you mean?" Thea was surprised by the emotion she saw on Hector's face.

"I was repairing some of the pistons on the milker when the stroke hit. I fell forward into it when I was doing a test run. Your brother pulled me out and called 9-1-1. The machine could have crushed me. He saved my life." He struggled to put his glove back on before tucking his hand into his pocket. "Anyway, give him a break if you can. He's taking this as hard as any of us."

"I'm so sorry," she said. And she meant about everything, not just the stroke.

Hector gave her a half smile. "It's not over yet. We're entering our busiest season. Maybe we'll find that miracle we were looking for. Hell, if your dad were here, he'd probably say that miracle was you."

Thea swallowed hard. That *was* something he would have said, and he would have meant it. If only she could believe it. "I'll do my best."

"I know you will," Hector replied. "We all have blood, sweat, and tears in this land. Your dad's and granddad's land. We'll figure something out. We'll find a way. I know we will."

Thea wanted to bottle up his positivity and carry it with her always. "I hope you're right."

"I am." He squeezed her shoulder. "Especially now that you're home."

Home. Thea wasn't sure this was her home anymore. And she wasn't planning on staying very long, either.

"Oh, looks like your mom's back from the store." Hector nodded toward the familiar old red truck that pulled up outside the family home a few hundred yards away. "She'll be happy to see you."

I hope so. Thea wasn't so sure about that.

"That's my cue. I'll see you 'round," she said as she gave him a wave.

"Bye, Dee." He headed toward the barn, leaving Thea to her thoughts.

That nervous energy and dread from before returned as she made the hike up the short hill to the home she'd grown up in. She wanted nothing more than to be back in Boston, not about to be within those four walls again. Because something told her that this conversation with her mother wasn't going to go well.

❖

Lauren tossed the file toward the edge of her desk in frustration, but she underestimated her force, and it flew beyond the desk's edge and onto the floor in a maddening pile of airborne leaflets.

"Fuck," she muttered. This was pretty on par for how today was going—shitty.

"That bad, huh?" Trina asked from her doorway, looking concerned.

"No. Yes." Lauren dropped her head into her hands. This week could go screw.

She looked up at the sound of Trina organizing the file. Trina's skirt was far too tight to accomplish this task—also on par for Trina—but she still managed to get it done and make it look good. Damn her.

Trina examined the papers, putting them back in order before closing the file and placing it at the edge of Lauren's desk. "Another one?"

"Another one." Lauren leaned back in her chair, resting her head as she tilted backward. "That's the fourth blown sale I've had in the last month. I'm averaging one fucked sale a week at this point. I might as well throw in the towel."

Trina frowned. "C'mon, Lau. We all go through slumps. Real estate is hard for that reason—sometimes shit just falls through last minute. People can be fickle. The market can be volatile. It's not a reflection on your ability to be awesome. You are awesome. This is just a rough patch. It'll pass."

She wanted to believe her, but she also wanted to have a pity party. She pointed toward the bag Trina had put on her desk. "Tell me they had my favorite salad today."

Trina winced.

"Fuck this day." Lauren had had it.

"Relax. And quit swearing. They had something new today that sounded good, so I got it. They'll have your favorite back in rotation again at the end of the week. I already checked." Trina held up her hand. "And yes, before you say anything, I fully intend on buying lunch that day as well."

Lauren smiled for the first time all day. Trina had always been generous, but she'd been even more so since her Realtor of the Year win. But Lauren didn't need her generosity, just her friendship, something she had grown to count on over the years. Trina was loyal, kind, and selfless when it came to her friendships. And Lauren knew without a shadow of a doubt that Trina would have her back—and tell her the truth—if she needed it. And right now, she really needed it.

"Ready to eat?" Trina motioned for her to join her on the chairs across from her desk.

Lauren took the seat across from her bestie and wiggled excitedly in her seat. She was hungry—one might say *hangry*, even—so this was the perfect antidote.

She opened the container Trina handed her and laughed. "Stone fruit with balsamic and mozzarella?"

Trina paused midbite. "You love peaches. Did I choose wrong?"

"No," Lauren said as she nibbled on the arugula. "Remind me to tell you about the other night."

"After the bar?" Trina leaned forward. "I'm dying. Tell me."

Lauren took a bite of the peach and smiled. "I will. But first I have to come clean about something."

Trina put her fork down. "That sounds serious. What's up?"

"You know that Heinz sale, the one from last week?"

"Yeah, you were pumped about it. I forgot to follow up—how'd that turn out?"

"I screwed it up." Lauren's shoulders sagged. "I wasn't watching the deadlines as closely as I should have been, and I missed a filing date with the estate. And, long story short, they broke their contract with us, forfeited their deposit, and used another Realtor to complete the deal. I lost the sale of my career over a formality because I'm an idiot."

The pity on Trina's face was from a place of love, Lauren knew that. But it still hurt all the same. "Why didn't you tell me sooner?"

"You were excited about the award and busy yourself, and I—"

Trina put her hand on Lauren's knee. "I'm never too busy for you. You know that. We're a team, Lau."

"I know." She looked down at the floor between them. "I just feel like, I don't know. Like I've lost my mojo or something."

Trina's hand on her chin guided her gaze up to look at her. "Tell me what I can do to help."

"Listen to me mope and bring me food." Lauren shrugged.

"Well, so far I'm killing this best friend thing," Trina teased. "Seriously, though, the Heinz family was giving you all sorts of trouble to start with. It sounds like that nasty daughter-in-law finally got fed up with her husband hitting on you and used whatever the excuse was to get out of dealing with you. Not that it's right, but you can't help your hotness."

Lauren laughed. "He was a total creep, and she was a total—"

"Bitch," Trina supplied. "Absolutely. There will be more sales."

"Okay, fine, maybe. But what about the other three failures in my immediate past? This can't just be bad luck," Lauren said, not feeling better just yet.

"You tell me. What happened there?" Trina asked. "Let's talk it out."

Lauren counted them out on her hand. "Last-minute seller cold feet, hidden bankruptcy past with resultant loan denial from bank, and a dead cockatoo."

Trina nodded along until that last part. "Say what, now?"

Lauren shook her head. "Remember that gay couple from Brookline? You know how one of them was really into crystals and auras and stuff? Well, they were all in on that Newton property until the seller revealed at the closing that her beloved cockatoo Coco passed away the week before after choking on a stale doughnut. The aura-reader guy lost his mind and stormed out, mumbling something about his grandmother Coco dying during Thanksgiving dinner or something and that it was a sign that the house was not right for them. They pulled out of the sale and put up a nasty review on Yelp claiming I'd misled them about a death on the property." She rolled her eyes.

Trina paused before bursting out laughing. "You're not serious."

"I am," Lauren said. "That's how my professional life has been the past month—indecision, a calendar error, bank fraud, and a dead bird. *F-M-L*."

Trina dabbed at her eyes with her napkin, still giggling as she took Lauren's hand in hers. "Look, we all make mistakes, but that Heinz chick was looking for a reason to dump you because of her horny toad husband. So don't worry about that for a moment longer. And people back out of buying and selling all the time—you know that. Sometimes for no reason at all. It sounds like the bank did you a favor catching that hidden bankruptcy because you know the seller would have come out swinging if the sale fell apart at the closing."

"And the death by stale doughnut?" Lauren asked, giving her a look.

"Okay, well, that one I can't explain. That's just ridiculous. And sad. The poor bird." Trina patted her knee. "But look on the bright side. Now you don't have to worry about burning sage at every place you show those guys because they don't want to work with you in the future."

Lauren had to laugh at that. "You make a valid point."

"I always do," Trina said as she nudged her knee again. "So, about the brunette from the bar…"

"Thea," Lauren said as she resumed eating her salad.

"Right. So, how did that go?" Trina gave her a mischievous look. "I assume from the ferocity of your making out that night that she helped you get home safely? I got the Uber itinerary, thank you for that."

Lauren nodded. "Oh, she was certainly helpful. Numerous times. Very hands-on. A true gentlewoman."

Trina cheered. "Good on you, girl. She was hot."

"Oh, you noticed that in between your death threats?" Lauren teased. Thea *was* hot.

Trina feigned offense. "I am your best friend, and though I am no knight in shining armor, I am your bitch in too tall heels, defender of your heart, and sometimes guardian of your coochie. It's part of the job." She deadpanned, "I take my responsibility very seriously."

"You're too good to me," Lauren said with a wink.

"So tell me about the sex." Trina wasted no time.

"It was incredible. Like, *so* good." Lauren forked a slice of fruit from her salad, holding it up before eating it. "And it started with a peach."

"A peach?" Trina asked.

Lauren let herself remember the seemingly innocent start of the night—a tall glass of ice water and a peach, sliced with care. But oh, how it had turned naughty.

"Well if that drooling faraway look is any indication, there's a story to the peach thing. And I need to know it," Trina said as she poked her leg with a fork. "Focus. More talking, less daydreaming."

Lauren rubbed her leg where she'd been assaulted. "Fine, fine. We were hooking up, and I told her I wanted to freshen up, and when I came back to the kitchen, she'd poured us some water and sliced up a peach from my fruit bowl."

Trina paused. "You left a stranger, unsupervised, in your home, near knives?" She shook her head. "You can't be trusted with your own safety. I'm driving you home next time."

"Shh." Lauren silenced her. "It was completely innocent and adorable. Until it got ridiculously hot. And suddenly naughty. And now I'll probably never look at a peach the same way again."

Trina slow blinked at her. "Is the peach an innuendo for oral or something? What exactly happened with the peach?"

Lauren thought back to that night. "Just about everything happened with the peach." She paused. "Let's just say there was nudity, and the peach paved the way for some really sexy and sticky foreplay that started in the kitchen and ended in the bedroom with orgasms sprinkled like glitter in between."

"Orgasms? Like multiple?" Trina asked.

"Mm-hmm," Lauren hummed in reply.

"Well, damn. That's awesome," Trina said as she leaned back. "I'm glad she didn't murder you."

"Me, too," Lauren said. "But she might have broken my libido. Because I can't stop thinking about her and the fruity seduction."

"That's a good thing, though, right? I mean, when are you seeing her again?"

Lauren frowned. That was the other thing about this week that had sucked. She hadn't heard from her. "I'm not sure. We texted a bit at the beginning of the week, but she's been radio silent. She mentioned she had to go out of town, but that feels like—"

"A brush-off," Trina said, looking annoyed.

Lauren was hopeful, but not foolish. She didn't even know Thea's last name. They hadn't had a lot of profound conversation before they'd started groping. This could very well be a memorable night and nothing else. She was a grown-up—she had to accept that. "I'm going to see where things go and try not to overthink it." Too late. "She seemed to have a good time, and I certainly did, so maybe we'll cross paths at The Mirage again sometime."

"Or maybe she *is* out of town and will text you when she's back," Trina offered.

"Maybe." Lauren could certainly use the distraction of great sex from her recent professional failures. She hoped that Trina was right.

CHAPTER FIVE

K athleen Boudreaux was solid in every sense of the word. She was strong, capable, reliable, and steady. Rock steady. But as much as she was the backbone of this family, Thea knew her father had been the whimsy. And though the backbone still stood, the fairy tale was gone.

That's all Thea could think about as she walked up the old, creaking steps of the farmhouse she'd grown up in. The house remained, aged and neglected but still standing. Something that was mirrored in the look of her mother's face from the kitchen window. She smiled when she saw her, but Thea could see a strain there. That strain had been there since her father had died and seemed to have deepened in the last few months since she had been here.

"Thea," her mother said with open arms as she stepped onto the porch.

"Hi, Mom." Thea relished the hug. Though she had been much closer to her father, her relationship with her mother had always been good. Just different. But her mom still gave the best hugs.

"I'm making your favorite. Come in." Her mother held open the door before ushering her into the kitchen. The smell of lasagna greeted her like an old friend, and she smiled as her mother handed her a dish towel. "Wash your hands and prep the garlic bread. I have to change over the laundry. I'll be right back." Her mother gave her a quick kiss on her cheek before disappearing toward the mudroom in the back of the house.

Thea washed her hands and walked around the kitchen, opening all the drawers and cabinets that hadn't changed since she was a little girl. The butter knives were over there, and the cutting boards were in the cabinet next to the frying pans. The fresh butter—churned a few hundred feet away—sat out on the counter, waiting for her. She grabbed a large knife from the block and started pressing the garlic, prepping it to warm and coat the fresh Italian loaf that sat on the butcher-block island her father had made for her mother's birthday, twenty or so years ago.

She ran her hand over the notched wood, remembering all the times she'd worked here with her mother making pastries, or helping her father prep vegetables for dinner. Her family had always divided the responsibilities evenly. Her father had cooked as much as her mother did. Everyone had an important role in this family, and no one was ever considered insignificant. That was something both her parents worked hard to remind her and Carl of.

"So, how's life in the big city?" her mother asked as she placed a stack of freshly folded towels at the base of the stairs. Thea knew those were for her. She'd take them up to her room later.

"Oh, you know, thrilling." She moved the butter and garlic around the frying pan, careful to keep it moving and not let it burn.

"Yeah? And have you met someone yet?" That question already? Wow. Her mom wasn't pulling any punches today.

"Uh, maybe?" Thea's mind went back to Lauren. And those lips she couldn't stop thinking about. She hoped to see her again soon. She really ought to shoot her a text.

"What does that mean?" her mother asked, leaning her hip against the kitchen table.

Thea placed the wooden spoon at the edge of the stove as she dug out her cell phone. "It means I had a nice time with a very nice woman the other night, and I'm hoping it leads somewhere." She fired off a quick text to Lauren. *Thinking of you. Will you be around next weekend?*

"What's she like?" Damn. Mom wasn't messing around.

"Um…" Thea stalled. She didn't know much about Lauren, so she decided to go with the things she did know. "She's about my height, a little shorter. She has dirty-blond hair and really beautiful hazel eyes. And she's bold." And adventurous. And delicious. And had seemingly endless energy in the bedroom. Well, that and about ten other things she didn't feel the need to mention to her mother.

"What's her name?" Why was her mother pursuing this so much?

"Lauren," Thea replied, not trusting her mother's interest. "What's with the third degree?"

Her mother paused. "I'm just curious about your life. That's all. Aren't I allowed to be?"

Thea dropped her head, feeling bad. "Yes."

"The garlic is burning."

Shit. She turned down the flame, attending to the forgotten simmer as Carl entered the house.

"How long until dinner, Mom?" he asked.

"Twenty minutes or so. Maybe longer if Thea scorched the garlic," her mother teased.

"Thanks." Carl didn't even look at Thea before he bounded up the stairs.

Thea sighed.

"I'm sure the garlic is fine," her mother assured her.

"It's not the garlic, Mom."

"It's Lauren?"

"What?" Thea pulled the frying pan off the burner. "No."

Her mother intercepted her, taking over. Thea sat at the kitchen table. It occurred to her that this was her usual seat here. How easy it was to fall into old routines, she mused.

"Mom?"

"Yes?" Her mother prepped the bread and placed it into the oven, next to the lasagna.

"What's going to happen to the farm?"

Her mother turned to face her. She suddenly looked exhausted. "Let's talk about it later. After dinner. Let's just have a nice, semi-normal meal as a family. Okay?"

"Okay, Mom." But Thea knew semi-normal was not an option. It hadn't been in a long time.

Thea found her mother on the porch swing outside. Dinner had been mostly civil. Carl only snapped at her twice before her mother reprimanded him, and he sulked until his plate was cleared. He disappeared when dish duty started, and Thea was fine with that. She'd rather work in silence with less hostility. Plus, she was sure there would be plenty of time to fight with her brother tomorrow, too, since she had taken a few days off from work to be here and figure things out.

"Here." She handed her mother a glass of iced tea.

"Thanks." Her mother smiled at her as she patted the space next to her. "Come sit."

She settled next to her, resting her head on her mother's shoulder.

Her mother's hand slid into hers, and they rocked in silence for a bit. It was nice. She'd missed this.

"I can't run the farm anymore, Thea. It's too much and too expensive, and I'm in so much debt that if I don't sell now, we'll be underwater on the whole thing. I don't think I'll have more than a few dollars to give either of you at the end of the day, and you deserve more than that. You deserve your daddy's legacy. But I've tried my best. I can't make the impossible possible." Her voice was soft, almost broken. Thea's heart felt as broken as her mother sounded.

She lifted her head to look at her. Her mother wiped tears from her eyes as she sighed a sigh as heavy as Thea had ever heard. "Why didn't you tell me it was so bad?"

"You were always a daddy's girl. And he doted on you. But he also knew that this life wasn't for you, Thea. I never expected you to stay here and keep the farm. That wasn't who you were. And your dad knew that, too. It's not my job to tell you how to live your life or who to be. When your dad died…" She paused. "I saw that part of him in you break. That connection you had to this land left with him. You aren't responsible for what happens. You never were."

Something about that angered her. Her brother's words from before flashed into her mind. "This is my home, too. Why doesn't anyone think I should be involved in what happens here?"

Her mother's hand stilled her fidgeting fingers. "No one said it wasn't. But the fact of the matter is that you left to start another life elsewhere, Thea. And I can't fault you for that. I don't. It's my decision to sell the farm. I'm fine with taking that responsibility. Of course"—she laughed—"it would feel less awful if your brother didn't hate me so much. But I know he's just mourning. We all are. But there isn't anything left to do."

"Why? How can you say that? What about a bank loan? What if I move back to help? What if—"

"I've exhausted my loan options. And I've already cut the staff here by more than half. We have the bare minimum coverage now, and everyone is doing double duty. We're only operating with a third of the cattle we used to have, and even that is too much to handle with such a small crew." She squeezed Thea's hand as she continued, "We're barely fulfilling our orders, as is. I haven't signed on for any new fulfillment contracts. This will be our last summer. It's best if you start accepting that now."

"I won't. I won't accept that," Thea said indignantly. She wasn't ready for this to all be gone.

"You're going to have to." Her mother kissed her forehead as she stood. "I'm tired. We can talk some more tomorrow. Don't forget to lock the front door when you come in."

Thea sat on the swing alone, lost in her thoughts. The night was warm with a slight breeze, but Thea found no comfort in that. Because her world was falling apart, and there didn't seem to be anything she could do about it.

CHAPTER SIX

Lauren's attempt at deep breathing was failing miserably. Every time she closed her eyes and tried to calm her mind, all she managed to do was picture herself breaking lots of fragile things. Over and over again. Which was sort of calming, until she opened her eyes and found herself sitting in her office, still frustrated and still a failure.

She shoved back from her desk with more force than was necessary and knocked her cell phone to the floor in the process.

"Fuck," she grumbled as she bent down to get it, only to slam her head on the underside of the desk in her attempt to get back up. "Double fuck."

The sound of someone clearing their throat interrupted her pity party.

"Oh, Ellison. Hi," Lauren said as she gingerly rubbed the sore spot at the back of her skull. Great. The last thing she needed was to be cursing like a sailor in front of her boss.

"Tough day?" Ellison asked, her tone neutral and calm. As usual.

"Tough month," Lauren conceded.

"Are you busy right now?" Ellison asked, and Lauren got a little nervous.

"I'm sorry about all the swearing," she blurted out.

Ellison laughed. "It's okay."

"But to answer your question, no, I'm not busy." That was the truth. She wasn't busy because yet another one of her sales fell through today. The fifth one in so many weeks. This was a record streak for being a loser.

"Good. I'd like you to take a ride with me. I want to show you something," Ellison said as she motioned for Lauren to follow her. "I'll meet you out in the parking lot."

Lauren gathered her cell and purse, closing her office door as she headed toward the back lot past Jax's desk in the direction of Ellison's Maserati.

Jax was sitting at their desk looking anxious.

"What?" she asked as she neared them.

"Nothing," Jax lied. Badly. She knew Jax too well to buy that. She would bet anything they'd overheard Ellison's request for a private conference.

"If you're nervous, I'm going to be nervous," Lauren reasoned. "This is just a friendly drive in her fancy car where she hopefully doesn't fire me."

Jax's eyes bulged. "You're getting fired?"

"No, I was joking." Lauren paused. "Oh my God, you think I'm getting fired?"

"Who's getting fired?" Trina walked up with a stack of files. She handed them to Jax. "Can you file these for me?"

"Lauren," Jax said as they took the folders from Trina with a nod.

"You're getting fired?" Trina didn't sound nearly as concerned as Jax, and now Lauren, was.

"Jax thinks I am." Lauren shrugged, now feeling as anxious as Jax looked.

"I didn't say that," Jax countered.

"Your face did," Lauren replied.

"You're not getting fired," Trina assured her. "I'm sure this is a pep talk of some sort. Oh! Maybe it's a secret project. She does that from time to time. She's tricky like that."

Lauren thought about the impromptu bet Ellison made last year for Trina, and her panic lessened. Ellison wasn't exactly prone to massive grand schemes, but she did seem to always have something going on behind the scenes. Maybe this was one of those things.

"Or maybe she's taking me off the premises so I don't make a scene when she fires me," Lauren said.

"I mean, that feels unlikely," Trina replied. "But if she does, can I have your BeDazzled stapler? That's the best stapler in the building."

"She's right," Jax added. "It's so smooth."

"No. Do you know how many times I glued my fingers together trying to customize Ruby so you fools wouldn't keep stealing her and feigning innocence? No way. If I'm going, Ruby comes with me."

Trina and Jax exchanged a look.

Lauren blew out a low whistle. "Wow, I see where I rank around here. You two are already conspiring against me to get your hands on my Ruby. I see how it is." She motioned between their eyes and her own. "I'm watching you."

"Hurry up and find out you're not fired, so we can keep using Ruby behind your back while you're out of the office without feeling bad," Trina said, playfully pushing her toward the back door.

"You two are evil," Lauren said.

"It's the best stapler!" Jax called out.

"So, I know you've had some setbacks lately, and I wanted to talk to you about them," Ellison said as she shifted lanes. The car drove like it was on a cloud, not unlike the way Ellison seemed to float places. This car was very much like Ellison herself—chic, expensive looking, luxurious, and powerful. Lest Lauren forget that.

"Yeah," Lauren said so as not to remain silent and seem rude. Dammit. She really wished she hadn't let Jax's doomsday mentality seep into her brain.

Ellison took a left, then a right. Lauren recognized the area, but she couldn't figure out why they were here.

"Where are we going?" Lauren asked.

"I want to show you something." Ellison drove in silence for a few more minutes until she pulled up to an old, boarded-up two-story building. "What do you think about this?"

Lauren looked at the building. It was overgrown with ivy and had a smattering of vandalized, broken windows along the wall facing her. The wood planks across the doors were warped and weathered. Spray paint covered the first-floor brick on one side of the building. This place was a dump. "I think it should be condemned if it isn't already."

"Yes, agreed. But what about the rest of it? What about the area? What do you think about that?" Ellison asked.

Lauren looked around again as she put the passenger window down, this time paying more attention to the surrounding neighborhood. The building was located on a side street, off a main road. She traveled this way often, but she'd never taken much notice of the surroundings before, and she'd certainly never noticed this rotting structure. She focused her attention on the area around them. There was a public park not too far away, with lots of fresh signage and welcoming benches. Children played in the greenway across from the building lot, and two dogs chased each other around a tree nearby while their owners talked and laughed. Lauren could make out a bronze statue of a firefighter nearby, and though she could see that traffic flowed constantly from the main street just a few blocks away, she couldn't hear much traffic noise.

"It's nice. Quiet, clearly well cared for, and regularly traveled by locals. The park is well-kept and a big plus. Is there a school nearby?" Lauren asked.

"Two within walking distance," Ellison said, looking at her intently. "What else?"

Lauren scanned her memory of the road they had turned off of. "I believe there's a few boutique shops over there, a dog grooming place, and a signature wine and brandy bar."

"There's a corner store, a drug store, two clothing boutiques, the dog place, the wine bar, and a Thai restaurant," Ellison replied.

"Grocery store?" she asked.

Ellison frowned. "No, not yet. There's talk of a bodega, and this greenway has a farmers' market in the warmer months."

Lauren stepped out of the car and soaked in the location a little more. She looked up, and she saw it now—just beyond the back of the property, at a slightly higher elevation, an acre of community gardens could be seen in various states of cultivation and growth. She stepped toward the intimidating and rusted chain-link fence bordering the lot and peered through the links. The gardens were bustling with people of all ages, shapes, and sizes. A small pond was at the center of the garden lot, and Lauren could see a little girl tossing what looked like stones into it and laughing at the ripples that formed.

The sound of the engine ceased, and Lauren heard Ellison's car door open and close. Lauren heard her heels as she approached from behind.

"There's no real housing over here. Most of those that have a plot up there come from all over the city, taking buses or trains to get here. This neighborhood outpriced its inhabitants," Ellison said.

Lauren turned to look at her. "So what's with the empty lot, then? I feel like a developer would have swooped in here and demoed this already. That garden view behind is beautiful, and with shops and a restaurant in walking distance, not to mention the parks and both schools, this lot must be worth a fortune."

"Oh, it is." Ellison gave her a small smile. "But the owner hasn't decided what to do with it yet."

"What are they waiting for? Do they want to sell the land?"

Lauren's sales brain kicked in, and the numbers circled before her eyes. "This place is worth millions, and if the community garden is linked to the land, that would triple the value of the square footage. I feel like I know a few people that would be interested in it. Is that why you brought me here?"

"No, I brought you here to remind you of how talented you are. And to show you that if you look past first impressions, something great might be waiting on the other side," Ellison said as she walked back to the car.

"This was a road trip pep talk?" Lauren asked, shaking her head as she climbed in next to Ellison. Trina was right, for which she was grateful.

"Of sorts." Ellison turned on the car and waited until Lauren was buckled before she pulled away from the dilapidated building.

Ellison was quiet for a moment before she spoke. "Lauren, one of the best things about you besides your incredible math skills is your humanity. You're kind and caring and gentle. You connect with your clients and your coworkers on a different level. And that uniqueness is invaluable. Your skill set is vast in that way. Your clients open up to you and let their guard down in ways they wouldn't with other people. That's because you are so sincere in all things that you do. You think outside the box. You problem solve like a champion, and you always come out on top because of it."

"Thank you." Lauren appreciated the compliments, but she wasn't feeling like much of a winner right now. "I hope you're right. Because it feels like I'm waist deep in a slump right now."

"I never worry about you. Do you know why?" Ellison cast her a brief glance before returning her eyes to the road.

"No. Why?"

"Because you're scrappy," Ellison said with a smile. "And beyond creative."

"Thanks." Lauren felt her confidence swell. "So what's the plan with that plot?"

"Probably some housing. Something affordable but also chic. Like a city suburb approach to luxury living. Something safe and welcoming for families but also for young professionals that want to live the luxury lifestyle without the steep price tag. The community gardens behind it are being renovated, and the space is being upgraded. New watering systems will be put in place, and all the garden borders will be reinforced. The city is planning on overhauling some of the forgotten parts of this historic area, and this building is the last eyesore left." Ellison turned on to the main road and seamlessly maneuvered into the midday traffic in front of them.

"That sounds lovely. I'm sure the neighborhood will appreciate it."

"That's the hope," Ellison said, and a thought occurred to Lauren. "Who owns the plot?"

"I do," Ellison said as if it was no big deal.

Lauren gaped. "That land alone is worth millions."

Ellison shrugged. "I got it at a steep discount a while back—I've been mulling over my options. But I think I've finally settled on a plan. That's where you come in."

"Me?" Lauren's head was spinning. What could Ellison possibly need from her? She had the plot and the plan. It sounded like she was all set.

"I'd like you to take the lead on selling the units once they're done. I need your people skills. And your unique way of thinking. And your incredible charisma to help me bring in the right clientele to match the already established neighborhood. These people deserve the right kind of neighbors. They've worked hard to restore their neighborhood to the charming, family-friendly area it is today. We need to find a way to make this affordable, but also luxurious and welcoming to young families. And you're the right person for the job." Ellison glanced over at her at the next light. "What do you think about that?"

Lauren tried to soak all the information in. She had a lot of questions. "First, yes. Totally yes. And I'm honored, and I think it's a great idea. But it's just an idea, right? Are you even in the building phase yet? Also, since when do you build things?"

Ellison laughed. "Good. And I'm moving out of the idea stage into the action stage. The building will be demoed in a week or so. And to answer your other question," she said as she eased the car back into the office lot, "I got inspired to get into the building world after Trina's bet last year. Clearly there's money to be made in new construction in the city. Why leave it all to old white guys like Charles Langley and his messy connections? We can make a real difference while also making a profit. That to me is a no-brainer."

Lauren agreed with that point.

"The building will take just under a year to finish. That will give us plenty of time to research the right types of residents and the sales or rental income necessary to make it available to a greater population without changing the neighborhood dynamic. Your super numbers skills will help with that."

"Okay," Lauren said, following along. "So what now?"

Ellison unbuckled her belt and turned to face her. "Now, I need a favor. And I need you to use that same creative approach we'll apply to the new building on a trial run first."

"I'm listening."

"There's a farm in Casterville, Maine, that is in desperate need of a bank loan to stay afloat, or they'll have to sell. I want you to check out the property and give me your thoughts on its value. Take a look at properties with similar acreage in the area, and do whatever research you need to in order to get me the full picture."

"Maine?" Lauren asked incredulously.

"Maine." Ellison nodded.

"I have no license in Maine. I can't operate as a Realtor there," Lauren pointed out.

"I don't need you to operate as a Realtor per se. I need you to operate as Lauren." She pointed to Lauren's head. "I don't think the farm will get that loan. But I need to know if the sale of the land will save the family. Even if just a portion of it." Ellison shifted in her seat, looking out toward the office before them. "I've racked my brain over this for a few months, but time is running out." She looked back at her, her expression more serious now. "I need your eyes and brain on the case. I need an outside-of-the-box approach. I think it's their last hope."

Lauren shook her head. "I don't get it. Why Maine? What's so special about this farm?"

"They're family friends, and they have an incredible and important legacy to Casterville. If they get torn down for luxury condos, then I want it to be because all other options were exhausted."

This was clearly important to Ellison, though Lauren couldn't figure out why. Not that she really cared. If Ellison needed her help, she'd help. "Okay."

"Okay?" Ellison's expression brightened.

"Yes," Lauren agreed. "I mean, I'll have to figure out some logistics and juggle some of my current client load a bit, but yes."

Ellison smiled broadly at her. "Let's get inside, and I'll give you all the information you need. I'll be announcing the new construction at tomorrow's staff meeting, and I'll be designating you as lead on sales at that time. I'd like you to think of a second chair to help you with the project."

"Jax," Lauren said without thinking. Trina was eyeball deep in high-rise sales and would have to sacrifice too much to make this kind of a long-term project work. Jax was exactly the person she needed to help with the research element Ellison was talking about. No one was better at social media management, internet searches, and data organization than Jax. They'd proved that last year when they'd helmed Trina's Harborside war room.

"I was hoping you'd say that," Ellison said as they exited the vehicle. "Jax will be an asset to you."

Trina was walking out of her office as Lauren and Ellison came in through the back.

"Did you get fired?" Trina asked with a smile.

"Who's firing you?" Ellison asked, looking scandalized.

"Well, you. If you were firing me. Which you didn't. So, thank you," Lauren said with a head bow.

"Why would I fire you?" Ellison looked puzzled.

"Because she can't sell a house to save her life." Jax's head popped up from behind their monitor.

"Rude." Lauren shot them a look.

Ellison placed her hand on Lauren's shoulder and gave her a quick squeeze. "I would never fire you for things that were outside of your control."

Lauren nervous laughed because that wasn't a promise not to fire her, just not to fire her if she wasn't directly the cause of the sales losses.

"Besides, I wouldn't take you out of the office to do that. What if I needed security?" Ellison gave her a wink as she walked away.

"See? I told you." Trina laughed as she slipped her arm around Lauren's waist.

Lauren rested her head on her friend's shoulder. "Not fired. But I am getting shipped to Maine."

Trina pulled away to look at her. "For lobster? Because I can get down with that."

"Nope," Lauren said as she pulled her bestie back in for a hug. "For a dairy farm."

Trina made a face. "Ew. You know how dairy bloats me."

"I've seen you kill an entire wheel of brie," Lauren said.

"Brie is the exception. But given the choice, I prefer the lobster option." Trina snuggled with her for a moment before separating. "But that doesn't mean you can't bring me home lobster."

"Fine," Lauren agreed easily. "But for the record, I know you're also obsessed with brie. Bloating or no bloating, you're a cheese plate and charcuterie whore."

Trina stuck her tongue out at her.

"What about me?" Jax asked.

"No lobster for you, traitor."

"I was joking," Jax whined, looking sad.

"Me, too. Fine. Lobster for you." Lauren loved her friends. And she was excited about the prospect of a new adventure and leadership opportunity. "Hey, you guys want to get drinks after work?"

"I'm in," Jax said.

"I'm buying," Trina replied.

Lauren had the best life.

CHAPTER SEVEN

I mean, I'm glad you worked it out. I guess," Thea said into the phone. "Your enthusiasm for me salvaging my relationship is overwhelming," Avni joked. She and Raj were back on good terms, which Thea was happy about because her friend was happy. Though she knew she was doing a bad job of expressing that.

"I'm sorry. I'm in a mood. Things have been tense here." That was an understatement. The past three days she'd been at the farm had been barely tolerable. Carl had warmed up to her some in that he now occasionally acknowledged her presence with a head nod, but there was still a definite wedge between them. Thea wasn't sure if or how she could fix it, but she was determined to try. And though things had been fine with her and her mom, Thea couldn't escape the sadness around this visit. Everything felt so heavy.

"What's happening there?" Avni asked. She was a good friend.

"Mom plans to keep the farm running through the summer if possible but wants to sell what she can and list the property to resolve the debt." Thea leaned back with a sigh. "My mother agreed to have some fancy big-city luxury Realtor come out and look at the place to help her determine its worth. There's been talk of tearing everything down and building luxury condos along the lake at the back of the property. The whole thing makes me want to vomit."

"Oh, Thea. I'm so sorry." Avni's voice was sympathetic. "How quickly is this proceeding?"

Thea stretched. "The Realtor gets in today, but I plan to discourage them as best I can. I just need a little more time. I know I can figure something out. My mom is overwhelmed and tired—I get that. But I've got the energy to keep trying. There has to be something I can do."

"Well, I'll make sure to hold down the fort here for you in your absence. Are you still planning on splitting your time?" That was the big question. Thea wasn't quite sure what her plans were.

"For now, yeah. As long as I can work remotely a few days a week, I plan to." Thea was scheduled to head back to Boston tomorrow. But she wanted to see about this smarmy Realtor first. "Ideally, I'd like to be in the office midweek and take longer weekends up here, working remotely on Friday and Monday. But I have to get Jeff to agree to that."

"Jeff will agree. I'll make sure of it," Avni said, and Thea felt a little lighter. Their boss was as easygoing as it got. She had no real concerns about him turning her down, but it was nice to know that Avni would advocate for her in her absence.

"I owe you a drink when I get back," Thea said.

"At least two," Avni replied. There was a pause. "Can we go to The Mirage for that drink?"

Thea smiled. "Of course. We can even go when Teagan is working."

"That's not...I wasn't..." Avni groaned, and Thea laughed. "I just like The Mirage, okay? The atmosphere is great, the drinks are strong—"

"The androgynous bartenders are cute," Thea supplied.

"I hate you."

"You love me." Thea heard the sound of a car door closing, and she sat up. "Someone's here. It might be that money-hungry Realtor. I gotta go make a scene."

"Call me with details later," Avni replied conspiratorially.

"Will do, bye." Thea disconnected and nearly tripped over her feet in her rush to get up. She raced to the front window of the farmhouse only to find Carl out front, unloading groceries from the truck. A part of her was relieved. Earlier she'd vowed to smooth things over with her brother today. This might be her chance. She jogged out to meet him.

"Let me help," Thea said as she reached to take a grocery bag from him.

He seemed to hesitate before handing her the bag.

"What?"

He shrugged, handing it to her. "I'm still not used to seeing you around. It feels, I don't know, weird."

Thea sagged a bit. "Can we talk?"

"We are talking."

She shook her head before grabbing another bag. "You know what I mean."

Carl closed the door to the truck, juggling the remaining bags in the process. "Okay."

Thea led the way into the house and placed the bags on the counter. She took the remaining bags from Carl and pointed to his usual chair in the kitchen. "Sit. Let me get you something to drink."

Her brother looked uncomfortable, but he did as she asked. She poured him some iced tea and handed it to him before she sat across from him.

"I know you're mad. I know you're mad at me for leaving and probably mad at Mom for deciding to sell the farm, and I'm in total agreement with you. On both fronts."

Carl put down his now half-empty cup and gave her a surprised look. "Really?"

"Really." Thea nodded. "I've been a shit older sister. I just left you and Mom to figure things out, and I never even asked if you needed help. I ran when things got hard, but you didn't. You put your head down and did the work, and it's probably devastating to think it was all for naught since Mom is selling the farm anyway. Am I close?"

Carl slouched in his chair, looking defeated. "I thought if I just hustled and did my best, I'd be able to fix this the way Dad always managed to. I was wrong."

Thea wanted to reach for his hand, but she wasn't sure they were there yet. "Look, Dad's gone. And he has been for a long time. The fact that you and Mom were able to keep this going all this time means you did it, Carl. You did it. You ran the farm and kept things going and honored Dad in the process. Which isn't something I can say for myself." Thea had been doing a lot of thinking since she'd shown up here. It was time she owned up to her own mistakes.

"We're still losing the farm, though," he said.

"Maybe. But you two ran it all alone for almost a decade," Thea continued. "Hector has been telling me all the stories, Carl. I've seen your handiwork on the fences, and I saw your engineering solution to the broken gutter off the milking parlor. Redirecting that rainwater to the barrels to help water the pastures was brilliant. You're good at this. You haven't just been filling Dad's shoes. You've taken a stand in your own. I'm proud of you."

Carl gave her a small smile. "The rainwater thing was pretty genius, right?"

"So genius," she agreed. "And don't even get me started on your grass-growing skills. Ridiculous," she said with a smile. "The back pasture looks like a jungle. The ladies are gonna mow that to shreds this week." Thea's family supplemented the cows with a diet that a nutritionist helped them hone over the years, but the majority of their food intake was still pasture based, which was a Boudreaux family tradition. They rotated the feeding areas between the three surrounding family-owned pastures to ensure all the cows had plenty to eat, and grass had plenty of time to regrow.

Carl's smile broadened. "Remember crazy Old Man Fuller?"

"The agriculture teacher at our high school?" Thea hadn't heard that name in years.

"Yeah." Carl leaned forward excitedly. "Anyway, he retired and has been working on developing some fancy new grass seed. I ran into him in town a few months ago, and we started working together. I'm trying out his seed on the back pastures between rotations, and he comes out and does a bunch of measurements and science stuff. He's talking about writing something for the *Journal of Agriculture*. I'm going to be mentioned in the research." Carl beamed.

"Famous? You're going to be famous?" Thea wiped her brow and pretended to be faint. "How will I ever handle your ego then?"

Carl laughed. "Shut up."

Thea smiled at him. "I really am proud of you. And I meant what I said before. I shouldn't have left you both all alone. I was wrong for doing that. I'm sorry."

Carl gave her a small nod. "Thanks."

Thea stood and started unpacking the groceries. "So, besides literally changing how the grass grows around here, what else is new?"

"Oh, uh, nothing really."

She pulled out a bag of onions and looked up at him. He was blushing. "What's that face? Is there a girl? There's a girl, right?" Thea prodded.

Carl rubbed the back of his neck and got even redder. "Maybe."

"Ha!" Thea did a victory dance with the artichokes. "I knew it. Tell me more."

"Thea," he whined, and the familiarity of that exchange from their youth made her smile. She was glad to be back in her little brother's good graces.

"Fine. I'll ask Mom, then."

Carl sat up straight. "No, no way."

"Well, if you won't tell me, she certainly will." Thea tapped her chin in consideration. "You know what? Don't tell me. Mom will have all the juicy dirt anyway."

Carl looked mortified. "Don't tell Mom. She doesn't know yet."

"She doesn't know?" Thea nearly dropped the yams. "This is a *secret* girl?"

"Shh." Carl held his finger over his mouth. "Keep your voice down."

Thea pretended to hide behind a stalk of celery. "It's just you, me, and the celery, Little C. We're good."

Carl still looked over his shoulder suspiciously before continuing, "Her name is Annie, and she works at the farmers' market in town."

Thea froze, holding up the fistful of radishes she had pulled from the bag. "Is this why we have so many vegetables? I mean, I've been a vegetarian a long time, and I appreciate all the freshy freshes in the house, but I was a little surprised as to why you bought enough produce to open a farm stand."

Carl's ears were the color of the apples on the counter. Thea picked one up and threw it at him.

"Hey," he cried out as he narrowly stopped it from hitting him in the face.

"Have a snack. You must be starving, living on vegetables alone," she said with a wink.

He took a bite and mumbled, "They sell fruit, too."

Thea laughed. That made sense. She opened the next bag and found the fruit bounty. "Plums, strawberries, more apples, mangoes, and grapes? Did you leave any fruit for anyone else?" she teased.

Carl nudged the sole bag left on the table in front of him, looking shy. "And peaches."

Thea reached into the bag, pulling out four perfectly round, plump peaches. She sighed. Peaches.

"Oh, now who's got a secret?" Carl said slyly. "I've seen that look before. You have a girl, too."

Thea raised an eyebrow in his direction. "You know nothing of the ways of women, mister."

Carl pointed at her while still holding his half-eaten apple. "You're a worse liar than me."

Thea contemplated tossing a peach at him, but she couldn't bring herself to do it. That peach reminded her of Lauren and the life she put on hold back in Boston. She wondered what Lauren was doing right now.

"Spill," he said.

"Okay, okay. I met someone, but it's really new. Like we haven't even gone on a date yet. That kind of new." Thea wanted to do lots of things with Lauren, and going on a date was one of the only wholesome things on that list. "But I barely know her, so we'll see."

Carl nodded. "That's cool."

"It is," Thea agreed. She thought about her night with Lauren often. A part of her really hoped that kind of chemistry translated into real life and not just the bedroom. Though she was more than happy to test that connection in bed again, she found herself hoping they could grab a bite to eat or something, too. She hadn't felt that way about another woman in a long time. Avni would be so pleased. She looked up at the clock in the kitchen. "When is Mom meeting that Realtor?"

"Now," Carl said, looking sad again.

"What do you mean now?" Thea asked.

Carl finished his apple and tossed out the core as he stretched. "She's meeting them now. I saw the fancy car pull up outside the barn. That's why I went to the store. I didn't want to be here. I figured that was why you were hiding in the house."

Thea shook her head. "I wasn't…I'm not hiding. I was working, sort of." She was on the phone with her bestie, not exactly working, but still.

"They're probably wrapping up now. I'm sure Mom will tell us about it over dinner."

Thea barely heard what he said as she flew out the front door in the direction of the barn. She had no intention of letting some slick rich-bitch Realtor talk her mother into selling the last of her father's legacy. No way in hell.

CHAPTER EIGHT

Lauren stretched in her seat. It had been a long time since she'd taken a road trip, and her body was sore. She was out of practice. She shut off the engine and grabbed her blazer and purse as she climbed out of the car. She checked herself in the mirror, adjusting her blouse before slipping on the jacket. She looked out at the dusty walkway up to the barn ahead of her and reconsidered her outfit. Maybe heels and a designer suit weren't the best choice for this meeting.

She glanced into the empty space behind the driver's seat where an overnight bag should have been had she packed one. Ellison had recommended she pack a change of clothes in case she was too tired to drive back. She'd even given her a list of local inns to reach out to if the meeting ran long, and she had already agreed to cover all of Lauren's expenses. But Lauren had no interest in sticking around in this sleepy little town. She was so sure she'd be in her own bed tonight that she'd even agreed to an early meeting with Ellison tomorrow to go over their upcoming project. Sure, the ride from Boston wasn't exactly short, but with some Starbucks, she could make it happen. She was a city girl, after all, and visiting the country was fine, but her high-rise apartment had a better view and probably better internet.

"Hi." An attractive older woman with graying blond hair waved as she walked up. "You must be Lauren. I'm Kathleen Boudreaux."

"Mrs. Boudreaux," Lauren said as she extended her hand. "It's so nice to meet you. Thank you for taking the time to chat with me today."

"Kathleen is fine," she said with a warm smile. "And thank you for making the trip. It's quite the haul from Boston when you aren't familiar with the roads."

"No trouble at all," Lauren lied. Ellison had undersold how much of the trip was back and country roads. Her Porsche was going to need a wash and a detailing to shine like it usually did. "So, tell me a little about you and this place. It's beautiful, by the way."

Kathleen looked at the acreage beyond them and gave her a small smile. "It is. But it's too much. And it's too expensive to keep running. So I need your help."

"I'll do my best," Lauren promised.

"I know you will," Kathleen said. "Ellie told me you were going to figure everything out, and I believe her. She's a great judge of character, that one. If she says you're the one for the job, then you're the one for the job."

"Well, that's nice to hear." Lauren didn't know what to say. Ellie? She had a hard time envisioning Ellison going by such a sweet, almost naive-sounding name. Nothing about Ellison Gamble was overly sweet or naive. Not one thing.

"Come on, it's hot out here. Let's head over to the office and talk numbers, and then I'll give you a tour of the grounds." Kathleen looked down at Lauren's feet. "We'll take the golf cart. Those shoes are cute, but you'll never make it out to the pastures."

"I really showed my city slicker today, huh?"

Kathleen laughed. "No comment."

❖

Lauren shrugged off her jacket and draped it on the back of her chair. She and Kathleen had been going over the operations details and numbers for over two hours now. And though the office was air-conditioned, the jacket was making her sweat.

"Anyway, this is probably more information than you needed, but Ellie told me to give you everything. So here it is," Kathleen said as she handed Lauren a glass of water.

"Thanks," Lauren said as she took a sip of the cool, refreshing beverage. "Can I take a look at the surveyor's markup?"

"Sure." Kathleen handed her the rolled document.

Lauren unrolled it and looked at the blueprint-like map in front of her. Each and every building and border of the property was identified on this sheet. She placed her finger over the barn to get her bearings— that's where they were now. The old barn had been converted into offices on the second floor, while the first floor operated like a small general store for all of the goods produced here: cheese, milk, ice cream, yogurt. Lauren thought it was a smart use of the historic space.

She looked back at the sheet and compared it to the aerial photos Ellison had provided in the Boudreaux file she'd given her. Her gaze fell to the large square designating the Boudreaux house. The family residence was only a few hundred yards away from the barn—a four-bedroom, one-and-a-half bath, beautiful old farmhouse with a wraparound porch that in pictures was stunning. Lauren wanted to see that part last. She loved old homes.

She pointed to the section of the property bordering the lake. "Tell me about all this open space."

Kathleen put on her readers and leaned forward. She pointed to the building labeled Milking Parlor, located just adjacent to them. "This is where the cows are milked, and these three plots of land are different grazing pastures for them to feed when they aren't fed in their stalls."

Lauren pointed to the largest back pasture. This one bordered the lake on two sides. "And this, too?"

"That's our back lot," Kathleen said with a nod. "That's the one Ellie said would be worth the most money if we broke things into pieces."

Lauren nodded. If the view from that property was unobstructed, the lakefront land was worth a fortune.

"Can you tell me about these other buildings?" Lauren asked.

"Sure," Kathleen said as she leaned closer. "This is where the cows are housed—there's a little medical station in here for them for when the veterinarian comes. The feed storage is in the back there, this is the cheese and dairy plant that also has the aging rooms, and this smaller building holds the mobile equipment like the mowers and such. And this little square is where Hector lives—he's our farm manager."

"And this?" She pointed to a large section with miniature cartoon trees on it.

"Those are the woods. They separate our land from the road."

Lauren took in the map and considered what Kathleen had said. The Boudreaux property had an oblong shape. The farthest-reaching edge of the property was that back pasture. Ellison had told her to be creative and do everything she could to help them figure out how to maximize their land sale. She wanted to see that part first, because that was going to be their moneymaker—she was sure of it.

"I think I have an idea of the property lines. Can we go on that tour now?" Lauren was eager to get started. She stood from her chair and grabbed her blazer as Kathleen rolled up the markup and put it back in the cardboard tube for storage.

"Absolutely." Kathleen led her out of the second-floor office and along the lofted balcony toward the stairs below.

They walked past another smaller office full of filing cabinets and a small desk. As they turned toward the top of the stairs, Lauren took the opportunity to look out at the floor below. The small store was laid out along the right side of the barn. She could see two customers perusing the items and a young cashier waiting patiently at the hand-carved wooden countertop. The rest of the open space was filled with what looked like old farm artifacts and merchandise all featuring something to do with the Boudreaux family.

She scanned the black-and-white photos along the wall as they got to the bottom of the stairs. Kathleen pointed to an aged newspaper clipping.

"That's the year my husband won the chili-eating contest at the annual Berry Festival around here."

Lauren leaned in for a closer look. She saw a tall, handsome man holding a trophy topped with what looked like a metal batch of blueberries. He was flanked by two little kids, a girl and a boy. The girl was smiling broadly with a missing front tooth and the boy looked like he had been crying.

"Are these your kids?" Lauren asked. The caption under the photo read *Carlton "CJ" Boudreaux Jr. takes top prize in front of his number one fans.*

Kathleen smiled. "They clearly had differing opinions about their father's win. I'm sure you'll cross their paths at some point. They're around here somewhere."

Another newer photo caught her eye. It was of Emerson Sterling posing with a handsome twentysomething-year-old guy. Even with a hat on and casually dressed, her perfect smile and Hollywood good looks were unmistakable. "Emerson Sterling was here?"

"Ah, that was an exciting day in Carl's life. It turns out she married one of our neighbors," Kathleen said, looking amused.

"Hayley Carpenter is your neighbor?" Lauren couldn't believe the coincidence. She'd just been talking about them with Trina last week.

"Her grandmother owned a place just beyond ours. Her family has a cabin there now. Hayley used to come here with her family all the time. Small world, huh?"

"Very."

They walked past an old saddle displayed on a shelf with a small placard, and a few shelves containing T-shirts and mugs featuring a picture of the barn they were currently in and the Boudreaux family name. Lauren touched one of the soft fleece pullovers.

"We used to sell a lot of everything out of this little store, but just before my husband died, we moved to more commercial sales. We don't keep much in stock on-site—just about everything is shipped to the surrounding towns and grocery stores. But in its heyday, the Boudreaux farm was a bustling place. A lot of that has changed as the times changed. In many ways, we're still stuck in the past." Lauren noticed Kathleen was looking at another framed picture as she spoke. The same man from before was pictured, with his arm around an old man's shoulders. "That's Grandpa Boudreaux, Carlton Sr. He built this place with his bare hands. My husband was so proud of his daddy."

"It's a beautiful legacy," Lauren said, because it was.

Kathleen sighed. "That makes it all the harder to let it go, though, right?"

"I'm sorry, I didn't—" Lauren hadn't meant to sadden her.

Kathleen raised her hand. "It's all right. The past is in the past. Maybe getting out from under it is exactly what me and the kids need." She reached out and squeezed Lauren's forearm. "I'm grateful you're here to help. Just knowing I'm not doing it alone makes it feel less overwhelming."

Lauren swallowed thickly. The kind, tired eyes looking at her were so sincere and genuine that she wanted to pull the other woman into a hug and promise her it would be okay. But she knew that probably wasn't the case. Ellison had sent her here to find a way to scrap and salvage. She was here to help Kathleen close this chapter in her life, whether she was ready for it or not. And she knew she would because she promised Ellison and because Kathleen seemed like a wonderful woman burdened by a farm that got to be too much in her husband's absence. But she would be lying if she denied that the faith this woman already had in her felt heavy.

"Hey, Kathleen. Do you have a minute?" an older man with graying dark hair asked as he wiped his brow with a gloved hand.

"Sure." Kathleen turned to Lauren. "This is Hector Alverez, our farm manager and all-around lifesaver. There isn't a thing Hector can't do."

Hector stood a little taller after the compliment. "Hi."

"This is Lauren Calloway. The Realtor Ellie recommended," she said to him.

His smile brightened. "Ellie? What's she doing these days?"

Lauren could not get over the Ellie thing. "Running a business and kicking butt," she said with a shrug. "But I don't get the pleasure of calling her Ellie."

"Oh." Kathleen pressed her fingers to her lips. "Don't tell her we called her that, then."

Hector laughed. "She'll always be awkward, gangly Ellie to me."

Awkward? Ellison? Never, Lauren thought.

"It's nice to meet you," she said as she shook Hector's hand.

"Oh, a good-bye handshake. Great. So I take it you're leaving, then? Because we're not selling," a familiar voice sounded from behind her.

"Theodora. Don't be rude," Kathleen chastised.

Lauren turned to the sound of someone running into the barn, shocked by what she saw.

"Thea, wait," a young man said as he skidded to a stop.

"What? I was just about to escort Mom's new friend off the prop—" The words died on her lips, and Thea's face was a mirror of how Lauren was feeling. "Lauren?"

"Thea?" Lauren felt like time froze, and everything was still, except for her racing mind. Talk about a small world.

Kathleen broke the silent spell. "Lauren? This is *your* Lauren?"

"I'm whose Lauren, exactly?" Lauren asked. She raised an eyebrow in Thea's direction. Had Thea been talking about her?

The young man burst out laughing. "This is the woman you were talking about? You have the hots for the Realtor Mom is working with to sell Dad's farm? Smooth, Thea. Really. Smooth." Well, that settled that. Thea certainly *had* been talking about her.

Thea's mouth remained open, her cheeks a deep pink. Honestly, Lauren thought she looked adorable while also managing to look super-hot in that casual linen dress shirt and jeans combo with those incredibly sexy work boots. But also, what was Thea doing here?

"This is a pleasant surprise," Lauren said, recovering quickly. "How are you?"

"I'm, uh, good." Thea looked embarrassed. The guy to her left started to cackle.

"Carlton Henry III," Kathleen snapped, and it was then that Lauren recognized him as the person in the photo with Emerson.

Carlton covered his mouth and nodded, appearing to strain under his attempts to stop laughing.

Kathleen sighed. "Well, this didn't go as planned at all, did it?"

Lauren let her gaze linger on Thea for a moment longer, still not quite over the surprise of seeing her here. "I take it these are the grown kids from the chili contest picture?"

Kathleen rubbed her forehead as she frowned. "Theodora and Carlton. Currently on their best behavior, it seems."

"You can call me Carl," Thea's brother said with a wave. "Carlton is reserved for when I'm being disciplined. It's nice to meet you." He elbowed his sister, who grunted in response. "I understand you and Thea are already acquainted."

She gave him a nod, her gaze settling on Thea again. "Theodora, huh?"

Thea rolled her eyes. "It's a family name."

"It's nice," Lauren supplied, enjoying the way Thea seemed a little uncomfortable. This was certainly not the Thea who was at the bar or in her apartment. She appreciated seeing this side of her.

Hector cleared his throat. "I don't mean to intrude, but I do need to go over a couple of things with you, Kathleen."

"Right, right. Sorry," Kathleen said as she touched Lauren's elbow. "I'll meet up with you in a bit. Thea will give you a tour of the grounds."

"I'll what?" Thea looked scandalized, and Carl was laughing again.

"Thea. Get the golf cart. Show Lauren around. Try to redeem your rudeness." Kathleen wasn't messing around.

"Yes, Mom," Thea acquiesced easily.

"Carl," Kathleen said, and the laughing stopped. "Check on the cows, and make sure the house is cleaned up for Lauren to have a look around."

Carl nodded and slinked off through the barn doors, his shoulders bobbing slightly as he chuckled.

Thea gave her a shrug. "I guess I'm your chauffeur."

Lauren was failing at trying to stifle a smile. "Seems like it."

"Right this way," Thea said as she stepped back, motioning for Lauren to join her.

They made it about ten steps outside of the barn before Thea turned to face her.

"Listen, I was rude before. Mom's right. I'm sorry about that. I had no idea. I didn't know it was—" She paused, seeming to collect her thoughts. "We aren't selling the farm. I just want you to know that up front. I'll take you on the tour or whatever, but we're not selling."

Lauren cocked her head to the side, contemplating what to say. She could tell Thea had as much emotion around this property as Kathleen did. Maybe more. "I'm not here to sell the farm."

"You aren't?" Thea looked relieved.

Lauren shook her head. "I'm here to help your mom figure out her selling options."

"That's the same thing," Thea argued.

"It's not." Lauren placed her hand on her hip. "I'm merely a consultant, trying to help your mom figure out what's best for the farm. And from what I've heard, that's her decision to make. Not yours."

Thea's face flashed with anger. "You don't know anything about that."

Lauren shook her head. "I know everything about that. That's why I'm here, to help everyone end up as well-off as possible. Your father left the farm to your mother. She's the one that reached out for help. I'm here to help *her*."

Thea looked at a loss for words. Her face was a mix of anger and pain, and Lauren felt bad for being so blunt.

She tried again. "Look, I am not here to step on any toes. I'm just here to try to help." She reached out to run her fingers along Thea's forearm. "I am happy to see you, though. This *is* a pleasant surprise."

Thea looked at Lauren's fingers on her arm, but she said nothing.

"I'm sorry. I didn't mean to make you uncomfortable." Lauren pulled her hand back.

"You didn't. You don't." Thea frowned. "I'm just—"

"Overwhelmed? Having a hard time with this? Feeling lost?" Lauren asked.

"Yes, actually." Thea looked up at her for the first time without seeming to mask her emotions. This was the Thea she'd met the other night, her steely blue eyes clear and open.

Lauren nodded. "That's what your mom said, too. Just, let me try to help. Okay?"

Thea watched her for a moment. "Okay."

CHAPTER NINE

Thea wasn't sure what to do, so she just played monosyllabic tour guide and tried to ignore the restlessness she felt. Her head was a mess of emotions, and Lauren smelled amazing sitting next to her in the golf cart, which didn't help at all.

The outfit Lauren was wearing didn't help either. She was completely ill-prepared for a farm tour in those shoes and those pants and that blouse, but damn, did she look good in them. Thea had tried not to notice that when her mother was yelling at her in the barn, but that was impossible. Because like the first time she'd met Lauren, she was struck by her beauty.

"Can we stop here a minute, please?" Lauren continued to be endlessly polite, and Thea hated that because she wanted to be mad at her, but she couldn't.

"Sure," she said as she eased the golf cart to a stop.

Lauren stepped out and pulled out her phone, taking panoramic photos and walking toward the back pasture. Thea followed because she felt like she should, even though the desire to brood in the golf cart and wait was also present.

"This lake is gorgeous," Lauren said to herself. Thea heard that often. And it was, though she realized she might have lost some of her appreciation for it over the years. It was part of the background of her life here. Maybe she'd taken it for granted all these years.

Thea's mouth moved before her brain could stop her. "I spent every afternoon in that lake after Carl and I finished our chores."

"I would, too," Lauren concurred. "It's so beautiful."

She stepped toward the embankment and squeaked when her heel sank into the wet soil, nearly toppling her in the process.

Thea rushed forward to grab her elbow to steady her, but Lauren rocked back, sinking her heel in deeper.

"Shit." Lauren lifted her foot, leaning into Thea as the heel stayed partially buried.

Thea laughed, her hands at Lauren's hips as she tried to help her get her balance on one foot. "Here, put your arms on my shoulders."

Lauren struggled to stay on one foot but seemed to hesitate at Thea's command.

"Come on," Thea coaxed her as she guided Lauren's arms around her neck. "I don't bite."

Lauren gave her a look. "I have on good authority that you do bite, and I got to experience a different kind of biting back at the barn. So that's not true."

Thea scrunched her nose. "Fair."

She reached down and scooped behind Lauren's legs, picking her up in a bridal carry as Lauren squeaked again. "It's easier this way, I promise."

Lauren looked skeptical but she didn't say anything.

Thea walked her back to the golf cart, depositing her on the seat before she went back and retrieved her heel from the mud. She used the side of her jeans to wipe off most of the gunk, but the heel would need some TLC back at the house.

"Thank you," Lauren said as she slipped her heel back on.

"You're welcome," Thea said as she climbed into the seat next to her, tapping the steering wheel just to give her hands something to do.

After a moment, Lauren said, "You know, I really thought when you texted me that you had family stuff to deal with that you were actually just blowing me off."

"I'm not like that," Thea said, realizing that Lauren had no way of knowing that. She turned to face her. "I'm not the ghosting type. Plus, I thought we had a pretty great night together…Don't you agree?"

"Oh, I thought so, but we didn't really talk about what would happen next. If anything. I didn't want to assume you owed me anything," Lauren said, and Thea appreciated that.

"Well, I certainly owe you a more polite greeting than the one I gave you in the barn," Thea replied, still feeling a little embarrassed.

"Thanks," Lauren said. "Maybe we should start over." She shifted, facing Thea with her hand outstretched. "I'm Lauren Calloway. I'm a Realtor for Gamble and Associates in Boston, and my boss asked me to come out here and help your mom navigate a sale if it comes to that. On a more personal note, I don't like mushrooms on pizza, I like rom-coms but I dislike Colin Firth, and my favorite color is yellow."

Thea laughed, shaking Lauren's hand. "I'm Theodora Boudreaux, but I prefer Thea. My family owns a dairy farm in Maine, but I live in Boston and am the head administrator to a biotech start-up. I like rum and charming, mysterious women who are fancily dressed and forward with their intentions. The smell of brussels sprouts makes me nauseous. And I've never watched *You've Got Mail* all the way through because the sound of the AOL dial-up gives me PTSD from my preteen years."

"Ooh, rough puberty?" Lauren asked.

"Rough coming-out," Thea replied, mostly over it. "I embarrassed myself in a chatroom once by professing my love to a classmate while using a fake screen name that wasn't nearly anonymous enough. It's safe to say that I never quite lived that down. I'm just grateful the internet exchanges were still in their infancy, and that Twitter and Instagram weren't a thing yet."

"Oh yeah. Good point. Teenage dating and social media sounds like a nightmare." Lauren nodded in agreement. "Although dating as an adult isn't exactly a cakewalk either these days."

"Truth," Thea replied. She considered that for a moment. This was another thing about Lauren she had no idea about. "Are you dating anyone?"

Lauren smiled at her as she leaned back. "Are you going to ask me out?"

This was the confident, sure-of-herself woman from The Mirage. Thea felt herself get excited. Gone was the hesitancy to engage from before. She found herself wanting to flirt back. "Mostly I'm gathering intel. But I certainly would be interested in seeing you outside the bedroom, yes."

Lauren fluttered her eyelashes playfully. "You didn't see enough of me in the bedroom?"

"I'm not sure that *enough* is an achievable thing when it comes to you and the bedroom. But I'd be willing to test that hypothesis," Thea replied.

Lauren gave her a broad smile, and Thea didn't miss the way she licked along her bottom lip. "Okay."

"Okay, what?" Thea realized she was staring at Lauren's mouth.

"Okay, you can take me out sometime," Lauren said before pointing to her shoe, "but only because you saved me from certain shoe destruction and a likely ass-plant in the mud."

"Only because of that?" Thea rested her arm on the bar between their seats, leaning in slightly.

"Maybe not only because of that." Lauren's hand briefly made contact with Thea's thigh before settling back on her own lap. "The whole carrying me like I weighed nothing thing certainly plays a part in my decision."

"You do weigh nothing," Thea pointed out. Lifting Lauren was as easy as breathing.

"Flattery will get you everywhere," Lauren said.

"Everywhere?" Thea asked, leaning in closer.

"Within reason," Lauren repeated from their first night together, and that brought a flood of memories to the forefront of Thea's mind. Suddenly the distance between them felt too vast.

"I can be very reasonable," Thea said as she placed her hand on Lauren's knee, pleased at the soft moan from Lauren that followed her touch.

"I bet," Lauren said, just inches from her face. "And I can be very persuasive."

"Sounds like we'd do just fine together, then." Thea moved her hand up Lauren's thigh a bit.

"We were more than *fine* together before," Lauren said, her voice thick and teasing.

"I'll say." Thea brought her hand from Lauren's thigh to her jaw, bringing her mouth closer. She ached to kiss her. "That was easily the most memorable night of my life."

Lauren's full lips parted, and Thea swallowed thickly as Lauren licked her bottom lip again. "So far, you mean."

Thea smiled because that was all the encouragement she needed to bring their lips together again, until the sound of someone coughing nearby ruined the moment.

Thea leaned back, whipping her head in the direction of the sound. Just behind the golf cart—standing with her arms crossed and a frown on her face—was her mother. Fuck.

"Kathleen," Lauren said as she straightened up. "I was hoping to ask you a few questions."

"Oh?" Kathleen asked, while her eyes shot daggers at Thea.

"Yes." Lauren exited the golf cart and gingerly walked toward her.

"About how much of those woods back there are part of your property as well?"

This question seemed to catch her mother off guard. It certainly caught Thea off guard. How did Lauren recover so quickly from the interruption? Thea still felt like all the blood had left her brain and was settled significantly lower.

"Uh..." Her mother considered this. "About twenty acres. There's an old wooden fence that runs along the border there, but it's not one we monitor or anything. There isn't anything on that side of the forest, really. It's rocky and dense. It would probably cost a fortune to make it habitable."

Lauren looked out at the area they were discussing and nodded. "I'd like to see it."

"It's best done via car. You'll be able to see the fence from the road," she replied.

"Great," Lauren said before briefly glancing back at Thea. "I think I have everything I need here. Can I see the last two buildings now? Your farmhouse and Hector's place?"

"Absolutely." Her mother gave her a quick look. "Climb in the back, Thea. I'll drive."

Oof. She could tell by her mother's tone that a discussion was on the horizon. Great.

"Sure thing," she said with a false smile as she climbed into the back, positioning herself in the middle of the rear seat.

Her mother got behind the wheel, and Lauren slipped easily beside her, not looking back. But Thea could see she had a small smile on her lips. She wondered what about.

They circled back to the main property, and her mother gave Lauren some of the details about the land. Things Thea should have mentioned on their drive to the pastures, but she had been too sore and embarrassed to be a good host. Thankfully, her mother was redeeming them both.

Thea waited in the golf cart as they toured Hector's place. She looked around and noticed that Lauren's blazer was draped over the back of the chair in front of her. She reached out to touch the fabric, pleased to see it was as soft and smooth as the material Lauren was wearing when she massaged up her thigh earlier.

"It's Chanel," Lauren supplied from behind her. She pulled her hand back, feeling like she was caught doing something she shouldn't.

"It's very nice," Thea replied.

"Only the best for me." Lauren had her forearm resting on the roof of the golf cart. Thea noticed the edge of a lacy nude-colored bra visible with the more obvious dip in her blouse this position provided.

"I'm discovering that," Thea said.

"I'd like the opportunity to continue our conversation from before," Lauren said, dipping her head to catch Thea's eye. She seemed unfazed that Thea's gaze was wandering.

"Was there much conversation occurring? Because I got the impression we were about to embark on a less chatty route," Thea replied, emboldened by Lauren's closeness again. It was like she couldn't help herself.

"Well, I'd like to continue that path as well," Lauren said, and Thea loved the twinkle in her hazel eyes.

The sound of Hector and her mother approaching drew her attention. "These interruptions are getting old real fast."

Lauren turned and waved to the two of them as she said under her breath, "Just think of this as foreplay. You know, just slightly less sticky than the peach."

"Fuck." Thea groaned at the reference. She wasn't so sure Lauren was right about that.

Lauren gave a not so subtle look to Thea's crotch as she replied, "Or maybe just as sticky."

Thea had to bite her lip to stop the next groan as she shifted uncomfortably. Lauren winked at her before innocently resuming her seat as Thea's mother climbed behind the wheel again.

"To the main farmhouse?" she asked.

"Yes, please," Lauren replied. And Thea felt like there was something naughty in her tone. Or maybe she was just imagining things because she was unreasonably turned-on. Maybe it was both.

"Off we go," her mother said, and Lauren chatted with her easily during the short drive to the house Thea grew up in. Thea was amazed how seamlessly Lauren switched from flirting with her to friendly, professional banter with her mother, and back again. That was not a skill Thea possessed. Especially not with her mother around.

She slumped back in the seat with a sigh as they rounded the gravel drive to her childhood home. Today had been a weird mix of emotions. In many ways, being in the back seat of this golf cart made her feel small and childlike. Hearing about the property she'd lived on as though it was being advertised for a sale made her sad, but she had to admit Lauren's way of engaging her mother felt more like a conversation than data collection.

She knew Lauren was there for a reason, but the more time she spent listening to her engage her mother, the less she saw her as a threat. There was a warmth in the exchange. It was much less transactional than she expected a Realtor to be. But then again, she'd noticed that warmth in her own exchange with Lauren. Albeit under much different circumstances, but still. When they'd first met, Lauren had quickly brought down Thea's guard. In every sense of the word. She'd easily connected with Lauren on lots of levels that night. It seemed that Lauren had that effect on her mother, who spoke candidly about the farm but also shared anecdotes and funny stories as well. Thea hadn't seen her mother this at ease in a very long time.

"Okay, last stop," her mother joked as she shut off the golf cart. "Dinner will be served immediately after the tour is completed."

Lauren laughed as she climbed out after her.

Thea picked up Lauren's blazer, thinking she'd forgotten it. Her mother called out to Carl and started talking to him as they walked in the front door. While she was distracted, Thea tried to hand the jacket back to Lauren.

Lauren looked at it and shook her head. "You can carry that for me."

"Oh? Did you expect me to join you on this tour?" Thea had no intention of going room to room with them as Lauren took stock of the space. She could mentally check out while they were at Hector's or outside on the grounds, but touring her *home* felt like it was a step too far. Even if she didn't find herself thinking of Lauren as a villain, she wasn't sure she could stomach that.

Lauren nodded. "Well, who else is going to give me a tour of your bedroom?"

Thea laughed. Flirty Lauren was back. This woman was incredible.

"Sorry for the delay. I'm ready." Her mother rejoined them with a tired smile. "Where should we start?"

"How about down here? I'd like to see the bedrooms last," Lauren said, her voice smooth like velvet. Thea shook her head. This was going to be a frustratingly torturous walk-through. She just knew it.

❖

"Mom, how brown is it supposed to be?" Carl's voice sounded from the kitchen below.

Kathleen looked panicked. "I swear, your brother can't cook to save his life."

Thea raised her hands seemingly in innocence as though not to get involved. She'd been mostly quiet on this tour, Lauren noted.

Kathleen turned back to her. "Sorry, I need to check on that. These last two rooms are the guest room and Thea's. Feel free to check them out. I'll be downstairs making sure Carl doesn't ruin dinner."

"Thanks," Lauren said as Kathleen scurried down the stairs.

She turned her attention to the guest room on the right. She gripped the polished antique knob, turning it slightly and sighing happily at the sight that awaited her. The room was beautiful and inviting with what looked like the original wide plank pine floors and minimal furnishings. The waning natural light of the day managed to cast a welcoming glow on the crocheted white throw that was draped on the queen bed. The late-day beauty told Lauren that midday this room would be the best room in the house to take a nap. In her opinion, there was nothing better than a nap in a room flooded in natural light.

She ran her hand along the hand-carved headboard, admiring the handiwork when Thea spoke for the first time.

"My grandfather made that for my grandmother when they were first married." She stepped over the threshold and leaned against the wall by the door. "He used to swear that elves helped him work on it in the nighttime while my grandmother slept, but the truth was he spent every waking hour—and what were supposed to be sleeping hours—making sure it was perfect for her. They didn't have any money, and they came from nothing, so everything they eventually had came from hard work. Blood, sweat, and tears."

"And love," Lauren said. "Love is what motivates a person to work well into the night and lose precious sleep to make something so wonderfully heartfelt for someone. Especially when they need that sleep to make their working hours productive. From everything you and your mother have told me, it sounds like your grandparents' hard work is what grew this family and this farm. Your grandfather sacrificing sleep and rest to make something that could be handed down for generations is an act of love."

Thea watched her for a moment, and Lauren wondered if maybe she'd overstepped.

"You really mean that, don't you?" she asked.

"Why wouldn't I?"

Thea crossed her arms, draping Lauren's jacket over her forearm in the process. Lauren let herself appreciate how strong Thea's shoulders looked in that linen shirt. "I don't know. I guess I keep expecting some sort of pitch from you. Like, I imagine you have to be poetic in your language to help people sell and buy houses."

Lauren perched herself on the edge of the bed, facing Thea. "You expect me to a be slimy used-car salesman, don't you?"

Thea shifted. "Not exactly."

Lauren could tell by her face that was precisely what she thought. This wasn't a new experience for Lauren. Lots of people had that prejudice toward her line of work. But for some reason the pushback from Thea bothered her more than usual. "Do you know why I got into real estate?"

Thea shook her head.

"I like making people happy," Lauren said. "Buying a new home or closing an old chapter and starting a new one with a home sale are some of the most emotional and frightening experiences you can have in this life. It's the commitment to embrace adventure or the closure necessary to find a new purpose. Homes like this—headboards like this one—are full of memories and milestones. This isn't some lemon on a car lot I'm trying to unload—this is your entire childhood and might have one day been the home you wanted to bring a family of your own to."

She stood, taking her jacket from Thea and slipping it on. "I'm not in the business of ruining lives, Thea. I'm in the business of helping people start new ones. Whatever that might be. That's not up to me to decide. But a used-car salesman I'm not."

She headed out the door, but Thea's hand on her wrist slowed her.

"I'm sorry." Thea's voice was small.

Lauren let out an exhale. "I know this is hard for you. And it will continue to be hard for you until you try to see things from your mother's perspective and try to see me as a person that isn't out to get you. Or anyone."

"I'm trying." Thea sounded defeated. Lauren felt for her, she did.

She turned to face her, surprised by the tears she found streaking down Thea's face. Her heart sank. She hadn't meant to wound her.

Thea broke their contact to wipe at the falling tears. She shook her head with an empty laugh. "You really got me with that line about never getting to bring my own family here. Like, right in the heart.

With a knife twist." She let out a shaky sigh. "Having to sell this land, running into you here—none of this was anything I was expecting. It feels like my life is slowly unraveling, and I'm on the outside looking in."

Lauren wanted to embrace her because it seemed like Thea might need that. And because she wanted to comfort her. But she realized this was bigger than her or anything she could do for Thea. This wasn't the sexy banter and verbal foreplay from before—this was Thea's life, and everything Lauren had just said, she'd meant. There was nothing easy about letting go of the past.

She stepped toward Thea, not being able to help herself. She wanted to comfort her—she had to. She reached out and took Thea's free hand. "I know we don't know each other very well, but I can promise you that your mom and your family are my priority in this. I'm only here as a consultant to help things transition in the best way for everyone. I'm not the bad guy. I swear."

"Okay." Thea squeezed her hand and nodded. Lauren kept that contact because it felt nice to hold Thea's hand. After a few moments she nudged Thea with her elbow, tugging her toward the hallway.

"So, I've sort of been saving the best for last," she said, eager to bring back the playfulness they'd shared earlier.

"Oh?" Thea's expression was lighter. Lauren noticed how she smiled when she looked at their joined hands. Good. Her plan was working.

"Yeah," Lauren said as she pulled Thea toward the last stop on the tour. "You think you're ready to show me that room of yours? Because I'm kind of dying to see it."

Thea covered her face with her free hand. "I don't think I can do it."

"Why? It's like a time capsule to your youth, isn't it?" Lauren asked, excited. "Do you have old *Baywatch* posters on your walls? Or maybe the Spice Girls? Wait, wait. Don't tell me." She released Thea's hand and stepped back to make a pretend frame between her fingers and thumbs and aimed it at Thea. "I know. It's angsty and Evanescence filled. That's it. You went through a dark, brooding stage, and the room behind this door shows all your innermost secrets."

Thea laughed. Good. Laughing was good, Lauren thought.

"Not exactly."

"No?" Lauren frowned. She'd really given that her best shot. "Am I close?"

Thea winced. "No."

"Really? 'Cuz I thought I really nailed the angsty part."

"Well, the way you made it sound so interesting and mysterious, I sort of wish you were right," Thea said as she opened the door and stepped back. "Just remember that this is my *childhood* bedroom and not what my *actual* bedroom looks like."

"I'll keep an open mind," Lauren said as she walked into the room to find a modest full-sized bed with a dark blue comforter and matching pillows. There was a trunk at the end of the bed, adorned with fading stickers and graffiti, upon which sat a small stuffed turtle with a welcoming smile. The far wall housed a bookcase with a medium-sized white dresser, and directly in front of her sat a matching white desk. The contents of the top of Thea's childhood desk caught Lauren's attention.

Lauren took two steps toward the desk and burst out laughing at the autographed, framed Justin Bieber photo there. "A Belieber? You were a Belieber?"

Thea was blushing. "It was a gift."

Lauren thumbed through the stack of comic books on the edge of the desk, nudging the Rubik's Cube and twirling the unicorn pen she found there before as she motioned back to the photograph.

"A gift because you were a Belieber. Someone went to a lot of trouble to get that for you, I bet." She picked up the photo, examining it more closely. "Wow, this was an early shot, too. Look at that blown-out hair! He was such a trendsetter." She fanned herself. "Dreamboat, amirite?"

Thea took the photo from her and placed it back in its central location on the desk. "Listen, we all made mistakes."

"No hate here. He's got some serious bops." Lauren pretended to hold a microphone as she swayed in place, singing the lyrics to his song "Baby" off-key and probably out of order. She threw in some smooth dance moves and hair flipping for good measure because she was not one to half-ass anything. Ever.

"You're mocking me," Thea said.

Lauren lost herself in a sea of giggles as she flopped back on Thea's bed, out of breath from her epic concert performance.

"I'm in a vulnerable state here," Thea reasoned. "Don't kick preteen Thea while she's down."

Lauren propped herself up on her elbows and deadpanned, "So that means you want an encore, right?"

"No, God no. Please don't." Thea barely got the words out before Lauren picked up her pretend mic again.

"What's another song he has? 'Boyfriend'? Let me see what I can make happen with that." Lauren knelt on the bed, hands clasping her invisible mic as she started warbling what were definitely the wrong words to a song she absolutely didn't know while substituting *girlfriend* for all the *boyfriend*s she thought were in the song. But she couldn't be sure. Because a Belieber she was not.

"I can't. If you continue, I'll die." Thea covered her eyes, laughing.

"If I was your *girrrrrrrrlfriend*—" She struck a ridiculous pose before falling down in another fit of giggles. "Omigod, I think I pulled something with all those hair flips."

"You're a mess," Thea said as she reached to help Lauren up.

"I'm not the one with an autographed Bieber photo addressed to *Thea* with a heart," Lauren said as she took Thea's hand, pulling Thea down to the bed with her. "I mean, he even signed it *Love, Justin.*"

"You're just jealous," Thea said as she leaned over her.

"Jealous of Justin? Unlikely," Lauren said as she traced her fingers along the lapel of Thea's linen shirt. "I'm the one who's got you in bed with me."

Thea looked between them, watching as Lauren toyed with the button on her shirt. "We do seem to keep finding ourselves here, don't we?"

"You say that like it's a bad thing," Lauren said, closing her hand over the fabric and pulling Thea closer. "I personally think it's probably destiny."

"Oh yeah?" Thea nudged her nose as she ghosted her lips along Lauren's cheek. "Are you saying Justin is some sort of modern-day cupid?"

"Not at all." Lauren cupped her jaw to stop her from all the non-kissing and teasing. "At this point, I'd say he's the full-blown real deal. I mean, how else would I get you on top of me on your childhood bed without his epic 'Girlfriend' lyrics."

"'Boyfriend,'" Thea corrected.

"I'm not interested in a boyfriend," Lauren said as she caressed up Thea's side.

"Neither am I," Thea said with a shudder as Lauren slipped her hand under the soft fabric to find even softer skin. "But if you were my *girrrrlfriend*—"

"Would you treat me *riiiiiight?*" Lauren pulled Thea's mouth to hers, reveling in the fullness of Thea's lips against hers.

Thea hummed into the kiss all too briefly for Lauren's liking before she pulled back to give her a suspicious look. "You totally know the lyrics to that song, don't you?"

Lauren shrugged—she'd changed them a bit for the occasion, but... "I mean, it was on all the time. I'm sure there's some Pavlovian Bieber trigger in here." She motioned toward her head. "But I don't think that warrants a cessation to the kissing."

"Agreed." Thea's lips descended on hers in a wonderfully passionate fashion that Lauren was absolutely here for.

"Five minutes until dinner!" Kathleen's distant call was like a bucket of ice water to the face.

Lauren pulled back, shocked. "Wait, was she serious about the dinner after the tour thing?"

Thea groaned, running her hand through her hair before falling back beside Lauren on the bed. "This cannot be happening."

Lauren sat up, pulling Thea to stand as she helped Thea rebutton her shirt in a slight panic. "Your mom literally made me dinner. While I was up here in your childhood bedroom with you about to get incredibly inappropriate."

Thea stilled her hands before looping her arms around her neck. "How inappropriate are we talking?"

"Super inappropriate. At least PG-13 with a strong chance of R because you look so sexy in that shirt and those jeans," Lauren said, flustered. "But that's out the window now that I have to sit across from her at dinner."

"You're going to stay?" Thea asked.

"How can I say no to your mom? She's so nice," Lauren said, as if the answer was obvious.

Thea dropped her hands to Lauren's hips pulling her close. "Okay. But about this shirt and these jeans..."

Lauren shook her head. "Oh no. No, you don't. Your mom is waiting for us. Don't start charming me out of my panties with dinner getting cold downstairs. That's rude."

Thea leaned in and kissed her neck, ignoring her protests. "What kind of panties are we talking about?"

"Lace, with a heart-shaped—hey! Stop distracting me. No kissing." Lauren leaned away from Thea's lips and slapped at the hands caressing up her sides.

"Are you sure?" Thea asked as she stepped back, giving Lauren some space.

"No. Absolutely not," Lauren admitted. The last thing she wanted to do was be away from Thea's lips and fingers. "Of course I don't want that. Clearly"—she pointed back to the empty bed—"I want to be over there, under you again. But that's not an option now."

"But it is an option for the future?" Thea asked, the smolder in her eyes making Lauren feel weak.

"You're killing me," Lauren said with a huff.

"I just want to make sure we're both on the same page here"— Thea motioned between them—"because I'm more than happy to skip a meal—or seven—if being with you is on the table."

Lauren paused, not wanting to miss the chance to flirt. "Just *being* with me?"

"Being on you, under you, in you. You know, all of the above." That smolder was winning her over.

"Fuck." Lauren stepped back into Thea's arms, walking her backward until her back hit the wall hard. Lauren licked across Thea's lips until she opened her mouth. She deepened the kiss, letting her hands explore Thea's chest and shoulders while Thea gripped her ass, pulling her against her in a rough and delightful grind.

"Mmm," Thea hummed against her mouth as she massaged her ass. It all felt amazing.

Thea slipped her thigh between Lauren's legs, using her hands to rock Lauren's hips against her muscled thigh. The strength and firmness of Thea against Lauren made her see stars.

"Ladies, dinner," Kathleen called out again. And this time Lauren swore her voice was closer.

"Okay, okay." Lauren pulled back, out of breath. Thea guided her into another grind against her thigh, and Lauren whimpered. "I don't want you to stop, but I need you to stop."

Thea dropped her head back against the wall with an ungraceful thud as she dropped her hands, seemingly begrudgingly, from Lauren's hips. "I hate my life," she muttered with her eyes closed.

Lauren got up on tiptoe to place a soft kiss to Thea's lips. "I'll make it up to you later, I promise."

Thea blinked one eye open. "Twice?"

"Three times," Lauren promised as she smoothed out the front of Thea's shirt. "Maybe four if you wear this shirt again. And these tight-ass jeans. And the boots. Don't forget the boots. This rugged farmer chic thing has me all kinds of turned-on."

Thea ran her hand through Lauren's hair before helping her adjust her own top. "Really? Because I was thinking that this designer suit and heel combo was kind of a dream come true for me. I'd let you boss me around in that suit any day."

"You should see the rest of my collection, then," Lauren said as she stepped back farther, putting plenty of space between her and the hands and lips she wanted all over her. "I have a closetful that would bring you to your knees."

"You say that like it's a bad thing," Thea parroted, and suddenly all Lauren could think about was how badly she wanted Thea kneeling in front of her.

Lauren closed her eyes, letting herself briefly enjoy that visual before saying, "Oh, certainly not. I'm counting on it."

"Later," Thea promised.

"Later," Lauren agreed.

"Okay, then dinner it is," Thea said as she extended her hand toward Lauren, leading her out of her bedroom.

"Sure. Good. Fine." Lauren was nervous.

"Why is it that you have no problem seducing me at every moment that my mother is around and even have no qualms grinding against me in my bedroom with her downstairs, but the idea of sharing a meal with her makes you nervous?" Thea asked, far too astute for Lauren's liking.

"You say that like all I've done today is rile you up just to leave you hanging."

Thea gave her a look.

"Okay, fine. Maybe I was enjoying our banter and our extracurricular activities rather fast and loose in the face of your family nearby, but this is different," Lauren reasoned.

"Why's that?" Thea asked as she motioned for Lauren to head down the stairs first.

"Because this is like, *meeting your mom*. And brother. *Over dinner*. At your house," Lauren said in a whisper over her shoulder.

"Oh," Thea said, seemingly catching her drift.

"Oh, good. I wasn't sure if you could hear me through the closed door to Thea's room," Kathleen said, and Lauren stifled a wince.

Oof.

Lauren mustered up all her courage to speak words. "I didn't realize you were serious about the dinner thing, Kathleen. I'd hate to intrude on your family meal."

Kathleen took her by the elbow and guided her toward the kitchen as the smell of something wonderful hit her for the first time. "Don't be silly. You're a guest here. And you drove all this way—it's the least I can do before sending you on the long ride back."

Lauren was hungry, especially now that she could see how great that casserole looked on the table. "Thank you."

"Plus, I'd be remiss if I let the opportunity to have a meal with Thea's girlfriend slip by." Kathleen's words hit her like a ton of bricks. Shit, how had she already managed to fuck this up? Ellison was going to kill her.

Thea coughed. "Mom, we're not—"

Kathleen held up her hand and shook her head. "Oh, please, Thea. You've been watching her like she's the sun, the moon, and the stars all day. And let's not even talk about what I interrupted in the pasture…"

Lauren dropped her head. She was wrong before—Ellison was going to kill her *twice*. "You saw that?"

"I see everything. I'm the mother." Kathleen patted her on the shoulder. "Wash up. Sit. Eat. Tell us about yourself." The command was gentle, but a command nonetheless.

"Yes, ma'am," Lauren said before risking a glance in Thea's direction. She looked just as nervous as Lauren had felt before.

Well, it's time to meet the family, I guess.

CHAPTER TEN

Thea heard her brother choking into his milk glass as she wiped tears from her eyes. Lauren was hilarious, on top of being gorgeous and charming. And this was the third time since they'd sat down that Carl nearly shot milk out of his nose.

"What? It's not my fault squirrels make garbage house pets. How was six-year-old me supposed to know that? He looked so cute in that little sweater I'd made him before he ripped it off. I wish I'd gotten a picture." Lauren gave her a wink as she dabbed at her lips with her napkin.

"I can't believe you tried to tame a squirrel," Thea said, shaking her head.

"He was a very friendly squirrel," Lauren reasoned. "He would visit me every day and had no problem taking some of my midday snack, so why would I think he'd dislike being trapped indoors and living with a first grader? I'm super likable—clearly he was the problem."

Carl lost it. Milk everywhere.

"Carl," her mother chastised as she got up to grab some paper towels.

Carl only sputtered and coughed in reply. Thea patted him on the back to help him clear his throat, but that only made him cough harder.

Her mom threw a pile of paper towels at him after cleaning up the table. She sat down with a sigh. "So, where is it your mom lives now?"

Lauren was suppressing a smile as she watched Carl try and fail to regain composure. "Scottsdale. She moved in with her partners, and they run a doggy day spa."

"Partners?" her mother asked, and Thea was glad because she had the same question.

"Mm-hmm." Lauren nodded. "My mother lives with her high school ex-boyfriend and her girlfriend. They have a really sweet poly thing happening. It works for them."

Thea was in awe. In the short time they'd had dinner together, she'd learned a hell of a lot about Lauren. Mostly because she gave so freely. Nothing seemed to be held back or embarrassing for her. It was like she was unfazed by life. Thea was captivated.

"That's nice. It's good to have extra help and support." Thea couldn't believe her mother was so agreeable about this. It's not that she was a prude or anything, but she wasn't aware of her mother being exposed to poly anything. Kathleen was surprising her at every turn tonight.

"They complement each other in the best ways," Lauren replied. "Greg is quiet and steady, always on time, and super responsible. And Lainey is, well, she's a creative in every sense of the word. Really in touch with her emotions and into nature. My mother falls somewhere in the middle—she's a free spirit and plenty opinionated. She's happy, so I'm happy," Lauren said, and it was that simple.

Thea looked at her mother and wondered when she had last been happy.

"Do you see them often?" Her mom was doing all the heavy lifting, so Thea let herself just be an attentive observer. She liked watching Lauren engage with her mother—it seemed so effortless. There were no nerves like Lauren showcased on the stairs. Those seemed to dissipate as the evening progressed, which Thea was glad about because she found herself enjoying Lauren's company more and more.

"A few times a year. I try to make the trek out there at least twice, and Mom will come out to visit me alone a couple times. She calls those trips her *vacays from the three-way*."

Carl gagged on his last bite, and Lauren giggled.

Thea felt like she should intervene as her mother shot Carl another death glare. "Lauren's had enough of the interrogation, Mom. Don't you think?"

Lauren leaned back with a smile. "Is this the part where I get to hear all the juicy gossip about you now?"

"What? No." Thea put that to bed real quick.

"Oh, c'mon. I just told your mom my mother's in a throuple," Lauren teased.

Carl shoved his chair back and sprinted to the pantry, hiding behind the door as he howled with laughter.

"Throuple?" Thea repeated with a laugh. "As in a three-person couple?"

Lauren shrugged as she sipped her water. "I don't make the rules."

Her mother crumpled up her napkin and stood, gathering some dishes. "Well, I think it's nice."

Carl poked his head out of the pantry but ducked back in when Lauren made what looked like a squirrel face in his direction behind her mom's back. She could hear him struggling to breathe.

"My mother is going to put him on manure duty if you don't stop making him laugh," Thea said quietly to Lauren.

Lauren's eyes twinkled as she smiled. "I've never had a little brother before. Are they always this fun?"

"No," Thea replied. "They mostly smell bad and ruin everything when you're younger."

"Hey," Carl said as he came back to the table, collecting the rest of their plates. "I resemble that comment."

Lauren laughed and gave Carl a high five. "Excellent."

"You're as bad as he is," Thea said.

Lauren surveyed her before saying, "He seems like good people. I'll take that as a compliment." She looked at Carl. "Okay, bud, spill. What's your most embarrassing Thea story for me?"

"Grossest or most embarrassing?" he asked.

Thea had to nip this in the bud. "Wait—"

"Both. All. Don't stop until I pee myself," Lauren replied.

"One time Thea was playing tag with me in the pasture when she accidentally stepped into a divot and pitched forward into a hot summer-sun-baked pile of cow pies. Face-first," Carl said from the sink. "You looked like a creature from the Black Lagoon. It was dripping off you like sludge. I could barely see your eyes."

"Oof." Thea cringed. "That wasn't pleasant."

"Try being the one who had to pull you out of it." Carl shook his head. "You pulled me down into it twice before we finally got you free. Do you remember how Dad cleaned us off?"

"Ice-cold hose water behind the barn." Thea shivered at the memory. There was so much filth in her hair, she wasn't sure she'd ever be rid of it.

"That's about the time you and Carl started doing your own laundry," her mother replied. "You two stunk to high heaven for days."

"Then there was the time she peed her pants during a track meet—" he started.

"Okay. That's plenty, thanks." Thea got up from the table with her hands raised in defeat. "There was awkwardness. It's in the past. I'm perfect now."

"Uh-huh," Lauren said, not believing her for a second.

Thea raised an eyebrow in her direction. "What flaws have you found?"

Lauren gave her a once-over as she stood. "I'm too polite to ever say."

"That's because there are none," Thea teased.

Lauren joined her at the sink, offering to help dry the dishes her mom was washing. "Okay, Belieber."

"Oh, burn," Carl said giving Lauren another high five. It was cute how quickly he'd taken to her. She hadn't seen her brother this playful in a long time. Lauren seemed to bring out the best in everyone.

"Thea, can you grab some whipped cream from the fridge for dessert?" her mother asked as she started working on the casserole dish.

"Sure. What's for dessert?" Thea asked as she grabbed the tub of cream made here at the farm. This was her absolute favorite.

"Peach cobbler."

This time Lauren was the one who burst out laughing.

❖

"I'm so full I'm going to burst," Lauren said as she leaned back on the porch swing, patting her belly contentedly. "I haven't eaten that much in probably a decade."

"That's a high compliment," Kathleen said with a weary smile. She yawned. "Off to bed for me, ladies. It's an early morning on the farm, as usual."

"Thanks so much for meeting with me and letting me stay for dinner. I truly appreciate it," Lauren said as she started to stand.

"Don't get up," Kathleen said as she placed her hand on Lauren's shoulder. "You're always welcome here. Say hi to Ellison for me." She paused. "Are you sure you won't consider staying the night? It's a long drive, and it's already so late."

Lauren frowned. The last thing she wanted to do was drive back to Boston tonight, but tomorrow was the start of planning for the new project at the office. And she knew Ellison was eager to get her perceptions on the farm as well. "I have a meeting tomorrow I can't miss."

"Another time, then," Kathleen said, and Lauren could tell she meant it. She looked at Thea and said, "Make sure she gets back to the main road okay."

"Yes, Mom," Thea said.

"Text Thea when you get home," Kathleen said to Lauren. "Don't forget."

"I won't," Lauren vowed.

"Good night, ladies," Kathleen said as she stepped behind the screen door of the farmhouse. "Don't stay up too late."

Lauren watched her disappear into the house, and she smiled.

"What?" Thea asked from her place, propped against the front porch railing, almost close enough to touch, but not quite.

"She's lovely," Lauren replied.

"She really is. I take her for granted," Thea admitted.

Lauren looked at her. Thea was looking through the screen door into her house, seemingly lost in thought. Lauren could appreciate how heavy all of this must be for her. "Come sit with me," she said, patting the space beside her.

"Hmm?" Thea replied distractedly.

"Come here," Lauren repeated.

Thea pushed off the railing and eased into the spot next to her, taking over the rocking duty as her long legs stretched out before them.

Lauren closed her eyes, enjoying the gentle sway of the swing and the warm night air. The heat from before had dissipated, the comfortable evening of early summer was upon them, and the slight breeze from the porch swing felt like heaven on her skin.

"This is where I used to come to think," Thea said.

Lauren opened her eyes to find Thea watching her.

"I can see why. This is heaven." Lauren placed her hand palm up between them. She wanted to touch Thea, but she didn't want to push anything. So far all of their interactions had been organic, and she didn't want this to be any different.

Thea traced her fingertips for a moment before intertwining their fingers. Her touch was gentle yet strong. Lauren was glad she'd taken the hand-holding bait.

"So, you're a vegetarian, huh?" she asked. She'd learned so much about Thea at dinner, but she was glad to have her alone. It was a little odd to have those first-date kind of conversations in the presence of Thea's family. Part of her felt like she was missing out on discovering who Thea was. But another part of her was thrilled at all those embarrassing childhood stories that came with family dinner conversation.

Thea nodded. "Since I was eighteen."

"Because of the dairy farm thing, or just…?" Lauren wanted to know all that Thea would share with her.

Thea shifted uncomfortably and started to release her grip. Lauren repositioned her hand to keep Thea in contact with her.

"What?" she asked.

Thea had that faraway look in her eyes again. "I never was a big beef eater. But I stopped eating meat entirely when my father died of a heart attack at forty-eight."

Oh. Suddenly this getting-to-know-you session had taken a turn. Not that Lauren minded—she wasn't afraid of hard conversations—but Thea had been through a roller coaster of emotions today, and Lauren hadn't meant to add to that. "I'm sorry."

Thea looked across the porch into the darkness beyond lights of the house but said nothing.

They'd danced around Carlton Jr.'s death all day, but Lauren hadn't had the nerve to ask what had happened. She hadn't wanted to upset any of the Boudreauxs, least of all Thea. Obviously, she was failing at that.

"He had a murmur and a weak valve from a bad viral infection as a kid. So I can't blame it on his diet, even though I want to. The truth was that my dad was in pretty good shape for someone who'd done physical labor his whole life. But he had his vices, and raw steaks, cigars in the field, and the annual competitive eating contests didn't help." Thea exhaled. "But Daddy was always more about quality than quantity. He used to tell us nothing was guaranteed but that hard work and a big heart would get you to where you were supposed to be in life. The irony of the enlarged heart comment is not lost on me."

Lauren let the words settle between them without disturbing their weight.

"Anyway, around that time I became a vegetarian and started working out more because I needed to have some control." Thea looked at her with a small smile. "Therapy taught me that."

Lauren squeezed her hand. "Therapy is the shit. How do you think I got to be so okay with my mom's throuple?"

Thea laughed, and Lauren was glad to see some of her somberness recede. "That's the coolest story ever."

"I didn't even mention that they live in a nudist colony," Lauren said. "I figured I'd save that tidbit for the next meal your mom cooks me."

Thea's mouth dropped open comically, and Lauren cracked up. "Seriously?"

"No," Lauren said between gasps for breath. "Not seriously. Ew. I can't even imagine Greg's shlong out in the open. Gross."

Thea palmed her forehead and fanned herself. "I was really trying to play it cool to impress you with how open-minded I was, but you lost me at the nudist colony. I started picturing campfires and s'mores and lots more sticks than were necessary for dessert."

"You just ruined s'mores for me," Lauren whined.

"For you? I ruined s'mores for me," Thea said, shaking her head.

Lauren pulled their joined hands onto her lap. "You're already thinking about meeting my family? This is the fastest moving relationship I've ever been in," she teased.

Thea shrugged. "Well, you met mine already. And we did have sex on the first date."

"Lots of sex," Lauren said, not missing the way Thea's gaze dropped to her lips. "And it was *so* good, too."

"*So* good," Thea repeated.

"But I would hardly call that a first date," Lauren replied, leaning back on the swing.

"Oh? What would you call it, then?" Thea asked as she turned to face her, propping her elbow on the swing back next to her.

"I don't know. I wouldn't call it a one-night stand anymore because—"

"You know how badly I want to repeat it with you." Thea released her hand to caress her leg.

She watched Thea's fingers boldly stroke along her thigh as she admitted, "I want that, too."

"Good." Thea leaned in, threading her free hand into Lauren's hair and angling her face toward her. "Because I think about that all the time."

Lauren loved how confident Thea was with her touch, and how her touch felt so electric, instantly. She managed to get her turned-on in no time, and this was no exception. "What do you think about exactly?"

Thea inched closer, and Lauren leaned into her touch. "Your lips. And how soft your skin is."

"Yeah? What else?" Lauren made the first move, kissing Thea softly. Teasingly. She took great pleasure in the way Thea chased her lips to deepen the kiss. She liked being pursued by Thea, especially by her mouth.

Thea abandoned her thigh to cup her jaw, and though she missed the kneading and teasing so close to her clit, she was glad to be anchored when Thea's tongue entered her mouth. Because this woman kissed like no one she had ever kissed before, and Lauren needed to be grounded during it.

"The way your body moves against mine. But the thing I think about most"—Thea breathed out as she kissed away from her lips to suck on the skin of her neck, grazing her teeth along the tissue in a way that made Lauren shiver—"are the noises you make right before you come."

Lauren's sex clenched, and she shifted, spreading her legs as Thea's mouth returned to hers.

"*So* not a one-night stand, then," she gasped out between hungry kisses as Thea's hand left her jaw to settle at her thigh again.

"I hope not." Thea rubbed along the inside of her thigh, moving closer and closer to where Lauren needed friction. "Stay tonight. Let's work on night number two right now."

Lauren felt dizzy between all the kissing and touching and dirty talking. Her aching clit was screaming *fuck yes* but her brain kept trying to chime in something stupid about meetings and Ellison.

Brains are overrated. She gripped at Thea's shirt, shifting to recline along the arm of the swing and pulling Thea against her. Thea wasted no time in rejoining their lips and, this time, pressed her fingers against the crotch of Lauren's skintight dress pants, causing her to curse and buck against the pressure.

"Maybe I was wrong about the sexy noises. Maybe this is my favorite part," Thea murmured against her lips, "feeling how turned-on you are for me."

Lauren would bet the heat Thea felt emanating from her was nothing close to the fire she felt burning within at the moment. "You're making leaving impossible," Lauren argued as she palmed Thea's breast through her shirt.

"And you make not kissing you impossible." Thea nipped at her lip as she pressed against her with more force, causing Lauren's breath to catch.

Lauren felt herself starting to lose control, giving in to the ecstasy that was Thea's mouth and fingers, when that annoying hum from her brain turned into a roar. She whined before placing her hand flat on Thea's chest and pushing her up a bit.

Thea stopped her affections, pulling back and looking concerned. "Did I hurt you?"

"No," Lauren said with a frown, sitting up and putting space between them. "Not at all. You are just too good at all the touching and the kissing, and I was probably going to come undone on this swing in about three more well-placed strokes and—"

"And you stopped me because...?" Thea asked teasingly.

Lauren let out a frustrated moan as she dropped her head into her hands. "Because I have to get back to Boston for a meeting, and the last thing I should be doing is letting you grope me on your mother's porch swing."

Thea gave her a wicked smile as she nodded toward the driveway behind her. "Well, I'd offer to fuck you in the back seat of your car instead, but you don't have a back seat in that fancy thing."

"You aren't helping," Lauren replied.

"Sorry, not sorry." Thea took her hand and kissed along her knuckles. "I can wait. Until there are four walls and fewer prior commitments, I guess."

"I don't even need four walls—one would suffice," Lauren said, closing her eyes at the sensation of Thea's lips on her skin.

"Up against a wall next time. Got it." Thea's lips pressed against her cheek, and Lauren turned her head to catch them.

"I'm so glad you get me," she said as she leaned her forehead against Thea's.

"So if not a one-night stand, then maybe a tryst?" Thea returned to their original forgotten conversation.

Lauren leaned back, letting her gaze trace over Thea's face before getting lost in the steely blue eyes before her that were much darker than before. "*Tryst* feels cheap."

"Rendezvous?" Thea supplied.

"Too fancy." Lauren scrunched her nose. "Plus, I feel like we should have ended up somewhere more exotic than my apartment."

"It is a great apartment," Thea reasoned.

"You saw none of it," Lauren argued.

"But you were there, so that was enough for me."

"You're so charming, it actually hurts," Lauren said as she clutched at her chest dramatically.

"I know," Thea said with a smile. "Let's call that first night the appetizer to this new thing we've got going."

"Appetizer?" Lauren asked, intrigued.

"Sure." Thea stood, pulling Lauren up and into her arms. "It's the start of something great with the promise of more. Something to entice and temporarily satiate."

"Is this about the peach?" Lauren didn't care what it was about because the way Thea was looking at her right now felt amazing.

"It's about you. And the peach. And about how I can't wait to see what the first course is like. Because the appetizer's got me hooked." Thea looped her arms around Lauren's waist, and the closeness of her made Lauren's lower abdomen ache in unfulfilled desire.

"Does this mean we're dating, then?" Lauren asked, hopeful.

"You already met the family, so obvs," Thea teased.

Lauren got up on tiptoe to bring their lips together once more for a slow but sensual kiss. "You know that means there might be a visit to a nudist colony in your future, though, right?"

Thea pulled back, looking suspicious. "I thought you were joking about that."

Lauren shrugged as she stepped out of Thea's embrace. "I guess you'll have to find out."

Thea laughed as she followed Lauren off the porch toward her car. "I guess I will."

Something in the way Thea said that made Lauren's heart skip a beat. Because this was new and exciting and fucking hot, and Lauren was here for it. All of it. Whatever it turned out to be.

CHAPTER ELEVEN

Thea watched the last drop of coffee drain into her cup as she yawned. "Late night?" Her mother's voice sounded from behind her.

Thea pulled the mug out from under the coffee machine and dumped two heaping scoops of sugar into it, stirring and sipping the brain fuel before she answered. "Sort of."

That was an understatement. After an all too brief make-out session against Lauren's car, she spent the rest of the night on the phone with her. Her intention was only to help her navigate the dark country back roads to the interstate. But then she found herself not wanting to get off the line. So they'd chatted the whole way back to Boston. The time flew, and before she knew it, the clock had struck midnight, and Lauren was already back in her apartment, getting undressed. Which nearly started a whole different conversation.

She turned to find her mother was leaning against the doorframe into the kitchen, cradling a pitcher of something.

"What's in the pitcher?" Thea asked.

"Fresh cream"—her mother held it out—"want some?"

"Oh, hell yes." Thea extended her cup and refrained from doing the happy dance she wanted to for fear of spilling the piping hot coffee. She normally drank her coffee with only a little skim milk and sugar at home, but when she was home on the farm, she always used their fresh cream. She was sad when there wasn't any in the fridge this morning.

"You're like your father with that cream," her mother said as she took back the pitcher and put it in the fridge. "He had a weakness for it."

"It's the best cream in the world, Mom," Thea replied confidently. "I've never found a better tasting product. And I'd count myself as an expert."

"Oh yeah?"

"I mean, I was raised with more cows around than people. I'm well versed in the way of the dairy," Thea joked. "Who else can say they had pet cows their whole life?"

"Hey, we had Sargent. You didn't have a childhood without a real pet," her mother countered.

"Sargent was deaf in both ears and almost blind by the time that old hound found his way into our lives. He nearly bit me out of ambush fear more times than he licked me," Thea said.

"That's because you used to always sneak up on him," her mother reasoned.

"From the front? While clapping to get his attention first?" Thea answered skeptically. "He was Dad's dog through and through. I think he faked the deafness part just so he didn't have to hang out with me and Carl."

"You two were rather rambunctious. But if you're right, Sargent was smarter than I gave him credit for."

"I prefer the term *energetic* to rambunctious. It implies less immaturity," Thea replied, inhaling the smell of her coffee and sighing happily.

"You mean like the immaturity you showed Lauren last night?"

Thea winced. She was hoping that misstep was forgotten.

"And when were you going to tell me that Lauren and you were way more serious than you let on?" Her mother had her hand on her hip. This was serious.

"I didn't. We're not—" Thea rubbed her hand over her face, not feeling rested enough for this battle right now.

"You're not what? Dating?" Kathleen crossed her arms. "Sleeping together?"

Thea choked on her coffee. The burning sensation in her nose made her gag and sputter. "*Mom.*"

"What? You think I'm oblivious to these things just because I'm your mother. I'm not. *Because* I'm your mother."

Thea staggered to a kitchen chair, her eyes watering from the coffee-boarding that just occurred. "You totally ruined this drink for me. And my now-burnt nose hairs. I'll never smell correctly again."

"You'll be fine," her mother said across from her. "How did you two meet? Really?"

Thea sighed. She never lied to her mother. It just wasn't something she felt comfortable doing. Or lying to anyone, for that matter. Her father had been morally against lies, especially lies by omission. He used to call that the action of cowards. And though Thea was many things, a coward she was not. "A bar."

"You met that beautiful, charming woman at a bar?" Her mother seemed skeptical.

"What? Did you think I was only capable of finding unattractive, socially inept women?" Thea feigned being hurt.

"Oh, far from it. You don't tell me anything about your life. As far as I know, you were living a life of contented loneliness."

"Well, that sounds...dull," Thea replied. "No, thank you."

Her mother smiled. "She's wonderful."

"She is," Thea replied. "She said Ellison Gamble sent her here. Is that true?"

"It is," she said. "Ellison owes us no favors, and yet she sent us Lauren."

"To consult on selling the farm," Thea reminded her.

"I haven't forgotten, Thea." Her mother's tone was weary.

"And as much as I'm glad that you like Lauren, I'm still not okay with her helping you find a way to sell Dad's farm."

Her mother sighed.

"Mom, I want to talk about this," Thea tried again.

"There's nothing to talk about. We're a few months away from losing the land to the bank. If we don't figure something out, you'll have nothing to hate me over except an eviction notice and whatever you can carry out of here."

"Have you all but given up?" Thea felt her anger bubbling up. This all felt so unfair. "Don't you want to save the farm?"

Her mother stood, heading for the door.

"Wait," Thea called out as she raced after her, barely catching her before she made it to the front porch.

"What choice do I have, Thea?" Her mother turned with tears in her eyes, and Thea immediately felt awful for challenging her.

"We took a big leap just before your father died. We commercialized the business like he had dreamed about for years and years. And just as we were getting off the ground, he died. He left a massive undertaking to me and this family as the undertaker took him. And I've tried. I've worked until my hands bled to keep you and Carl happy and healthy and keep this farm running. And none of it mattered because at the end of the day I couldn't make your father's dream a reality." She wiped at her eyes with the back of her hand and shook her head. "So to answer your question, no. I don't want to sell the farm. Because this is as much my home and my livelihood as it ever was your father's. Maybe even more so, because in the time he's been gone, we've grown and done so many wonderful things, all in his name. And in his legacy. But it wasn't enough. I researched every option. I'm not *just* giving up. It's over."

"Mom," Thea said as she reached for her, and for the first time she could remember since her father died, her mother broke. But this time Thea wasn't a teenage girl anymore. She was an adult, and she could take some of this burden. And as she held her mother, feeling her sobs resonate through her own chest, she made a promise to do whatever she could to help. Even if that meant to help unload the burden. Even if it killed a little part of her in the process.

❖

Lauren checked the clock again. Where the fuck was Trina? She grabbed her cell to fire off a text to her when her familiar rap at the doorframe drew her attention.

"What's up, buttercup? How'd it go?" Trina asked as she carried in a coffee Lauren assumed was for her. "I figured you could use a pick-me-up after your haul to and from Lobstah Land."

"Yes, thank God. You're a shero. Now shut the door," Lauren said.

Trina paused. "Oh, damn. Okay. A closed door kinda thing, huh?"

Lauren waited until she closed the door to blurt out what she'd been stifling all morning. "Thea from the bar is the client's daughter. I slept with the client's daughter before she was a client and before I found out that the client is a close personal friend to Ellison. And I am so fucking screwed because I almost hooked up with her again while I was there on the porch swing because I have no self-control. And I sort of wish I did because now I'm just horny and worried about losing my job. When I'd rather just be worried about losing my job."

Trina's eyebrows were practically at her hairline. "I need you to back up a bit. That was a lot to unpack. Hot Thea, the leather jacket wearing, fruit foreplay woman from the other night lives in Maine?"

Lauren shook her head. "No, she lives here in Boston. But her family owns a dairy farm in Maine. *The* dairy farm that Ellison sent me out to consult on. And she was there, ready to sling insults and eject my ass from the property because she doesn't want her mom to sell."

Trina looked confused. "What do you mean she was there?"

"I mean she was there, in the flesh, looking amazing and sexy in this shirt and jean combo—" Lauren shook her head. She was getting sidetracked. "That's not the point. The point is she was there, on the farm. And this whole thing nearly erupted in my face."

"Until it didn't," Trina noted.

"How can you be so sure of that?" Lauren felt like Trina was missing the big picture.

"Well, you're here, right? And you almost hooked up with her again? On a porch swing, which sounds interesting and makes me question the physics involved…Like, I could see the swing part of it being very sexy. All that rhythmic movement and sway." Trina seemed distracted.

"Did you just mentally order a sex swing for your apartment?" Lauren gave her a look.

"I'm suddenly strongly considering it," Trina replied bluntly.

"T," Lauren whined.

Trina perched herself on Lauren's desk. "I'm joking. Well, maybe not about the sex swing—that seems like something I should explore. But I'm kidding about the rest of it. Tell me what happened—spare no details. Least of all the porch swing part."

Lauren laughed. She loved this woman. "I got to the farm, and I met the matriarch, and we crunched some numbers for a bit. Then she started giving me a tour, and Thea just marched into the barn ready to brawl. Until she noticed it was me, and then she was sort of super adorable and shy. And then her mom got mad and made her give me a tour of the farm instead." Lauren thought back to their mostly silent ride out to the pastures. "Then my heel got stuck in the mud, and she carried me back to the golf cart, and it was like we hit a reset button. Suddenly she wasn't so broody, and I momentarily forgot I was there to do a job. And her mom walked up on us almost kissing."

Trina winced. "Did the heel survive?"

"That's your priority?" Lauren asked.

"Shoes are always my priority. What's life without a little sole?" Trina joked.

Lauren rolled her eyes. "Anyway, her mom, *the client*, nearly interrupted us kissing and then demanded I stay for dinner because evidently Thea had been talking about me before I got there. Long story short—I ended up staying for dinner with her family, who are absolutely lovely, by the way, and now we're sort of definitely dating, but also, I haven't told Ellison I'm sleeping with the client's daughter. Because she'll kill me."

Trina was watching her intently.

"Okay, I'm done rambling," Lauren said.

"So what I'm hearing is, Thea didn't blow you off with some fake excuse about visiting family out of town. She was, in fact, visiting family out of town, and you just happened to drive into town and find out she was telling the truth."

"Trina. I'm fucking the client's daughter. The client. Ellison's close family friend. That's the big reveal." Lauren wasn't sure why she had to spell it out. Trina was usually better about these things.

Trina sighed. "Lauren. You slept with her before taking on her mother as a client. And you *slept* with her—you aren't sleeping with her on the regular yet. And even if you are, so what? Before this trip your biggest concern was that the best sex of your life seemed to be ghosting you. Now we know that's not the case. And I suppose she mentioned that she wanted to have more sex with you since you're, like, a couple now, right?"

"Yes," Lauren replied slowly, not quite sure what Trina was getting at.

"Then, awesome. More sex for you with the hot farmer chick. Boom. All good things. Let's research sex swings now."

Lauren felt like she had whiplash. "Fine. Yes. Let's celebrate the end of my celibacy, along with the end of my career. One door opens..."

"I think you mean legs, not doors," Trina said with a playful nudge.

Lauren put her head in her hands. This wasn't helping.

She looked up when she felt Trina's hand on her shoulder.

"Hey, I'm just being silly with you because I want to celebrate the small victory of awesome sex with the promise of more," Trina said, her tone soothing. "But as someone who famously made out with her literal competition and got caught by Ellison potentially sabotaging a bet that Ellison put her legacy on the line to help me win, well, I can say mistakes happen. And sometimes they aren't mistakes. You met Thea before you knew about the farm. Just because she is somehow connected to that farm doesn't mean that you did anything wrong. And if you continue to see her, that doesn't mean you're doing anything wrong either." Trina took her hand in hers. "Did you do everything that Ellison asked? Did you get the information or read the numbers or do the things?"

"Yes." Lauren nodded.

"And are you ready to answer any question she has with information from your data collection trip?"

"Yes," Lauren confirmed.

"Then you're all good." Trina squeezed her hand before releasing it. "Trust me when I tell you Ellison has no time for our messy dating lives. Ever. As long as you boning the dairy princess doesn't impact whatever it is Ellison has in mind, you are fine. She's not interested in our drama. If she was, she could have tried to put a stop to me and Kendall that night at the fundraiser. And she didn't. But she certainly had every right to raise the alarm or can my ass."

Lauren thought about that. "Well, when you put it like that..."

"So," Trina said as she rubbed her hands together excitedly, "about that porch swing."

Lauren laughed. "In the interest of full disclosure, I should first mention her childhood bedroom and Justin Bieber."

"Are we ready for the big reveal?" Ellison asked as she sat across from her and Jax in the large conference room.

"Lay it on me," Lauren replied. She'd been anxiously anticipating this meeting for a number of reasons, but today was a big day. She'd find out the name of the project, and they'd start the planning process. She was more than ready.

"The working title for this project is Newbridge on the Gardens. I wanted to make sure the name of the building reflected our plan—to bridge varying communities around the beautiful natural space behind the property," Ellison said as Jax handed Lauren a printout with full color pictures of a computer-generated building on the site Ellison had taken Lauren to. The gardens behind the property were still there, but in this image, they were lush and overflowing with greenery and vibrant colors. This was the prettiest fake garden she had ever seen.

"Like I mentioned before, I don't want this to be any ordinary new-build luxury condominium. I want to ensure that the community benefits from this project and that the residences are available to all people and financial brackets. That means there needs to be something for everyone, and we'll need to do the work to make sure the right people find their way to our building.

"On the second and third pages you'll see some loose sketches and mock-ups of what a few of the condos will look like. This is to give you an idea of the spaces and general layouts of the apartments. Like we discussed, the building is projected to be complete in a little less than a year's time. Newbridge on the Gardens will be entirely helmed by our realty office. More specifically you and Jax." Ellison looked directly at Jax as she said, "As you know, Lauren has chosen you to help her run the numbers and lead the sales."

Jax had been beaming since Lauren gave them a heads-up this morning. She hadn't had a chance to say anything before the trip to Maine, and she'd wanted to wait for Ellison's go-ahead, but waiting to tell Jax had all but killed her. So she broke the rules a little and told them she needed help on a project. She just didn't mention how big this could be for Jax. And her. Jax's excitement made hers bubble over even more.

"Wait." Jax spoke for the first time. "Does that mean I'll be handling some sales as well?"

This had been a stipulation of Lauren's, though Ellison had not fought her. Jax had operated as a junior agent at this point. Their sales were always done under the supervision of a Realtor in the office, but Trina and Lauren had mentored Jax over the past year and worked hard to make sure Jax was ready. And they finally were. Or at least, they would be by the time the building was done.

Ellison motioned for Lauren to answer.

"We need to build your portfolio, Jaxy. It's time you take the lead on some of the bigger projects. Between now and the launch, we'll make sure you run point on as many sales as possible." She dabbed at her eyes playfully. "You're growing up so fast."

Jax laughed and cheered. "Yes! Hand me the keys."

"Not so fast, champ," Ellison said with a good-natured smile. "We have a lot to get done before we're at the sales stage."

Jax straightened up, all business once again. "What do you need from me?"

"I was really impressed by the war room you set up for Trina during the Harborside project," Ellison said. It was not lost on Lauren that the Harborside was now being referred to as a project and not a bet, like it had been originally. A lot had changed in a year. Trina's involvement in the Harborside deal was the catalyst for this opportunity for Lauren and Jax. Lauren had no plans to squander that.

Ellison continued, "I'd like you to set up a more mobile version of that for this project as well. I want to make sure it's mostly digital so we can regularly access and update it as we go."

"Can there be a whiteboard? I'm partial to a whiteboard," Lauren chimed in.

"As long as it doesn't take up one whole wall of my conference room for a year, then sure," Ellison replied, and Lauren did a victory dance in her chair.

"What?" she asked when Ellison gave her a look. "The whiteboard was how Trina was so successful. The whiteboard was the magic. Ask Jax."

"I can't confirm or deny this, but I did like using color-coded markers for things," Jax replied noncommittally. Traitor.

"Yes, we need lots of bright colors. Maybe more neons," Lauren replied.

"Whatever you need, I'll make sure you get it," Ellison said.

Lauren loved that Ellison never stood in their way about anything. She was quite simply the best boss Lauren had ever had, and she hoped that continued for a long time.

"Okay, let's address any questions you might have." Ellison redirected the conversation back to the task at hand.

Jax raised their hand.

"You don't need to raise your hand, Jax. There's only three of us here," Ellison said.

"Right," Jax said as they lowered their hand to their side. "How do we get started?"

Ellison nodded. "Construction is already underway, and we're incorporating prefabricated building sections to complete the build. So the foundation will be laid and the supports installed, and then these partial prebuilds that have been completed off-site will be brought in by trucks and cranes and integrated into the construction process. It's a new approach that was invented by Zander Alter, the main architect for the project."

"Zander from the Harborside project? That Zander?" Lauren recognized the name right away.

"One and the same," Ellison said with a sly smile. "I poached him for his downtime between Langley's big projects. That narrows our window a bit, so he came up with the new construction approach to get this done in half the time."

Jax said, thinking out loud, "So by building off-site and bringing it in, he's going to cut down noise and traffic and people standing around and—"

"Just about everything annoying about construction in the city," Lauren completed.

"Exactly." Ellison drummed her fingers on the table. "The only caveat is that this requires an incredible amount of precision. So Zander and I will be working closely while the foundational construction phase is happening. That's where you and Jax are going to take the lead on the preparation front."

Jax pulled out a notepad that Lauren hadn't realized they had on their person. "I'm ready."

Ellison laughed. "I'll send this in an emailed memo, but I'm glad you're enthusiastic."

Lauren nudged Jax as she stage-whispered, "You're making me look bad."

Ellison rolled her eyes before continuing, "I've reached out to a friend who works at Clear View Enterprises. As you know, Clear View has done all of our marketing and PR since the beginning, but this is a bit different. Lauren, I'd like you to set up a meeting with one of their executives to work on the Newbridge project."

"Done. My friend Claire Moseley is one of the senior execs there. I'm on it." This would be a cinch. She was planning on seeing Claire later this week at their softball game anyway. She loved the idea of collaborating with her professionally. Claire was amazing. And she was the best hitter on their team, but that was beside the point.

"Great. I'll let Lucinda know, and she'll forward all the project specs to Claire so you two can get started. Check back in with me on what you two come up with." Ellison checked her cell with a sigh. "I have a meeting in a bit, so I need to cut this short."

She turned to Jax. "I have a list of things I need you to get a jump on as well, but I'll email those to you later on today. I need to meet with Lauren for a second—can we have the room?"

"Sure thing." Jax jumped up and disappeared faster than Lauren could process what was happening.

Lauren tried not to fidget now that she and Ellison were alone. Even though talking to Trina had helped, she'd be lying if she said she wasn't still a little nervous about talking to Ellison one-on-one.

"What did you think?" Ellison asked, looking at her intently.

"About the Newbridge drawings? They're great," Lauren said.

"Thanks. But I was talking about the Boudreaux farm," Ellison replied.

That made sense. Duh. Lauren shook her head. "Sorry. It was a long drive and a late night." *And I was really hoping you wouldn't bring that up.*

"It's a big trip to make in one day," Ellison agreed.

"It is," Lauren agreed. "The farm is really beautiful, and Kathleen and her son are lovely." She intentionally left out Thea.

"Kathleen is wonderful. Losing CJ really rocked that family. I know the community helped out as much as possible, but the kids were still teenagers when it happened, I believe. I'm sure that was exceptionally hard on Kathleen—raising a family and running a farm." Ellison frowned, and Lauren wondered what her connection to the farm was.

"Did you know the Boudreaux kids?" Lauren asked, unable to help herself.

Ellison shook her head. "Not exactly, they were very young when I was there last. They were just babies, really."

"Hector says hi," Lauren said, her curiosity getting the best of her again. "He called you Ellie."

"Did he now?" Ellison gave her a secretive smile, like she was withholding something. That only made Lauren want to know more. "What else did he say?"

"He mentioned that you had an awkward stage. I'm having a hard time believing it, though."

"You're very kind. But I think we all have an awkward period in our lives, don't we?" Ellison seemed unfazed by Hector's remark. If anything, she seemed amused by it.

"My adult life is one giant awkward phase most days," Lauren replied, thinking back to Kathleen nearly interrupting her and Thea's everything, all day.

Ellison laughed before getting more serious. "How bad is the situation there?"

"You mean debt-wise or morale-wise?" Lauren asked.

"Both," Ellison replied.

"Well, on the debt front, saying they're underwater is an understatement. They're in deep, and I can see why Kathleen is considering selling the property."

"And morale-wise?" Ellison asked.

"The kids don't want her to sell, and everyone seems pretty upset about having to unload the father's legacy," Lauren replied honestly.

Ellison leaned back, seemingly burdened by this information. "Tell me about the land. What did you see?"

"Pastures, a barn, some commercial kitchen and cheese-aging spaces, Hector's farm manager house, and the old farmhouse. Plenty of fields and space. All of which are well manicured and cared for, given their age. A beautiful forest area and the lake." Lauren nearly forget to mention that. "The lakefront land is their gold mine for sure."

"Tell me more." Ellison closed her eyes, listening.

"There are three pastures in the rear of the property, one of which is right on the lake's shore. It's a gorgeous plot of land, spacious and open. The perfect spot to build on. And behind it, heading back toward the main road, are twenty or so acres of woods, unkempt and natural. If someone developed the pasture, they could wind a long drive through those woods and make a spectacular entrance view for whatever build they have planned." Lauren had no trouble visualizing the potential of the space prior to getting her heel stuck. After that, she'd had trouble focusing on anything other than Thea.

"What does Kathleen want?" Ellison opened her eyes. Her attention was intense.

"Whatever is best for the kids." Lauren shrugged. "Part of her seems like she's ready to close this chapter of her life. But I got the feeling that she wasn't exactly gung-ho about it. It was as if she was accepting a fate she seemed to think was unchangeable."

Ellison seemed to consider this. "What do you think is the best move for them?"

Lauren had given this a lot of thought since she'd returned home. She spent some time this morning going over the land surveyor's report and copies of the drone photos of the property that Ellison had provided. "If they break it into pieces, they could probably clear the majority of the debt. But I doubt they'd be able to keep the farm functioning."

"So sell the land, save the bank account, but lose the livelihood and the legacy in the process," Ellison summarized.

"Exactly." Lauren frowned. "When you put it like that, it seems like a lose-lose, not a win-win, to be honest."

Ellison was quiet for a moment. "There's a Realtor there that specializes in large land sales, particularly agricultural ones. Her name is Faith Leader. I'll have Jax get you her number. I'd like you to set up a call with her and find out what type of interest there is in the area for property like the Boudreaux farm." Ellison's phone buzzed on the table, and she reached for it. "That's my next meeting—I have to go. Let's get together again after you and Faith talk. I'd like to hear your thoughts on what she has to say."

Ellison glided out of the room with her usual grace, before she reappeared in the doorway to add, "And thank you for taking this on. I really appreciate it."

"Of course," Lauren replied before Ellison stepped out of sight.

Once alone, she considered all the events that made up the last two days. It was incredible to her the difference a day made. A moment, even. Before running into Thea at The Mirage, she'd been mostly happy, though unhappily single. In meeting Thea, she'd found a fiery connection and a more than satisfying bedroom partner, but her professional life had been a disaster. But then Maine happened. And in that moment in the barn—when Thea walked in—her personal and professional lives overlapped in a way she never would have expected. Just one moment, and all the loose ends suddenly weren't loose anymore. And the weight that came with that realization sat heavily on her shoulders.

"Life is weird," she said to herself as she gathered up her papers and headed back toward her office, feeling more confused than she had been in days.

CHAPTER TWELVE

Thea was staring off into space when the balled-up piece of paper hit her in the side of the head.

"Ouch," she said as she rubbed the spot.

"Liar," Avni said with her hand on her hip from the doorway to Thea's office. "That didn't hurt."

Thea ran her hand down her face trying to massage herself awake. "Okay, that was a surprised *ouch*, not a hurt *ouch*."

"You'll live," Avni said as she plopped down in the seat across from Thea's desk. "In my defense, I started talking to you long before the aerial assault. You were just in a fog. I was trying to resuscitate you."

"By hitting me with a receipt?" Thea asked as she uncrumpled the paper before balling it back up and throwing it at Avni.

Avni caught it easily. "I figured that would be less jarring than shaking and slapping you to make sure you hadn't had a stroke at work."

Thea considered this. "Thank you for not slapping me. Even though I can't believe that was on the table."

"It could have been a matter of life and death," Avni said with a shrug. "My parents are doctors. I know not to mess around when someone is frozen in time like that. You could have been in the midst of a medical emergency."

Thea leaned back with a yawn. "Well, when you put it like that…"

"Another late night?" Avni looked concerned.

Thea nodded. "All my nights seem that way these days." Thea had been home from Maine for about a week catching up on life and work around here. But she'd spent a few hours every night trying to help manage some of the farm remotely, to unburden her mother. And in the time she wasn't monitoring order numbers and bills, she was trying to find ways to save the farm, even entertaining the idea of community milk farming as a way to offset some of the challenges of keeping and maintaining cows. But she kept coming up empty-handed. The idea of maintaining their dairy production line with someone else's harvested dairy had promise, but there wouldn't be enough debt relief in the sale of the cattle and the milking parlor equipment. Still, she fired off a text to Lauren featuring the suggestion. If she could help at all, she wanted to.

"You can't keep straddling both these worlds," Avni warned, and Thea knew she was right. "Something has gotta give. Your mom is the one who wants the farm to sell, and maybe it's time you made peace with that."

"You sound like her." Thea sighed. She wasn't ready to give up just yet. Plus, she had an ace in her pocket working on her side—Lauren.

"Speaking of *straddling* things, that faraway look makes me think you're running down memory lane with that hottie Realtor woman."

Thea gave her a look. "Don't make me regret telling you about her."

"It's not like your ass was in a rush or anything."

"I literally called you the day after she showed up at the farm. That's still a hot take, I promise," Thea said.

"Not as hot as the make-out session on the porch, it sounds," Avni teased.

Thea couldn't stop the stupid grin on her face. "That's true."

Avni slapped her knee. "I'm so mad I missed her that first night. I'm dying to meet the woman who has you so damn gaga already. She must have a magic vagina."

"I probably wouldn't have had the chance to talk to her if you'd stayed. So I'm glad you left," Thea said before quickly adding, "no offense or anything."

"None taken," Avni replied. "But about the magic—"

"The whole package is magic. Yes," Thea replied. "I mean, at least it is so far."

"You say that like you expect this new thing to crash and burn."

"It's not that. It's just, I don't know. Running into Lauren felt like an exciting and serendipitous accident. And the immediate chemistry felt like really good luck. But then seeing her on the farm, making my mother and brother laugh and helping everyone feel at ease, that was something else. Something special."

Avni was on the edge of her seat, cradling her face in her hands as she said, "Aww. You really like this girl."

Thea looked for something to lob at her but found nothing. "Shut up."

"No, it's cute. I'm not mocking you. I'm just, aww. You're like all grown up now."

"You are mocking me," Thea said, crossing her arms.

"Maybe a little." Avni left a tiny space between her first finger and thumb. "But I do think it's cute. I've known you a long time, and I haven't seen you stare off into space thinking about anyone else."

Thea laughed. That was probably true. "I was thinking about the farm when you assaulted me, though."

"And not Lauren?" Avni challenged.

"Okay, maybe a little about Lauren, too," Thea admitted.

Avni fist-pumped and stood with a stretch. "I knew it."

"What's on your agenda today?" Thea asked, glad to be back in this life at this moment. She'd missed her friends and work while she was in Maine. And she knew she'd be going back shortly, but she didn't want her life here to suffer because of it. Especially if her Maine life was going to change forever soon.

"Gonna go run some tests in the lab. Take down some data. Save the world. You know, brilliant scientist stuff," Avni said as she pretended to admire her manicure. "Then Raj's parents are coming over for dinner later. So that'll be a barrel of laughs."

Raj's parents never quite seemed to approve of Avni for some reason. Raj was a total mama's boy, and Thea knew Avni hated when his mother was around because Raj became almost infantile in her presence. "Does she still taste his food for him and cut the big pieces on his plate if she thinks he might choke?"

"It's gross. Their relationship is gross." Avni moaned. "How am I supposed to plan a life with a man that reverts to a child when his mother is around? I can't compete with Saanaa. She's the perfect Indian wife and mother. The standards are too high. I'm a woman of the twenty-first century, goddamn it. I have needs and am an independent thinker. There is nothing about that woman that encourages any type of individuality."

"You're preaching to the choir, sister. You know how I feel about Mama S. I don't trust her as far as I could throw her." Thea had met her three times, and each time she'd left feeling insecure and emotionally battered. She wasn't sure how Avni did it.

"She's the worst. She sent ahead a list of ingredients she wants on hand because she doesn't think I'm capable of cooking Raj's favorite meal without help. I'm to gather the supplies and sit in the corner looking pretty." She tossed her long dark hair over her shoulder. "Luckily, I have this pretty thing down. Now all I have to do is sit and block out everything passive aggressive she has to say tonight."

"Will there be wine? I feel like wine might help."

"I bought a whole case," Avni said with a broad grin. "Let's just hope I don't get too sauced and start airing my true feelings."

"If you do, please record it. I don't want to miss that."

Avni saluted her. "You got it, Captain."

"Good luck," Thea called out after her as she disappeared toward the lab.

Her phone buzzed beside her. It was a text from Lauren. *Busy tonight?*

Thea wasn't busy. Not that she wouldn't cancel any plan she had if she was. If seeing Lauren was an option, she was available. No matter what. She hadn't seen her since Maine, and though they'd talked a few times since, she was eager to be back in her presence again.

I'm always free for you, she replied.

Lauren texted back: *Does that make you easy? Or just cheap?*

Thea laughed. *Easy. But free implies no cost. So I guess cheap, too.*

Ooooh, the total package. I like that, Lauren replied.

What did you have in mind? Thea texted back.

After a few floating dots for what seemed like forever, Lauren finally wrote back: *I have a softball game later. Wanna come watch? We can grab drinks after.*

Softball? Lauren played softball? Thea smiled. She liked finding out new things about Lauren. And she happened to love softball. So obviously she was in.

Sounds great. What are your team colors? I want to rep accordingly.

More text bubbles showed up and disappeared before finally Lauren replied: *Wear that leather jacket I like so much. And those sexy boots from the farm. If all goes well, maybe after the game and drinks we can find a wall.*

Thea bit her lip at that last part. *Just one wall?*

Lauren's reply came instantly. *That's all we'll need* ;)

Thea was vibrating with excitement now. *I can't wait. Where and when should I meet you?*

Lauren texted back the time and location, and Thea plugged it into her cell calendar immediately. Not like she was going to forget or anything. She couldn't think of something she'd been this excited about in months.

Thea looked at the clock on the wall. She still had half a day between now and the time and place Lauren told her to be later. She sighed. This day needed to hurry up and be over. She had a game to catch.

❖

"Who are you waiting for?" Trina asked as she handed Lauren the work folder.

"Thea," Lauren replied, not bothering to lie. Trina could sniff out a fib on her a mile away.

Trina clapped. "Hell yes, a game and a booty call in one night? My girl can do it all."

Lauren pretended to brush dust off her shoulders. "Now all I have to do is make sure we win, so I can secure a victory lap dance."

"You devil, you." Trina gave her shoulder a squeeze. "I expect details over coffee, if you can make it to work in the morning."

Lauren laughed. "I'll be there—I have another meeting with Ellison about the Newbridge project."

"That project is going to be awesome. I'm so excited for you," Trina replied, and Lauren knew she meant that. Trina had been so supportive about Lauren and Jax working together on this that Lauren had almost been overwhelmed. Not that she expected Trina to mind not being included or anything, but the genuineness of her enthusiasm had touched her.

"Thanks, T. I don't know what I'd do without you."

"You'd probably be bored. And you'd certainly be without the necessary paperwork you need for tonight," Trina teased.

Lauren had been distracted all afternoon after her brief flirtation with Thea via text. She was going to go over a few things tonight with Claire before her follow-up meeting with Ellison tomorrow, but she'd foolishly left all the paperwork at the office. Thankfully, Trina was working late and could swing by. She was a lifesaver.

"You sure you can't stay?" Lauren was in no rush to see Trina leave. This new project meant that she was spending even less social time with her bestie. And as much as she didn't want Trina grilling

Thea the whole night, part of her really wanted Trina's opinion about Thea. Because Lauren had a feeling that this Thea thing could be more than just amazing sex.

"I can't," Trina said with a frown. "I'm watching the boys tonight while Calvin and Lisa go to Hannah's dance rehearsal. I would totally bring them and let them wreak havoc in the stands, but Henry has a cold."

"I miss the kids," Lauren whined. It had been forever since she'd seen Trina's adorable niece and nephews. Henry must be so big now.

"Listen. I owe you some best friend time and some pseudo-auntie time. Let's not combine the two because I want to get drunk and talk about all the awesome sex you're going to have tonight, and that's not appropriate around my babies. Look at your schedule for next week, and let's carve out time for both. I'm sure I'll have no trouble convincing Calvin and Lisa to go on a date."

"I'd really like that."

"Then it's happening. Okay, I gotta split. Win big, get laid, tell me everything. Deal?"

"Deal," Lauren said as she extended her hand toward Trina.

Trina slapped it away and stepped into her arms for a hug instead. "Have fun tonight."

"I will." Lauren didn't doubt that for a minute.

"Meow," Trina said with a playfully cat-clawing motion.

"Good-bye," Lauren said as she rolled her eyes.

"Does your sex kitten drive a pickup truck? Because a truck just pulled in, and it's got dairy farm written all over it," Trina said as she walked away backward.

Lauren snapped her head in the direction of the parking lot, frowning when she didn't see any trucks at all. Trina was teasing her.

Trina smiled and shook her finger in Lauren's direction. "Maybe get laid before the game. You seem distracted."

Lauren flipped her off with a chuckle before jogging toward the dugout to drop off the paperwork.

"Trina looks great, as usual," Claire Moseley said from her seat on the bench, as she finished braiding her hair.

"Annoying, isn't it?" Lauren replied, checking her own reflection in her cellphone's glass front to makes sure she was looking good for Thea.

Claire laughed. "Have you convinced her to join the team yet? Now that Kelly is a new mom, we're down a player."

"Trina?" Lauren nearly dropped her phone from laughing. "Trina's a hell of a golfer, and though she's a natural athlete, she's not exactly into team sports. Softball is far too dirty for her."

Claire frowned down at her stained knee socks. "This game is deceptively filthy. I need to up my bleach use."

"They look like that because you play all these games like they're the Olympic trials," Lauren teased. Claire was easily their best player. She was the best hitter, the best catcher, and the fastest base runner. Claire gave all the credit of her athleticism to being the younger sister to four much older brothers, which might very well be true, but the end result was that Claire was an absolute badass. And Lauren, well, Lauren liked hanging out and drinking with the team. She wasn't bad, by any measure, but she was here for the social aspect. She didn't hate the fitness that came with it, but she wasn't exactly hitting up the batting cages or doing drills or anything when they weren't at practice or in a game setting.

Claire gave her a look. "That's a bold statement coming from the woman who intentionally tripped Helga from Osterville last week in our pickup scrimmage."

"Hey," Lauren argued, "that was mostly self-defense. Who runs like they have windmill arms? She nearly took me out."

Claire tapped her chin before saying, "She did have a wicked weird gallop."

"Exactly. And I wasn't trying to trip her. I just didn't know whether to duck or dive out of the way of her flailing limbs. Mostly I misjudged my foot placement," Lauren replied.

"Uh-huh, sure." Claire stood and stretched, waving to her girlfriend Shelly White in the stands.

"You two getting married soon?" Lauren asked as she rolled her shoulders, loosening up her neck.

"I hope so. She's my everything," Claire said with a dreamy look. She and Shelly were adorable together. Lauren figured it was just a matter of time before they tied the knot.

"I'll give her a not so subtle nudge to propose," Lauren said.

"Oh, man. Make sure I'm there when you do. I'd love to see the look on her face." Claire scrunched her nose with a laugh.

"She's going to hate me," Lauren replied, shaking her head.

"No way. You're her favorite numbers gal. No one humors her love of math like you do. She's got a soft spot for you and that Pythagorean theorem or whatever nerdy math shit it is you two talk about."

Lauren laughed. She knew that was true. She'd called in a Shelly favor last year when she'd needed some digital intel on Kendall before she and Trina got together. Shelly was a computer whiz and inventor among a dozen other brainy accolades—when Lauren had asked her for help, Shelly had found what she was looking for in a matter of minutes.

"I did bring her a math puzzle tonight, actually."

"Of course you did," Claire said. She was looking over to where Shelly was sitting when she asked, "Who's the hottie in the leather jacket?"

Lauren knew who it was without even looking. But that didn't stop her from admiring tall, dark, and gorgeous.

"Oh, that's Thea," she said as she waved to her. Hottie was an understatement. Thea looked amazing tonight in those dark jeans and Lauren's favorite boots of hers.

"Oh?" Claire gave her a playful nudge. "Will she be joining us for drinks later?"

"That's the plan," Lauren said with a smile. She had every intention of getting over there and greeting her before the game started.

"Good, I want to meet her," Claire replied.

"Don't let me forget about the Newbridge thing. I do need to do a little brainstorming tonight," Lauren said, more for herself than for Claire. She could see herself easily forgetting her work responsibilities now that Thea was here looking fine as hell.

"No worries. I won't let you forget," Claire said, giving her a knowing look.

"Thanks. Be right back." Lauren hurried out of the dugout to give Thea a proper greeting. Or at least a proper safe-for-public greeting.

CHAPTER THIRTEEN

"You made it," Lauren said as she trotted over to her.

"I wouldn't miss it," Thea said, appreciating how great Lauren looked in her uniform.

"Hi," Lauren said, stopping just short of her reach.

She stepped toward her. "Hi."

Lauren reached out and played with the zipper on Thea's jacket. "I see you wore my favorite jacket."

"And your favorite boots," Thea said as she stepped closer.

Lauren flattened her palm over Thea's chest, pulling aside the jacket to caress along the red shirt she wore beneath. "I see you wore the team's colors."

"I looked you guys up online when you neglected to reveal the proper attire. I didn't want anyone getting confused about who I was here for." Thea put her hand on Lauren's hip, guiding her closer.

"Oh? And who's that?" Lauren leaned against Thea's front, and Thea held her close, loving the feeling of her body against her.

"You," she said as she squeezed Lauren's hip.

"Is that right?" Lauren asked as she looped her hands around Thea's neck.

"I'm all yours," Thea said as she lowered her head, bringing her lips to Lauren's ear. "But the question is, will you be *all* mine later?"

Lauren tightened her hold around Thea's neck, bringing her hips closer. "How am I supposed to focus on the game when you say something like that?"

Thea turned her head to catch Lauren's lips, kissing her slowly and deeply before pulling back to say, "You're right. Less talking is a much better option."

Lauren reconnected their lips in an exchange that was all too brief for Thea's liking before huffing in frustration. "That is certainly not any better than all the talking. Just so you know."

Thea shrugged, feigning innocence. "Really? I thought it was pretty PG."

Lauren stepped out of her arms. She had her hand on her hip as she wagged a finger in Thea's direction. "Nothing about that tongue near my body is PG."

"Near isn't close enough." Thea took Lauren's hand and toyed with her fingers. "I prefer *in*."

Lauren moaned. She took Thea's jaw in her hand and pulled her close as she promised, "I am going to exhaust you tonight."

"Not if I exhaust you first." Thea eased out of Lauren's grasp, kissing her lightly. "Save some energy for after the game."

Lauren dragged her thumb across her bottom lip as she stepped back. "I will."

"Good luck," Thea said with a wave as Lauren turned back toward the ball field.

Thea watched as Lauren's teammates met her with catcalls and cheers when she stepped into the dugout. The look Lauren shot her afterward was probably supposed to be menacing, but all it did was make Thea want to give her more reasons to be teased by her teammates.

She surveyed the small bleachers to her right and chose an empty seat by the end on the top row. She'd have a great view from up here.

"So, you're with Lauren, huh?" an attractive brunette in glasses asked as she sat down.

"I am," Thea said without hesitation. Her seatmate was holding a tablet and typing something on it with one hand. "And you?"

"Claire. Auburn hair. First base." She smiled broadly as she said it.

Thea looked up in time to see Claire waving to the woman next to her.

"I'm Shelly, by the way."

"Thea," she replied.

"Is this your first time here?" Shelly asked as she continued to type on the tablet in front of her. Thea noticed she was barely looking at the screen.

"Yes," she replied before nodding toward the tablet. "Busy?"

Shelly laughed. "Always."

"How do you type so fast and not look at what you're doing?" Thea leaned back. "I'd be lucky to not have a typo every other word."

"I'm coding," Shelly said with a shrug. "I could do that in my sleep."

"Ah, you're one of those," Thea said with an easy smile.

"One of those what?" Shelly asked as she put her tablet down for the first time since Thea had sat next to her.

"The genius type," Thea replied. "My best friend is like you."

"Oh?" Shelly slid her glasses up into her hair, looking amused.

"Yup. Certified brainiac." Thea stretched. "Do you forget to do things like close the refrigerator door or leave your keys in the lock?"

Shelly looked scandalized. "I do."

Thea nodded. "All you genius types do. You're too busy being superhuman to remember to be human."

"Wow." Shelly said, seeming to consider this.

"It's a burden for the rest of us mere mortals, to remind you to put your shirt on the right way, but we all make sacrifices," Thea joked.

Thea didn't miss the way Shelly glanced down at her own shirt before replying, "Well, you mustn't be a box of rocks or anything if Lauren likes you."

"Why do you say that?" Thea wanted to know more about Lauren—that was one of the reasons she came tonight.

Shelly repositioned her glasses on her nose as the game got underway in front of them. "Lauren's brilliant with numbers. And people. She's got a way with people that I've never seen before. Well, maybe once, but that's a story for another day and involves a matchmaker and a dancer and..." She shifted. "Sorry, I get distracted."

"Par for the genius course," Thea replied. "No worries."

Shelly laughed, and Thea was glad her humor hadn't offended her. "Maybe you're right."

"So, tell me about Lauren." Thea leaned in toward her new friend as she watched Lauren make a particularly impressive lunging catch near second base. On top of brains, beauty, and charm, Thea now had her athleticism to admire as well. Lauren seemed to be the total package.

❖

"So, what do you think?" Lauren asked Claire, hopeful that she'd like her ideas.

"I think it sounds great. This is an exciting project." Claire took the folder Lauren had placed on the table and slipped it into Shelly's messenger bag. "I already did a few mock-ups after our initial conversation, but I'll input this stuff into my marketing vision. I should have a preliminary write-up for you to present to Ellison in the next day or two."

"You're a lifesaver," Lauren said, glad Claire had been willing to become part of her professional team.

"No sweat. Working with you outside of these dusty uniforms is going to be fun." Claire drained her martini glass as she nodded toward Thea and Shelly, who seemed to be deep in a conversation about God knew what. "Thea's great. No one gets Shelly to loosen up the first time they meet her."

Lauren smiled as Thea used one hand to express whatever animated thought she was getting across. Her other hand had been resting on Lauren's thigh under the table since they'd sat down as a group. The warmth of her continued touch was comforting, and exciting. Since it reminded Lauren about the plans she had for after this meeting with Claire.

"She is," Lauren agreed.

"They're talking about us," Shelly said with a small smile.

"Don't be an egomaniac," Claire said as she kissed Shelly's cheek. "We were talking about Thea."

"Oh?" Thea asked, and that killer smile doubled in wattage when Lauren squeezed the hand that was on her thigh.

"All good things, I promise," Lauren said as Thea intertwined their fingers.

Shelly yawned.

"That's my cue," Claire said as she slid off her chair. "Time to get you home before you turn into a pumpkin."

Shelly tried and failed to stifle another yawn. "Yes, mistress."

Claire laughed as she waved to Lauren and Thea. "It was nice to meet you, Thea. I hope we see you again soon."

"Same," Thea said, as she stood to hug Lauren's friends. "Hey, Shel, don't forget to send me that video."

"On it," Shelly said with a nod.

"What?" Thea asked as she resumed her seat and took Lauren's hand again.

"Nothing. You're just cute," Lauren said, glad to have Thea's hand back again.

"I mean, duh," Thea said with a wink. "But besides that, what?"

Lauren pulled her close, kissing her sweetly. "I like that you get along with my friends."

Thea nuzzled her nose. "Well, your friends are awesome. So that's an easy task."

Lauren warmed at that. Her cell phone buzzed, and she checked it. It was a text from Claire.

"Did I pass the friend approval test?" Thea asked.

Lauren turned the screen toward her. Claire's text had Thea's name next to heart-eyes and flame emoji. "I'd say so."

Thea cheered. "Now I just have to get your award-winning friend to like me—then I'm set."

"Trina?" Lauren asked. It was funny to her that Thea was nervous about that.

"Um, yeah." Thea finished her last sip before discarding her glass. "She's the one to impress."

"Why do you say that?" Lauren asked, though she wasn't wrong.

"I got to the game early tonight. I saw you two chatting in the dugout." Thea looked a little shy. "I ran up to her as she was leaving, just to say hello."

Lauren gaped. "You did? What did she say?" She was almost afraid to ask.

Thea got very serious "She threatened me with death. And told me she had people that could make me disappear if I hurt you."

Lauren slow blinked. She was going to kill Trina.

Thea burst out laughing. "Oh my God, your face." She paused. "Wait. Did you really think she said that to me?"

"She didn't?" Lauren let out a relieved sigh.

"No." Thea wiped at her eyes. "But maybe I should count myself lucky since you weren't shocked that she could have. Which means she might have said that in the past. Which means she might be a sociopath. But I digress."

"She's not a sociopath. She's just protective." Lauren playfully slapped her arm. "What did she say, though?"

Thea gave her an embarrassed smile. "She said she was sorry to have missed hanging out tonight, but that she hoped we could get together sometime soon."

"Aww." Lauren was glad Trina decided to extend an olive branch and not bare her teeth tonight.

"She also told me to put tonight's cocktails on her tab, but Shelly beat me to it." Thea frowned.

"Shelly can afford it," Lauren said, touched that Trina wanted to pick up the bill even though she wasn't there.

Thea nodded. "She said she worked in technology. And that her office is nearby. But I would never assume—"

Lauren shook her head. "She said she worked in technology?"

"Yeah. Does she not?" Thea asked.

"Oh, she does." Lauren slid off her chair, reaching for her coat. "But maybe she undersold it a bit."

Thea helped Lauren into her jacket as she asked, "Why do you say that?"

"Because Shelly practically *invented* technology." Lauren reached for her purse as she added, "Or at least has been a major player in the field for long enough to be on the cover of *Forbes* before age thirty-five."

Thea froze. "What's Shelly's last name?"

"White," Lauren replied with a smile as recognition spread across Thea's face.

"I thought she looked familiar. Avni is going to kill me," Thea said as she palmed her forehead. "Are all your friends award-winning?"

"Trina, Kendall, Shelly, Ellison," Lauren said, counting out on her fingers. "Seems like it, huh?"

"Damn." Thea shook her head. "I just casually had cocktails with the tech goddess of the modern world and had no idea. I will never live this down. That does explain the cool camera glasses and the tablet, I guess." Her phone pinged, and she held it up excitedly as she said, "My video has arrived."

"What video?" Lauren stepped into Thea's space, loving the way Thea immediately wrapped her arm around her.

"The one of you hitting that game-winning home run tonight," Thea said as she swiped across the screen, turning it to face her. "My favorite part is your victory dance at the end."

Lauren took the phone and laughed as she saw the final hit from the game from Thea's perspective. Or rather, Shelly's glasses' perspective. And though she was happy to see the play again, what she was most excited about was when Shelly looked to her left and recorded Thea standing and cheering for her. It was one of the most genuine things Lauren had ever seen.

Lauren pulled Thea to her lips. "Be honest, you just liked watching me run the bases, right?"

"Your ass does look incredible in those pants." Thea kissed across her lips before asking, "But is it time to get you out of them yet? Because I am very much interested in that."

Lauren savored the feeling of Thea's tongue against hers for a moment longer before she nodded. "Let's go to my place. I need to shower."

"You'll need more than just a shower after I'm through with you." Thea's tone made Lauren wet.

"Let's get out of here."

CHAPTER FOURTEEN

Thea was having a hard time keeping her hands to herself, but in her defense, Lauren wasn't exactly doing much to deter the groping and caressing. Except this time Thea was driving, and not a passenger like before. So that made things rather interesting.

"We're here." Lauren was out of the car and yanking open Thea's door before she'd even had time to shut off the ignition.

"Excited much?" Thea asked as she climbed out the driver's side of her car.

Lauren answered by pushing her up against the side of her car and kissing her hard. Thea dropped her hands to Lauren's hips and ass, palming greedily as Lauren opened her mouth wider, inviting her in.

"I don't know how I couldn't be. You were about an inch away from getting me to orgasm in your passenger seat, while you were driving, mind you. So yeah, you could say I'm primed and ready." Lauren breathed out against her lips, and Thea reached between them with the intention to finish what she started. Lauren caught her wrist and shook her head. "Not here. I want to be loud, but that's hard to do in an echoey parking garage."

Thea didn't argue. Because the prospect of Lauren coming undone, loudly, was right on the top of her priority list right now. "Lead the way."

Lauren's apartment, though familiar, was still a new space for Thea. She hadn't exactly seen anything more than the kitchen and the bedroom the first time around. So when Lauren opened the door and began to shuffle things around, she took in the contents of the space for the first time. A large flat screen was mounted over the gas fireplace on the far wall, and a soft looking cream-colored sofa faced it. The couch was flanked by two dark wood end tables, of which the one closest to her had ceramic photo coasters of Lauren doing various things with various people. Thea recognized Trina, a photo of Claire and Shelly at one of Lauren's games, and that younger friend of Lauren's who'd been at The Mirage the night they'd met.

"Who's this?" she asked as Lauren deposited a dining room chair in front of the fireplace.

"Jax," she said with a broad smile. "We work together. They're my partner on a new project."

"You mean you are doing things outside of trying to save my family home?" Thea teased.

"Imagine that, huh?" Lauren nipped at her ear, and she turned to face her.

"What's with the chair?" Thea asked as she pulled Lauren close.

"That's for you," Lauren said, as she tapped her nose and stepped back. "It's the seat for the guest of honor."

Thea regarded the chair with a raised eyebrow. "Okay?"

"Don't ask too many questions," Lauren said as she eased Thea's jacket off her shoulders, then tossed it to the couch. "Sit, wait. I'll make it worth your time, I promise."

Lauren slipped out of her grasp, and she whined.

"Shh." Lauren's finger pressed against her lips. "Don't argue."

Thea let herself be guided to the chair. If Lauren had something in mind, she would go with it. She was pretty sure she'd go along with anything Lauren wanted at this point. She was more than desperate to get her hands and mouth back on Lauren's body. She could wait, right?

"I'll be right back. Don't move," Lauren said as she used the remote to start the gas fireplace behind her.

Thea reached out for her once more. "You'll be fast?" she asked, caressing Lauren's side. "Because as much as you might like being touched, touching you drives me crazy. And I'm already at, like, a ten from that car ride here."

"Are you saying you're feeling impatient?" Lauren asked as she guided Thea's hand between her legs, pressing her fingers against the damp fabric of her pants.

"Yes." Thea leaned forward to increase their contact, but Lauren stepped back.

"Just think about how bad you want it," Lauren said as she gave her a once-over. "And when I get back, I want you to tell me in detail what it is you were thinking about."

Thea swallowed thickly. That would be a short conversation if she had any say in it. Largely because what she wanted was Lauren, spread out in front of her, crying out again and again. That didn't seem like too much to ask.

"Stay. Wait," Lauren said again as she walked out of the room toward her bedroom, before disappearing behind her bedroom door. Thea waited. She did. Well, she sort of did. But she was endlessly thirsty after all that making out and almost fucking. So when she heard Lauren's shower turn on, she slipped off the chair and headed to the kitchen, grabbed a glass from the cabinet, and poured herself a quick drink. She swirled the contents of her glass, letting herself get lost in the smoothness of the water's motion. She smiled as she remembered the last time she had a glass of water in this kitchen. After draining the glass, she washed her hands and the glass, before drying it and returning it to the cabinet in the hope that Lauren wouldn't notice.

She made it two steps toward the living room when Lauren's voice stopped her in her tracks.

"I thought you said you were great at taking directions."

Thea winced. She had said that the first time she'd been here. And usually, it was true. "I am."

She felt Lauren step up behind her. "And yet, you aren't in your seat."

"Headed there now," Thea said as she started to turn, but Lauren stopped her.

"You left your seat."

"Am I going to be punished?" Thea asked, part of her hoping she would be.

"If you're lucky." Lauren's lips were by her ear. "Go, sit."

Thea did her best to restrain her body's desire to sprint toward the chair. As she lowered herself into the seat, she caught a glimpse of Lauren for the first time. She was draped across the arm of the sofa, wearing some silky-looking bathrobe thing that was obstructing the nudity Thea knew awaited her underneath. She took a moment to appreciate the beauty of the lingerie, even if it was standing between her and what she most desired.

"You're staring," Lauren said.

"You're beautiful."

Lauren smiled and stood. Thea's lower abdomen tightened at the way the almost too short robe framed Lauren's sexy legs.

"Why are you so far away?" Thea asked, placing her elbows on her knees and leaning forward.

"I'll be plenty close, I promise." Lauren picked her cell phone off the narrow table behind the couch and she thumbed over the glass. "I just need to pick some music first."

Thea leaned back, spreading her legs to relieve some of the ache that Lauren's near-naked form was causing. "Music for what?"

Lauren looked up, a mischievous smile on her face as she replied, "For your lap dance, silly."

"Fuck." Thea had never had a proper lap dance. Sure, she'd gone to a few strip clubs, and yes, she'd paid for a dance or two, but never had she had one in private. And something told her this was going to be something else entirely. As Lauren bent over, depositing her phone on the side table as music filled the room, Thea caught a glimpse of what was under the robe—nothing. And suddenly the prospect of a lap dance was even more exciting.

Lauren looked over her shoulder and smiled when she caught Thea staring. Something told Thea that her action was planned, and she'd fallen for it. Seemingly to Lauren's delight.

"Are you ready?" Lauren asked.

Thea was practically drooling at this point. "Yes."

"Good." The music picked up, the beat gradual but heavy as Lauren stepped toward her painfully slowly.

Thea reached for her when she was close, but Lauren pressed against her sternum, pushing her back against the chair.

"Hands behind your head," she commanded, and Thea had to bite her bottom lip to keep from moaning.

She nodded and obliged as Lauren walked her fingers along Thea's jaw, tipping her chin up before placing a gentle kiss to her lips.

"I love you in that jacket and those boots. But I'd be remiss to leave out how sexy I think you look in these dark jeans," Lauren said as she dropped a hand to Thea's waistband, unbuttoning them before dipping lower. She rubbed her fingers along the seam of Thea's crotch, and the moan she was trying to stifle spilled out.

"Lauren," she gasped. She was heating up fast, and she knew it wasn't from the gas flame behind her.

"Soon," Lauren promised as she stepped back, swaying to the music. Thea watched as she turned, lowering herself slowly onto Thea's lap as she rolled her hips forward and back, moving to the music and frustrating Thea's clit more and more.

"Can I touch you?" Thea's hands were clenched behind her head, her fingers aching from the restraint she was employing at that moment.

"No," Lauren said as she looked over her shoulder, licking her lips as she pressed her ass against Thea's crotch in an exaggerated roll. Thea closed her eyes and hissed at the sensation of Lauren's ass against her sex and her back rubbing against Thea's chest. All the while her hands clutched at nothing. This was maddening. She needed to touch her.

Thea felt Lauren briefly leave her lap before feeling her climb back on her, this time facing her and straddling her legs.

"Open your eyes." Lauren's lips were at her ear.

Thea blinked and found heaven awaiting her. Lauren was fully naked now, her robe forgotten on the floor next to them. Her eyes were dark, and her lips were wet, and Thea felt like her whole body was on fire with Lauren pressed against her.

"My God, you are gorgeous," Thea said as she leaned in to connect their lips.

Lauren leaned back, dodging her mouth, to Thea's frustration. "You left the chair."

"I was thirsty." Thea let her gaze drop to Lauren's chest.

"I bet you're thirsty now," Lauren said, leaning back and exposing her sex.

"So thirsty."

"Good." Lauren rolled her hips forward again, draping her arms over Thea's shoulders and grasping the wrists behind Thea's head. "Keep your hands here, and I'll make sure your thirst is quenched."

Thea didn't have time to agree before Lauren's lips connected with hers. Lauren's tongue entered her mouth and massaged against hers as Lauren continued to move to the beat of the music, grinding and rolling against her body.

She hummed against Lauren's lips as Lauren's fingers worked under her shirt, pressing against the skin of her abdomen before moving up to her chest.

"Do you know what touching your body does to me?" Lauren asked as she stripped Thea of her shirt, helping her reclasp her hands behind her head—hands that now ached from diminished blood flow.

Thea dropped her gaze down to Lauren's swollen lower lips. "I have a pretty good idea."

"Do you want to touch me?" she asked as she rolled one of Thea's nipples between her fingers through the soft cotton fabric of her bra.

"Y-yes," she said as she jolted at the contact. Her hips thrust up as Lauren ground down again.

"What do you want to touch?" Lauren asked as she leaned forward and licked the fabric of Thea's bra, causing her nipple to rise at the contact. The now wet fabric brought a rush of sensation to her chest that caused her to shiver.

"All of you." Thea struggled against her own restraint.

Lauren sucked on her nipple through her bra once more before reaching up and freeing one of Thea's hands. She brought it to her chest, and Thea exhaled at the soft fullness of Lauren's breast in her palm. Her hand tingled as the blood flow returned, and her fingers felt clumsy as they massaged Lauren's flesh. But Lauren didn't complain if she'd noticed.

"And this hand?" Thea asked, flexing her shoulder as Lauren's lips returned to hers.

"Here." Lauren guided Thea's hand between her legs, and Thea nearly climaxed from the feeling of Lauren's arousal on her fingertips.

"Fuck." Thea gasped for breath against the insistence of Lauren's lips on hers.

The music picked up, and Lauren rolled her hips, rubbing herself onto Thea's hand before pulling back again. Thea reached for her, abandoning her breast to grip her hip. As she slipped lower, to press against Lauren's opening, Lauren pulled back and shook her head.

"Tonight is about exhausting you, remember?" Lauren rubbed herself against Thea's hand briefly before shifting backward to dance on Thea's lap.

"You're driving me crazy," Thea said as she leaned back, enjoying the view and the feeling of Lauren straddling her and moving to the music in what was the hottest lap dance Thea had ever had. She reached out to stroke Lauren again as she said, "I want to taste you."

Lauren slowed her movements, guiding Thea inside her as she set the pace and rolled against Thea's hand. But before Thea knew it, Lauren was just out of reach again.

"Just a taste, love." Lauren brought Thea's hand to her mouth, and Thea closed her eyes at the delightful torture of barely tasting Lauren against her tongue.

Thea hummed, opening her eyes as Lauren helped her out of her bra. Lauren slipped off her lap, pulling her up by her unbuttoned pants before leaning in and licking the shell of Thea's ear. "Get naked, baby."

Thea did as she was told, and Lauren pushed her back onto the chair as a new song started. This one was similar to the first one, though the beat was heavier, and Lauren immediately synced her hips to the new sound.

Thea gripped her own thighs as Lauren swayed in front of her, loosely resting her forearms on Thea's shoulders and bending forward to bring their chests together before easing back. Teasing. So much teasing. Thea reached for her, caressing along her sides and cupping her ass, until Lauren turned, sitting back on Thea's lap and grinding that amazing ass against her swollen clit and making her see stars.

"Lauren," Thea warned as Lauren increased her pace. She felt herself start to tremble as her lower abdomen tightened.

Unable to stop herself, Thea bucked her hips to meet Lauren's motion. Lauren looked over her shoulder, kissing her briefly before she asked, "What do you need?"

"To touch you." Thea wrapped her arm around Lauren, pulling her flush against her as she cupped her breast. She reached her free hand down along Lauren's abdomen to settle at her sex, her excitement building as she found Lauren was as turned-on as she was.

"Yeah, baby. Like that." Lauren continued to circle her hips as Thea caressed her. Thea felt her pleasure skyrocket with each intentional roll of Lauren's ass against her. Between that and finally being able to touch Lauren, Thea knew she wouldn't last much longer.

Thea brought her lips to Lauren's shoulder, sucking on the skin as she felt herself start to climb too fast. Lauren must have realized it too because to Thea's relief her hand slipped between them, rubbing Thea's clit as she continued to grind on Thea's lap. Her body felt like it was on fire, and the combination of Lauren's touch and breathy pants caused her to come hard. Her body shook as she wrapped her arms around Lauren, leaning forward against Lauren's back to catch her breath.

Lauren kissed the hand Thea had pressed against her chest, holding her close. It was a small gesture of affection, but Thea relished it. Because holding Lauren like this as she recovered felt incredibly intimate for some reason. Maybe it was because Lauren let herself be held. Or maybe it was because Thea needed to feel grounded, to come back to Earth from that stratospheric orgasm, and feeling Lauren's labored breaths under her palms helped her feel tethered to this planet. She wasn't sure what it was, but she was sure that she hadn't felt anything like this before.

After a long few moments, Lauren turned in her lap, straddling her again. It was only then, when she was looking her in the eyes, kissing her lips and cradling her jaw, that she noticed the *literal* heat of the moment. She could feel sweat dripping down her neck and back as she became aware of just how hot that fire was burning behind her. Or maybe she was still burning from the inside out. It didn't matter. Either way she was sated and hot as fuck. But none of that mattered while Lauren was naked on her lap, kissing her like she held all the air in the room.

"Still thirsty?" Lauren asked against her lips.

Thea nodded, holding her close in another embrace, not ready to let go just yet. "I've never been so thirsty."

Lauren pressed one last lingering kiss against her lips before she eased out of her embrace, stepping gingerly on the carpet as she shut off the music playing from her phone, which Thea had forgotten was on in the background.

"Me, too," she said as she reached for Thea's hand. "Let's get you cleaned up and cooled off in the shower."

"Is that all we'll be doing there?" Thea asked, aware that Lauren hadn't had her chance in the spotlight yet.

"Oh no," Lauren said as she walked backward toward her bedroom. "First I'm going to clean up that mess I made while I'm on my knees. Then you're going to fuck me against the wall like you promised on your porch swing." She tugged at Thea's hand. "My shower has two walls that aren't glass. I'll let you pick which one to pin me to."

"I'm probably going to die from overstimulation tonight, and I'm surprisingly okay with that," Thea said, hurrying her pace.

Lauren didn't miss a beat. "Just make sure if you do, it's after you've been inside me."

"I'm so glad you invited me to that game tonight," Thea said as she followed Lauren into the massive walk-in shower.

"Oh, you have no idea. We're just getting started," Lauren said as she turned on the water and knelt before her. "You're about to learn a whole new definition of exhausted."

"I can't wait," Thea said as she threaded her fingers through Lauren's hair, closing her eyes and hoping this night would never end.

CHAPTER FIFTEEN

"When can I see you again?" Thea asked as she kissed along Lauren's neck.

Lauren brushed her hair back to give Thea more access. "You're seeing me right now."

"I'm kissing you right now. But I'd like to see a whole lot more of you very soon." Thea closed her lips around Lauren's earlobe, and Lauren's clit throbbed.

"Don't start the earlobe thing—I have a meeting," Lauren said as she grabbed a handful of Thea's shirt.

"Well, I'd rather suck on other things, but you have so many clothes on. I'm limited." Thea nibbled, and Lauren's knees almost buckled.

Lauren braced herself against Thea's strong torso, wrapping her arms around her waist and leaning back against Thea's car for support. "I want to hear all about those things, but—"

"You have to go." Thea pulled back, and Lauren missed her mouth.

"It's true." Lauren caressed along her jaw before running her hand through Thea's thick, dark hair. She playfully tugged it. "Will you think about me while I'm working?"

Thea smiled, and Lauren wanted to jump her. She had the sexiest mouth. "I think about you when I'm waking, sleeping, driving, and dreaming. You name it, and I can guarantee I'm only paying half attention to whatever it is because you hold every free thought in my mind."

"And when I'm with you?" Lauren cocked her head, watching her.

"When you're with me, I'm thinking I'm the luckiest girl in the world. And I'm wondering how I can make all these incredible things we share happen over and over again."

Lauren felt herself melt a little more. She'd never been with anyone as smooth or charming as Thea. "Tonight. Come by tonight. Tomorrow is Saturday—we can spend the whole night and next day in bed. No work. No responsibilities. No distractions—"

"No clothes."

"Exactly." Lauren was glad they were on the same page.

"I'll bring dinner. You be dessert."

Lauren moaned. "You're going to break me."

Thea kissed her long and slow. "I'll fix you afterward, I promise. But I might break you again, just to put you back together. If you're all right with that, that is."

"I am," Lauren replied against her lips.

"Then I'll see you tonight," Thea said as she pulled back. "I'll call you later. You sure you're okay to get your car?"

Lauren nodded. She'd left her car at the softball field last night, to be groped by Thea in hers. "Jax will take me. I have to swing by the Newbridge site anyway. We'll have an adventure."

"Everything with you is an adventure, huh?" Thea asked as she stepped back, trailing her fingers along Lauren's arm until Lauren intertwined their fingers.

"You never know what you'll get with me," she said.

"That's my favorite thing about you."

"Your favorite? Really?" Lauren teased.

Thea laughed. "Okay, one of my favorite things. But I admit, I have many."

"I'm okay with that," Lauren said.

"Me, too." Thea had the most interesting eyes. Lauren could stare at them forever, she thought.

"Hey, Thea." Trina's voice sounded nearby.

"Trina." Thea looked momentarily nervous. "How are you?"

"I'm good." Something about Trina's smile told Lauren she'd been there awhile.

"How much of that did you see?" Lauren asked, hiding behind her hand.

"Mostly just the moony eyes. And the flirty kisses. Oh, and the goofy smiles." Trina turned her attention back to Thea. "How do you take your coffee?"

"Caffeinated," Thea said, seeming to regain her swagger.

"Then this is for you." Trina handed over one of the coffees she held. "You look tired. And you're wearing the same clothes from the game last night. So you probably need this more than me."

Thea took it with a bashful smile. "Thank you."

"You're welcome," Trina said, seemingly sincere, and Lauren nearly squealed. "I'll see you inside, Lau."

Once Trina said her good-byes and was out of earshot, Lauren cheered.

"What?" Thea said after sipping her new coffee. "Damn, this is good."

"Trina gave up her beloved coffee. That's an olive branch, an entire tree, and a freaking grove. Hell, that is as precious as a new Birkin bag to her. She likes you." Lauren was thrilled.

"She likes me." Thea beamed before doing a celebratory dance. "Yes! Best friend approval, check. Now you're stuck with me."

"That doesn't seem like such a bad thing," Lauren said before stealing one last kiss. She savored the delicious taste of coffee on Thea's tongue before stepping back. "Call me later, and don't forget about tonight."

"I promise I won't think of anything else," Thea said.

"Good."

Trina was perched on Lauren's desk when she finally made it inside, hustling to get ready before the morning meeting.

"Please tell me that coffee is for me," Lauren asked as she reached for it.

Trina pulled it just out of her reach. "Pssh. I gave your coffee to Thea. What kind of fool do you take me for?"

Lauren's heart broke. "Seriously?"

"No," Trina said as she handed her the coffee. "I gave her mine, relax. But that means we need to take a walk after your meeting, because I'm undercaffeinated now and no one wants a cranky, half-awake Trina."

"Agreed. She's a real downer," Lauren said as she cradled the cup in both hands, inhaling the robust aroma before taking a hearty sip. "My God. I'm alive again."

"Long night?"

"Shh, don't ruin this for me," Lauren said as she took another sip. She let out a sated exhale. "Okay, ask me again."

Trina crossed her legs with a laugh. "Long night?"

"So long. The longest. The longest night, the longest morning, the longest orgasms. All of it. Long and lovely and happening again tonight, hopefully," Lauren said as she stared out the window, remembering some of her favorite moments.

"I'm happy for you." Trina stood, kissing Lauren on the cheek as she headed toward her office door. "Bask in this sexiness for another moment or two, but don't forget about your meeting."

"Shit." Lauren palmed her forehead.

"I'll go chat up Ellison. That should buy you a few minutes to temporarily suppress your lingering horniness."

"You're the best," Lauren called out after her as she rushed to her desk to gather her notes.

"I know," Trina called back, and Lauren laughed. Where would she be without her best friend?

Lauren tapped the desk as she waited for the voice on the other end of the line. She'd missed Faith Leader's phone call while she was meeting with Ellison and Jax this morning. She wanted to get Faith's perspective on the Boudreaux property so she could get the info to Ellison and start to formulate a more serious plan to help Kathleen. And Thea. Lauren chewed her bottom lip. The Thea thing certainly complicated matters.

Lauren wanted to help Kathleen. And impress Ellison with her creative thinking. But now, she was also worried about appeasing Thea, which was an unexpected consequence to their budding relationship. Largely because she'd had no intention of dating a client's daughter. Or bedding her. Again and again. And yet here she was with a handful of lusty orgasms and sexy exchanges that she couldn't ignore. And they were all connected to Thea. Who was connected to the Boudreaux farm. Fuck.

"Faith Leader, how can I help you?" a surprisingly sultry voice said over the line.

"Faith, hi. This is Lauren Calloway with Gamble and Associates in Boston. How are you?"

"I'm good. I'm glad we were able to connect. I reviewed the things you sent over to me. I have some numbers for you, and some potential buyer interest, if you're ready."

"I am." Lauren scribbled notes as Faith spoke, thanking her as the call ended.

She leaned back and looked at the messy script in front of her. She stared at the numbers, circling a few of them as she did the math in her head. This was not what she was hoping to hear. "Goddammit."

There was a knock at her door. Jax poked their head around the doorframe. "Ready for that ride?"

"Hell yes. Can we put the top down? I need to think, and my brain needs air." Lauren stood, slipping on her blazer as she grabbed her sunglasses.

"Top down, you got it." Jax held out their elbow for Lauren to take. "Trina had to rush out to a meeting, but she'll be back afterward. She said something about coffee and sexy-time chat."

"I owe her both."

"Why don't you ever include me in the sexy-time chat?" Jax pouted as they opened the passenger door for her.

"I do," Lauren said.

"After you tell Trina." Jax pouted more.

"That's only because she doggedly pursues the topic. And because her office is next to mine," Lauren replied.

"You walk past my cubicle on the way to both of your offices," Jax countered as they lowered the top to their Mini Cooper and Lauren stretched.

"All right. I've registered your complaint and will rectify my conduct moving forward," Lauren said. "Starting now. What do you want to know?"

Jax smiled as they slipped on their sunglasses. "Everything."

"So, I'm sort of dating Thea from that night at the bar."

Jax winced. "That night is kind of a blur to me."

"You didn't miss much," Lauren said.

"That's a lie. The one thing I do remember is there was lots of kissing with a hot stranger." Jax eased out of the parking lot and onto the main drag. "But I know all that. I want to know about Thea."

"She's great. She's smart and funny and enigmatic. She's just the right amount of sarcastic and playful while still managing to be sexy as fuck. She's sensitive and kind. And she loves her family. There's a loyalty there that's admirable, like you can tell she was raised well. She respects her mom, and she mostly gets along with her brother, which is cute. And she's strong. She's got these incredible shoulders and confident hands and—" Lauren stopped, feeling like Jax was watching her. "What?"

Jax smiled as they pulled through the now green light. "Nothing, it's just like you're so cutesy about it. I don't know that I've seen that side of you before."

"What do you mean?"

Jax merged into the next lane, speeding up. "I mean, you have, like, this glow about you. Like you *like* her. I've talked sexy times with you before, but you never started describing relationship qualities. It's nice."

Lauren wanted to argue, but Jax was right. She did like Thea. Like, *like* her, like her. So much so that she was hoping tonight would lead to more sex but would also maybe be a cuddle sesh with a movie or two first. "I'm totally in a relationship, huh?"

"Oh yeah." Jax gave her a fist bump. "You're practically domesticated."

Lauren had to laugh at that. "Well, what about you?"

"Am I domesticated?" Jax asked as they pulled up to the Newbridge property.

"You've been domesticated," she teased. "I meant, are you dating anyone?"

Jax parked the car and slid their glasses into their hair. They looked down. "Maybe soon? I mean, I like someone. And we are currently in the friend zone, but I'm hoping for more."

This was big news. So big, Lauren was surprised it hadn't come up yet. Jax hadn't been in a serious relationship since before their top surgery last year. "Whoa. Talk about being left out of the loop," she said with a nudge. "You failed to mention that, Jaxy."

"I'm trying not to jinx it," Jax said with a half smile. "In a lot of ways, I think it's all in my head and that there can't be anyone who would be interested in me. Things are still so new, you know? But at the same time, I'm physically happier and more comfortable than I've ever been…"

"But it still takes some adjusting."

"Right." Jax looked relieved that she got it. "So there's nothing to report yet. But I'm hopeful. Cautiously optimistic, even."

"Well, you're a total catch. So whoever this person is, they better realize that from the jump." She lowered her glasses, giving them a look as she said, "Or I'll sic Trina on them."

Jax snorted. "That's so mean."

"I stand by my threat," Lauren said. She looked up at the site for the first time. "Oh, shit."

"Yeah," Jax said, leaning back. "Ellison isn't messing around. She must have them working double and triple time. This building is flying up."

Lauren had to admit, she wasn't sure how Ellison could have been this productive this quickly. That woman was some kind of magic for sure, but even this seemed unreal. The foundation was down, and the first floor was already in skeleton form. There appeared to be twice the usual number of workers moving around as usual, so maybe that was how.

Lauren noticed the main architect, Zander Alter, walking toward them, and she climbed out of the car to meet him.

"You guys aren't fooling around, are you?" she asked.

He tipped back his hard hat and gave her a broad smile. "Make sure you tell Ellison that."

"Something tells me she comes around plenty often to get the inside scoop," Lauren said. Ellison wasn't known for skipping steps or cutting corners. In all the years that Lauren had known her, she had never seen Ellison miss a meeting or a phone call. Something this big was not a project Ellison wouldn't handle personally. No way.

"You're right," Zander said as he shook Jax's hand. "You look sharp, Jax. New suit?"

Jax struck a brief pose before rebuttoning their blazer. "Straight from Paris...Avenue in the South End."

"Well, it looks great." Zander was such a sweetheart. He and his wife had attended Jax's fundraiser. That made him even more awesome in Lauren's book.

"Seriously, though, how are you this far along?" Lauren asked again as two burly guys handily maneuvered a giant steel beam.

Zander watched them hoist the beam before he replied. "We're doing a lot of it off-site, which helps. Once it's here, it's mostly like a giant LEGO build with some fine tuning. That seems to be contributing to it." He paused. "But Langley wants me back earlier than expected, so we increased our workforce to hurry things along."

That explained all the extra hands and feet Lauren could see. "So that means an earlier completion than was previously expected?"

"Looks like it." Zander grabbed a pencil from behind his ear as he checked over his clipboard. "Of course, things could come to a screeching halt, and everything could fall behind. That's always a possibility, I suppose."

Jax coughed. "Ellison would have an aneurysm."

Zander laughed. "I'll do my best to keep that from happening." He looked back at Lauren. "You guys are here for a quick tour of what's happening out back, right?"

"Yes, please." Lauren was excited about this. Zander had been working with a landscaping crew in the back to help jump-start the community garden space, and Ellison had asked her to come snap some pictures to send over to Claire for the marketing write-up. She was eager to see what he'd accomplished and even more eager to get those pictures to Claire. Once this was out of her hands, she could focus on the garbage numbers that Faith had just given her related to the Boudreaux farm. Which overwhelmed her immensely. So having one less thing on her to-do list was ideal.

"Right this way," Zander said as he took them toward the back lot.

Lauren exhaled and rolled her shoulders. She needed to put Thea's family farm on the back burner and get her head in the game on this project. Newbridge was her future, and as much as she hated to admit it, Thea's family farm might soon be part of everyone's past.

❖

Thea keyed into her office and flicked on her light, nearly screaming when she found Avni stretched out on her couch.

"Sonofa—"

"Can you shut off the sun, please?" Avni groaned as she covered her eyes and rolled to face the back of the couch.

"What's going on?" Thea asked as she shut off the light. She used her cell phone to guide her to her desk since it appeared that Avni had quite literally dumped all her things on the floor in front of the couch.

"You want the long or the short version?" Avni asked before seeming to reconsider it. "Forget that, my headache has voted, and it appears you are getting the short version."

"Short version of what?" Thea plopped in her chair, scooting toward her friend.

"I lost it. I lost my cool with Saanaa and stormed out of the apartment, but not before breaking up with Raj and dropping the dinner his mother made in the trash on my way out," Avni said, still facing the back of the couch.

"You what? Back up, what happened?"

Avni rolled over, and Thea had a hard time seeing her face in this darkness. She had no idea the blinds in her office were adept at room darkening.

"I told you—my hangover brain is only allowing the short version of events to be relayed. But the real question should be, *Avni, my greatest and dearest friend, why have you chosen the couch in my office as the destination for your fall from grace?* To which I would reply, *Because I went to your apartment and you weren't home.* At which point you would say, *That's because I was getting laid.* Right?"

Thea cringed. "Uh, yes."

"Let's talk about that. That sounds more interesting than me being single, homeless, and hungover." Avni laughed before gripping her head and groaning. "No laughing. Got it."

"Avni—" Thea tried but Avni held up her hand.

"Gossip talk only. Until I get coffee and my weight in greasy bacon," Avni mumbled.

Thea grabbed her cell and placed a food delivery order on the app from their favorite breakfast joint down the street. In fifteen minutes there would be coffee and food, which Thea certainly wouldn't mind since she only had time to shower and change today. Well, that and drink Trina's coffee, that is.

"You're doing that thing where you don't talk out loud but instead have an inner monologue that is super annoying to other people." Avni sat up, rubbing her forehead.

"Sorry. Food is en route. You have my undivided attention."

"I don't want your attention. I want gossip. Tell me about Lauren. How is she? Are you getting married yet?"

"Married?" Thea laughed. "That's a little quick, even for you."

Avni shot her a look.

"Too soon?"

"A bit." Avni leaned back with a stretch. "So you had the best night, and there was lots of sex, and I bet there was even cuddling, too, wasn't there?"

Thea nodded. "There was totally cuddling."

Avni sighed. "This is just one more reason why being straight is overrated. You know the last time Raj and I cuddled? 2017. And I'm pretty sure he was just trying to read his cell phone screen on the table next to me. It was an around the shoulder, one-armed, kinda half-assed approach like all things he does in his life. Except be a mama's boy. He does that full tilt. Totally committed there."

Thea's heart broke for her friend. She never really liked Raj, but he wasn't a bad guy. He just wasn't the right guy for Avni. Not that she'd say that right now or anything.

Avni paused. "I just hijacked your floaty lust cloud with my rainstorm of disappointment and jadedness. My bad." She waved her hand at Thea. "Continue."

"There's nothing else to say. It was nice. I had a really nice night."

Avni leaned her elbows on her knees as she tried to sit forward. "That's it? I carried all of my most sacred belongings and camped out on your super uncomfortable office couch because of a nice night?"

"To be fair," Thea started, "you could have called me. And I would have brought you back to my place. At least the couch in my apartment pulls out to a bed."

"When was I gonna call you? In between round two and round three?" Avni challenged.

"What makes you think there was more than one round?" Thea asked, curious.

Avni laughed. "I mean, first of all, I know you. And I have never seen you spend a night with any one of your conquests. So if I had to sleep on this rock-hard piece of cardboard, you had better have had sex all night. Otherwise I'll never forgive you."

Thea thought about what Avni had said. She couldn't remember the last time she'd spent a full night with someone. And she'd now spent two with Lauren.

"So?" Avni pushed again.

"I did," Thea conceded. And she'd enjoyed every moment of it, too. But again, that seemed best left unsaid right now.

"Thank the heavens for that." Avni yawned. "At least someone is getting laid around here."

Thea's office phone line rang, and Avni jumped.

Thea tried to muffle out Avni's curses as she answered the line. "The food's here. I'll be right back."

She scooped up the food and jetted back to her office, surprised to find the blinds cracked a bit.

"We're doing light now?" she asked as she closed the door behind her.

"It's in the trial phase. I'm still doing data collection regarding this hangover and its response to the sun." Avni sipped a bottle of water before making a face. "I'm tired of water. Tell me you have bacon in that pile."

"Extra bacon on your plain bagel, egg, and cheese sandwich. Toasted twice, just like you like it." Thea handed her the sandwich wrapped in tinfoil, suppressing a laugh when Avni practically lunged for it.

"Thank you," she mumbled between bites. Thea handed her a large iced coffee with extra sugar and a napkin because what she was doing to that sandwich was damn messy.

She nibbled on her own meal as they sat quietly, wondering when she'd get the full story but too afraid to ask.

"That was amazing," Avni said, leaning back.

"I got you a doughnut, too—extra sprinkles, double chocolate," Thea said as she tossed the small wax bag at Avni.

Avni nearly missed it, juggling the bag briefly before catching it. "I appreciate the doughnut. I do not appreciate the shitty throw."

"Sorry, my arms are tired," Thea joked, and Avni gave her a playful glare.

"I hate you," Avni said before being silenced by the doughnut. "I take it back. I love you. This doughnut is orgasmic."

"Fatty foods, lots of sugar, and caffeine should fix you right up," Thea said as she tossed the wrapper from her own sandwich in the trash. "So, almost human again? Are you ready to tell me what happened now?"

Avni wiped her mouth with her napkin before giving her a small nod. "Look, I know that things between me and Raj haven't been good for a long time. But honestly, I think we were both just comfortable in our unhappiness. Or at least Raj was. But I don't think I was, not entirely. I swear his mother has been trying to break us up for years, and last night, I think I'd just had enough.

"She started in with her usual critiques about my height and weight and clothes. Then she rounded off the insult party by criticizing the way I organize my spice cabinet. Then it was over the quality of paper towels we use. And Raj just nodded along like a bobblehead. He even made the comment that he didn't like the paper towels when I brought them home but that he hadn't wanted to offend me." Avni ran her hand through her hair. "They're fucking paper towels, and last time I checked, his lazy ass hadn't grocery shopped in months. But I digress."

She took a big swig of her coffee before continuing. "I'd killed a bottle and a half of wine before the dinner finally hit the table, and Raj had one bite and was all, *This is so much better than the way Avni makes it.* And I lost it. I saw red. Maybe it was the merlot, maybe it was rage. I don't know. All I know is I started screaming and then the trash got the remainder of the meal, and I grabbed anything and everything I could get my hands on."

She motioned toward the eclectic mess on the floor—a laptop, a cell phone charger, random clothes, a mismatched pair of slippers, and a small stuffed bear lay before her. "I told him when he drops his mother off at the airport tomorrow, he might as well get on a flight, too. Our lease is up at the end of the month, and I told him he's moving out."

Thea was stunned. Avni wasn't the spontaneous type. She wasn't the one to make the first move or pull the rug out on you. She was a planner, a nester, a long-term relationship guru. Thea had never seen her friend this way. "What happens now?"

Avni checked her cell phone and turned the screen toward Thea. Thea could see an alert from American Airlines on the screen—the reservation for Saanaa had been confirmed. "Now you pretend to work, and I hang out here until he takes her to the airport. Then we go over to my place, so I can pack with more intention, and I move in with you until Raj is out of the apartment."

"Move in with me?" Thea squeaked, before backtracking. "Of course. Sure. Definitely. Screw Raj."

Avni deflated. "I wouldn't ask if I didn't need the help."

"Well you didn't ask, you told me, and that's totally fine. I'm in a sleep-deprived sex haze—I can't be expected to operate fully just yet." Thea joined Avni on the couch, wrapping her arms around her. "Anything you need, I'm here for you."

"Thanks." Avni leaned into her, and for what Thea suspected was the first time since last night, she finally let go and cried.

"We'll figure it out," Thea whispered, and she hoped they would.

CHAPTER SIXTEEN

I miss you," Lauren said, surprising herself with her candidness.
"I miss you, too," Thea replied. And the sigh that followed told
Lauren that Thea was on the same page as her.

Thea had called her the afternoon after they'd parted ways to
tell her about her friend Avni. She'd felt like Avni was in too fragile
a state to be left alone, so they'd rescheduled their date night. Which
was certainly a bummer, but Lauren got it. She'd been able to crash
Trina's auntie duties that night, so she'd soaked up the baby snuggles
and kicked some serious ass at Uno. But not seeing Thea had affected
her more than she'd expected.

"I feel like it's been a week," she complained.

"It's been *half* a week, and I hate everything," Thea said.

Lauren smiled. "What are you doing right now?"

"Pretending to work. Failing miserably. Thinking of you. Wishing
you were here."

"How's Avni?"

"I think she's working through her third stage of grief at the
moment. We're done burning his things and have now moved on to
wondering whether we made the right choice. We think we did. But
we're sorting through it."

"I love how you say *we*," Lauren replied.

"Well, I kind of feel like the other woman in the situation. Since
she's bunking with me while this whole thing goes down, it certainly
feels like I'm involved."

"It's good of you to do that. You're a good person," Lauren said.

"Thank you," Thea replied. "But I don't feel like a good person
when I'm thinking about ways I can sneak out and see you without her
noticing. That makes me feel bad. Very bad."

"Why does that turn me on?" Lauren asked, teasing.

"Because you are sick and twisted and perfect for me," Thea replied. "That's why."

"Are you free for lunch?" Lauren asked as she looked at the clock. She had an appointment in a couple of hours, but right now she was just cold-calling some people for Newbridge research.

"Define *free*," she teased.

"This is that cheap date conversation again when I just want you to be easy, isn't it?"

"Oh, we both know I'm easy."

"Then say yes."

"Yes."

Lauren cheered. "I'll be by in thirty."

"I can't wait."

Lauren called in a lunch order at the deli a few doors down as she packed up the contents of her desk. She could do most of her work remotely, as long as she had a cell signal. As she shuffled the files into her bag, she paused. The Boudreaux file was the thickest, most complicated file on her desk. And there was still no answer to be had regarding the future of the farm.

She'd met with Ellison and gone over the numbers that Faith had given her. Now she was just waiting to hear back about the potential interested buyer Faith had mentioned. She had every intention of tagging along to that walk-through if it ended up happening, but she hadn't relayed that information to Kathleen yet. Or to Thea.

Thea. She had a feeling Thea wasn't going to like what she had to say. But the truth was, the numbers weren't working out in her family's favor. If they couldn't sell off pieces of the land for a large enough profit, they wouldn't be able to keep the farm running. And it seemed like unless there was something she'd missed the first time around, this was the end of Boudreaux farm.

"Have you decided when you're going to tell her?" Trina asked from her doorway.

Lauren looked up at her bestie and shook her head. "I don't think I have the guts."

Trina walked into the room and helped her pack her bag. "When will you hear back from Faith?"

"Sometime tonight," Lauren said as she grabbed her purse. She had every intention of talking to Thea, but she was waiting on Faith's call first. "If there's any sort of concreteness to it, I'll be heading up there to observe—"

"And judge, I hope."

Lauren had every intention of judging the hell out of whoever was undoubtedly going to lowball Kathleen, but that wasn't what Trina meant. "Absolutely. I'll see how legit this guy is and do my best schmooze work to pull all his secrets to the surface. If I can sniff out a way to get him to bleed more money, I will."

"Smell that weakness and desperation and attack like the shark I know you can be," Trina said with a smile. "There is no one better than you when it comes to judging someone's intentions and character. You got this. This might be exactly what you need to solve the saving-the-farm puzzle."

"Your positivity is infectious," Lauren teased as she kissed Trina's cheek.

"As long as that's the only thing about me that's infectious, we're good." Trina followed her toward the front of the office. "Where are you off to?"

"Lunch with Thea." Just saying it out loud made her feel giddy. She felt the stress of a few minutes ago start to melt away.

"Afternoon delight with Thea is more like it," Trina said with a wink. "Have fun."

"I will," Lauren replied with a wave. She had no control over the future, but she could enjoy a few stolen moments here and there. And she intended to.

❖

"Special delivery," Lauren said as she knocked on the glass of Thea's open office door.

"I'll say," Thea said as she stood. "You look amazing. Like, seriously. Wow."

"If you keep telling me things like that, lunch won't happen," she said as she closed the door behind her and met Thea in the middle of her office.

"Because dessert will happen instead?" Thea asked. "Lunch is sounding kind of overrated."

"How come food and sex are so closely intertwined with you?" Lauren asked, not actually caring because Thea was looking at her lips like she wanted to devour them.

"Anything that intertwines me with you is fine by me," Thea said. "Food can be an aphrodisiac, right? Not that I need that with you.

Just thinking about you gets me hot. Put you in front of me and"—Thea kissed her, and Lauren felt her clit throb—"the attraction is all-consuming."

"More consumption talk," Lauren said as she leaned back in for a kiss. "You sound hungry."

"I'm insatiable for you," Thea replied, and Lauren glanced back at the door, wondering if it had a lock.

"It does," Thea said.

"It does what?" Lauren asked, enjoying the feeling of Thea's arms around her waist.

"Have a lock. That's what you were thinking, right?"

Lauren licked her lips. "What else am I thinking?"

"Naughty, naughty things that we probably don't have time for over this lunch break. But know that I see that tongue move over my favorite lips, and I hear those thoughts loud and clear," Thea said as she rejoined their lips. "And I am all in."

Lauren moaned as Thea deepened the kiss and she started to second-guess Thea's warning that they wouldn't have time for *things*. She certainly could make time. And the way Thea's hand was creeping up her rib cage made it seem like Thea was interested in making time.

"I can't," Thea said, dropping her hand to Lauren's hip. "I want to. I need to feel you. And yet, I really can't be caught with you naked and splayed out on my desk right now."

"Is that what you would do with me?" Lauren asked, pulling Thea back for one last quick kiss.

"To start," Thea said with a smile. "I've always wanted a reason to throw everything off my desk with a dramatic, sweeping arm motion."

"You'd mess up this office for me?" Lauren asked as she stepped back.

"I'd probably mess up my whole life for you," Thea replied, and Lauren laughed.

"Fine. Lunch it is." Lauren pointed to the bags she'd left at the doorway. "Ready to eat?"

"Hell yes," Thea replied, and Lauren was glad she'd offered to stop by. This was exactly the kind of boost she'd needed. Thea made her feel rejuvenated. Amongst other things.

Once they'd settled on the couch, Lauren broached the friend topic. "How's Avni?"

Thea looked toward the door, almost as if expecting her to be there. "Better? I'm not sure, honestly. I've never been in a long-term committed relationship the way she and Raj were. There's a lot of history and loose ends there. And emotions. So many emotions."

"How long were they together?" Lauren asked.

"Ten years."

Lauren almost choked. "Damn. That's a lifetime."

"I know," Thea said between bites of her salad. "I'm not sure where she's going to even start. I mean, that's all of her twenties to this point, and the end of her teen years. It's practically her whole adult life."

"Ten years. Wow." Lauren couldn't imagine what that must be like. "What's the longest relationship you've ever been in?"

Thea gave her a sly look. "This one."

"Shut up," Lauren said, shocked.

"I'm kidding," Thea replied. "I once dated a girl for two years, but it didn't work out."

"Why?" Lauren asked before adding, "Not that I'm complaining."

Thea gave her a small smile before directing her attention toward her meal. "My dad died, and having a girlfriend seemed overwhelming. I was young, and I think it was the right decision at the time. But I don't know if I would have come to it so abruptly had he not passed."

"I'm sorry," Lauren said, reaching out to take Thea's hand. "I can't imagine what that must have been like."

"It was awful. But I suppose awful things have to happen from time to time to make you grow as a person. I needed to grow up. I think if you asked my mother, she'd say I still have some growing to do. And I wouldn't disagree with that," Thea said, looking up at her. The emotion in those stormy eyes nearly caught Lauren's breath. Thea had a depth that continually caught her off guard, and this time was no different.

"I wouldn't have the life I have now if he was still here. And though I miss him every day, I don't know what it's like to have him in my adult life either. It's like a wound that's mostly healed but scarred. Like I don't know who I'd be without the scar, but at the same time, I wish I didn't have it."

Lauren got that last part, in her own way. "I never knew my father. You can't miss someone you never had, right? But sometimes I think about how differently things would have turned out for me if I'd had one. I know it's not the same thing that you've experienced or are going through, but—"

"It's a missing piece that makes you wonder if you'll ever feel whole," Thea said.

"Yeah, maybe." Lauren hadn't considered it that way. She didn't feel like she needed to know her father, but she did feel as though she didn't know a part of herself. "I don't think I've ever told anyone that before."

Thea smiled. "I'm glad you told me. You can tell me anything."

"I think you're right about that," Lauren said. "I don't seem to be able to stop myself around you, anyway."

"I'm magnetic in the most frustrating ways. I know," Thea joked, lightening the mood. And being perfect.

"This also seems to be true," Lauren said as she popped a cherry tomato into her mouth to keep herself from kissing Thea.

"All right, so my dirty laundry is aired. What about you? What's the longest relationship you've ever been in?" Thea turned the tables on her.

"A year and a half."

"Ooh, I got you beat."

Lauren waved a forked cucumber as she added, "But in my defense, I've successfully managed that three times."

Thea laughed. "What happens at the eighteen-month mark?"

"The relationship seems to combust." Lauren counted them out on her fingers. "One girlfriend cheated. One took a job across the country and didn't want to try long-distance. And one, well, let's just say the last one fizzled out."

Thea looked offended. "Well screw the first two, ew. And what does *fizzled* mean, exactly?"

Lauren tried to find a delicate way to word this. "We had different, uh, bedroom interests."

Thea's eyebrows were at her hairline.

"Wait, that came out wrong," she backtracked. "We had different sex drives. That's probably more accurate."

"Meaning?"

"She was happy with being intimate once a month." Lauren wiped her mouth with a napkin. "I'd prefer—"

"Once a day?" Thea asked with a mischievous smile.

"I was going to say at least once a week," Lauren said. "Though I'll admit that doesn't feel like enough with you."

"I hope that doesn't change," Thea said, putting aside her meal and scooting closer to Lauren. "Because I'm really having a hard time being in the same room with you and not helping you out of those clothes. And I can tell you that I haven't experienced that before."

"Having to wait?" Lauren teased as she shifted on the couch, turning to face Thea more fully.

"Having such a hard time waiting."

Thea's eyes were on her lips. She licked them for good measure. "I like knowing that you want me so badly."

"Sometimes it feels like *need* more than want. Which is new for me, too. It's like I can't get enough of you. But I don't want to, either."

"That sounds unhealthy," Lauren said as she pulled Thea to her lips.

"It doesn't feel unhealthy," Thea murmured across her lips as she leaned into her. "It feels fucking amazing."

Lauren's hand dropped from Thea's cheek to her collarbone, quickly finding the warm flesh of her upper chest. She eased her fingers under the lapels of Thea's dress shirt and relished the softness of Thea's skin.

As she inched lower, unbuttoning one button, Thea stopped her.

"If you do what I think you're about to do, I'm going to get fired."

"Why's that?" Lauren asked, though she respected Thea's request and pulled her hand back until Thea stopped her again.

"Because"—she brought Lauren's hand over her heart—"I'm already too excited, and if you touch me, we won't even make it to the desk. And it'll be awfully loud, at that."

Lauren loved the fast beat of Thea's heart under her palm. She loved the effect she had on Thea and how clearly Thea's body communicated that effect. "You don't think I can be quiet?"

"I don't want you to be," Thea said, her eye contact so intense that Lauren shivered. Suddenly being loud with Thea was all Lauren could think about.

Lauren brought her lips to Thea's ear, keeping her hand on Thea's chest as she asked, "When can we make that happen?"

"Tonight?" Thea turned to meet her lips, but Lauren moved just out of range, drawing a smile from Thea at the tease.

"My place?" Lauren nuzzled her nose, not giving in to Thea's attempts to kiss her just yet.

"Well, since I have a roommate currently, yes." Thea's hand found the side of Lauren's breast, and Lauren moaned. "Because I really want that moan, times ten. All night."

"Okay," Lauren acquiesced, giving in to Thea's affections and savoring the passion of Thea's mouth on hers. This woman kissed like no one else.

A knock on Thea's door jolted them apart.

"Yes?" Thea called out, as breathless as Lauren felt.

"It's Avni. Can I come in?"

Thea glanced down at her shirt, fixing her button as she scrambled off the couch to smooth out her shirt. "Uh." She looked over at Lauren, who was trying not to laugh.

"It's your office. Your call," Lauren said as she stood. She pressed a quick kiss to her lips before assuming her most casual lean against Thea's desk.

Thea gave her a look.

"What? I don't want you to blow off your best friend on account of me groping you on the couch. And since that moment seems to have been placed on pause until later, I say let her in. I'd like to meet her."

Thea looked momentarily panicked.

"What? I met your mom and brother, and that went fine."

Thea strode to her office door, her hand on the doorknob as she said over her shoulder, "Yeah, but I don't talk to them about our sex life."

"And you do with Avni?" Lauren asked, laughing.

"With Avni what?" Avni walked through the now open door and froze on the spot. "Oh. You have company."

Lauren waved. "Hi. I'm Lauren. It's nice to meet you."

"Avni. The work and life bestie," she replied with a smile.

"Yeah, yeah." Thea observed her briefly before asking, "Who told you?"

"Who told me what?" Avni asked.

"Who told you I had a lunch guest?" Thea asked, her hand on her hip. The tone she had was accusatory. Lauren was enthralled.

Avni feigned looking innocent before conceding, "Fine. Sarah at the front desk."

"I knew it," Thea said with a shake of her head. "She's off the Christmas cookie list. That's it."

"Don't do that," Avni cried. "She'll never forgive me."

"Christmas cookie list?" Lauren asked.

"Thea makes the best Christmas cookies ever. It's like some secret farm girl recipe or something. Being on that cookie list is like achieving the ultimate orgas—" Avni paused. "Wait. Why was the door closed just now?"

"We were having lunch," Thea said, not sounding convincing in the least.

Avni looked between them before a realization hit her. "You were shacking up on my breakup couch, weren't you."

Lauren laughed. "I like her."

Thea shot her a look. "Don't encourage her." She looked back at Avni. "We weren't."

Lauren could see that Avni didn't buy a word of it. "We kind of were."

"Ha! I knew it," Avni cheered. She looked at Lauren as she said, "You're much more honest than she is. I'm sorry my friend is a jerk."

"Thanks." Lauren accepted the compliment before she stage-whispered, "She's not really a jerk, right?"

"Nope. She's the real deal. Betty Farm Girl Crocker and all." Avni went to sit on the couch before seeming to second-guess that.

"Am I going to be on the cookie list?" Lauren teased when Thea still looked a little flustered.

"That depends," Thea replied.

"On what?" Lauren had to know the terms of this cookie list deal.

"On whether I still have a family farm. The secret is in the milk, butter, and cream we make at the farm. I can't bake my famous cookies without them. It just wouldn't be the same." Thea's words hit like a punch in the gut.

"Oh, damn." Avni looked devastated. "Christmas cookies are ruined forever."

"Maybe not, right?" Thea looked to her with a hopeful expression. "Lauren's been working on helping Mom figure out a way to save the farm through some smart real estate moves. So there's still a chance, right?"

Lauren reached out to touch Thea's forearm, though she wasn't sure what to say. She didn't want to lie to her, but she couldn't ignore Faith's numbers from earlier either. "I'll certainly do my best."

"Well, that's something," Avni said, looking encouraged, and Lauren felt like the weight of the world was settling on her shoulders.

"She certainly is." Thea was looking at her so affectionately that Lauren almost felt sick.

"Oh, wow. You two are disgusting," Avni joked. "I'd say get a room, but I think I'm in it."

Thea laughed. "Hey, I'm not going to be home tonight. Try not to burn the place down in my absence."

"Wait, aren't you going to Maine tonight? Because I totally planned on you being gone for the weekend," Avni said.

"Are you having a party at my place without me?" Thea asked, clearly scandalized, seeming not to notice the first comment.

"No, I just, you know, need some me time."

Thea's face morphed into a horrified expression. "Are you implying you're going to mast—"

Lauren put her arm on Thea's again. "Babe, that's totally none of your business, and it's probably best if you two hash that out after I'm gone."

"This isn't over." Thea shot Avni a look before nodding.

"But about Maine…" Lauren nudged.

"Shit." Thea palmed her forehead, dragging her hand down her face in an almost comical fashion. "I promised my mother I'd help her organize for the Berry Festival." She looked at Lauren with a frown. "I can't come over tonight. I'm going to Maine."

"Oh." Lauren tried to hide her disappointment. "Well, another time then."

"Or maybe go up first thing in the morning?" Avni suggested. "I'm sure Kathleen can manage until then."

Thea's shoulders slumped. "She's meeting a vendor at eight. I'd have to leave at like five to get there in time."

Avni leaned against the door. She raised an eyebrow as she asked, "What are you worried about? Not getting a full night's sleep first? Because something tells me that you probably weren't gonna lock down an eight-hour slumber regardless."

Lauren burst out laughing. "She has a point."

"Don't side with her," Thea said, gesturing her hands in frustration.

"I'm not wrong," Avni said, crossing her arms over her chest.

"She's not," Lauren agreed.

Thea looked between the two of them as she said, "You two just formed a bestie bond right in front of me, didn't you?"

"I think so," Lauren said, walking over to Avni and slinging an arm around her shoulder.

"Oh, man, I'm keeping her." Avni turned into her embrace, snuggling close for a hug. "Look, I'm already boob height, just like with you, Thea. Come on over—let's make an Avni sandwich."

Thea scowled.

"C'mon," Lauren coaxed, reaching her free arm out. "Your friend is recovering from a major life change and making new friends in the process. Don't be a hater."

Thea hesitated.

"You know you wanna," Avni said as she grabbed Thea's hand, pulling her into their three-way snugglefest. "That's better."

"I'm so screwed," Thea said with a small smile, and Lauren could see her stress start to melt away.

"You totally are," Lauren replied, happy to have a moment without worry. If even if it was just one moment.

CHAPTER SEVENTEEN

I'm really glad this worked out," Thea said, reaching across the center console to caress Lauren's thigh.

"Me, too." Lauren's smile was as gorgeous as the first night Thea had met her. Even with those oversized sunglasses, Thea could tell her eyes were sparkling with that smile.

They'd hung out with Avni until Lauren's afternoon meeting. Which meant that Thea had gotten nothing done and had twice the work to take to Maine with her than she'd previously anticipated, but it'd been worth it to see how well Avni and Lauren got along. Even if they picked on her a bit. It was good-natured, and a part of her felt more complete with Avni throwing her support behind this new relationship with Lauren. Which she did—endlessly—after Lauren left.

"What time is your meeting with Faith?" she asked. Lauren had called her later that afternoon and told her that she'd been in touch with a Realtor in Maine who specialized in large land sales and commercial farming property estimates. She said that the woman had availability to meet the following day, and that if Thea was open to it, she'd be happy to make the trek up with her in the morning. At first mention of it, Thea had recoiled, not ready to embrace the sale idea. But she remembered the conversation at her office and tried to be open-minded. Plus, that meant that she could spend the night with Lauren and still spend at least part of the weekend with her as well.

"Around eleven. I want to see that property line by the main road that I didn't get a chance to before." Lauren took her hand and held it on her lap as she looked down, shuffling through some papers with her other hand. "That'll give me the morning to wander the property a bit and take in some things that I might have missed."

"Because of all the kissing on the porch?" That was one of Thea's favorite go-to memories.

"That, or the making out in your childhood bedroom. Either one, really." Lauren rubbed her thumb along the back of Thea's hand. "But I don't regret any of it."

"Me neither," Thea said.

"You sure you don't mind driving?" Lauren asked with a yawn.

"Not at all." Thea liked driving. And it was exponentially more enjoyable with Lauren next to her. "You should close your eyes and capitalize on the chance to sleep."

"Why? Aren't you just as tired? Last time I checked, you were up just as long as me," Lauren said, stifling another yawn. Though Thea had been able to negotiate a later arrival with her mother and shift back the first vendor meeting by an hour, they were still on the road by six a.m. But they'd desperately needed that extra hour of sleep, so she was grateful.

"We surely didn't do each other any favors, did we?"

"On the contrary, there were lots of *favors*, just not in the sleep department," Lauren said, and Thea laughed.

"We did manage to squeeze in a movie, though," Thea noted. She had been thrilled when Lauren had suggested still getting together for a quiet couch and movie date night before the trip up to Maine together. She'd been even more excited when the movie Lauren chose was *Clue*, which was her all-time favorite campy comedy flick.

"I mean, like half a movie," Lauren said.

Thea clicked her tongue. "I distinctly remember eating dinner on the couch and then snuggling up with some popcorn and a blanket with you leaning against my chest, laughing at Yvette's French maid outfit."

"Right," Lauren agreed. "But what happened after she got locked in the attic?"

"Uh…" Thea paused.

"I'll tell you. Groping. Groping happened, and suddenly there was popcorn everywhere, and the next thing I knew it was after midnight, and we were stumbling to the bedroom for round whatever it was," Lauren said. "I'm going to be finding popcorn kernels in the couch cushions until I die. I'm sure of it."

"Okay, fine. So we didn't get through the whole movie. But at least we both know how it ends," Thea said.

"I mean, Mr. Body dies. Sure. That's a given."

Thea released Lauren's hand to stroke along the inside of her thigh. "You can't blame me for ignoring Mr. Body in favor of your very alive body when it's so touchable and close and soft."

"And occasionally very wet," Lauren added with a cheeky smile. "But all of those are things not for you to talk or think about while you're driving because I'm precious cargo, and I don't want you to careen off the road into some wild animal or road sign."

"Or wooden moose," Thea said.

"I mean, that's pretty specific, but okay."

Thea shook her head as she pointed at a side road off in the distance. "There's a life-sized wooden carving of a moose that marks the edge of one of our neighbors' property. Stan is kind of a legend in these parts."

"Is Stan the neighbor?"

"No, the moose."

"You Maine-iacs are weird," Lauren said, and Thea laughed.

"You're not wrong."

"I almost never am," Lauren replied.

After a few moments of silence, Thea glanced over at Lauren to find her on her phone, scrolling quickly. "Something up?" she asked.

"Um, no." Lauren shifted. "I was just looking up places to stay."

"Where?" Thea asked as she turned off the main road toward the one that led to her family farm.

"Here."

Thea hazarded another glance at her. "What do you mean here?"

Lauren shifted again. She seemed anxious. "I mean, you drove us in your car—"

"Because yours doesn't have a back seat."

"But it does have a trunk with plenty of storage, if that's what your back seat comment is about."

"It's not, necessarily. Maybe I just really want you in a back seat this weekend."

Lauren slid her sunglasses up into her hair. "I feel like this is an unfulfilled fantasy we keep revisiting."

"I'm hoping to make it less of a fantasy and more of a reality at some point," Thea said with a wink. "But back to the first topic, about a place to stay. You were saying?"

Lauren worried her bottom lip. "Look, you're driving us up here, and I know that you're planning on staying for the weekend—"

"As are you. I know since I almost bulged a disk in my back lifting your suitcase."

"Listen, a girl needs things," Lauren said. "I didn't want to be underprepared."

"For a weekend getaway in Maine? Because it felt like you packed gold bars."

"I happen to have on good authority that all those dreamy shoulder and arm muscles are plenty strong enough to lift me up, let alone my measly suitcase."

"I mean, you weigh nothing at all," Thea said. "That suitcase, on the other hand, is a different story entirely."

Lauren laughed, and Thea loved the melodious sound. There wasn't anything about Lauren she didn't like. Which should probably cause her alarm, but it didn't. Things with Lauren were easy and fun. Nothing about being with Lauren felt like work. Ever.

"You didn't answer my question," Thea said.

"I didn't pack gold bars," Lauren answered.

"Why are you looking for a place to stay here?"

"Oh, right." Lauren shifted again. "I didn't want to just assume that I could stay at the farmhouse. That would be rude. And I'll admit I'm far too much of a princess to sleep in your car for the night, so I was just seeing what's available in town."

Thea very nearly swerved the car. "You can't be serious."

Lauren looked out the windshield, her eyes wide. "Is there a moose or something? Please tell me no. I'm not all that interested in dying by a hoof to the face."

"No moose," Thea said as she took them the final few hundred yards down the road to her family farm. She put the car in park outside the farmhouse and turned to face Lauren. "Hey, listen. I don't want you to do anything you don't want to do."

"I sense a *but* coming," Lauren said, looking amused.

"But," Thea said, "I will be totally offended if you don't stay here with me. As a guest. As my adorably overpacked girlfriend. You can stay in the guest room if you want, and I can text you naughty pictures from across the hall if you'd prefer, but I'd like the chance to show you how the dawn creeps in like a slow-burning fire over the lake, igniting the day. And I can't do that if you're staying at Penny Prebble's two-bit bed-and-breakfast twenty minutes away."

"Wow," Lauren said.

"What?"

"That was incredibly romantic." Lauren gave her a small smile. "I certainly want to experience that with you."

"So you'll stay?" Thea asked, hopeful.

"As long as I get naughty pictures, I'm in."

"You're my favorite," Thea said, leaning in.

Lauren kissed her, smiling against her lips. "Good, because I expect you to carry that bag up to the guest room for me."

"And what do I get for my troubles?" Thea asked between kisses.

"Maybe you'll get some naughty pictures, too." Lauren touched her jaw, trailing her fingers down her neck to the V of her T-shirt. "Or maybe you can give me a tour of that roomy and luxurious-looking back seat."

Thea stopped Lauren's hand just short of reaching her breast. "If you start that, I'll never get to my meeting, and you'll probably miss yours, too."

"You'd think after last night you'd be satiated," Lauren said with a quick kiss as she pulled her hand back.

"And yet here I am, thinking about all the ways I can get you naked and under me."

Lauren motioned for her to lean in. She whispered into her ear, "I think you underestimate how great it is when I'm naked and on top."

"Fuck," Thea said as Lauren licked her earlobe before slipping back into her passenger seat like nothing happened. "This is going to be a long day."

Lauren merely smiled at her as she brought her sunglasses over her eyes again. "Ready?" she asked as she opened the passenger side door.

Thea laughed and shook her head. Lauren Calloway was something else.

CHAPTER EIGHTEEN

Thea's head was swimming. There was a lot to get done in preparation for the Berry Festival, and the many moving pieces highlighted in this morning's meetings made her feel overwhelmed. She'd been impressed with her mother's cool, calm, and collected demeanor—she handled everything like a consummate pro. Which made sense since this was nearly her fortieth Berry Festival, and almost number one hundred for the Boudreaux Family Dairy Farm. That thought made her sad since this was also probably her last as a commercial vendor. And that the hundredth showing of the Boudreaux farm at the festival was not a milestone that would be reached.

"I'm glad Lauren came up with you," her mother said, jarring her from the melancholy that threatened to settle in her chest.

"Me, too." Thea couldn't stop the involuntary smile if she tried.

"She makes you happy," her mother said, looking pleased as they headed out of the second-floor barn offices.

"She does." *So happy*. Thea was more and more aware of that fact with every passing day. As much as she joked in the car this morning, last night had been special to her. Sure they'd fooled around and spent lots of time not sleeping like they should have, but last night had been different. The evening had felt so complete. She'd felt like everything was unhurried and pure. Thea had loved holding Lauren close on the couch, and feeling her soft, naked body behind her in the bed. Lauren was a cuddler—pre-sex, post-sex, whenever. She was affectionate and loving in every exchange she had with Thea. That was a nice change to what she'd been used to. Up until now, almost all of Thea's interactions with beautiful women were short, sweet, and sweaty. But not with Lauren. What she had with Lauren was special. And she knew it. Because last night was the first night she'd realized she was falling in love with her. And as she watched her sleep this morning, waiting to wake her until the last possible second so she could rest, Thea felt her heart race. Because the beautiful, seemingly perfect woman so contently sleeping next to her held her heart in so many ways she couldn't remember what it felt like to beat without her. Because in that moment, Thea felt like her heart beat exclusively for Lauren. And that scared her a little.

"You're thinking about her," her mother noted, holding the door open for Thea to pass through.

"I'm always thinking about her," Thea said candidly. "She's just about always on my mind."

Her mother smiled. "I've never seen you so smitten. It's refreshing."

"Refreshing?"

Her mother seemed to hesitate. "Don't take this the wrong way."

"I'm certainly going to if you preface it with that," Thea replied.

Her mother laughed. "I'm used to you being, you know, a little broody."

"Broody?"

"Yes, broody." Her mother touched her arm. "Relax, Carl does it, too. So did your father. You three feel things so deeply. It must be the Cancer in you. All emotion and passion, straight across the board. It's one of your best and most challenging qualities."

Thea let that sink in. Growing up, they'd always had a birthday week in the house since they had birthdays within a week of each other. She missed those days. She regretted not coming up for her birthday this year, since it might have been the last one she would have had in the house.

"Anyway," her mother said as she kept walking, "I think it's great that you found Lauren. She's wonderful and smart, and she's clearly bringing out the best in you. I'm glad she's here for the weekend. Selfishly I've been looking forward to getting to know her better. The last time she was here was the first time in a long time there was so much laughter and joy in that house. She just bubbles over with life."

Thea couldn't argue with that. Even with all the things going on with the farm and Avni and work, Thea had felt like Lauren was her life's missing piece. She felt grounded and content, even finding happiness when she hadn't expected it. And she had Lauren to thank for that.

Thea let herself think of all the ways she planned to do that as she followed her mother to the cheese and dairy kitchen located just off the milk parlor. She pulled on the hairnet and mask, slipping on her gloves as she kicked her boots clean before following her inside. The space was cool and sterile. The walls were a pristine white and the gray slate floors had been recently scrubbed. She followed her mother past the ghost crew of workers around the various cheese-making machines and refrigerators to the aging room in the back. She'd never seen this place so understaffed.

"This room still stinks," Thea complained, as all her dreamy thoughts of Lauren were thrust out by the intrusion of cheese stank.

"It's full of aging cheese," her mother said. "That stink is a sign of success."

"If you say so." Thea wanted to hold her nose, but the mask and gloves prohibited that. "Let's get in and out of here before we pass out."

Her mother laughed as she read a few of the signs on the rack next to her. Thea was largely removed from the cheese business, but she knew the basics. They had a few different types of cheeses at different stages of aging in this refrigerator. The signs denoted the type of cheese, the age, and when they would reach premium quality and should be pulled to package and sell.

Looking around, Thea could see the once filled shelves were sparse now. She knew her mother had slowed the production of everything on the farm, but she hadn't realized by how much until now.

"Will there be enough for the Berry Festival?" she asked, recalling the orders they'd gone over in the meetings earlier.

"There has to be," her mother said from behind her mask. "We made enough for every order and a little more. But that's it. We'll be cleaned out after that weekend."

Thea hated hearing that. "And the ice cream and butter, too?"

"And the yogurt and cream," her mother replied. "We'll keep the cows milking until it's time to sell them off, too."

"Unless Lauren finds a way to save the farm, you mean," Thea said.

"Perhaps," her mother said as she pulled a tray off the rack and motioned to the door. "Can you get that for me?"

"What do you mean *perhaps*?" Thea asked as she held open the door. "That's what Ellison sent her here for, right? I thought you were on board."

Her mother carried the tray to one of the prepping stations and waved over Cynthia, their head cheese master. "Hey, Cyn, can you get this started?"

"Sure thing," Cynthia said as she started gathering materials.

"Mom," Thea said, trying again.

Kathleen stripped off her mask and hairnet, depositing them with her gloves in the nearby wastebasket before answering. "I ran into Faith Leader in town last week. She'd been in touch with Lauren already. Her face told me everything I need to know—the land value isn't what we were hoping it is."

"What do you mean?" Thea felt blindsided. Lauren hadn't said much about the farm to her, but she'd figured that was because her mother was the point person. And she knew Lauren was meeting with Faith today, but she hadn't realized they'd done more than have a brief chat.

"I mean," Kathleen said as she headed out of the dairy kitchen, "Lauren is meeting with her and a potential buyer today to iron out details, but the land sale probably isn't going to solve all of our problems."

Thea ripped off her protective gear and tossed it in the trash to chase after her mother. "You don't know that. You can't know that."

"I do," Kathleen said, looking weary again. "I let myself believe that there might be another option, but I knew deep down there wasn't. I'd hoped that maybe if we sold enough of the land off, we'd be able to keep part of the farm up and running. But that's not going to happen. And now my greatest fear is that even if we sell everything off, we still won't reach our goal." She looked back at the farmhouse and her lip quivered. "I'd hoped we could save the house, but I think that has to go, too."

"Mom." Thea reached for her. "We haven't even heard about the meeting yet. Let's just see how it goes before we start giving up. Lauren will find a way—she's got that same magic Dad had. She'll help us figure it out."

Her mother looked at her, her eyes wet. "You have your father's optimism. Maybe you're right."

"I am," Thea said, not quite believing herself. "Look, the vendor meetings this morning were long and hard. And you have a lot of work to get done in a short time. But I'm here. Go rest, and I'll help you finish whatever else needs to be done."

Her mother reached out and touched her cheek. "No matter what happens, I want you to know that your dad is proud of you. He always was. And so am I."

"We're not losing the farm, Mom," Thea said because she needed her to believe it. Because she believed it.

Her mother gave her a small smile in return. "Go into town and pick up some fresh vegetables. We're having tofu stir-fry tonight, but the green beans look a little wilted. I'm going to lie down. I think that's good advice."

"I love you," she said to her mother, feeling like she should say it more often.

"I love you too, Sweet Girl."

And as she walked away, Thea's heart broke. Sweet Girl was one of the many pet names her father had had for her. She looked at the red barn that was so much a part of her history, and she felt that melancholy from before sneak back in.

"I can't lose this farm. I just can't." Because she had no idea who she was without it.

CHAPTER NINETEEN

"Thanks for taking me out," Lauren said as she tightened the laces on her boots. She'd packed more sensible shoes this time around, especially since she knew she'd be going into less manicured territory to get the full picture she wanted.

"Of course," Carl said. He adjusted his cap as he maneuvered the cart in the effortless, familiar fashion of someone who had spent their whole life on this land. "Anything to get out of farm chores."

Lauren thought about that. Carl's whole life—much like Thea's—started on this soil. The literal ground under the cart's wheels was the same ground their grandfather razed by hand with what would be considered antiquated tools today, plodding across night after night, day after day as he built the legacy that they continued. Though maybe not for long.

She would be meeting with Faith shortly, and this was her last chance to get a feel for the land. She wanted to be prepared for the potential buyer Faith was bringing with her. This would be his first time touring the property, and Lauren wanted to make sure she was on her A game and fully versed in the Boudreaux land so she could find a way to make Kathleen—and Thea—feel like they had a fighting chance.

"It's just a bit farther," Carl said, his voice a soothing rumble.

"Great."

She was glad Carl was her tour guide—he wasn't overly chatty, but he managed to say plenty in the few words he shared. And selfishly, she wanted to get to know him better. Thea had talked about growing up with Carl with such fondness, and she wanted to see the part of him that Thea treasured so much. And she felt like they were making good ground on that front. So much so, she decided to dig a little deeper.

"How's Annie?" she asked, and he gave her a surprised look. "What? I know all about the fruit stand girl."

"Man, Thea's got a big mouth," he said, but he didn't seem put out. If anything, he seemed shy. "She's good. We've gone out with a bunch of friends a few times, but I'm working up the courage to invite her as my date to the Berry Festival."

From what she could gather, and from what Thea had mentioned, the Berry Festival was the highlight of the Casterville summer. And the final celebration of the season as well. Everyone looked forward to it, even though it signified the end of summertime. But on a more somber note, the Berry Festival was the deadline that Kathleen was using as the last event for the Boudreaux farm. She planned to sell the farm shortly after she'd fulfilled all her obligations for the weekend. That was the working timeline she had discussed with Ellison and Lauren. And that date was creeping up faster than Lauren liked.

"That's just a few weeks from now," Lauren said, already feeling stressed. "How are you guys doing with getting ready for it?"

Carl frowned. "You mean like are we selling farm equipment off just yet? No. But Mom's calendar is empty afterward. All orders have been suspended." He sighed. "I think we're doing our last cheese and ice cream batches this week. Then..." he trailed off.

Then it's over, she thought. Unless she could see something today that she'd missed. That was the whole purpose of going out with Carl before her meeting with Faith—to discover something she might have overlooked. Anything that might have more value to it than the underwhelming numbers Faith had proposed. And Carl's quiet, calm demeanor helped her think a hell of a lot more clearly than had Thea been her guide. Because when Thea was around, she couldn't think of anything else. And she didn't want to. Which frightened her a bit. Last night had been different. It had felt a lot more intimate and real. Not that all the orgasms hadn't felt *real* before, but this was something else. Last night was magical.

"Okay," Carl said as he pulled the cart over, pulling her out of her reverie. "This is it, the unkempt, wild woods."

"Wow." Lauren stepped out of the cart and walked toward the old wooden fence in awe. "It's gorgeous."

Before them lay acres of wonderful, untouched Maine woods. A slight descent from the fenced plot led into the moss- and underbrush-covered vibrant green woods full of tall, narrow trees with opulent treetops that cast a lovely shaded coolness on the lush land below. This looked like a snapshot right out of a Twilight novel. She half expected a vampire and an insecure teenage girl to scamper by.

Carl kicked at the aging post, adjusting one of the lateral beams and realigning it. Lauren looked at his hands. They were slightly dirty and tanned from working. Scars lined his knuckles, some faint, some seemingly fresh. Carl had clearly put his blood and sweat into his work here. Those were the hands of someone who knew how to get things done even when those things were difficult to do.

"Why didn't your father or grandfather ever expand into this land?" she asked, watching him closely.

Carl secured a loose piece of wire around the newly adjusted post with some tool he'd pulled from his pants pocket. "Granddad didn't have the ambition for an operation any larger than the one we had. And though Dad doubled it over time, he never got the chance to grow it any larger," he said as he stared off into the woods before them. "Once they got into more commercial sales, the plan was to cultivate this space as well. But that never happened."

After a brief pause, he said, "In some ways, I'm glad it didn't. I like the quiet of the woods. This little forgotten part feels welcoming in a way." He shrugged. "Like it wasn't left behind as much as it was left alone to just be what it was supposed to be all along."

"Is that a metaphor for you and your situation?" she asked quietly.

He looked at her, confused. "What do you mean?"

"Well, had your father not passed, would you have taken over his role at the farm? Or would you have left, like Thea did? Or did the change in circumstances force you to be something you weren't?"

"No one can take over for what my dad left behind." Carl took off his hat, combing through his sandy blond hair before putting it back on. "We are all just doing our little parts to fill in some of the void. And sure, we've managed. But it's not like it used to be."

"Things change," she said.

"That's the damn truth," he said. "But to answer your question, I was always going to be a farmer. It's in my blood in a way it's not in Thea's. I knew I'd run this farm with Mom and Dad. That was a given. I just didn't expect that responsibility to come on so soon." He gave her a charming smile, not unlike the one his sister melted her heart with. "But we don't get to decide when the world spins and sends everything we planned crashing to the ground, do we?"

"You're like your sister," Lauren said, seeing more of Thea in him than just his smile.

"How's that?"

"You're like this subtle poet. The still waters run deep in this family. You're all flirty smiles and easy teasing, and then *bam!* it's heartstrings and sonnets about the fiery dawns and the untouched beauty of nature. You two are triple threats—smart, sincere, and artfully seductive. Poor Annie doesn't stand a chance."

Carl stood a little taller, giving her a boyish smile. "You think so?"

"I know so," Lauren said, taking the arm he offered her as they headed back to the golf cart. "What's she like? Tell me everything. We have three weeks to figure out how to sweep her off her feet and make this the best Berry Festival of your damn life."

"He should be here any minute," Faith said as she leaned against her SUV. Her large sunglasses nearly obstructed her enviable cheekbones.

"Have you worked with him before?" Lauren asked.

"Once," Faith said before removing her glasses. Her dark brown eyes were so expressive. She was beautiful. "He's unique. He has a, uh, different perspective."

"Ah," Lauren said, understanding. "That means he's difficult. But quirky difficult. Right?"

"You got it," Faith said, and Lauren appreciated that she was being candid.

Lauren observed her for a moment. She was impeccably dressed and incredibly fit. Her fitted sleeveless blouse gave Lauren arm and shoulder envy, and that skirt was incredible. She looked almost out of place on the farm. Not unlike how Lauren imagined she looked herself the first day here. "You're nothing like I expected."

"You mean because I'm a drop of chocolate in a literal town of milk?" Faith said with a playful tone as she waved to the barn behind them.

Lauren laughed. "No, I mean in-person you is very different than on-the-phone you."

"Oh, because I have a phone sex operator voice, right?" Faith said with an understanding nod.

"Well, certainly that," Lauren said with a laugh. "But more I meant your style and look is much more like what I'm used to in Boston. I guess I kind of figured you'd be in plaid and more sensible shoes like I was told to change into," she said, pointing to her boots.

Faith pretended to squint at her shoes before laughing. "Those are Prada, doll. They're boots, but I wouldn't call them sensible."

"See? That's what I'm talking about. You've got flair *and* an eye for quality. Two talents that I'm hoping will help with the land tour today."

Faith raised an eyebrow in her direction. "You're good. Charming but not pushy about it. You managed to compliment me—highly—while also laying the groundwork to get me to help you in your endeavor."

"Which is to say, I hope you'll see the beauty and character of this property as much as you clearly see quality and value in a good pair of designer boots," Lauren said. She could tell she'd hit her mark when Faith laughed.

"I see why Ellison chose you to come up to the country," Faith said with a wave of her hand, gesturing around them. "She never lacked in brains or boldness. It appears that she sees those qualities in you as well."

"Do you know Ellison well?" Lauren was still mystified that Ellison had an existence outside of Gamble and Associates. Though she hadn't had the opportunity to inquire what Ellison's connection to this land was, she felt like she was learning more about her every day.

"You could say that," Faith said with a smile that told Lauren there was more to that story.

Out of the corner of her eye she noticed movement by the back of the barn. Thea was deep in conversation and carrying something for her mother. The two of them were seemingly oblivious to the fact that Lauren and Faith were only a few hundred feet away. Lauren let herself appreciate how strong and capable Thea was. She thought back to their conversation this morning, and to that magical night they'd shared last night, and she wanted to be under those capable hands sooner rather than later. Something about this place made her extra horny, and she had no idea why. Maybe it was because Thea was here.

"Something going on with you two?" Faith asked, and Lauren nearly bit through her lip.

"What's that?" She soothed her tongue over her sore lower lip.

"Mm-hmm," Faith hummed with a knowing nod. "Ah, it appears Mr. Egbert has arrived."

Edmund Egbert pulled up too quickly in his black sedan, kicking up dust and debris in the process. When he excited the vehicle, Lauren was struck by how much he looked like, well, an egg.

"You must be Lauren," he said as he extended his hand to her. "Ed Egbert, nice to meet you."

"You, too," she said as she examined his appearance more closely. He was nicely dressed, clearly having chosen fabrics and cuts that flattered his broad shoulders and narrow waist. A full head taller than her, he was over six feet in height and his posture was perfect. With his bald head and V-shaped torso, he looked like a better dressed Mr. Clean.

"I'm anxiously anticipating this walk-through," he said to Faith as he stepped forward, putting on black-rimmed glasses as he went. "This property looks great on paper."

"Wait until you see it in person," Lauren said, encouraging his enthusiasm. "There are some real hidden gems amongst the acreage. I'm sure you'll find them as lovely as I have."

"Oh, let's get started, then. Shall we?" He rubbed his palms together excitedly.

After they finished the barn and milking parlor tour, they headed toward the back pastures. This was the first of the two money spots— the lakefront acreage that housed Carl's experimental grass endeavor at the moment.

"Well now, this is something, isn't it?" Ed wiped his brow as the midday sun started to creep over the tall trees. "Look at that lake. Beautiful."

He paused for a moment, taking in the view until his watch pinged. "Oops, time to keep moving." Lauren glanced down at his wrist as he shuffled forward, walking toward the edge of the property line.

The smart watch wasn't anything new or exciting to her, but she recognized the app and the chime right away—her crazy, tiger-obsessed, wannabe psychic Aunt Carole used that app after her double knee replacement as a way to get back in shape and moving again. Ed wasn't just in good shape—he was someone who was closely tracking his activity as well.

Faith excused herself to take a call, and Lauren jumped on the chance to chat him up.

"So, Ed," she said as she joined his side, "how many steps a day do you average with that thing?"

Ed stood a little taller as he smiled. "Twenty thousand on a good day. If I've gotten my midday jog in, that is."

"Impressive."

"What made you ask?" The way he asked, looking momentarily insecure, made Lauren wonder if perhaps this lifestyle was new to him.

"My aunt wore that smart watch and had the same movement chime to meet her daily exercise goals after her knee surgery. It worked wonders for her. Now she ambles around her dozens of acres with no knee pain or shortness of breath." She left out the part about her collection of illegal wild cats and her belief she could see into the future.

"That's great to hear. This app is new to me, but I like it," Ed said, beaming. "I've recently embraced some big changes and reclaimed my fitness after years of neglect from working all the time. I feel like I have a new lease on life now."

Lauren could see he meant that. "So—if you don't mind me asking—what were you thinking about doing with this land? If you had the chance."

His expression became more bashful. "I'd like to make it into an exercise retreat and spa. A place to learn some new, healthy skills and develop one's acceptance of self. Someplace to escape to when you need to find yourself, you know?"

Lauren forced a smile. That sounded nice and seemingly was coming from a good place, but that also meant that the Boudreaux farm would no longer exist.

"It's time we abolished this archaic dairy industry anyway. All it does is negatively impact our digestion and our waistlines. My dietician and life coach Adrian agrees." He puffed out his chest as he said, "I'd be doing good while doing away with some bad. Really, I'm doing the world a favor. The sooner we tear down these ancient institutions that encourage the production of excess fat, the better."

"Is that so?" And just like that, Ed didn't seem all that different from loony Aunt Carole and her menagerie.

"Sorry for stepping away," Faith said as she rejoined them. "Did I miss anything?"

"Ed doesn't like cheese and milk. He believes dairy farms are the work of the devil, and his dietitian and life coach Adrian agrees," Lauren said as sweetly as possible, trying to convey her feelings for Faith's benefit.

"Oh," Faith said, understanding. "Well then, we can skip over the detailed milking parlor information and dairy kitchen then, right? I assume you have no interest in retaining any of the equipment."

"None," Ed said as he wiped his sweaty hands on his pants. "I plan to mow this entire place flat. I'll make sure every building comes down to the dust to start over. I want to purge the soil of this fat-inducing, mammalian lactose plant."

"This is someone's home and legacy," Lauren bit back, not able to help herself. "Have some respect."

Ed looked embarrassed. "Oh, uh, sure. Right. Sorry."

Faith raised an eyebrow in her direction but said nothing.

"Let's take a look over here, shall we?" Faith directed his attention toward another section of back pasture, and Lauren kicked herself for mouthing off. The last thing she needed was to offend the one person that could dig the Boudreauxs out of their debt.

She sighed. This was going to be a long property tour.

CHAPTER TWENTY

I was hoping I'd find you here," Thea said when she found Lauren swinging on the front porch swing, looking off into the distance.

"Oh?" Lauren smiled at the sound of her voice. "Have you been looking for me long?"

"No," Thea lied. She'd wanted to tag along and listen to what Faith had to say during the meeting Lauren had earlier, but she'd gotten back from her green bean errand just as Faith and that bald guy were driving away. When she'd gone to seek out Lauren, she couldn't find her anywhere.

"You're a terrible liar," Lauren said as she held out her hand to her.

"You figured that out already, huh?" Thea said as she sat beside her, cradling her hand.

"I'm a good reader of people and body language. It's part of the business," Lauren said, resting her head on Thea's shoulder.

"Where were you before?" Thea asked as she wrapped an arm around Lauren's shoulders.

"I went for a walk. I needed to clear my head."

"Is it clear now?" Thea asked, kissing her temple.

"No. But the buzzing thoughts have stopped now that you're here being so sweet and lovely," Lauren said as she turned to face her. "How was the vegetable run?"

"Who told you?" Thea asked, amused.

"Your mom," Lauren said as she picked up a mug Thea hadn't noticed on the small table nearby. "She made me a cup of tea before she went with Carl to pick up some feed."

Thea accepted the cup Lauren offered her and took a sip before something Lauren said dawned on her. "Why did she send me into town for green beans if she was going to go with Carl anyway?"

"To keep you out from underfoot with the potential buyer walk-through here," Lauren said, scrunching her nose. "That was my idea."

Thea nearly choked on her sip. "You're conspiring against me. With my own mother, no less."

"She likes me more. What can I say?" Lauren took the cup back, cradling it before taking a long sip.

"What's not to like?" Thea said, brushing an errant hair off Lauren's forehead.

Lauren placed the cup down and looked at her. "I don't deserve you."

Thea laughed. As if that was the case. "If you keep sending me on fool's errands, then I'll have to agree."

"It wasn't a fool's errand," Lauren countered. "Your mom needed green beans, and I needed to make sure you didn't greet Faith the way you greeted me the first time."

Thea winced. "That wasn't one of my proudest moments."

"We all have them—it's no big deal."

Lauren was quiet as she looked off the porch again. She was seemingly lost in thought. Thea was taken by how beautiful she was even when she was doing something as simple as thinking. She somehow made thinking look sexy.

"How did the meeting go?" Thea asked after she watched her for a while. She'd been dying to know, but she hadn't wanted to come across as needy or desperate. Even if she felt that way.

"We'll find out if he generates an offer letter, I suppose," Lauren said, looking at her again. "Your mother hasn't formally listed any-thing yet, so at this point, all there would be is an interest letter from him."

"That's a good thing, right?" Thea still had no interest in selling, but everyone kept reassuring her that the investigative process was for her family's benefit, so she was trying to go with it.

"It can be," Lauren said. "Without a formal listing, you can't know the interest in a property, particularly a unique property like this. But having someone come in before a listing goes up can help to gauge the value of the property in the eyes of someone other than the seller. Oftentimes the seller and the buyer have differing opinions in value—an early, interest-generating walk-through with someone in the market for a property like this can determine market viability from an outside perspective."

"Which is why Faith is involved and not just you," Thea replied, trying to understand.

"Yes, partly." Lauren squeezed her hand before releasing it. "I'm not licensed here, and my specialty is smaller plots and mostly city-based residences. Whereas Faith operates up here full-time and knows the culture and pulse of interest better than I do."

"And the *partly*?"

Lauren's eyes traced her face before she replied. "The *partly* is that I'm here as a consultant to ensure your mother's best interest is met. I'm an outsider trying to make sure she gets the best deal possible."

"When she sells the farm, you mean," Thea said, still not okay with saying that out loud.

"Maybe, yes," Lauren said, looking pained. "But we aren't there yet."

"But we're running out of time." Thea looked away. She wasn't ready to talk about that.

Lauren's hand on her jaw carefully guided her gaze back to her.

"We'll figure it out," she said, and Thea wanted so badly to believe her, to get lost in those gorgeous eyes and escape the unknown for just a few moments, or a lifetime, so she nodded.

"Okay," she said as she leaned in and placed a delicate kiss to Lauren's lips because she needed to. She pulled back to ask, "Are you doing anything right now?"

"You mean, besides kissing you?" Lauren asked, bringing their lips together again.

Thea allowed herself to enjoy Lauren's affections until she needed to break for air. "Come with me—I want to show you something."

"All right," Lauren said without hesitation.

Thea swooned. She was falling in love with her. How could she not? Lauren trusted her. She wanted Lauren to know she trusted her, too. "Do you know how to swim?"

Lauren followed as she led her beyond the perimeter of her house toward the shed. "Is this a leading question? Like are we talking about actual water? Or, like, wetness?"

Thea stopped short, and Lauren bumped into her back. "I, uh, meant actual water. But now my mind is in the gutter."

"My mind never leaves the gutter, so welcome." Lauren slipped her arms around Thea's waist.

"We'll never get to our destination if you keep flirting with me and touching me like that," Thea pointed out, while doing nothing to stop her.

"Touching you like what?" Lauren slipped her hand under Thea's shirt as she bit down gently on her shoulder.

"Like that." Thea closed her eyes at the sensation of Lauren's fingers dancing across her abdomen.

"Okay." Lauren kissed her cheek and withdrew her hands, much to Thea's dissatisfaction. "For later, then. After you send me those sexy photos you promised."

Thea took her hand and pulled her toward the shed. "I'm going to regret saying that, aren't I?"

Lauren shrugged. "I'm certainly not."

She released her hand to pull open the old shed door, straining against the rusted hinge before it eventually opened. She peered inside and let out a relieved sigh. The door hinge needed some TLC, but the interior of the shed was mostly clean and free of cobwebs. She smiled when she saw what she was looking for.

"Do you trust me?" she asked, looking back at Lauren.

"I do," Lauren said definitively.

I'm not falling in love with her. I am in love with her, Thea thought. And in that moment, that was all she needed to know.

❖

Lauren could find her way around Home Depot in a pinch. And she could maneuver through an outlet store with the best of them, but she wouldn't call herself particularly useful or handy. And though she'd been in a Bass Pro Shops once to use a bathroom on a road trip, she certainly wouldn't call herself outdoorsy. Like, she could probably pitch a tent to save her life, but not without maiming herself in the process. So when Thea asked her if she trusted her and then proceeded to pull out an old canoe, Lauren had her reservations.

Yes, she trusted her. But she did not trust herself. Or her balance. Or that she wouldn't flip that cute but ancient-looking canoe and drown them both in this gorgeous lake. Because though she was confident that she would still look good in a life vest, she wasn't confident she wouldn't need it to survive.

Thea took off her boots and socks, rolling her pant legs up to her knees as she said, "Don't worry about it. I'll hold the canoe, and you get in. I promise not to let it tip."

Lauren looked at the boat and shook her head. "You can't promise that."

"I can," Thea reassured her as she coaxed her down the short dock. "Then why did you take your boots off, like you plan to get wet?" Lauren asked.

Thea pointed to her boots. "Because they have steel toes, and if something bad were to happen, they would pull me under."

"And the rolled pants?" Lauren asked, still skeptical.

Thea guided her to the end of the dock, toward the waiting boat. "I'm going to help you into the boat by holding on to it with a hand and a foot. Just to make sure it's extra stable. The pants were just in the way."

Lauren looked down at the boat, and her stomach flipped. She backed up, crossing her arms. "I don't know about this."

Thea's expression was patient and understanding. She was so sweet. "Would you rather I get in first?"

"Yes." Lauren surprised herself with the quickness of her response.

"Okay," Thea said, still so sweet. She stepped to the edge of the dock and eased into the boat, like it was nothing at all. She reached a hand out to her. "I'm ready when you are."

"What if I'm never ready?" Lauren asked, half kidding.

"Then I'm on a lake alone, barefoot, with my pants rolled up like I'm in a flood."

"Or about to stomp some grapes," Lauren said.

"Or that." Thea smiled up at her. "Trust me. I won't let you fall."

In the late day sun, Thea looked incredible on that boat reaching out to her. She was like some dark-haired goddess—all confident and sexy with that flirty smile and those sparkling eyes. Her skin glowed with a light tan, and Lauren knew it was as soft as it looked.

"I'm ready," she said more for herself than for Thea. "Just a sec."

She stripped off her boots and rolled up her pants as well before double-checking the clips on her life jacket.

She looked up to find Thea giving her an amused look. "What?"

"You took off your boots," Thea said.

"They're Prada," Lauren replied, before adding, "I'm also ready to stomp grapes with you, in case you didn't notice."

"That might rock the boat a bit," Thea joked, and Lauren hesitated. "I'm kidding. No boat rocking. Come on, come to me."

The gentle command made her feel unreasonably turned on, so she must have been ready to get in the boat, right? "Okay, I'm trusting you," she said as she took Thea's hand.

"I won't let anything happen to you," Thea said, and Lauren believed her.

She took a tentative step down into the boat, shifting as the boat swayed slightly underneath her. But true to her word, Thea braced the boat to the dock, steadying it as best she could, and soon, Lauren was safely seated across from her, in awe that she'd actually done it.

"Wow," she said, looking around for the first time. "It's beautiful here."

"Wait until I show you the best part," Thea said as she grabbed the paddle. "Are you ready to leave the dock?"

"Yes," Lauren said confidently.

"Good," Thea said, her voice gentle. "You need to let go of it, then."

"Oh, right." Lauren released the vise grip she had on the nearby dock, and her hand throbbed as the blood rushed back into it. "We're good. Everything is good."

Thea laughed as she pushed off from the dock, slowly paddling them farther from land into the calm waters of the lake. "Everything is good," she said, reassuring her.

Lauren watched the shoreline as they paddled toward the center of the massive lake, finally relaxing a bit in her seat when the steady movements of the paddle in the water and gentle rhythmic lapping became soothing background noise. "This is nice."

"I told you before that I like to go to that porch swing to think, and though that's true, sometimes I do my best thinking on the lake," Thea said as she continued to paddle. "It's so peaceful out here. I feel like I can just breathe in the clean air and nothing else matters in that moment. Like I can forget all my worries."

"The lake is your happy place," Lauren said. She could see why Thea felt that way.

"It is," Thea said as she took them out farther. "And I thought maybe you could borrow it for a bit."

"Oh?"

Thea turned them back toward the shoreline before pulling in the paddle and leaning it against the seat as she said, "You seemed lost in thought on the porch. I wanted to show you my favorite view of the farm. I thought maybe a different perspective would help you find what you were looking for."

Lauren heard the words she was saying, but she was lost in the vision before her. Thea was so, so beautiful. She was so at home in this role, guiding them out onto the lake, paddling like it was effortless. She was strong and confident and oh so sexy at the same time. And the background only enhanced that image. As the sun began its slow descent in the sky, the red barn and Thea's family home seemed to shimmer in the distance. Thea had positioned them perfectly to showcase the beauty of the farm under the slowly setting sun, and Thea was front and center, completing the picture. Looking perfect.

Lauren thought about what she said, and Thea was right.

"I *have* found what I was looking for," she said.

"You're fast. I usually spend an hour or more out here trying to collect my thoughts," Thea said, looking adorable.

Lauren reached for her, scooting forward as much as she dared. "I don't need an hour. I think I knew all along, but you just really helped put things in perspective for me."

"Oh?" Thea asked, leaning toward her. "And what did I put into perspective, exactly?"

Lauren caressed her cheek. "How much you mean to me. How much this means to me. How you were what I was looking for."

"We're not talking about the porch, huh?" Thea asked with a knowing smile on her lips.

"Nope," Lauren said, daring to lean closer. "We're talking about how glad I am that you were at The Mirage that night."

"And that you had fresh peaches at home," Thea replied, hovering her lips close.

"I'll never look at peaches the same way again," Lauren said.

"Me neither." Thea's hands fell to her hips as she connected their lips. "Come here."

Lauren felt herself being moved, but she didn't care because Thea's mouth was on hers, and breathing was already challenging enough.

"I've never met anyone like you," Thea said, kissing away from her mouth to suck on the skin under her jaw.

"That's a good thing, right?" Lauren moaned when Thea lightly bit down on her pulse point.

"So good." Thea moved back to her lips, and Lauren leaned into her kiss until she felt the boat rock much too far to one side, reminding her that she was on a fucking boat.

"Jesus." Lauren pulled back in a panic, rocking the boat in the opposite direction, the result of which was her spilling off Thea's lap and onto the tiny sliver of floor between their respective seats.

Thea lunged forward to slow her fall, causing the boat to sway some more, and Lauren watched in horror as the paddle went overboard, splashing into the water as Thea landed on top of her. Which only made the boat tip more to the right.

Lauren closed her eyes, waiting for the water to consume them both.

"Hey, babe." Thea's voice was far too calm for the impending drowning they were faced with.

Except there was no water. Just the very pleasant weight of Thea's body on hers. She dared to open one eye, finding an amused-looking Thea looking back at her. "We're alive."

Thea laughed. "I'm alive. You—on the other hand—are as pale as a ghost."

Lauren blinked open both her eyes, surveying the scene. They were still in the boat, which was happily absent of excess water. But the paddle was missing. And while having Thea draped across her felt nice, the seat she used to be inhabiting did not feel nice digging into her rib cage. "I'm good."

"Yeah, you look good," Thea teased. She started to lift herself off Lauren, but the boat rocked, causing Lauren to clutch her forearm to keep her close. Thea winced.

"Sorry," Lauren said, not letting go.

"It's okay." She felt Thea's muscles rippling under her touch. "You're safe with me. I promise."

"We don't have a paddle," Lauren said. "We're going to die out here."

Thea shook with laughter.

"This is not the time to mock me," Lauren scoffed. "These pants are too tight to swim in. I had no idea I'd be taking my life into my hands when I put these on today. If I had known we were going deep-sea fishing on a toy raft, I would have chosen a different outfit *and* politely declined your proposition."

"We aren't fishing, nor are we in the sea. And this boat is plenty sturdy enough for two people—one could argue even three."

"Three!" Now she was being ridiculous.

"Well, not if you plan to make out with me on it, no," Thea said, that flirty smile returning.

"You made out with me," Lauren said.

"Did I?" Thea tapped her chin. "Or did you tell me I was what you were looking for all along, and then *you* kissed me."

Lauren shook her head. "I said that, and I meant it. But you kissed me, and you pulled me onto your lap, disturbing the delicate balance of weight distribution, and now we are in the middle of the lake without a paddle and going to die."

"But at least we'll be together."

Lauren huffed. "Not the point."

"C'mon." Thea tickled along her side. "If I hadn't taken you out here, you wouldn't realize how incredibly special and sexy I am. I think that's totally worth aimlessly floating on the lake until a rescue boat arrives."

"That's an option?" Lauren was horrified.

"No. Sadly, there are no rescue crews assigned to this lake. We're on our own."

"I left my boots on the dock," Lauren said sadly.

"That's your priority?"

"I really like those boots."

"They'll be there when we get back, I promise."

"You're making a lot of promises for someone missing a paddle," Lauren pointed out.

Thea attempted to get up, but Lauren stopped her. "I can't get the paddle if you keep that death grip on me."

"The paddle is gone. Accept defeat. We're doomed."

"The paddle floats and is right over there." Thea motioned with her head. "And I can get it, if you let go. Then you can be reunited with your beloved boots."

"And stay dry in the process?"

"I mean…" Thea licked her lips. "Are you saying the kissing did nothing?"

Lauren slapped her arm. "So not the time."

"Is that a no, then?"

"Yes, the kissing was great. I really enjoyed it until we almost tipped the boat. Can you please get the paddle now? I'm too pretty to freeze to death in the sea."

"Lake," Thea corrected.

She shot her a look.

"I'm going to get up now," Thea warned.

"Okay," Lauren said, releasing her hold on her. "I'm ready."

Thea paused, making sure Lauren didn't change her mind before slowly easing off her. Lauren grabbed the sides of the boat as it swayed slightly, only exhaling once Thea had resumed her seat.

"Can I help you back into yours?" she asked.

"I'm good here." Lauren wasn't about to move, even if her ribs were throbbing.

"You sure?"

"Just get the paddle."

"On it."

Once Thea maneuvered the boat and leaned too far for Lauren's liking toward the water to retrieve the paddle, she finally started to relax again. That's when she noticed how low the sun was now. The already beautiful view was somehow more breathtaking, and with Thea's back to the barn and farmhouse, the angle was perfect.

"Don't move," Lauren said as she reached into her back pocket, sitting up. "I need this picture in my life." She shifted, making sure she got the perfect shot. "Got it."

"And you managed to get off the floor and back into your seat without tipping the canoe. Congrats."

Lauren looked down and saw that Thea was right. "Huh. Would you look at that?"

"I'd look at you all day, if you let me."

She looked up to find Thea watching her. "Take me back to shore so I can kiss that charming mouth of yours," Lauren said.

Thea leaned toward her. "You sure you don't want to plant one on me now? I did save the paddle and our lives."

Lauren rolled her eyes. "I'm not making that mistake again. Once I'm back in my beloved boots, I'll reward you for your heroism."

"Deal," Thea said with a wink as she rowed them back to shore.

Lauren took a few more pictures on the journey, enjoying the calmness of the water and the unparalleled beauty of the Boudreaux property line along the lake.

"This place really is magical," she said as they approached the dock.

"It is." Thea looked nostalgic.

Once they were anchored to the dock's edge, Lauren got brave. "Take a picture with me."

"Sure," Thea said.

Lauren braced herself against the dock as she stepped into Thea's space, lowering herself onto Thea's lap. She leaned against Thea's chest as Thea's arms wrapped around her waist, and she took a few pictures of them with the lake in the background.

"Those came out great," Thea said, kissing the side of her head.

"We are a very photogenic couple," Lauren agreed. Thea's stomach grumbled against her back, and she laughed. "Your digestion seems to agree."

Thea patted her belly. "I worked up a real appetite saving us from certain death."

Lauren laughed. "C'mon. Let's get you some dinner for your troubles."

As Thea helped her out of the canoe, Lauren felt braver than she had before, pushing off with a quick leap and hopping up on the dock with what she would call the nimbleness of a gymnast. As she cheered midturn, she heard the crash of something hitting the water hard.

"Oh, shit." Lauren's Olympic finish to the dock had tipped the canoe and deposited Thea in the water.

Chapter Twenty-one

D inner was great—so great, in fact, Thea was almost sad it had ended. She'd never had a lover like Lauren. Someone so comfortable in their own skin that they so easily meshed with her family. It was like Lauren had always been in her life. Her mother adored her, and Lauren and her brother seemed to have endless inside jokes. Thea thought back to how, not so long ago, their family dinners had been tense. Long gone were those days. The days before Lauren so seamlessly intertwined herself within her family and her heart.

"This long, romantic walk into the woods at night is just that, right? Romance? You aren't taking me out here to murder me for submerging you with your phone in the lake, right?" Lauren joked as she slipped her arm into the elbow Thea offered her.

"There's no murder on the agenda tonight. You're good," Thea said. "I need to walk off that dinner a bit. Even when cooking vegetarian stir-fry, my mother manages to make it hearty." Her mother had gone off for her weekly bridge night, and Carl was lovestruck in the parlor on the phone with Annie. She'd been looking for a way to get Lauren alone, and a walk seemed like the perfect way to do just that.

Lauren teased as she guided Thea's arm up over her shoulder, "We could always go back on the lake and paddle around a bit. That'll burn some calories."

"Until my phone emerges from the rice bowl on the counter—in full working order—I'm all set with the lake," Thea said, not upset about it in the least. She'd had a wonderful day with Lauren today, even if she got unceremoniously dunked. She wouldn't change a moment of it. And she didn't have anyone to worry about regarding the phone, except work. If they needed her, they could call the house. The only person she would be concerned about reaching was Lauren, and she was nestled in her arm right now. All was right with the world.

"I'm sorry about that." Lauren scrunched her nose. "It really was an accident."

"I know," Thea said. "You do know what this means, though, right?"

Lauren frowned, sagging. "No naughty pictures from across the hall."

Thea laughed. "I was going to say you were due for some payback, but that is so much sadder a realization."

"Liar," Lauren said as she nudged her. "Now you don't have to stay true to your naughty picture threat. Come to think of it, I'm reevaluating the whole accidental dunking thing. Maybe this was all part of an elaborate plan to get out of sending me the crotch shots I'm going to so desperately need later."

"Crotch shots?" Thea said, scandalized. "I was maybe going to send you some cleavage pics. I had no idea your expectations were so high."

Lauren shrugged, snuggling closer as they strolled along the water's edge toward the back pastures. "A girl has needs, love. How am I supposed to get off with you across the hall if I can't see what I want most?"

"Is that what you want most?" Thea asked as she slowed their progress to lean against one of the nearby fence posts. She looped her arms around Lauren, pulling her to her chest as she waited for a reply.

Lauren caressed her jaw as she replied, "What I want most is you. Kissing me. Touching me. Over me. Under me. *In* me. But if I have to settle for a photograph, then, I mean, why not ask for the whole picture?"

She dropped her hands to Lauren's ass as she said, "Well, that wouldn't be the whole picture, though, would it?"

Lauren bit her bottom lip when Thea squeezed lightly, and Thea repeated the action with a bit more pressure because watching Lauren do that was something she never wanted to not see.

"Mmm," Lauren hummed. "I mean, my perfect fantasy picture of you would be you stretched out naked on the bed with a hand behind your head, sitting up a little so those tight abs of yours pop, with your legs casually out in front of you, and your free hand at your clit. But that might be a hard picture to take alone. So I'd certainly have to help. But if that was the case"—Lauren brought her lips just short of Thea's—"I'd probably have a hard time just watching."

Thea connected their lips, moaning at the passion Lauren met her with. "You've given this some thought," she said between hot, openmouthed kisses.

"I think about the ways I want to fuck you and please you, often."

"How about the ways I can please you?" Thea slipped beneath the waist of Lauren's jeans and thong to grab at the flesh of her ass. "Do you think about that often, too?"

"More and more each day," Lauren said with a throaty moan as Thea tugged at the back of her thong.

"Walking is fine and all, but since we've stopped making forward progress, I can think of a better way to burn off those calories from dinner." Thea needed Lauren out of these clothes, now.

"Take me," Lauren said, and from the darkness in her eyes, Thea knew she meant that in every way imaginable.

She pressed one last, blistering kiss to Lauren's lips before taking her hand and doubling back toward the farmhouse. As they passed her car, she noticed that Lauren's gaze seemed to linger on the back seat. She smiled when Lauren slowed her to whisper in her ear, "Next time. I promise."

I love you. Lauren just got her, in so many ways. She had to slow to keep from running into the house.

Carl was on the phone in the parlor when they walked through the door, but he didn't look up. His smile told Thea he was still talking to Annie. He seemed the happiest in those moments. She was glad he'd found someone that made him as happy as Lauren made her.

"He's adorable," Lauren whispered over her shoulder.

"Don't tell him that—you'll kill his game," she said.

"Adorable is plenty sexy—don't worry." Lauren nipped at her ear as they climbed the stairs. "I'm speaking from experience—I've been bowled over by that Boudreaux charm more than once."

Thea paused at the top of the stairs to take her hand. "Do you regret that?"

"Not one bit," Lauren said, taking the lead.

They hadn't discussed their destination, but Thea noticed Lauren was leading her to the rear guest room, not Thea's room. Which was fine by her, but—

As if reading her mind, Lauren turned. "The guest room is the farthest from the stairs and at the farthest corner of the house. Plus, it's got a nice big queen bed, versus the full in yours. And something tells me we're gonna need room to spread out."

"I like the way you think," Thea said, kissing her as Lauren stepped through the open guest room door backward, closing the door behind them.

"And I like the way you taste," Lauren said as she pulled back the covers and pushed her back onto the bed. "Now get out of those clothes, and let me show you just how much."

Thea laughed as Lauren climbed over her, playfully kissing her while helping her out of her shirt. Lauren's hands found the warm skin of her abdomen, caressing up her sides and over her cotton bra as she palmed the flesh underneath. Thea arched at the contact, loving the way Lauren paid such great attention to her breasts and nipples. Kissing Lauren got her plenty hot, but being teased and stroked by her ignited her insides. And if the increased attention she was paying to her nipples tonight was any indication, Lauren had figured that out.

"You feel so good," Thea said as Lauren stripped her of her bra, dropping her mouth to the pert nipples Lauren had teased into attention. Thea wove her fingers through Lauren's hair, keeping her mouth close as she squirmed with delight.

Lauren flicked open her jeans while continuing her affections, and Thea had to force her brain to concentrate long enough to shimmy them off her hips and lose them to the floor with her boots and Lauren's cashmere sweater.

She bucked her hips when Lauren grazed the front of her underwear with her fingers, and she moaned in ecstasy as Lauren kissed down her abdomen to take the waistband of her panties in her teeth, dragging them down and off so artfully that Thea was momentarily distracted from her aching clit and throbbing center.

She reached to pull Lauren back to her, but Lauren shook her head.

"You owe me a picture," she said as she kicked off her boots and stepped out of her pants. She pulled her phone out of the back pocket of her jeans before she cast them down with Thea's.

"Do I?" Thea could stare at Lauren in her designer lingerie all day and never get bored of it.

"You do," Lauren said as she stepped close enough for Thea to touch.

"Seems like we could be doing more than just taking pictures."

Thea reached out and ran her fingers along the damp front of Lauren's thong. "Seems like you're plenty ready for that."

Lauren closed her eyes, stepping forward. Thea teased over the silky fabric before slipping beneath it, relishing the wetness she found there.

"Come to bed, baby," Thea said as she dipped lower.

Lauren's breath was short as she braced herself at the edge of the bed. Her legs shifted apart slightly, and Thea leaned forward to get more of Lauren in her hand.

"Wait," Lauren said, her eyes flicking open as she panted. "My picture first. Then you can have your way with me. I promise."

Thea smiled. "You might regret that."

"Oh, I doubt that," Lauren said as she pushed her thong off her hips before stepping out of it. "I've never regretted a moment I've spent in your presence. I sincerely doubt tonight will be any different."

"And why do you think that is?" Thea asked as she leaned back on the bed, putting her hand behind her head like Lauren had mentioned before. She bent one knee, dropping her leg out to the side as she rested her hand on her lower stomach.

Lauren licked her lips, seemingly captivated as she shrugged off her bra and exposed that perfect, perky chest that Thea literally dreamed about. "Because you are every naughty fantasy I have ever had. Right down to the steel toe boots."

Thea moved her hand lower, nearly touching herself, but pulling back. "Even when I'm out of them?"

"Especially when you're out of them," Lauren said, bringing her phone back into view.

"Just a picture," Thea said, feeling exposed but also somewhat emboldened by the prospect of documenting this moment.

"Just a picture," Lauren confirmed, licking her lips again.

Thea gave her a wink as she dipped lower, moving over her own arousal to stroke her swollen clit with a pleased exhale. Lauren stayed true to her word, climbing back over her in a moment's time, crashing their lips together as she palmed Thea's breasts. Thea continued to rub her clit until she started to climb too quickly. She pulled her hand back only to feel it guided between Lauren's legs and inside her.

The hot tightness that greeted her sent a shock of excitement through, bringing her back up to the precipice. Lauren rode her hand hard. Lauren's hot, openmouthed kisses suffocated her as Lauren's fingers found her clit, quickly bringing her to her breaking point.

"Lauren," she warned as her body started to tremble. Lauren ground her hips down faster, rolling forward so the heel of Thea's hand pressed against her clit.

"Come with me," Lauren panted, and Thea couldn't have resisted if she tried.

She came hard under Lauren's touch, her body quaking as Lauren came undone in her hand, Lauren's tremors moving through Thea, too, as if by extension. She stayed inside Lauren as she rolled her to her back, so that she was on top and looking down at the most beautiful woman she had ever seen.

Lauren shifted beneath her as her sex clenched around Thea's fingers. Thea could tell she could go again. Lauren always seemed ready to go a second time. She lowered herself onto Lauren, sucking on her earlobe in earnest as she stroked over her clit, and within seconds, Lauren's nails were in her back, and she was climaxing again.

The tremors were smaller this time, but Lauren's breaths were coming short and fast as she pushed Thea's hand away from her with a sated laugh. "Don't break me."

"I don't think that's possible. I've seen what little recovery time you actually need," Thea said as she obliged. She ran her fingers along Lauren's still heaving rib cage, tickling the skin as she settled at her side, draping her leg across her in a comfortable embrace.

Lauren closed her eyes as her breathing slowed, smiling when Thea intertwined their fingers.

Thea's breath caught as Lauren looked up at her. The faint perspiration along her hairline and the healthy pink glow on her cheeks were highlighted so picturesquely by the full moon's light coming through the windows. Lauren was so gorgeous. She was so *everything*.

She touched her jaw infinitesimally, almost afraid that if she used any more pressure, the dream that was Lauren would disappear before her eyes and under her touch. Because this felt like a wonderful dream. Too wonderful to be real. Too real to be hers.

Lauren rose slightly, bringing their lips together, and Thea melted into her kiss.

"I love you," Thea said as her heart hammered in her chest, unable to stop herself from saying what she had been thinking since last night.

Lauren pulled back, her hazel eyes watching her intently as she ran her hands through Thea's hair and along her jaw, guiding Thea's lips back to hers. She smiled as she placed a delicate, almost too soft kiss to Thea's lips as she said, "I love you, too."

Thea let herself luxuriate in Lauren's embrace, snuggling into her neck as Lauren traced circles up and down her naked back. As her heart rate slowed, she slid off to Lauren's side, facing her. "Hi," she said as Lauren scooted close, slipping her leg between Thea's.

"Hey," Lauren said in that sex-drunk way that made Thea never want to leave the bed she occupied.

"Are you okay?" Thea asked, feeling insecure. Yes, Lauren had reciprocated her *I love you*, but she was still grappling with what that admission meant.

"I'm more than okay," Lauren said, looking flawless even with her hair a sex mess. Her kiss-plump lips were the most delicious dark pink right now, and those perfect white teeth were on full display with her easy smile. "I'm with you. And there's no place I'd rather be."

Thea closed her eyes as Lauren tucked her head under her chin. She pulled the covers over them as she held her, so grateful Lauren had entered her life. So grateful that this wasn't just a dream. So grateful that for once, things seemed to work out just as they should.

CHAPTER TWENTY-TWO

Thea was hot. Like, so hot. Her body was constantly warm, at all hours of the day and night, and Lauren fucking loved it. As someone who was always a little chilly, Thea was the perfect antidote as a literal human furnace. And after a night of lovemaking and snuggling, naked Thea, with her arms wrapped around her protectively as Thea lightly snored, was the warmest and best Thea there was. Though, admittedly, awake and horny Thea was also a favorite of Lauren's. So was lovingly affectionate Thea. This Thea. It was a tie.

Because Thea loved her. And she loved Thea. And that was amazing and complicated for so many reasons. But mostly amazing. And right now, that's what she chose to focus on. Thea feeling amazing wrapped all around her like the sexiest, hottest blanket there was.

She closed her eyes, and when she blinked them awake, the sun was higher outside the window. She had no idea what time it was, but her bladder told her it was time to pee. That was when she noticed the repeated buzzing of her phone, somewhere on the floor in the abandoned clothes pile.

Thea shifted. "Is that your cell or mine?"

Lauren brushed Thea's dark hair out of her face. "If it's yours, then congrats—your phone is working again."

Thea palmed her face. "Oh, the lake. Right. I forgot."

"Why? Are you finding yourself distracted?" Lauren asked as she danced her fingers along Thea's naked chest.

Thea blinked sleepily. "Very."

Lauren smiled when Thea reached down to run her hand along Lauren's hip, pulling her leg across her hips.

"How do you feel about morning sex?" Lauren asked as she toyed with Thea's nipple.

"The same way I feel about afternoon and evening sex," Thea said, stilling Lauren's fingers and bringing them to her mouth. "I love it."

Lauren moaned as Thea sucked on her fingertips. There was nothing this woman did that didn't turn her on. "And what about me?"

"Well, you," Thea said as she ran her tongue along Lauren's first two fingers, "you I love even more than sex."

Lauren's heart swelled at Thea's words, and her lower stomach tightened at Thea's teasing. "And what about sex with me?"

"That I love best of all," Thea said, her gray-blue eyes alert and darkening by the second.

Lauren's phone began ringing again, and Thea stopped what she was doing to look down. "Should you get that?"

"It's probably just the airline confirming my flight tonight," Lauren said, bringing her lips to Thea's. "But you're here, and this is much more important."

"Are you sure you have to fly home tonight?" Thea asked between kisses.

"I have meetings tomorrow and a showing. This weekend escape wasn't originally on my calendar. Plus, you'll be back in Boston on Wednesday, right? That'll give me plenty of time to miss you."

"So I should surely give you something to miss, then." Thea stroked below her navel, and Lauren remembered she had to pee.

"Hold that sexy thought," Lauren said, stilling her hand. "I really want to start my day that way, but I also really have to pee."

Thea laughed. "Same, girl. Same."

Lauren sat up and stretched. "Shit."

"What?"

"We're naked."

"That usually happens during and after sex," Thea said, reaching out to touch her.

Lauren swatted her hand away. "This is an old farmhouse without a guest bathroom en suite."

"I'm not seeing the problem here," Thea said, oblivious to all the issues that she posed.

"That means we have to get dressed to pee, just to undress and do whatever it is your filthy mind has in store," Lauren said, gesturing to Thea's incredibly hot naked body.

"We could make a run for it," Thea proposed.

"That doesn't sound like a bad idea at all," Lauren said, rolling her eyes.

"What could happen?" Thea joked.

"Your mother or brother could be brushing their teeth or wandering through the hallway and suddenly—boom—*Hi, Lauren. Nice tits.*"

"I mean, they're easily the best I've ever seen. And the softness. Don't even get me started on the softness." Thea caressed the underside of her breast as she leaned in to kiss her sternum, and Lauren contemplated just how badly she had to pee.

"Don't start," she demanded half-heartedly.

"You sure?" Thea's mouth was quickly moving toward her nipple.

"Not really, no." Lauren's phone buzzed again, halting Thea's progress. Lauren frowned because...obvious reasons. She flopped back on the bed, pulling the sheet up to her neck as she pointed toward the floor. "Okay, let's see what's so urgent. Then a pee break, then maybe breakfast."

"No morning sex?" Thea looked devastated.

"I mean, probably. I can't exactly resist you."

"So after the pee break..."

"And before breakfast, a quickie," Lauren agreed, because nothing about that felt like a compromise.

The ringing stopped, but a new sound replaced it—the sound of fast approaching footsteps. Then a knock.

"Thea? Are you in there?" Kathleen asked, sounding out of breath.

Thea gave Lauren a horrified look before calling out, "Uh, yes?"

"Are you decent?" Kathleen asked.

"Just a sec." Thea's eyes were wide as she pointed frantically to her naked chest. She tugged at the blanket, uncovering Lauren in the process. Lauren snatched the covers back, nearly knocking Thea to the floor as she pointed toward Thea's shirt and jeans. Thea nodded, pulling on her clothes in an unbelievably fast and coordinated way that at any other time would have impressed Lauren to the point of arousing her, except right now wasn't the time. With her mother literally knocking at the door.

Thea took a breath, and Lauren made sure she was covered before nodding her begrudging approval.

"Hey, Ma," Thea said, trying to sound casual as she cracked open the door. "What's up?"

"I need you to take me to the hospital."

"The hospital? What's wrong? Are you okay?"

"I'm fine. But Hector isn't." Kathleen's voice sounded fragile. "He had another stroke this morning. We just found out. Carl's there now, but he took the truck."

"Jesus." Thea looked like she might faint. She turned back to Lauren, her mouth agape.

Lauren mouthed *go* as she waved her off.

Thea nodded before looking back at her mother. "Okay. Let's go."

"Thanks, honey," Kathleen said. "Oh, and good morning, Lauren."

"Morning," Lauren said, wincing. But in that moment, her embarrassment was the least important thing.

Lauren checked her phone. Still no calls from Thea. Today was really not the day for Thea's phone to still be buried in rice.

"Thanks for meeting me," Faith said as she placed Lauren's coffee on the table between them.

"Sure, yes. Of course. Thanks for the coffee." Faith had been one of the many missed calls on her phone. Kathleen had been the remaining four. After trying Thea's phone and realizing she couldn't reach her, she smartly started to call Lauren's. Except Lauren had hers on vibrate. Because she was in bed with her daughter.

"Well, I can't say I expected to hear back from Edmund that quickly, but he's an odd guy. So I guess I shouldn't be surprised," Faith said as she took the seat across from her. Faith had recommended Life's a Grind, a quaint little coffee shop in town. And to Lauren's relief, Cynthia the cheese master from the farm was headed into town to pick up supplies, so she scored a ride.

"Well, time is certainly of the essence here," Lauren said, trying to be open-minded even if her heart and brain were worried about Hector and the Boudreaux clan. She took a sip of the coffee and tried to ground herself. She just needed to focus. This was how she could be helpful to them right now. "I appreciate his interest."

Faith seemed to hesitate.

"What?"

"It's just an initial offer. Keep that in mind," she said as she slid the documents across the table.

Lauren opened the folder and scowled. "You're kidding me."

"It's a starting point," Faith rationalized. "A place where we can start and negotiate around."

"Negotiate around?" Lauren shook her head. She did some quick mental math and had to bite back the bile that started to rise in her throat. "You can't negotiate around a number that is less than fifty percent the value of the square footage alone. Forget about the lakefront acreage and the forest area."

"It's not a final offer yet."

"It's insulting," Lauren growled, angry for Kathleen. "This family has been through so much. And continues to go through so much." She shook her head. "This isn't anywhere near even the numbers you quoted me."

"That was just an estimate for the value of the land in a perfect world," Faith said, sitting a little taller. "An estimate is only as good as the interest. You know that."

Lauren did know that. And she also knew that she shouldn't be shooting the messenger. Faith had gone above and beyond to try to help the Boudreauxs out. The least she could do was try to be gracious.

She took a breath. "I'm sorry. It's been a tough morning." She glanced at her phone again. Still nothing. "Okay, I'll run this by Kathleen and see what she thinks."

"I know you were hoping for more," Faith said, looking sympathetic. "But maybe this can help to keep expectations more realistic."

That was exactly what Lauren would have said to her client, were she trying to convince them to consider the offer on the table. But Lauren wasn't there yet. And she had no interest in trying to coax Kathleen into selling her livelihood and still not ending up better off in some way.

"Is there an expiration on this offer?" she asked as she thumbed through the forms.

"A week from tomorrow."

Lauren looked up and saw annoyance on Faith's face this time.

"I know, I know. It's ridiculous," Faith conceded. "Look, see what Kathleen says, and let's maybe list her property to generate some counterinterest so we can force his hand a bit."

"All right," Lauren said. That was the best course of action, even if presenting this to Kathleen right now felt like the shittiest timing ever. "Hey, are you busy right now?"

"Um, no. What's up?"

They weren't going to get anywhere sitting around, and truthfully, Lauren felt like she needed to be somewhere else. "Can you take me to the hospital?"

CHAPTER TWENTY-THREE

L auren," Thea said, relieved. Seeing her walking down the lonely hospital corridor was exactly what she needed.

"Hey." Lauren greeted her with a kiss. "What's the news?"

Thea sighed. "Hector had a headache last night and asked Carl to close up the farm. Sometime during the night he had a stroke, but we didn't find him until this morning. He's stable but still sleeping."

"I'm so sorry," Lauren said, touching her arm. "Does he have any family that should be called? I can do it. I'll do whatever you need."

"He has a daughter in California. She's on her way now. But that's it. We're his family," Thea said, feeling emotional.

"And you are his, too." Lauren stroked her arm. "He loves you guys. And that farm."

Thea nodded. She knew that. She also knew that Hector was the glue that held the patchwork farmhand work together. Carl couldn't do it alone. Hector had the experience and know-how like her father always had. In a lot of ways, he'd made losing her father a little less painful since she saw so much of her dad in Hector. "I don't think I can lose him. He's as essential to that farm as any of us. He was there before Carl and I were even born. What will happen if…?"

"We're not there yet," Lauren said, and the kindness in her eyes made Thea want to cry for a different reason. "Come on. I brought you all some food. You need to eat something."

She held up a large brown bag from Life's a Grind that Thea hadn't noticed before. She'd been so relieved to see Lauren, she'd ignored the luggage-sized bag entirely.

"I wasn't sure what everyone liked, so I bought a little bit of everything." Lauren looked around. "Where are Carl and your mom?"

Thea motioned around the corner. "In the family waiting area. I needed to take a walk."

"Let's go eat a little—we can wait and pace aimlessly once we've had sustenance," Lauren said. "Listen to your girlfriend. She's brilliant."

"And so modest," Thea said, glad Lauren was here.

"It's a talent, I know." Lauren gave her a wink before she embraced Kathleen and then Carl.

Thea watched as she maneuvered a few chairs together and cleared a small end table of magazines to make a mini dining area for them all. Lauren unpacked the collection of sandwiches—and she hadn't been joking, it was a full collection of the café's offerings—handing them out with napkins and beverages. She produced an assortment of chips and cookies from a bag within the giant bag, and she handed Carl an apple with a note attached to it.

"I assume that's from Annie. I found it on the front porch on my way here. I think it's a love note," she said with a shrug.

Carl grabbed it and turned to read it out of sight.

Her mother laughed. "Thank you, Lauren."

"Glad to help," she said as she settled next to Thea. "This is for you. Portobello mushroom on ciabatta with mozzarella, balsamic glaze, and arugula." She leaned in conspiratorially. "The girl behind the counter told me it's the best thing on the menu. But I bought the whole menu, so we can determine that ourselves."

"It sounds great," Thea said, surprised by how hungry she was. "I'm sure it's delicious."

Thea took a bite, closing her eyes at the delightful combination of flavors in her mouth. "This is so good." She looked up to find the room watching her. "What?"

"You just moaned into that sandwich like you were making out with it," Carl said, snickering.

"Says the guy who nearly fell out of his seat to read his apple's love note," Thea teased. "What did it say? Are you the apple of Annie's eye?"

"That's some big talk coming from someone wearing the same clothes as yesterday." Carl gave her a sly smile as he asked, "How *was* the mattress in the guest room? Comfy?"

Thea launched a bag of chips at him, and Lauren ducked to avoid getting hit.

"Hey," Lauren said with her arms stretched out between them, "no projectiles. We're in a hospital."

"One could argue that's the safest time for projectiles," Thea said as she tossed an oatmeal raisin cookie in Carl's direction.

Her mother caught it handily. "I think it's safe to say that we all needed to eat and laugh a little." She reached out to squeeze Lauren's knee. "You're a lifesaver. I'm not sure what we'd do without you."

Lauren smiled, but Thea noticed her smile didn't reach her eyes. She also noticed she wasn't eating.

"Aren't you going to have something?"

Lauren crossed her legs, leaning back. "I had a snack over coffee with Faith before I got here. I'm good for right now."

"Faith?" Thea asked. "You met with Faith today?"

"She called this morning," Lauren said. "Cynthia gave me a lift to meet her on her way into town."

Her mother paused between cookie bites. "Oh, right. I was supposed to go shopping this afternoon."

"She's got it all under control," Lauren reassured her. "She told me all the cheese things on the ride. I'm like a junior cheese master now."

"She does have a love of cheese," her mother said, looking amused. "What did Faith have to say?" Thea asked.

Lauren reached over and wiped something off Thea's lip. "We caught up about yesterday."

"And?" her mother asked. "Did she feel it went well?"

Thea sat forward. Her feelings about yesterday's showing were still complicated. But she wanted to be in the know.

Lauren hesitated. "Maybe this isn't the best time."

Thea didn't like that answer. "What does that mean?"

"Lauren, I appreciate your attempt at discretion and your sensitivity about what's going on, but I think I can speak for all of us"—her mother's tone was gentle as she looked between her and Carl—"when I say we could probably use the distraction. And I have no intention of keeping any of this a secret from my kids."

Lauren sighed. "He submitted an offer letter."

Her mother's eyebrows shot up to her hairline. "That fast?"

"It's a tactic some more aggressive buyers will use to try to sway a listing price in their favor or try to stave off a listing at all. Usually it's a generous offer to dissuade the seller from posting the listing and encouraging any sort of competition."

"And this offer, was it generous?" her mother asked, and Thea wanted to know that as well.

Lauren's face fell. "Not particularly."

"What does that mean?" Carl spoke up, catching Thea off guard. She hadn't realized he was paying attention.

"It means you have a few choices to make." Lauren uncrossed her legs, sitting up straighter. "You can accept the offer. You can dismiss it without further consideration. Or you can list the farm and see if anyone else shows interest, then use that interest as a bargaining tool to drive up the offer you received today."

"And the benefit to listing it is what?" Thea asked, feeling betrayed. "I thought the plan was to get creative and try to find a way to save the farm while getting us out of debt enough to continue to run it."

"Thea." Her mother's tone held a warning. "Let Lauren talk."

"It's okay," Lauren said, looking at Thea for the first time since she'd started talking. Her expression was unreadable. "This is part of the process. Finding out the best offer for the property was part of the long-term plan."

"Of selling off my family's livelihood, you mean. That plan," Thea said, her annoyance mounting.

Her mother shot her a look.

"I want to hear what Lauren has to say," Carl interjected. The seriousness in his expression made him look so much like their father, it was almost eerie. "What should we do?"

Lauren glanced at Thea briefly before facing her mother. "Faith and I think you should formally list the property. Let's see what kind of interest there is in it, and I'll work with Faith to determine if dividing up the land at that point will be more or less beneficial based on the interest. The offer letter gives us a jumping-off point and also, in some ways, a backup plan. There was never a guarantee the land would sell, but now we at least have *some* interest in a sale. And a whole land sale, at that. Which is something you can use to your advantage."

"A whole land sale?" Carl asked.

Lauren nodded. "The offer was for all that is contained within the borders of the property."

"So the farmhouse and Hector's place, as well. That's what you mean." Thea felt her blood pressure rising.

"It's the only way he would make an offer—all or none." Lauren held her gaze, but that only made Thea more upset. How was she okay with this?

"Then list it," her mother said without hesitation. The tenor of her words was far too final for Thea's liking.

"You can't be serious," Thea said, sitting at the edge of her seat. "We're at the hospital waiting for Hector to wake up, and you've just decided to sell the farm out from under him. And us?" Her mother raised an eyebrow in her direction, and she knew she'd overstepped. But she couldn't stop herself. "The Berry Festival is right around the corner. If we work hard, we can make it our most profitable one yet. We can still save the farm."

"Without our general manager?" her mother challenged. "We're currently down the one person who is instrumental in helping us accomplish the work that we're already understaffed to do. And Hector being sick is exactly why we should list the property. We have no idea how he'll be when he wakes up. Who he'll be, even. At least if we sell, then we can give his family the money he will need to get back on his feet. We can't do that now, Thea. We can't do anything but watch everything we've worked for slowly disappear."

"Mom—" Thea started to argue.

"Enough," she said, raising her hand. "Your brother and I can't keep this up any longer." She looked at Lauren. "List the farm. Get whatever paperwork you need me to sign, and I'll sign it. I trust you and Faith and Ellison will make sure we're treated fairly, and we'll see the best outcome possible."

"I promise," Lauren said, and Thea felt betrayed all over again. Because Lauren had promised her more than once that she'd do everything she could to keep the farm intact. And listing it was the very opposite of that.

The room was silent and tense when the doctor walked in at that moment to tell them Hector was awake. Thea was the first one out of her chair to see him. She couldn't sit here anymore. She couldn't sit next to Lauren and act like everything was okay. Nothing was okay. And it never would be again.

❖

"Thea," Lauren tried again, fruitlessly. "Talk to me."

Thea had been icing her out since the hospital, and Lauren, although initially hurt, was now starting to get angry.

"You're just going to drop me off at the airport without so much as a few mumbled phrases between us. And what? Send me on my way?" At this point she wished she was already on the plane.

"I am talking to you," Thea said through gritted teeth.

"You aren't. At least not about the important stuff. I don't care about the amount of seasonal rainfall you get here or how many fucking goat yoga retreats are around. I care about you and—"

"Do you?" Thea bit back. Finally, some emotion.

"Of course I do," she said.

Thea pulled into the small airport and put the car in park. She twisted in her seat to face her as she replied, "Really, though? Because all along you've been trying to convince me that things were going to work out just fine, yet you also said today that the long-term plan was to list the farm anyway. So how are those two things both possible? And where in there did you give a damn about me? Or was sleeping with me to get closer to the farm and this potential sale part of the long-term plan too?"

Lauren recoiled. She expected resistance from Thea about the listing, but what was this bullshit about not caring about her? Or leveraging their relationship for some professional advancement? Did last night mean nothing to her?

"First of all, I met you and slept with you long before the farm even came on my radar. And you had no trouble continuing that sexual relationship after it was clear I would be working with your family, so you can dissolve that false narrative right now." She shook her head, angry. "I was honest with you from the start. I told you I would try my best to help your family, and I'm doing that. I'm doing my best. No one said this was going to be an easy process or a bump-free ride. Listing the property was always on the table, and I told you that as well. If you chose to ignore it, that's on you."

Thea scoffed and leaned back in her seat, staring out the driver's side window, brooding. But Lauren wasn't done.

"And just to clarify things, I do care about you. A fucking lot. And the last two nights with you have been nothing short of wonderful, but maybe I'm the one who was deceived all along. You had no trouble telling me you loved me last night, but you're so quick to jump to all these awful conclusions about me today. What's changed?"

"Last night was a mistake," Thea said to the window.

That was all Lauren could take. She'd been patient with Thea's constant insecurity around the potential farmhouse sale. She'd been gracious despite the repeated insults to her character and career in the process. And today she'd carefully listened when Thea needed her to, she'd been there when Hector woke up, and she'd tried to help them navigate the uncertainty that awaited them all. But she couldn't take this. She couldn't take Thea breaking her heart out of spite. She deserved better than this.

"Look at me when you say that," Lauren said, trying to keep the tears at bay.

Thea sighed before turning to face her. She looked weary. "This isn't going to work. Now that Hector is out of commission, I'm going to be staying up here indefinitely. They can't get ready for the Berry Festival without me. This"—she motioned between them before letting her hand fall limp to her lap—"there isn't any time for this. I have too much going on."

"Wow," Lauren said, having had her fill. "Okay. So you regret telling me you love me, and being in any type of a relationship with me is a burden. Did I miss anything? I'd hate for there to be anything unsaid."

Thea looked straight ahead, saying nothing.

Lauren unlocked the door and slipped out. She opened the rear door and pulled out her suitcase with more force than was probably necessary.

"Wait, let me help." Thea climbed out of the car as Lauren slammed the rear door shut.

"Don't worry about it. This nice, roomy back seat made it easy for me to get all my baggage out of your life." Lauren got no satisfaction from the wince Thea gave her at that remark.

"It's heavy. Let me at least get you to the gate," Thea said as she trotted up behind her.

Lauren spun on the spot, her voice louder than she planned when she said, "I somehow managed before you entered my life. I'll be fine with you out of it."

Thea looked hurt. "I didn't mean—"

"Oh, but you did. You were plenty *mean* whether you meant to be or not. Don't worry. The point was well received. Good-bye, Thea."

"Lauren," Thea called out, but Lauren kept walking. She couldn't stop from crying any longer, and she was damn sure not about to let Thea see that. She'd seen and done enough. She wouldn't give her the satisfaction of knowing that her heart was broken.

Chapter Twenty-four

L auren had managed to keep it together in the lobby, but now that she stood outside Trina's door waiting for her to open it, the floodgates opened again.

"Oh, Lauren." Trina's arms were around her, and she couldn't remember another time when she needed a hug so badly. "Come in, let's sit."

"I'll get the bags," Kendall's voice said from nearby, and Lauren sat on the couch with her face in her hands as another wave of sadness washed over her. Because she was alone again. And crashing what was probably some cutesy date night between her best friend and her girlfriend.

"I should go," she said as she started to rise, but Trina's hands pulled her back down.

"Stop that nonsense. Don't be ridiculous." Trina brushed a hair off her forehead as she inspected her undoubtedly puffy face. "Are you all right?"

"No." Lauren laughed before crying some more.

"Okay, obviously you aren't all right," Trina said, guiding her face up with a gentle touch to her chin. "But I mean, physically, are you hurt?"

"I'm fine," Lauren said.

"Have you eaten?"

Lauren sniffled. "No."

"On it," Kendall said from the kitchen.

Lauren leaned back against the couch and closed her eyes. "The little cooler has perishables in it."

"Lobsters?" Trina asked, and Lauren could hear a smile in her voice, as she felt a blanket draped over her lap.

"Alas, no. I made friends with Cynthia the cheese master when she drove me into town today, and she dropped off a cooler full of Boudreaux farm specialties at the house before my flight."

"Oh, damn. There's cheese, ice cream, yogurt butter...I had no idea yogurt butter was even a thing," Kendall said.

"I think there's some whipped cream in there, too," Lauren said, rubbing her forehead.

"Found it," Kendall replied.

"Good," Lauren said with a yawn. Her eyes hurt from crying, and her head felt so heavy. Today had been the longest day ever.

When she opened her eyes again it was dark out. Well, it had been dark when she'd arrived via the car service from the airport, but now, it was darker. She shifted on the couch and nudged something with her foot.

"You're awake." Trina blinked, sleepy, from her end of the couch.

"What time is it?" Lauren asked, stretching.

"Let me check." Trina reached for her cell phone with a yawn. "Midnight."

"Oh my God, Trina. I'm so sorry." Lauren started to get up. "I didn't mean to crash on your couch."

"It's fine," Trina said, yawning again. "Clearly you needed to rest."

"Which I could have done in my own place," Lauren said, feeling bad again.

"But you came here instead. Which it seems like you needed to do, too." Trina slipped out from underneath their shared blanket and padded into the kitchen. "It's probably too late for wine, but would water suffice with your pizza?"

"Pizza?" Lauren heard the refrigerator open and close.

"Yeah. Kendall ordered your favorite from that place around the corner when you got here. You just didn't last long enough to get it while it was hot." Lauren watched as Trina popped a few cheese slices into the toaster oven. "There's salad, too."

"Oh gosh, Kendall." She looked around, worried she'd find her on the floor.

"Relax," Trina said with a laugh. "She's in bed, probably snoring away."

"Which is exactly what you should be doing," Lauren said.

"And yet I'm making you midnight pizza and going to snuggle right back onto the couch next to you while you tell me why you showed up at my door on a Sunday night in tears with a cooler full of farm goods."

"Cynthia sent the cooler," Lauren replied.

"I do recall you mentioning that. The rocky road ice cream was legit," Trina said patting her belly.

Lauren gave her a look.

"What? I had to eat something while gossiping about you with Kendall. I could only watch you sleep so long before I got bored."

Lauren was horrified.

"I'm kidding." Trina took the now hot pizza out and brought the plate with a glass of water to Lauren. "I ate the ice cream after Kendall went to bed. It's too good to share."

Lauren smiled as she inhaled the smell of her favorite slice. "This cheese pizza is the best in the city."

Trina handed her a napkin. "You're such a weirdo. It's cheese pizza. That's like impossible to fuck up."

"You'd be surprised," she said before taking a bite. "Oh, this is heavenly."

"Good." Trina sat facing her at the other end of the couch with her knees brought up to her chin.

After she finished the second slice and declined a third that Trina offered to warm up, Trina finally asked, "So, are you ready to tell me what's going on?"

Lauren sighed as she placed the empty plate on the table in front of them. "I told Thea I loved her."

"Well, damn. Okay. And?"

"I should probably back up," Lauren said, starting over. "We had a great afternoon on Friday—"

"Ah, the afternoon delight," Trina said.

"Right, except that didn't happen because Thea was at work, and her friend walked in, and"—Lauren shook her head—"that's not the point. She came over that night, and we sort of watched *Clue* but mostly we made out, and then we had, like, the sweetest, most intimate night that we'd ever had. Only to then drag our exhausted asses out of bed to drive up to Maine."

"Where you met up with Faith, right? How'd that go?"

"Well, not great, actually." Lauren frowned. "The guy she brought was kind of a jerk, and then he submitted an offer that was a total lowball."

"Ew," Trina said.

"But before that, I had the most incredible afternoon on the lake with Thea. The sun was setting, and she was perfect, and I realized how much she meant to me. And then I sort of knocked her into the lake and waterlogged her everything, but that was an accident."

Trina whistled. "Classic Lauren."

"I know, right?" Lauren laughed. "Then we had dinner with her family once she dried off, and it was so nice, T. Like, so nice. Her mother and brother are so sweet and lovely, and it never feels like work with them. They eat together for every dinner over there—it's like a small holiday feast nightly. I can't remember the last time I broke bread with my mother."

"With or without Greg and Lainey?" Trina asked.

"Either, really. It's probably been a year." Lauren made a mental note to call her mom. "But being around Thea and her family, it's been so wonderful for so many reasons."

"Because you love her," Trina supplied.

Lauren nodded, sad again. "We went for a walk after dinner and started talking. I knew something had changed the night before, and I knew on the lake how I felt, but we hadn't talked about it yet. Until last night."

"So sexy times and I love yous?" Trina asked with a smile.

"Thea said it first, but only because I was breathless." Lauren bit her lip. "But she took it back this afternoon, so…"

The smile dropped off of Trina's face. "She did what?"

Lauren rubbed her eyes, trying to erase the look on Thea's face when she told her their relationship wasn't going to work anymore. Her words had hurt, but that face seemed to haunt her still. She felt like it might always.

"Hector had another stroke, and the family rushed to the hospital to be with him."

"Oh no," Trina said, looking surprised. "That's awful."

"Yeah, it's pretty serious. He woke up while we were there, but it's still too early to tell how he'll be." She took a breath. "On the way to the hospital, I met up with Faith, and we went over the offer letter. We made the decision to convince Kathleen to list the farm, or at least consider it."

"Because the offer sucked. That's what you should do to drum up some interest to get a counteroffer," Trina replied.

"Right. Well, Thea got wind of it and freaked out. After giving me the cold shoulder all day, she chose to wait until we were in the airport parking lot to tell me that I was being duplicitous and screwing her while planning to sell the farm all along." Lauren got angry. "Which is bullshit, because *I* can't sell the farm, I'm a fucking consultant. And also fuck her for accusing me of sleeping with her to secure the sale of anything."

Trina's mouth opened before closing.

"What?"

"Did she really say that?"

Lauren looked down. "She said that I had betrayed her by encouraging her mother to list the property and acted like I didn't work hard enough to stop it from getting there. And then she walked back her I love you, telling me that last night was a mistake. Then she dumped me, saying she was going to have to stay in Maine now until the sale or the Berry Festival or whatever and that she didn't have time for a relationship with me. Which is fine since she fucking took back an I love you. Who even does that?"

Trina handed her a tissue. Lauren hadn't realized she was crying again.

"Okay," Trina said, scooting closer and placing her hand on Lauren's thigh. "First off, she's clearly under duress with the whole Hector and potential sale thing, but"—she dipped her head to catch Lauren's gaze—"that doesn't give her justification to be a jackass to you or try to break your heart. Which you wear on your sleeve, and anyone with eyes could see that you were in love with her."

Lauren sniffled. "How long did you know?"

Trina contemplated this. "Probably since the night after the softball game. You just seemed different."

"I don't think I knew yet," Lauren said, letting herself briefly remember that night and that lap dance.

"Well, it doesn't matter," Trina said, shaking her head. "What matters is you've been busting your ass to try to save that farm and help that family. And Thea is foolish to let you go."

Lauren exhaled, feeling marginally better. She looked at her friend who was saying all the right things but still had a slightly homicidal look on her face. "You're going to kill her, aren't you?"

"Oh, no doubt," Trina said. "I'm just working out ways to make sure I get away with it. I'm too pretty for prison."

"I love you," Lauren said, glad to have Trina in her corner.

"I love you, too," Trina said as she wrapped an arm around her shoulders before pulling the blanket over them. "What do you say to a quick episode of *The Simpsons* and then a couch sleepover until Kendall wakes us up for work tomorrow with coffee and breakfast?"

"Sounds perfect," Lauren said. Tomorrow was a new day, and for the first time in a few hours, she didn't feel alone going into it.

Chapter Twenty-five

I overnighted your package from work yesterday. They assured me it'd be there by tonight," Avni said.

"Thanks. You're a lifesaver." Thea was grateful now more than ever that Avni was staying at her place. She'd been gracious enough to send along some more clothes for Thea and had even gathered all the remote working equipment she was going to need to do her job from up here. Her boss had been more than understanding, and everyone had been really accommodating over the last two weeks.

"I'm watering all the houseplants, and I even took out the trash this weekend," Avni said.

"Oh, wow. You've become a real domestic goddess," Thea said, impressed.

"I'm killing it at this single life thing."

"Have you heard from Raj?" Thea wanted a distraction from her new venture into singledom. Or really, Thea wanted any distraction from the depression of missing Lauren and her life falling apart.

"Not this week. Maybe he finally got the hint," Avni said. Thea knew he'd called her numerous times after she'd left, but that seemed to have slowly tapered off. "I guess we'll find out if he actually moved out. The lease is up next week."

"What did Mrs. Jenks say?" Avni's across-the-hall neighbor had been reporting information since the day Avni left. She and Avni had gotten close over the years when Avni often took her to medical appointments on her days off. She never took to Raj, so she was more than happy to spy at all times as a favor to Avni.

"Jenksie said his mother was by again last week, but that it'd been quiet since then. Of course she fell asleep in the middle of the day, so she couldn't confirm if he'd actually moved anything out yet. So we'll see." Avni didn't sound nearly as upset or anxious as Thea would have expected.

"Why are you so calm about this?" she asked.

"I guess because I realized it's the right decision. I don't regret it. At all," Avni said. "I mean, I miss my view and my bomb-ass bathroom. No offense," she said.

"None taken." Avni's place was much nicer than hers. She could afford it as a brainy scientist and all, even alone. Thea's place was fine, but it was small. Being back in her childhood home confirmed that. Even her bedroom here was bigger than the one she had in Boston.

"But I'm glad to have a place to stay while this all unfolds. Hopefully he's out next weekend, and I can give you back your space."

"It's your space now," Thea said, not meaning to sound so jaded.

"This is all temporary, Thea," Avni assured her.

"I suppose it is." That's what worried her. Her life felt like it was in complete flux right now.

"How's Hector?" she asked.

"Better each day. Though he had a rough beginning, he's already starting to walk more every time I see him. His daughter moved in with him, so she's taking him to his rehab appointments. He's in good spirits, considering everything that's happened."

"That's good," Avni said before asking, "and how have the property tours been going?"

Thea frowned. "Fine. There's been a lot of interest, actually. It feels like every other day Faith is bringing someone by."

There was a pause. "Have you heard from Lauren?"

Thea sighed. "No. I don't think I'll be hearing from her anytime soon. Or ever again."

"It couldn't have ended that bad," Avni argued. They'd talked about what happened when Lauren left, but Thea had been pretty vague. Mostly because she'd felt guilty about what she'd said. And left unsaid.

"I told her I loved her the night before she left, and then the next day I told her the relationship wasn't going to work," Thea hurried out, feeling ashamed all over again.

Avni was silent.

"Are you there? Did you hear me? This phone cuts out every now and then since it took a bath in the lake. Shit. You're not there, are you? I need a new phone," she rambled.

"I can't believe you," Avni said, her tone serious.

"You *are* there."

"Yes, I'm here. What is wrong with you?" Avni asked.

"I mean, mostly nothing," Thea joked.

"*Wrong*. So much is wrong with you," Avni clucked.

"That's a little harsh," Thea said in defense.

"Not really. I think it's pretty on point." Avni opened and closed something on her side of the line. "You know what? Now I'm mad at you."

"Why?" More opening and closing. "What are you doing?"

"Looking for a fucking bottle opener." Avni sounded pissed.

"The drawer next to the sink by the pans."

"Thank you." The distinctive noise of a bottle cap popping off sounded on the other end of the line. "You're an asshole."

"Are you talking to me or the bottle?" Thea asked, confused.

"You. I can't…Why did you—?" She huffed. "When was the last time you told someone you loved them?"

"You mean, like, besides my mom?"

"Yes, obviously," Avni said.

"Um, I don't know."

"Never," Avni supplied.

"It can't be *never*—that seems ridiculous."

"As ridiculous as you are, you mean."

"Hey," Thea started to argue.

"Listen, I'm going to be blunt with you. That was a shitty thing to do and say to Lauren."

"You don't understand," Thea started. "She told my mother to list the property—"

"Are you done?" Avni was having none of it.

"Yes," Thea said with a frown. She couldn't even listen to herself make excuses anymore. She knew she was wrong. She knew she'd acted out of anger and insecurity, but she had no idea how to fix it. And she was worried she'd lost Lauren forever.

"Regardless of what you think might have happened or what your ego wants to defend you from, the fact of the matter is that you told her you loved her because you do. Right?"

"Yes," Thea said, frowning deeper. "I do."

"And as long as I've known you, I have never, ever heard you be vulnerable and honest with any woman. Especially one you were sleeping with regularly. Because you keep all these walls up and do that sexy, mysterious, tall, dark, and good-looking lesbian thing that you do, and people just get naked in front of you."

"Thank you?" Thea wasn't sure if this was a compliment or the start of more tough love.

"You're welcome. But you fucked up, too. Don't get distracted."

"You're really coming in hard, Avni."

Avni's tone was softer when she said, "Listen to your best friend who's awesome at monogamy and long-term relationships—"

"Until she's not," Thea pointed out.

"Too soon and not the point," Avni replied. "What I was trying to say before you so rudely interrupted me is this—relationships are hard. They take work. But when you put in the work, they can be so incredibly rewarding."

"So what happened between you and Raj, then?"

"I was doing all the work, and he was doing none of it. And I let it get that way. That's on me. He was always who he was, and I just ignored it. But I'm telling you this because you need to hear it—you are the runner here. You got all up in your feelings and overreacted. This is on you."

Thea let that sink in. She'd replayed the events of the night Lauren left over and over, and though she knew she'd been rash, she still in some ways tried to justify her reaction. Now she wasn't so sure those justifications were valid.

"My mother is so mad at me," she admitted. "When she found out I ended things with Lauren, she actually stormed out of the room."

"I bet," Avni said, though she didn't sound unsympathetic. "How did she know?"

"I was a blubbering mess on the front porch after I dropped Lauren off, and Carl ratted me out."

"I always wanted a little brother. Carl's a good guy," Avni said.

"He is." She'd been working side by side with him nonstop these two weeks. She was up at four in the morning and working until six every night with only a short break for lunch in the middle where she did some of her actual Boston-based work while choking down food. Her back hurt, her shoulders ached, and she'd never been so tired, but she was so proud of her brother and the man he'd grown into. He truly had learned every aspect of running this farm from her father and Hector. They'd managed to keep the farm running—it hadn't been easy, but with the remaining workers and her mother, they'd managed. Barely. But they wouldn't have if Carl wasn't so good at this work. "Anyway, she gave me a tissue, then called me a fool and went to bed."

"How are things with her now?" Avni asked.

"Better. She's talking to me, and we're all working together fine. But from time to time I catch her giving me this disappointed look. I know she wants to talk about things, but she hasn't. And I'm a coward, so I'm okay with that."

"Sounds like maybe you aren't okay with it," Avni said.

"Yeah, maybe I'm not," Thea agreed.

"Oh, I have another call. I have to run. Look, it'll all work out. I'm sure of it. But you needed to own your decision and figure out what you want in life. The farm is getting sold. That seems inevitable. But you don't have to be miserable in all avenues of your life. Like, maybe you might want a life to come back to in Boston. Call Lauren."

"Maybe," Thea said noncommittally.

"Just do it. I gotta go. Call me after you talk to her," Avni said.

"Bye," Thea replied, disconnecting the call.

She sat on the porch swing, thinking about everything that had happened over these past few months. She had a good life in Boston. She liked her job and her friends, and she was mostly happy. Mostly. But when her mom called about the farm, everything had changed. Suddenly, the *mostly* happy didn't seem like enough. And when Lauren entered her life, she realized it hadn't been enough. Because with Lauren she was truly happy. Maybe for the first time she could ever remember. And a life knowing that Lauren was out there and not a part of hers seemed bleak. Avni was right—they'd done everything they could to save the farm. The end was inevitable. But maybe the end of her relationship with Lauren didn't have to be, too.

Now if only she could gather up the courage to call her.

CHAPTER TWENTY-SIX

Jax nudged her arm. "Are you in there?"

"What?"

"I said two hilarious things in a row and nothing. Crickets," Jax said rubbing their chin.

"I love that little soul patch—it's adorable," Lauren said.

"I'm going more for sexy than adorable." Jax frowned, looking more adorable.

"It's very sexy," Lauren backtracked. "But also adorable. It can be both."

Jax gave her a look.

"What? It totally goes with the whole image," Lauren said, holding up her hands to frame Jax. "It's very dapper. This suit fits you like a glove, and that fade is tight. And the soul patch is sexy."

"And adorable," Jax said, giving her another look.

"Adorable to me," Lauren reasoned. "But only because I'm so proud of you and I think you're awesome and such a catch—"

"Fine, fine." Jax held up their hand. "I accept your compliment. Thank you."

"You're welcome." Lauren paused. "What were you trying to tell me before?"

"Oh," Jax said, nodding. "Zander said we can start doing walk-throughs of the inside now that all the walls are up. There's still a lot to do, but we can start going over Claire's mock-ups and making sure the spaces match the advertising materials."

"That's great. I still can't believe how fast this place has gone up," Lauren said. It was astonishing really. Ellison had so many people working in rotation on this that her head must be spinning. Not that she ever seemed stressed or even put out by anything. But this was freaking masterful. They were going to be ahead of schedule somehow. Lauren had no idea how she did it.

"I know." Jax stretched. "It's a good thing we've been busting our butts and getting that client information together."

"Seriously." After her initial sad sack night on Trina's couch, Lauren had doubled her focus at work. She'd been working around the clock on the Newbridge project, even managing to close on three of her other sales in the process. Faith had been updating her on the showings in Maine, but Lauren had done her best to remove herself. It was too painful to think about. It was too painful to think about Thea.

Ellison poked her head into the conference room. "Lauren, can I borrow you?"

"Sure." Lauren stood, heading toward the door.

"Oh, Jax," Ellison said with a smile, "Talia is coming by to drop off some new stuff for me in a bit. Can you make sure to greet her?"

Jax was out of their seat so fast, the chair almost tipped. "Absolutely."

"Thanks," Ellison said.

"Talia French, huh?" Lauren said with a smile as she walked into Ellison's office.

Ellison sat at her desk as she nodded. "I noticed Jax tripping over themself when she came by a few months ago. And then I caught Talia giving Jax dressing tips after their top surgery—tips I saw immediately integrated into Jax's wardrobe. I figured putting them in the same room together might lead to something. Seems I'm not wrong." Ellison pointed to her still open office door.

Lauren leaned to the right to see Talia smiling shyly as she handed Jax the garment bags. Jax was standing tall, adjusting their lapels as they talked. The body language between these two was beyond cute. They were so into each other. Trina was gonna love this.

"Wow. You've got matchmaking in that arsenal of yours, too?" Lauren whistled. "Boss bitch indeed."

Ellison laughed. "I'll leave the matchmaking up to the professionals. Let's just say I pay attention to people, and I saw two people that had interest in each other." She paused. "Speaking of paying attention, I wanted to talk to you about the Boudreaux property."

Lauren tried to keep the smile she had plastered on her face even though her instinct was to frown. "What's up?"

"I wanted to commend you on the work you've been doing with Faith. She's told me that you have been instrumental in helping her prepare the property for sale and that your creativity has led to some new avenues for her to pursue. That's high praise from someone with such incredible attention to detail like Faith."

"Thank you," Lauren said, feeling proud. She'd given Faith all of her ideas for the property, including its potential viability for commercial farming. Which was an idea that Thea had brought to her attention. "She seems pretty amazing all on her own, though, honestly."

"She is." Ellison leaned back in her chair. "She called a few minutes ago to let us know that they received a serious offer today from a developer. A good one. They're going to show it to that Egbert fellow and see if he'll counter. But this offer will afford them the opportunity to break even."

"Oh. That's, uh, great." Lauren meant that. But she also knew what that meant.

Ellison watched her for a moment. "You aren't happy about this."

"I am," Lauren said. "I'm sure Kathleen will be relieved that she can start with a clean slate."

"But maybe Thea isn't so happy about it?" Ellison asked and Lauren froze. "In addition to complimenting your creative sales approach, Faith mentioned that you seemed more invested in the farm and the Boudreaux family than she was anticipating. Namely, that you and Thea seemed to have a connection."

Lauren swallowed, unsure of what to say.

Ellison leaned forward. "Is she wrong?"

"No." Lauren had been dreading Ellison finding out that she and Thea were an item, but since they weren't anymore, maybe that wasn't such a big deal. "But things have changed, so that's less of an issue now."

"Is it?" Ellison asked, though her tone wasn't challenging.

"If you're asking if I can remain professional and still do my job even if we did have a connection—granted, one that is in the past— then yes. I am capable of that," Lauren replied honestly. At least, she hoped she was being honest.

"I don't worry about you in that regard," Ellison said, her expression compassionate. "I only worry about you in regard to you."

"What do you mean?" Lauren asked.

"Do you know why I asked you to consult on this for me?"

"To prove I won't fuck up the Newbridge account?"

Ellison laughed.

"And because I'm creative, and you needed a creative solution.

Because I think outside the box. But I didn't do that here," Lauren said with a frown. "We've gone by the book all the way, and we've still ended up in the position of having to sell the farm for minimal profit for the Boudreauxs. So minimal that they won't be able to carry on their legacy or their livelihood or even keep their house. So"—Lauren sighed—"basically I failed at the one job you gave me, and if you want to hand all of Newbridge over to Jax, I'd understand. They certainly deserve it."

Ellison shook her head. "You deserve it. And you deserve to be happy, too." She stood, walking to the opposite side of her desk. She perched on the edge of it in front of Lauren's chair. "You haven't failed at anything. You did exactly what I needed you to do, and you've shown yourself to be the hard worker and the talent that I knew you to always be. Faith sees it. Kathleen sees it and trusts you. And I see it. I've always seen it.

"Without you hustling and advising and adding your expertise to the conversation, they might not have found a buyer at all. They might have lost the property to foreclosure, and the legacy still would have been lost. But now they have the chance to walk away debt-free with a fresh start. And sure, it's not the fairy tale we might have hoped for, but it's far from a failure."

She sat next to Lauren in the empty seat, turning her body to face her as she said, "Did I ever tell you about CJ Boudreaux and the chance he took on me?"

"No," Lauren said. She'd been more than curious, but Ellison kept lots of things close to the vest, only revealing what was necessary. She had figured whatever it was that connected her to that farm was for her and her alone to know.

"I grew up a town over from Casterville. My mother and I were alone, and she worked hard to make sure I had every opportunity. But when I was old enough to work, I had to. There was no other way for us to survive." Ellison gave her a sad smile, and Lauren couldn't picture Ellison being impoverished, ever. The woman who sat before her was the picture of success. She had no idea Ellison'd had such humble beginnings.

"CJ Boudreaux hired me when no one else would. I was gangly and awkward and inexperienced. But I was willing to work hard, and though I lacked the natural talent that some of his other workers had, I showed up early and stayed late. Because CJ told me something once that I never forgot. He told me he took a chance on hiring me because he could see I had a drive and a fire. And he told me that hard work beats talent when talent doesn't work."

Ellison briefly touched Lauren's forearm. "You are hardworking *and* you are swimming in natural talent. You're the whole package. You put everyone at ease the minute they meet you, and you're damn good at what you do. That's why I asked for your help. You *are* hard work and talent. And you can't lose because of it."

Lauren let that sink in. Ellison had had faith in her all along, even when she'd doubted herself. Even when she'd let her emotions around Thea cloud her judgment and make her feel insecure.

"And even if there is something brewing between you and Thea, I never question the choices you'll make. Because you've made the right ones all along, and you always will," Ellison said.

"Thank you," Lauren said, feeling honored that Ellison thought so highly of her. She also felt like she needed to clarify something. "In the interest of full disclosure, I'd already slept with Thea before I met Kathleen or knew Thea had any connection to a dairy farm in Maine that would suddenly consume my entire world."

"The night at The Mirage, right? After the award ceremony?" Ellison asked. "Jax sort of told me by accident."

"Traitor," Lauren said, looking back at Jax and Talia laughing in the room beyond.

"Go easy on them," Ellison said. "It was an honest mistake. They were really worried I was sending you to Maine to fire you."

Lauren laughed. "Weren't we all?" She watched Jax and Talia for a moment more, and her heart hurt as her mind wandered briefly to Thea. "They're going to be a gorgeous couple."

"That they will," Ellison said. "She's stunning like her aunt. And so smart and talented, too."

"Her aunt?" Lauren asked.

"Faith," Ellison said with a small smile.

Lauren looked back at Talia and could see it now—the perfect complexion and unbelievably beautiful arms and shoulders. And that style. "Ah, that explains why Faith has such awesome clothes."

"All Talia specials," Ellison said. "When Talia got out of fashion school and moved to Boston, Faith asked me to give her a chance as a personal stylist while she immersed herself in the fashion business. It was an easy decision and one I've never regretted. Talia is incredible."

"Like her aunt," Lauren said, picking up on more than just admiration.

Ellison said nothing, but her smile said everything. If Faith had noticed something between her and Thea, Lauren figured it was because she knew what to look for. She'd been coy about how she knew Ellison—maybe that was because there was something there. Lauren knew Ellison was into women and had been married to a woman in the past, but she kept her personal life very private. This was like a glimpse behind the curtain. Lauren had to know more.

"So, you grew up a poor country girl, in the sticks of Maine, and you"—she took a stab in the dark—"somehow managed to date the prettiest girl in school before becoming a luxury real estate tycoon and general badass?"

"Oh, she wouldn't date me until after school ended. But that was the best summer of my life," Ellison said, and Lauren believed her. "We weren't meant for forever, but we've managed to stay friends through all of life's little challenges."

"Just friends?" Lauren hoped for Ellison's sake there was more there. Faith was hot. And charming. And hot.

"Mostly." Ellison gave her a wink. "Don't tell Talia—she'll be mortified."

Lauren crossed her heart and made a zipping motion over her lips. "Your secret is safe with me."

"Thank you." Ellison's cell rang on the desk. She checked it briefly before silencing it. "That's Zander. I should probably take that."

"I'll leave you to it," Lauren said, excusing herself.

"Thank you for everything," Ellison said as Lauren made it toward her office door. "I'm so grateful that we'll be able to help the Boudreauxs find closure. That wouldn't have happened without you— I'm sure of it."

Lauren nodded, still not feeling right about them losing their legacy and livelihood. Maybe some space between her and the project would help her feel better. Maybe once the sale was finalized, her gut would stop aching so much.

"Oh, and I hope if whatever was going on between you and Thea is meant to work out, that it does. Because I meant what I said before— you deserve to be happy, too."

"Thanks," Lauren said but she wasn't so sure that Ellison was right about this one. She wasn't sure about anything regarding Thea anymore. And that made that pit of her stomach feel even deeper.

CHAPTER TWENTY-SEVEN

Thea had never been this tired. Not once in her entire life could she recall another time when everything hurt this much and she had this little energy to focus on anything else. The ache in her back and shoulder muscles was so constant, it was almost numbing. If it wasn't so fucking uncomfortable.

She popped two more Tylenol and walked out to the porch swing to think. She'd go to bed soon, another early night, out of necessity. And she'd go to bed alone. Another night, out of stubbornness. And location. There weren't exactly a million women into women up here, but also, she had no interest in just any woman anyway. She only had interest in one woman. And she was too much of a coward to reach out to her like Avni had demanded she do. Instead she filled her days and nights with as much busywork as possible, until the sun went down and her body quit. Like right now, as she sat battered and exhausted, even the swinging of the porch swing brought her no comfort.

"You used to help me think, but now all you do is force me to remember," she said to the swing, recalling her time here with Lauren. "I'm going to have to find a new place to collect my thoughts."

The irony of that statement was that she'd have to find a new place regardless. Her mother had sat her and Carl down today and told them that the Egbert guy was currently in a bidding war with some luxury condo builder. It was just a matter of time before they settled on a deal and the farm was demolished for something shiny and new. The porch swing was about to be a part of her past, just like her time here with Lauren.

Lauren—who filled her mind all day and all night. She stalked her dreams and stole her heart over and over. And yet, Thea had let her slip away.

"You threw her out, dumbass," she said to herself. Because slipping away was too gentle a description of what had happened. And as the days between that night and now grew in number and those until the end of her life here grew fewer, Thea was panicking.

She placed her hand on her heart and swore she could feel it falter. The beats weren't strong and deliberate. They were sluggish and tired. Like she was. Like a heart that had lost its reason to beat.

She picked up her phone and drafted a text, like she had a million times before. But just like before, she deleted it before sending it. Her life was a mess right now. What good would reaching out to Lauren do? She was in no place to be in any sort of a relationship, and why would Lauren even consider taking her back? She'd been a first-class asshole. Avni had been right. And yet she hoped above hope that maybe Lauren could forgive that. Because her heart didn't beat like it used to now that she'd given a piece of it to Lauren. And she didn't want it to. Because she wanted Lauren. And she knew that.

She loaded Twitter to distract herself from all the feelings when a text from Shelly White interrupted her mindless scrolling.

Sorry you missed the game tonight. They're going to the finals! Here's your girl making a killer save.

The video that came through showed Lauren making a diving catch at third and the bench erupting in cheers. Thea smiled. The athleticism of the catch was truly remarkable. But the fist pump and victory dance Lauren did after the catch were what Thea loved the most. It was *so* Lauren. How did she manage to be dorky and sexy at the same time?

Thea watched the clip about a dozen times before she made up her mind. This weekend was the Berry Festival. And though it was normally a joyous time, this year it was bittersweet. Even more so without Lauren here to share it. It was now or never. She'd never forgive herself if she didn't try.

❖

"You were an animal tonight," Claire said as she patted her shoulder.

Lauren winced. "Oof," she said as she reapplied the instant ice pack from the training bag they kept in the dugout for emergency collisions and general clumsiness. It was already warm. She needed something colder for her shoulder and something stronger in her glass.

"Oh, sorry," Claire said with a frown. "But still, amazing catch."

"Thanks." Lauren was proud of herself. Considering how the week had started out, things had been going really well. And tonight was no different. She was glad to be back at The Mirage with Claire and Shelly, unwinding after a big win.

"Back to the state finals again," Claire said, beaming. "Champions again, too. I just know it."

"I wouldn't hate that." Lauren would be happy for more successful, positive distractions.

"Where's that winner I know and love?" Trina's voice was a welcome sound.

"Here." Lauren foolishly raised her hand, paying for it immediately. "Sonofa—"

"I'm back with fresh ice and an even fresher lemon drop." Shelly showed up like an adorkable knight in shining armor, wielding what Lauren needed most in the world.

"My shero," Lauren said, taking a large sip before discarding the warm pack and replacing it with the freezing ice bag. "Damn, this is cold."

"That's the point, right?" Trina shrugged off her jacket and joined them at the tall bar top. "What happened this time? Helga from Osterville try to take you out?"

"She would never. She learned her lesson last time," Lauren joked.

"That sore shoulder was earned fair and square when Lauren caught the game-winning final out off a pop fly. No big deal or anything," Shelly said as she pulled out her phone to show something to Trina.

"You recorded that?" Lauren said, leaning over to see the screen.

"I record everything," Shelly said. "I test out all my new gadgets at your games."

"Damn, girl. That's some catch," Trina said, looking impressed.

"Don't worry, I've already forwarded it to all necessary media outlets and fangirls," Shelly said as she kissed Claire on the cheek.

"Fangirls?" Lauren said with a laugh.

"Yeah. I figured Thea would want to see it since she wasn't there tonight," Shelly said, and Lauren choked on her lemon drop.

"You did what?" she managed out between coughs. Trina ineffectively patted her on the back, making her shoulder hurt.

Claire let out a low whistle, and Shelly looked between them.

"I did something wrong, didn't I?" Shelly asked.

"I mean, it was thoughtful. You were being thoughtful," Claire said as she squeezed Shelly's hand.

"Uh-oh. That's not good." Shelly looked at Lauren. "Why wasn't Thea at the game tonight?"

"Because I had her killed," Trina muttered into her cosmo before flashing a bright smile to a mortified looking Shelly. "I didn't really. Not yet. She can have her Berry Festival first."

Lauren rubbed her forehead as she chuckled, trying to focus on Trina's humor and not the hurt that came with the admission. "We broke up, Shel."

"Oh, I'm sorry to hear that." Shelly frowned. "And I'm doubly sorry I sent her that video."

"It's okay—your heart was in the right place," Lauren said, holding no grudges about it. Part of her hoped Thea was sad to have missed the game. A part of her hoped Thea missed her in general. Because she sure as hell missed Thea. But she wasn't sure what there was left to say about the topic. Thea had made herself clear—Lauren was not what she wanted.

Trina touched her lower back as she guided the conversation into happier, lighter matters, and Lauren was grateful for her bestie. She didn't want to let tonight's big win get bogged down with memories of Thea. And she knew that Trina would make sure of that.

By the time Lauren keyed into her place, it was late—much later than she'd anticipated getting home. But tonight was a night for celebrating. Not just the softball win, but the past few weeks. Because even though her romantic life was in shambles, her professional one was soaring for the first time in a long time. The Newbridge project was coming together without incident, and she'd even heard from Ellison that Egbert was in a bidding war with a developer for the Boudreaux property. That was good news for Kathleen. And Thea, by extension.

Lauren dropped her keys on the kitchen island as she rubbed her shoulder. It was significantly less sore after two rounds of martinis and enough ice to build an igloo, but she knew she'd be hurting tomorrow. A nice hot shower before bed would surely take some of tomorrow's pain away today, so she stripped as she walked, heading toward her en suite.

She looked at herself in the mirror as she waited for the water to warm up. She had a smudge of dust by her forehead from the game, and her french braid was starting to come undone. She was still cute, though, and she smiled at that. Getting drinks with her friends tonight had been the right decision. She was glad she'd gone out, even if she was a little dirty from the game.

She stepped into the hot shower and let out a happy sigh as she rolled her neck and let the water wash over her. This felt great. Her shoulder momentarily protested the contrasting temperature from the hours of icing, but soon, that relaxed as well, and the nagging background anxiety of Thea and the farm's sale drifted away along with the ache in her shoulder, all lulled by the heat of the water on her naked skin. She stood under the water after showering away the grime of the game, leaning her forearms on the tiled wall before her. She blinked open her eyes as the water ran down her back, and a flash of Thea crossed her mind. They'd made excellent use of this shower wall together. And though that felt like a distant memory, her lower stomach tightened at the vividness of it. She could practically feel Thea's mouth on her neck and her hands moving over her possessively before pleasuring her thoroughly. This shower was full of sexy, naughty memories of Thea, and Lauren sighed again, this time in sadness.

"Well, it was good while it lasted," she said to herself as she shut off the faucet and stepped into the steam-filled bathroom beyond the shower. She grabbed a towel and dried her body before wrapping up her hair to get it off her back. She slipped on the terry cloth robe on the back of her door as she made her way into her bedroom.

She stepped toward her bedside table to check her cell phone when the screen lit up before her. It was a text message. And it was from Thea.

She paused, her hand hovering in midair as she contemplated what to do next. She couldn't see the full text, but the brief notification window revealed the words *I'm sorry* and *I miss you.* Lauren's heart rate picked up as she reread the words on the screen, still unsure of whether she wanted to read any more. Thea missed her.

"It's just a text. What can it hurt to check it out?" Why did she need a pep talk to open a damn text? After another moment, she nodded, feeling ready. "Okay, let's just see what she has to say."

After swiping the screen to unlock it, Lauren found a sweet and thoughtful message waiting for her.

I hate the way things ended and I know I'm to blame for that. I'm sorry. I miss you. I miss your voice and your smile and your touch. And I miss how much being with you made every moment feel so full and alive. I have a lot going on in my life right now and I know it's selfish to expect you to understand that, but I hope that maybe you'll be open to talking at some point. If you're okay with that. I'd really like the chance to redeem myself.

Lauren reread the text a few times as she sat at the edge of her bed. Though she wholly disagreed with Thea's dismissal of her the last time she'd saw her, she did understand that emotions had been running high for her. Not that that was an excuse for her to be so freaking rude, but— *I'm sorry. And I miss you. So, so much. I'm so sorry.*

Thea's second text broke her heart. Before she could stop herself, she swiped the screen again, and soon Thea's voice was on the line.

"Hi."

"How sorry are you really?" Lauren asked as she leaned back on her bed, her heart seeming to beat in her throat.

"The sorriest I've ever been. At least the most *sincerely* sorry I've ever been. I'll admit to being really sorry after I got caught borrowing my dad's work truck freshman year in high school before I got my license. But that was a hugely different kind of sorry."

Lauren smiled at the visual of young Thea trying to discreetly motor off in a noisy pickup truck, of all things. "What did you steal the truck for?"

"There was a party in the cornfield behind the old high school." Thea chuckled. "Wow. Saying that out loud makes me realize how much of a farm girl I actually am." She let out a low whistle. "On second thought, you shouldn't accept my apology. I'm a loser."

"You're not a loser," Lauren said. "Maybe just a country bumpkin."

Thea laughed. "That's fair. So, what do you say? Do you accept the apology of a foolishly rash and overly stubborn country bumpkin? Because I meant what I said. I have never been sorrier in my life than watching you walk away from me that night."

"Do you mean that?" Lauren wanted nothing more than for that to be true.

"More than anything I have ever said. Except telling you I love you. That moment was special. And it still is. That was real."

Lauren brushed a tear from her cheek, glad to be in the privacy of her bedroom for this conversation. Thea had really hurt her, in part, she realized, because she felt so strongly about her. Things weren't perfect between them, and she knew they had definite work to do to recover what they'd lost, but she was willing to try. She wanted to try. Because she loved her, too. And something Ellison had said earlier had stayed with her—she deserved to be happy. And with Thea, she really was.

"Okay."

"Okay? As in you accept my apology?" Thea asked, sounding hopeful.

"I do."

Thea let out a long exhale. Lauren could hear the smile in her voice when she replied, "You are everything I've ever wanted. And I probably don't deserve you."

"Probably," Lauren teased, though Thea had her swooning once again.

Thea's laughter was a melodious sound. Lauren settled back on the bed, feeling lighter.

"How have you been?" Thea asked, her voice soft.

"Busy. Work has been a lot."

"Yeah, I know that feeling. The farm and my full-time job have been my only mistresses of late. Early mornings, late nights, no sleep. I much prefer my sleepless nights to be because of you."

"Always the charmer," Lauren said, though she loved it.

"Only for you," Thea said before adding, "oh, I got the video from tonight. Looks like you had a great game."

"Is that why you messaged me?" she asked, curious.

"I mean, that catch was beyond sexy. But no, I had drafted and deleted that text to you a hundred times over the past week. Today was just the day I finally built up the courage to be let down. If it came to that."

"Lucky for you, it didn't," Lauren replied.

"I'm feeling very lucky at the moment, yes," Thea said, the low timbre of her voice lulling Lauren into a yawn. "You sound tired—do you have to go?"

"I am tired," she admitted. "But I'm in no rush to get off."

"Really? Because the Lauren I know and love is always in a rush to *get off*." Thea's tone was teasing.

"Oh no. Don't start with that. Just because I'm lying in bed postshower, nearly naked save for this very soft robe, doesn't mean you can start in with the innuendos and try to seduce me. We're working back toward sexy times and sweet lady kisses. No phone sex for you tonight." It wasn't lost on Lauren that Thea had told her she loved her again.

"Well, that visual certainly does nothing to keep my mind out of the gutter," Thea said. There was a pause. "Are you above or below the covers?"

"Thea," Lauren complained.

"Fine, fine," Thea agreed. "But you should know I'm currently replicating that particularly salacious picture of me that you have on your phone."

Lauren didn't have to pull up the image to recall it. Though she hadn't looked at it since that night, she was sure she'd remember that sight until she went to her grave. "Is that so?"

"It is. Of course, I'm in my childhood bedroom, alone with the Biebs. But I'm a lot less lonely now."

Lauren warmed at that. She loosened the tie on her robe and shifted, revealing a bit of cleavage as she snapped a selfie. She fired it off to Thea before saying, "Now you're not alone."

"This is my new favorite picture," Thea said.

Lauren sent her one of her favorite pictures of the two of them on the lake. "Even more than this one?"

"Nope. I take it back. This is my favorite picture."

"Mine, too," she admitted. This photo she *had* looked back at several times since they'd broken up. It hurt just as much each time. She wasn't ready to move forward completely. They really needed to talk some more, but she wasn't sure she had it in her tonight. She yawned again. "I'm serious about needing some time to feel comfortable hopping back into bed with you, though. You really did hurt me."

"I get that. And I hope that my flirting doesn't make you feel like I'm being out of line. I think I'm still a little nervous about how things are between us, and flirting is just comfortable and easy. With you, I mean. I haven't been flirting with anyone else. I didn't mean—" Thea sighed. "I'm rambling. The point is, I get it. And I know. I'm so sorry. I think I'll always be sorry," Thea said, sounding sincere. "I'm willing to take this at any speed you feel comfortable with."

"Thank you." Lauren was having a hard time keeping her eyes open.

"Go to sleep. Call me when you're free, if you want to catch up. No pressure. I'll be here waiting, when you're ready."

"Hey, Thea?" Lauren said as she slipped beneath the covers, settling into the soft sheets.

"Yeah, babe? What's up?"

"Will you stay on the line with me until I fall asleep?" Lauren wasn't sure why she wanted that so badly. But she did.

"Of course. Good night, love." Thea's voice sounded softer and farther away than before.

"Good night."

CHAPTER TWENTY-EIGHT

"Hector, you look great!" Thea was shocked to see him walking outside with his walker. He almost looked like his old self. He was truly a miracle man.

"Thanks," Hector said with his signature squinty grin. "She's a real taskmaster. No rest for the weary," he said, nodding toward his daughter.

Christine gave him a look. "You'll get nowhere sitting around watching HGTV, Dad."

"You're right. I've got a farm to help run," Hector said, looking as earnest as ever.

Thea kept the smile on her face even though that comment threatened to cripple her. Tonight was the start of the Berry Festival weekend, and by Monday morning, she knew her mother was going to sign the farm away. Hector would be displaced with the rest of them. And though they'd been as transparent with him as possible, he insisted on being hopelessly optimistic that they'd find a way to save the farm at the last moment. Thea wanted to soak up that optimism, but she'd walked in on her mother crying too many times the last few nights to have any flicker of hope left. It was over. This was their last Berry Festival, and Hector would do well to accept that, too.

"Hector," she started, and his daughter looked away. She was just as emotional as any of them. Christine had spent her summers on this farm. Thea had watched her grow up here. They all had memories on this soil.

"It's not Monday yet," Hector said, pushing his walker and swinging his left leg to complete his now altered gait. He struggled to maintain the walker's upright position now that his left hand worked even less than before, but he managed. He always seemed to make the best of whatever was thrown his way. This was just one more example of that. "We have the weekend to enjoy every moment. I intend to."

Thea nodded. That's all any of them could do, she supposed. "You'll be by the booth tonight?"

"Not even a stroke could keep me away," he said.

"Thank you for staying on and making sure we didn't foul this place up after Dad died. We couldn't have done it without you," Thea said, getting emotional.

Hector shifted his walker toward her and took a strong, confident step in her direction. "This farm is my life. And you and your family are, too. It's not over yet. Let's have the best Berry Festival ever."

She closed the distance between them to place a kiss on his cheek. "We love you. So much."

"And I love you, too."

She embraced him gingerly, careful to respect his altered balance as she let out a sigh that felt like it came from her soul. This was the beginning of her closure. She could feel it.

"Okay, enough mushy stuff. Someone has to double- and triple-check the inventory for the booth. And Carl is awful at math, so that means I'm up."

Hector wiped a tear from his eye with his right hand as Christine helped him stabilize. "You're right about that. Don't let him be the final word on what's on the truck, or you'll be missing all the ice cream."

"Aye, aye, Captain." She saluted him. "I'll see you tonight."

He gave her a wave before refocusing and trying to walk down his paved driveway toward the dirt path between their houses. She watched him for a few moments, in awe of his determination and strength. No battle had ever come easily for Hector, yet he always seemed to prevail.

She headed back toward the barn to do one last sweep of the general store section to see if she'd forgotten anything. They would be selling off the remaining T-shirts, sweaters, and hats tonight. She knew they'd sell out—everyone in town knew about their situation by now. And everyone would want a piece of history to remember the Boudreaux place by. She and Carl had picked out their favorite pieces and tucked them away. But folding them and putting them into her dresser drawers had been excruciating.

"Thanks, Faith. Will we see you this weekend?" Her mother descended the stairs from the offices with her cell phone pressed firmly to her ear. "Great. See you then."

Thea leaned against the wooden bar top her grandfather had carved from a downed tree at the edge of their property. The remainder of the tree made up their dining room table and the island in their kitchen. She wondered if she could take this counter with her when they sold the farm. She'd spent every moment not in school manning this counter and selling ice cream or butter or cream. She'd even carved her initials under the cash register after one particularly bold night in her late teens. That meant this counter was hers, right?

"What did Faith have to say?" she asked as her mother gave her a quick kiss.

"She sent along the two final offers. I'm to choose one and sign off on it. Then the sale process can begin." She looked weary. "It won't happen overnight, thankfully. That will give us time to find somewhere to land."

Thea hated that idea. "Do you know which offer you plan to accept?"

Her mother shook her head. "Faith and Ellison weighed in with their opinions, but I have a call out to Lauren. I'd like her input as well."

Thea perked up at that. "You called Lauren?"

Her mother gave her a look. "Well, I wasn't going to die waiting for you to come to your senses and call her."

Thea hopped up on the counter with a grin. "For your information, we've talked every day this week."

Her mother paused, looking shocked. "Really?"

"Really," Thea said with a nod. "I called and apologized for being a total ass, and we're working it out."

Her mother put her hand on her hip, looking pleased. "Good."

"That's it? Just good?" Thea felt like there was more there.

Her mother shrugged. "She's wonderful. You were a fool to let her go. Maybe if she's fool enough to take you back, you'll do better this time around."

"Ouch, Mom." Thea put her hand over her heart, wounded. "Have you no faith in me?"

"Oh, please. I have all the faith in the world in you," her mother said as she patted her arm. "I just have no faith in your ability to hold on to a good woman."

"Mom."

"I'm kidding." Her mother gave her a sly smile. "I'm glad to hear you're working it out."

"Thanks," Thea said, blushing.

"Is she coming up for the weekend?" her mother asked, and Thea frowned.

"I don't think so. She's got a big project she's working on in Boston. And her softball team is in the state championships." Though Thea wanted nothing more than to have Lauren here, she knew she didn't have the right to ask her to drop everything and show up. She'd lost that right when she'd let her walk away at the airport.

Her mother matched her frown as she caressed her cheek. "I'm sorry, honey."

"Are we ready? I want to get there early," Carl called out from the opening of the barn, looking frantic. And surprisingly dapper.

"You showered, shaved, put product in your hair, and are wearing new boots?" Thea shook her head. "Wowza. What a stud."

"Shut up." Carl toed the dirt before seeming to think better of that. He dusted off his new steel toed boot and stood up, fixing his shirt. "I have a date with Annie tonight."

Thea looked at his shirt and cocked her head. That was new, too. And the jeans, as well. Come to think of it, she'd never seen her brother look so put together. "When did you learn to dress yourself so well?"

Carl looked everywhere but at her face. "Since Lauren taught me my color wheel and helped me pick out my outfit for the night."

Thea's jaw dropped. "You've been talking to Lauren this whole time, too?"

Carl looked nervous. "I mean, just because you screwed things up didn't mean I had to give up Lauren, too. Right? She's kind of awesome."

"You two had no confidence in me. None." Thea couldn't believe the betrayal.

They both shrugged.

"We like her," her mother said.

"A lot," Carl added.

"We're talking again," Thea said, waving her hands in frustration. "I didn't totally blow it, guys. Jeez."

Carl looked relieved. "Oh, good. Because I really wanted her opinion on which jacket to pair with these boots."

Thea laughed, hopping off the counter to throw her arm around her brother's shoulders. "You could have asked me, you know. I do okay with the ladies."

"Lauren's a keeper, that's for sure." Carl elbowed her ribs. "But I can't rely on leather jackets and smoldering looks alone."

She pushed him as she said, "You're such an expert, huh?"

He gave her a broad smile. "I've been trained by the best."

"Stop fighting—we're going to be late." Her mother clucked as she walked past. "Don't forget to lock up. I'll meet you at the truck in five." She paused before disappearing to add, "I think you look great, honey. Lauren gave you terrific advice."

"Thanks, Mom," Carl called out before sticking his tongue out at Thea.

Her family loved Lauren as much as she did. There was nothing better than that. "Hey, I'm glad you're in your own boots now. They look good on you."

Carl gave her a nod. "Lauren told me I couldn't spend my whole life in Dad's shoes. She said I had to walk the world in my own boots, and that I'd find my way easier that way. The more I wear them, the more I think she was right about that."

Thea's heart swelled. "She's pretty great, huh?"

"She is," Carl said before motioning toward the truck. "Let's get on the road. I want to be ready for Annie."

"Okay, Romeo."

Thea gave one last look inside the barn before flicking off the light and closing the door, not sure how many more opportunities she'd have to do just that.

"I'm going to be late," Lauren complained, looking at the clock on the dash for the millionth time.

"You're not. You can't be late to a festival. It's, like, all weekend long." Trina's voice over her Bluetooth sounded much calmer than Lauren felt.

She switched lanes as she glanced at the GPS. "You say that like this isn't a giant romantic leap or something."

"Is it?" Trina asked. "I mean, she's been telling you she loves you every night you talk to her. I suppose you have to decide when you're going to start saying it back. Is that why you're nervous?"

Trina was right. Lauren and Thea had talked every night for the past week—even texting occasionally throughout the day—but Lauren couldn't bring herself to return the phrase Thea expressed so easily. She loved talking to Thea and she was glad they'd reconnected. But she wasn't ready to put herself out there yet. Not fully. Though, driving up to the Berry Festival to surprise her sort of spoke volumes, she supposed.

"It's not that I don't love her—"

"Oh, I know, girl. I have never seen you so gaga over any woman before. Let's not pretend here. It's just about the time and the place, right? Getting back to that groove you two had."

That was what Lauren was worried about. Their flirtations had been brewing to the point of near explicitness all week. She'd had to repeatedly walk them back to the line of friendly-with-feelings and not full-fledged phone sex. "I'm afraid I'm going to see her and just jump her on the spot."

"You two do seem to be rather combustible. I, for one, am thoroughly enjoying the recaps after the fact. But that's probably selfish, huh?" Trina teased.

"Being compatible in the bedroom has never been the issue." Lauren had never been with anyone like Thea. Somehow, even while talking about the most mundane things, Lauren found herself wanting to touch and taste Thea. Something that this long-distance phone relationship was making difficult. That was part of the reason she wanted to see her this weekend, because she missed her. But she also knew how important and emotional this weekend was going to be for the entire Boudreaux family. She just hoped she hadn't made the wrong judgment call and that her arrival would be a negative reminder of the impending sale. "What if seeing me just makes things worse? I guess I'm afraid of getting hurt."

Trina was quiet for a moment. "You told me back when I was figuring out things with Kendall that taking a leap was the only way to know if the risk was ever worth it in the beginning. When she dropped that gift off for Henry and left that note, you were the one that told me to call her and give her a chance to explain herself. That wasn't a decision I might have come to entirely on my own."

"Yeah, but you're much more of a gambler than me. That was sound advice for Trina. Maybe not so much for me."

"Why? Because you don't wear your heart on your sleeve? Because you do. Or because you're weak? Because you aren't. We work in the business of bold, luxurious leaps. Don't bet against yourself, Lauren. You're worth everything you want in this world. The gamble isn't on whether Thea is the right person, the gamble is on whether you think you're worth it. And I'm your best friend—who is never wrong, I might add—and I say you are. You are worth the leap. And I think Thea knows that." She paused. "At least, she better."

"Or you'll kill her?" Lauren asked, knowing her friend was all talk.

"Maybe just injure her. You're my girl, I gotchu."

"Thanks, T."

"Don't sweat it." The distinct sound of a bottle being uncorked sounded in the background.

"Celebrating tonight with your favorite cab sav?" Lauren asked as she took the exit off the interstate toward the back roads leading to Casterville.

"I had a good week. And suddenly, my girlfriend is no longer filling in for my bestie during her state championship softball game. So my evening plans have taken on a much sexier agenda."

"I owe her a million thanks for volunteering." Lauren had found out yesterday that their game had been pushed. It seemed that the field they usually used for their games was rented out for some film, and the production had run long. The game was rescheduled until next week, which was more than fine by Lauren. Graciously, Kendall had offered to sub for her so they wouldn't be short a player, since they were already barely filling the roster slots. Lauren secretly had hoped that if it went well, Kendall would take Kelly's old spot and join the team on a more permanent basis. That would mean more Trina on the sidelines and more cocktails at The Mirage afterward. Both of which were highlights, if you asked her. "I still can't believe how easily she agreed."

"She was thrilled. She must miss all those old tennis-playing, richy-rich days at the club," Trina joked. "I have to admit, I love the outfit on her. It's so *sporty*. I'm certainly down with seeing her bring some of her competitive nature to the softball field. I'm getting hot just thinking about it."

"You two are quite the pair," Lauren said, glad for her friend. "And we're still down a player. So work on convincing her to join for the finals, anyway. I can't be the only one making sure Helga from Osterville is eating dirt."

"I'm on it."

"So, is tonight the night?" Lauren asked as she turned on her high beams. She had reached the portion of the drive that was much less lit and much more animal filled.

"I think so." In rare form, Trina sounded a little nervous.

"You know she's going to say yes. Right?"

"What if she doesn't?" Trina sounded like she was pacing now.

"Well, ask her about the more permanent softball position first. You know, in case it goes badly."

"Lauren."

"I'm kidding," Lauren reassured her. "She's never at her apartment anymore. Asking her to move in with you is the financially responsible thing. Besides the fact that you two are madly and insufferably in love with each other. That's reason enough to live together."

"She doesn't need to save any money, Lau. She's a Yates." Trina seemed unconvinced.

"Okay, fine. But think about how many more Birkins you can get if you have someone helping with the mortgage."

"The Fall line is promising to be a banger, that's for sure."

"Right. But again—madly and insufferably in love. You always want to fall asleep beside her and wake up next to her, right?"

"I do."

"Then tonight is the night." Lauren was proud of Trina. She'd come a long way in the years that she'd known her, but the growth she'd seen in her last year, with Kendall, was exponential. Trina had always been warm and protective and loving toward her, but now that Kendall was in her life, she shared so much more of that version of herself with others.

"Okay. She's going to be here any minute. I have to go and...I don't know, light candles or something."

Lauren laughed. "Just get naked and hold out a key. I'm sure that will be romantic enough. And much less flammable."

"I like the way you think," Trina said, sounding more confident.

"You bought her a fancy key ring, didn't you?" Lauren asked, knowing her best friend all too well.

"And six dozen roses. You think that's too much?"

"Nope. I think it's perfect," Lauren said. "I love you. Good luck. Let me know how it goes."

"You, too," Trina said before adding, "Thea is going to be thrilled you're there. Honestly. This is super romantic and adorable. You're the best."

"Thanks, T." Lauren disconnected their call after saying goodbye. She checked her GPS again. She wasn't so comfortable with the new route she had planned, and she was already feeling stressed about the time. As she pulled up to Penny Prebble's bed-and-breakfast, she remembered what Thea had said about staying anywhere but with her when she was in town. But her intentions this weekend were to support Thea and her family. And not about jumping into bed with her. Though, if that happened organically, Lauren was okay with it. But that's not why she was here. The Berry Festival was about helping the Boudreauxs find closure. And maybe reconciling some of her own feelings around her relationship with Thea along the way. But she knew she'd have a lot more opportunity to do that with some distance between them. At least sleeping distance, that was.

❖

The room was cozy and comfortable. She had a small private bath and a faux porch outside her bedroom window. She opened the windows, letting in the warm, late summer evening air. The bed-and-breakfast was on the main drag in Casterville. She could see Life's a Grind—where she'd met up with Faith—just a few doors down. And a charming little mom-and-pop shop sat on the corner next to a small apothecary and a dog groomer. A local hardware store was across from that, next to an ice cream parlor. The quaintness of this little strip was enhanced by the hundreds of hanging lights between the buildings and signposts. Those lights weren't there last time she was here, but if the many signs advertising the Berry Festival were any indication, they were part of the celebrations as well.

She walked over to the mirror and smiled at the Lauren reflected before her. She double-checked her outfit one last time before deciding it was now or never. The young man at the front desk told her she could walk to the festival from here, but she knew she needed caffeine first. As she stepped out the front door she walked straight into a familiar face.

"Lauren?" Hayley Carpenter asked, looking as shocked as Lauren felt.

"Hayley," she said with a smile, reaching out to hug her. "What are you doing here?"

"I was going to ask you the same thing," Hayley said, adjusting her messenger bag.

"I'm here for the festival." Lauren paused. "But first, coffee."

"Oh, I'll join you." Hayley walked beside her toward the café. "What brings you to Casterville?"

"Work-ish."

Hayley gave her a look. "Oh?"

Lauren nodded. "I'm helping the Boudreauxs out."

Hayley frowned. "I heard they might be selling. I love that place. It's like an institution around here."

Lauren stopped short, remembering the photo in the barn. "I remember seeing a photo of Emerson at the farm, but I didn't realize you were so familiar with the town or the family," Lauren said while holding the door open for Hayley to enter before her.

"Of course. I grew up here." Hayley waved to the barista behind the counter, chatting animatedly with her as though they were old friends. She placed their drink order before saying, "I try to get back every once in a while. My family owns a cabin along the lake, near the Boudreaux place. I spent my summers here. And a Boudreaux farm ice cream was the best part of my summer nights."

Lauren accepted the coffee Hayley handed her and looked out the window at the town that bustled with activity. She knew word had probably gotten out about the farm's impending sale, but she wasn't sure how Kathleen had decided to deal with that. "I wasn't sure if they'd told anyone they were planning to sell yet."

Hayley looked sad as she said, "It's a small town. News travels fast."

Something about the way she said that made Lauren feel like maybe she knew about that firsthand. As she took a sip of her coffee, a thought occurred to her. "Where's Emerson?"

"She's wrapping up some work in Boston. Their filming went a bit long. She's supposed to be here by tomorrow. We try to catch the Berry Festival every year if we can. That doesn't always work out with her filming schedule and my writing deadlines. But we try. Though we get here a lot more often now that we have a place in the Seaport. Much thanks to you and Trina." She raised her coffee cup in cheers.

"That was all Trina—she's a genius. But I'll relay the thanks and take all the credit in her absence." She tapped her lidded cup to Hayley's. "How's the production company going?"

"Busy. Super busy. Which is great. And even greater that we can spend so much time together since my work is essentially all remote right now. I love being here. It's such a nice change from the fakeness of Hollywood. The escape—even if brief—always feels like a chance to recharge."

Lauren loved the way Hayley described things. But she'd been a massive fan of her last two film projects, too, so there was that. "And how's the new place working out?"

"It's gorgeous and super over the top, right up Emerson's alley," Hayley joked as she held the door for Lauren this time.

"Liar. You know you love the view. I remember your plans for your writing room facing the water. I bet you've crafted many a story with that backdrop in mind," Lauren said, teasing her a bit.

"I do have an idea for a small-town romance. Maybe someplace coastal," Hayley said with a wink. "But I have to work out the details a bit."

"I'm sure you'll kill it," Lauren said as they walked along Main Street, following the signs to the festival ahead. Before she knew it, they were in a crowd of people slowly making their way into a large, converted cornfield that was lit with stadium lights and filled with sounds of music and cheering. They descended a small hill toward the entrance, and from her vantage point, Lauren could see dozens of large, tented booths in organized lines and alleys in the field. Along the edges were carnival-like games, a petting zoo of sorts, some small rides for kids, and—"Holy crap. Is that a dunk tank?"

"Mr. Forrester—the high school agriculture teacher—dresses up like a clown and gets up on that platform year in and year out. No one knows why he volunteers to have balls pelted at him and to get dunked in ice cold water. But we all sort of go with it."

"Oh, wow." The massive entrance arch had to be fifteen feet high. It was made of braided wood and fake ivy with smatterings of plastic versions of all the local berries farmed in the area. A greeter with a bright smile handed them each a map of the field and a raffle ticket to win something, though Lauren missed what she said it was for. She was too distracted by the booths before her: each one was uniquely decorated, advertising the wares available but also showcasing the booth owner's individual flair. Many of them were adorned with fairy lights, making the aisle before her glow in a warm and welcoming way. The first booth to her left sold berries—blackberries, blueberries, raspberries, boysenberries, you named it and they had a berry for it. To her right was a bakery booth. She recognized their logo from Life's a Grind. They must have provided the baked goods there. Someone handed her a sample of still hot sourdough, and she nearly died.

"Damn. This place is like heaven."

"Your first time, I assume?" Hayley asked. "It's great, isn't it?"

"Totally," Lauren said as she dodged two kids playing tag between the booths. Music was playing from what she assumed was the gazebo she'd noticed on the map. The happy hum of people's voices all around her made her smile. She could see why Hayley came back for this and why it was so important to Thea. There was something about this place that was magical.

"Hayley!" An excited twentysomething brunette rushed toward them, wrapping her arms around Hayley and lifting her off the ground.

"Hey, Annie." Hayley swayed with her for a moment before introducing her to Lauren. "This is my friend Lauren, she's here—"

Annie's jaw dropped. "Oh, man. You're way prettier than he let on."

"Who let on?" Lauren asked, but her answer approached with a giant hug of his own.

"You came," Carl said, lifting her off the ground, not unlike what Annie did with Hayley. "Thea's gonna lose it."

"In a good way or a bad way?" Lauren asked, kissing him on the cheek.

"Totally a good way. She's been all moony eyes this week. Which is a major improvement to the sulking and broodiness of the past few weeks. We blame and thank you for both," he said, flashing her Thea's signature smile.

"You're welcome," Lauren said. She turned toward Annie. "So you're the famous Annie I've heard so much about."

Carl blushed, looking down.

Lauren reached out and slipped her arm into his. "How do you and Hayley know each other?"

"She's my cousin," Annie and Hayley said at the same time with a laugh.

"Hayley went off and became all Hollywood on us, but she comes back from time to time and buys all the fruit when she's around," Annie said, bumping her cousin's shoulder.

"You mean any fruit that Carl hasn't bought just as an excuse to be around you, right?" Lauren said as she playfully pushed Carl toward Annie.

"Maybe you should have stayed in Boston," Carl joked.

"You'd be lost without me," she said, glad to be back in his presence.

Carl took Annie's hand as he said, "You're probably right."

"We're going to grab a quick bite, in case you want to join us," Hayley said, rolling her eyes at Carl and Annie, who seemed to be in some sort of young lovers' trance. "Please say yes, so I don't have to be the awkward third wheel."

"Sorry." Lauren laughed as she noticed the Boudreaux booth just a few tents away. Thea was handing a pint of something to an older gentleman. "I'm sure I'll catch up with you later. But first, I need to see a girl about some dairy."

"Fine," Hayley said with a wink. "It was great seeing you."

"You, too." Lauren gave her a wave good-bye before taking a deep breath. She was oddly anxious about approaching the booth even though Carl had assured her Thea would be happy to see her. It wasn't like she could turn back now—there were far too many witnesses.

"You can do this, Calloway," she said to herself as her heart rate picked up.

Thea didn't notice her at first. She was busy working the digital cash device and negotiating a sale. Kathleen's back was to her as she spoke to a short-haired woman in a brightly colored sweater that seemed too heavy for the warmth of the night's air.

Lauren picked up a wedge of cheese and asked, "Is the cheese any Gouda from here?"

Thea turned at her voice and her face lit up. "I'm pretty biased, but I think it's the GOAT. You know, greatest of all time."

"Well if you can Muenster up that kind of enthusiasm, it must be amazing," Lauren said.

"I'm usually pretty Chilton about these things, but I feel strongly about this."

"Wow. You really blue me away with the Wisconsin cheese reference."

"You should see what I can do with cheddar. I'm absolutely Brie-illiant." Thea put her hand on her hip as she asked, "Can I come kiss you now? I've had a lot of ice cream and feta lotta people today, but I'm most hungry for your lips."

Lauren laughed as she placed the wedge back on the pile. "I can honestly say I've never flirted using cheese puns before."

Thea stepped out from behind the counter, striding up to her confidently as she cupped her jaw. "That's because up till now, all of our foreplay has involved peaches. But cheese and peaches pair well together."

"Do they?" Lauren pulled back teasingly.

"I mean"—Thea gave her a once-over—"I'd eat just about anything off you."

"Damn," Lauren whispered as Thea guided her mouth closer. "That's a visual I intend to revisit often."

"Or..." Thea paused, pressing a kiss just to the left of Lauren's lips. "Maybe instead of visualizing it, we just put the theory to the test?" The want was greater than the desire to fight it anymore. And though she intended to take things a little more slowly with Thea this time around, kissing her was all she could think about. Lauren turned her head, connecting their lips, and her knees nearly buckled. Because no one had ever kissed her the way Thea did, and damn had she missed this talented mouth.

"Ladies." Kathleen's voice sounded behind her. "Maybe take that to anyplace that's not directly in front of the sales counter."

"Sorry, Mom," Thea said, breaking the kiss and tugging Lauren with her away from the booth.

"It's nice to see you, Lauren," Kathleen called out, and Lauren wanted to die.

She covered her face with her hand and buried her head in Thea's shoulder once Thea had finally maneuvered them into a more private area.

"What?" Thea asked.

Lauren smacked her arm and pulled back to say, "Once—just once—can we not be making out or naked when your mother is around. Just once? Maybe?"

Thea looked her up and down again. "I mean, you look dressed to me. But I'm always envisioning you naked. So I'm not a reliable judge of your clothedness."

Lauren buried her head against Thea's shoulder again. "You know what I mean."

"I can't help it. You're so kissable and touchable. I'm powerless around you." Thea wrapped her arms around her. "And truthfully, I've really missed you. So grant me a bit of forgiveness for my forwardness. The knowledge that I might be able to kiss you again has been the only thing keeping me sane these days."

Lauren looked up at Thea to find her tearing up. "I forgive you."

"For the way I acted, too? Because I honestly thought I'd lost you. And I'm so sorry. I'd never intentionally hurt you," Thea said.

"I know," Lauren said, kissing her. "It's going to be okay."

"Thank you," Thea said against her lips. "Because even if it's not, just hearing you say that makes things feel better already."

Lauren pulled back, caressing her cheek. She so wanted things to be different. She wanted to take Thea's pain and sadness away and go back to the simpler time when they'd first met and life didn't feel so heavy or hard. But her heart wasn't invested back then, like it was now. And now when Thea hurt, she hurt, too.

"It's going to be okay," she repeated, because she needed to hear it for herself, too.

"Okay," Thea said as she wiped a tear from her cheek.

"Can you slip away from the tent for a bit? I'd kind of like to walk with you under all these fairy lights and see what this festival has to offer," Lauren said, feeling like they both needed a little escape.

"I'd love nothing more than that," Thea said, taking her hand and leading her back into the main strip of tents and people.

And under the lights, surrounded by the laughter and joy of the people enjoying the festival around them, Lauren felt some of the magic from earlier seep back in again.

CHAPTER TWENTY-NINE

Thea smiled as Lauren charmed another massive sale out of a passerby. She was a born saleswoman and people loved her. In the two hours since they'd returned to the booth, Lauren had sold out nearly every item they had. She could not be stopped.

"That'll be sixty-two fifty," Lauren said as she handed a bag over to one of the festivalgoers.

"I still don't get how you can do that," Thea said, stepping forward with the electronic payment device. Lauren had been doing a mental tally of the totals and taxes due for each person that came to the booth. Thea always doubled-checked her numbers, but she hadn't been wrong once.

"It's good to exercise the mind as well as the body," Lauren said, giving her a wink. "I like numbers."

"And I like you," Thea said, kissing the side of her head.

Lauren leaned against her before shivering. "Ooh, the temperature dropped quick, huh?"

Thea reached under the table and pulled out a black fleece zip-up with the Boudreaux Family Dairy Farm logo on it. "We only have black and red left, but this one is your size, and it'll keep you warm."

She helped Lauren into the fleece, zipping her in with care. Lauren pulled her hands into the cuffs so only her fingertips were exposed as she snuggled into the jacket. "This is heavenly."

Thea watched her for a moment, loving the way the logo sat over her heart. She looked adorable in this fleece, and Thea was proud to see her grandfather's farm memorialized in the embroidery.

"You look good in that," she said, running her fingers over the image of the barn.

"Well, you've certainly branded me now, haven't you?" Lauren said as she took the credit card device from Thea. She swiped her card and punched in a total before Thea could stop her.

"Hey, you don't have to pay for that," Thea said.

Lauren shook her head. "I intend to keep it. So I'll pay my way, thank you very much." She paused. "Don't worry, I calculated the tax."

"I bet you did," Thea said as she put her arm around Lauren's waist.

Lauren rested her head on Thea's shoulder, and Thea inhaled the scent of her perfume and shampoo. She'd missed her. She'd missed her smile and her laugh and the way she fit so perfectly in her arms. Being with Lauren had never felt like work, and that was something she had never experienced before in a relationship. It was also something she never wanted to lose again.

"Hey, Mom? Can you cover the booth for a few minutes? I want to show Lauren something," Thea said.

"Of course," her mother said as she patted Hector on the knee. Since Lauren had taken the sales reins, her mother had been able to socialize with the townsfolk and Hector, once he'd arrived. She was so happy to see the two of them laughing and chatting with all the familiar faces of people she'd grown up with. But there was something sad about it, too. Something finite.

"Ooh, is this a surprise?" Lauren asked. "Because I love surprises."

"It is," Thea said, taking her hand.

She guided her along the path in front of the stalls, stopping occasionally to point something out or pose for a picture. Lauren had been taking tons of pictures and videos, and Thea was looking forward to seeing what she'd captured. There was something special about your first Berry Festival. She wanted to see it from Lauren's perspective.

"Here you go," she said, handing Lauren a bright pink fluff of cotton candy on a hollow paper stick.

"My teeth hurt just looking at this," Lauren said before taking a big bite. "This is amazing," she mumbled.

They paused at the table of Killinger's Dairy. Mr. Killinger smiled at her and said a few words that were heartfelt and sweet. He wasn't much of a talker, but he'd been good to them after her dad died.

"He seemed nice," Lauren said as they walked.

"He is. He has a dairy farm about a hundred miles from here. It's a lot bigger than our operation. But he mostly does milk collection and transport and not production stuff. His market is broader than ours.

Where we supply locally and produce cheeses and other dairy goods, he mostly just breeds cattle and ships milk." She adjusted the hold she had on Lauren's hand. "He stepped in when my father died and helped Hector figure out some of the more complicated milking parlor issues. I'm sure Mom already talked to him about helping offload some of the milking supplies and cattle. He's good people. I'm glad that some of Dad's stuff will find its way back to him."

Lauren kissed her cheek, and Thea knew she understood how complicated that realization was for her.

They walked farther, and Thea took her along the side of the dunk tank before taking a hard right and stepping off the designated path. She helped her climb up the grassy hill until they'd reached the near top.

"Don't turn around yet," she said, holding Lauren still. She stripped off her jacket and laid it on the grass. "Close your eyes."

"That feels like a dangerous command on a hill, babe," Lauren said, though she complied.

Thea helped her sit and joined her on the jacket as she leaned over and whispered into her ear. "Okay. Open your eyes."

Lauren obliged and her jaw dropped. "Oh my God. It's beautiful."

"This is my favorite spot in the whole festival," she said, watching Lauren's face as she spoke. "You have an unobstructed view of all the people and the lights and the Ferris wheel. You can smell the apple cider and the roasted nuts. You can hear the music at the bandstand and watch the dance competition under the bright lights. There is nothing more beautiful in the whole world."

Lauren looked at her. She was so close, Thea could kiss her. And she would have, had Lauren not taken her breath away.

"I love you," Lauren said. "And I never want this night to end. Or this feeling to go away. Because up here with you feels like the perfect place, with the perfect person, on the most perfect summer night. I thought this town and this festival were magic. But I'm starting to think maybe it was just you all along."

Thea rested her forehead on Lauren's. "Best. One-night stand. Ever."

Lauren laughed, but Thea silenced her with a kiss. She tasted like cotton candy and summer and it was a taste Thea hoped to never forget.

"I love you, too."

She sat with Lauren for a long time before the chill of the night traveled up her now naked arms. She shivered and Lauren was on her feet in a flash.

"Come on," Lauren said as she pulled her up. She dusted off her jacket and handed it to her as she said, "Let's go check on your mom and Hector. It's getting late."

Thea appreciated the warmth of her jacket as they descended the hill. "Maybe we should find Carl."

After a few hundred feet, Lauren pointed toward the picnic tables by the sausage stand. "There he is."

"Is that—?"

"Emerson," Lauren said as they approached the small group. "I thought you weren't getting in until tomorrow."

"Hi, Lauren." Emerson Sterling addressed her girlfriend with such familiarity that Thea nearly fainted. Thea knew she'd visited the farm once or twice in the past and even knew she'd married their neighbor, but she'd never been in the presence of Hollywood royalty before. Her dark hair, pouty lips, and light eyes were stunning. Thea could see why she was chosen to portray a younger version of Angelina Jolie in her biopic, *Lip Service*. Their physical similarities were uncanny.

"You two know each other?" Thea asked.

"Hi." Emerson extended a hand toward her. "You must be Thea. Your brother has been telling us all about you and how your mom caught you shacking up with Lauren in the guest room."

"Carl," Lauren scolded, and she watched as her brother raised his hands in surrender. "Rude."

"Sorry? I mean, she's Emerson Sterling. I had to tell her something amusing to keep her from thinking I was a dud," he said, looking sufficiently rebuked.

"He's dating my cousin-in-law—go easy on him. He's sweet," Emerson said, and Carl looked bashful again.

"It's official?" Lauren asked, pointing between him and Annie. When he nodded, she cheered. "Hell yes!"

He high-fived her, and Thea recognized Hayley Carpenter approaching with a tray of hot dogs. Though she'd seen her in tabloid photos with Emerson and knew she was some big important screenwriter, she most vividly remembered her as Ginny Carpenter's granddaughter from when they were younger. They were far enough apart in age that they never hung out growing up, but Hayley'd always been kind to Thea when she came around the farm.

"Thea, wow. You've grown up," Hayley said with a broad smile. "How are you?"

"I'm good," she said as she reclaimed Lauren's hand. "And you?"

"Good." Hayley started handing out food as Lauren talked animatedly to Emerson.

Thea watched them all interact, feeling like a bit of an outsider until Lauren dragged her into the conversation.

"So, anyway, I met Emerson and Hayley in Boston while they were house hunting," she said.

"We weren't, but Trina convinced us we were," Emerson said with a laugh as she put her arm around Hayley.

"She's very convincing, that Trina," Thea said, still a little worried about seeing her again after the sort of breakup with Lauren. She had a feeling she should make sure she wasn't alone and cornered by her anytime soon.

"You say that like you've been on the wrong side of her," Hayley said.

"She's a protective best friend," Lauren said before kissing Thea. "Let's just say, she takes a little while to warm up."

"You two are super cute," Emerson said with a yawn.

"And you drove super far after a long day of work when you were supposed to rest at the condo before heading up here in the morning. Come on, let's get back to the cabin," Hayley said to Emerson.

"It's not my fault that the production kept getting delayed by onlookers and traffic issues. I love it—don't get me wrong—but Boston is a bustling place this time of year. It's no LA when it comes to the privacy invasion we're used to, but I'm glad to be here—where I can just be your lovely wife and not worry about having my photo sold to *TMZ*. That's why I love it here—it's the only time I feel like I can be normal and live my life without intrusion." Emerson yawned again. "Okay, I'm cooked. I claim defeat. Please take me home," she said, and they said their good-byes as the festival started to break down around them.

"I think we closed the joint," Lauren said to Thea as they ambled back to their booth.

"You're right," Thea said. All around them tables were emptied and decorations were removed. And the once bustling festival grounds were now only filled with vendors and festival workers. The emptiness and the quiet hit her harder than she'd expected. That mean that another day was behind them now.

"This is the best sales night we've ever had. Hector and Christine had to make a trip back to the farm just to get some more goods. We put a sizable dent in tomorrow's festival supply," her mother said as she stretched.

"Does this run all day tomorrow, too?" Lauren asked.

"One more full day and night, then a few hours on Sunday," Carl said, looking tired. He'd said good-bye to Annie when the rest of that crew left, and Thea could have sworn he'd floated the whole way back here. It was cute.

"Well, let's get home and get some rest, then," her mother said with a yawn. "We'll need to be rested if tomorrow is anything like today."

"I'll load the truck," Carl said, grabbing one of the last few boxes and heading toward the parking area off to the left.

"Are you coming back with us?" her mother asked Lauren, and Thea stopped clearing the space because she hadn't even considered that Lauren might not be coming home with her.

"I have a room at Penny's," Lauren said, and Thea's heart sank. She'd thought they'd made up. Why wasn't Lauren staying with her tonight?"

"Okay, dear," her mother said, looking between them before busying herself at the edge of the tent.

Lauren's hand found hers, and she looked up at her. "I was hoping you might stay with me tonight. If you're okay with that."

Thea's heart rate picked up. "I'm more than okay with that."

"Good." Lauren looked pleased.

Thea broke down the tables and folding chairs before helping Carl finish loading the remainder of the supplies on the truck and waving to her family as they drove away. She and Lauren took a leisurely stroll back through the now sleepy main strip, chatting and teasing along the walk. Lauren's hand never left hers as Thea told her story after story of her hijinks here as a child. They laughed so hard, she cried, and before she knew it, they were at the bed-and-breakfast and tiptoeing up to the second-floor rooms.

"You seemed genuinely concerned that I was bunking away from the farm," Lauren said with a nudge as they walked down the hallway toward her room.

"I was. I mean"—Thea ran her hand through her hair—"I kind of absolutely and totally panicked."

"Because you'd miss me?" Lauren said, batting her eyelashes.

"Because I'd wake up without you," Thea admitted. "I want to be with you, Lauren, and not casually. I realized that in our time apart. I hated it. And I have no desire to know what my life would be like without you in it."

"How do you always manage to say the most romantic things?" Lauren asked as she opened the door to her room, ushering Thea inside.

"I don't know. I guess you bring out that side of me," Thea said, losing her breath as Lauren pushed her back onto the bed.

"Do you know what side you bring out in me?" Lauren asked as she climbed up on her lap and began kissing along Thea's neck.

"I'm more than willing to find out," Thea said as she gripped Lauren's ass, moaning at the feeling of Lauren's lips along her pulse point.

"Good. Because sleep is a long way away." Lauren looked down at her, and Thea's fatigue from the day disappeared when Lauren licked her bottom lip. "And I have a lot to show you."

"I'm ready," Thea said, and she'd never meant that more in her entire life.

CHAPTER THIRTY

L auren woke up with a start. Her body was tired, more tired now that she'd made love with Thea for the last few hours. But her mind was buzzing—buzzing with numbers. And she knew if she continued to lie here, she'd eventually wake Thea up with her restlessness.

She remembered falling asleep quickly after their last round, something that never seemed hard while wrapped in Thea's arms, but then the dream set in. It was a vague fog of memories from the night—glimpses of screenshots from the evening. And numbers. So many floating, brightly colored numbers. And now, after only a few hours of sleep, her brain was in high gear even though her body was protesting fiercely.

After reviewing an email from Jax with updated pictures of the Newbridge project and community garden space, she opened her phone and scanned through the photos she'd taken last night to try to quiet her brain. She was surprised by the number she'd taken—over a hundred. Some of them were shots of the crowd, or background shots of the festival grounds. She had pictures of the dunk tank and the raffle station, the fried dough stand, and a few carnival games. She had one of Hayley and Emerson holding an oversized stuffed teddy bear that Emerson had won for Hayley that they soon gifted to a little girl and her mother walking by. She had a few of Thea being all sexy and salesy at the booth and more than one of Carl staring affectionately at Annie. She had candids of Kathleen laughing with Hector and some artsy shots of the full Boudreaux farm table, showing off their products.

She paused when she got to the pictures she'd taken at the top of the hill with Thea. These were spectacular. The lights were vivid in the clear summer night sky, and the scene was so welcoming and joyful. She could almost taste the cotton candy that appeared in the next photo of her and Thea, snuggling close and looking very much in love.

Love. She went back to the panoramic shot of the festival before quickly scrolling through the hundred-plus photos again. That was what she'd seen there—a *love* of community. Farmers and bakers, local dog groomers, florists, and restaurant owners all showed up. The Berry Festival was the event that brought all the best parts of Casterville and the surrounding towns together, and she had seen firsthand the impact and presence the Boudreaux farm had on the community. They were the busiest booth, without a doubt. People came to chat and reminisce. They purchased snacks and posed for pictures. Kathleen and Hector knew everyone's names and family stories. And though she'd spent most of her time with the Boudreauxs, she'd seen the same thing at every table and stand there tonight. The theme of the night was one of caring and love for community.

Love for community. That was it. That was the answer. That was how she was going to save the Boudreaux farm. There was still time, but she had to hustle.

❖

"Lauren, you'd better be dying if you're calling this early. Otherwise I'm going to kill you," Trina's sleepy voice sounded over the line.

"I know. I'm sorry. But if it makes you feel any better, I called Ellison first. Then I paced for an hour and a half, *then* called you. So this is like my *late* phone call." Lauren paused. "Wait. More importantly, did she say yes?"

"I did," Kendall's equally sleepy voice replied. "You're on speaker. Good morning."

"Yes! I mean, hi. Also, I told you not to worry, T."

"Aw, were you worried?" Kendall asked Trina, and Trina grumbled something inaudible.

"She was. She loves you so much she can't stand when you sleep anywhere else, but she's too much of a wannabe cactus to tell you that. Even though we all know she's a giant softy with a heart of gold beneath all those prickly spikes," Lauren said.

"This is so true," Kendall replied.

"You're lucky I love you both," Trina said with a yawn. "What's up, Lau? You okay?"

"Yes. No. I mean, yes. But I need your help," she said, her mind racing as it had been for the past few hours. She'd literally watched the clock tick minute by minute as she formed her plan, waiting for it to be an appropriate time to start calling in favors.

"Can I have coffee first?" Trina asked.

"Sure. I just sent you some. It should be arriving..." Trina's doorbell sounded in the background. "Now."

"I'll get it," Kendall said, and there was a shuffling in the background.

"It's a good thing you called first, because I definitely would have slept through that," Trina said.

"Kendall would have heard it," Lauren said confidently. Trina mentioned often that Kendall was a light sleeper.

"I certainly would." Kendall's voice rejoined the conversation. "I probably would have smelled the coffee, too."

"Ooh, this is my favorite. And bagels? With lox? Chive cream cheese..." Trina sounded wary when she asked, "What kind of help requires this much buttering up?"

"The kind that might take a good chunk of your day. I'm calling in a favor," Lauren said, hoping her bestie wouldn't let her down.

"I'm listening," Trina said while chewing something.

"I had a numbers dream last night," Lauren said.

"Oh, damn. This is serious. Were they doing all the floaty enchanting things?" Trina asked.

Lauren smiled. Trina knew her so well. "So much floaty enchantment. And bright colors, too."

"Numbers dream? I'm lost," Kendall said.

"Lauren's best and brightest ideas happen around her numbers dreams. Whatever this is, it must be genius. Lay it on us, girl," Trina said, and Lauren knew she was on board.

"You know how I was researching all those alternative sales options? Like the community farming and the land rental option? Or selling a piece of the land to the state for a cell tower. All that?"

"Yeah. Didn't you even research medical marijuana farming for distribution?" Trina asked, stifling a yawn.

"Among other things, yes. Well, I think I figured out how to save the Boudreaux farm, but I can't do it alone. And now that Ellison gave me the okay to try one last Hail Mary on this project, I need to call in the troops. Do you have any of that cheese and ice cream from the farm that I brought back with me?" she asked.

"I'll be honest with you that the rocky road ice cream didn't survive the second night. It's long gone. But there's a lot still here. Why?" Trina asked.

"I need you to share it with Claire. And Shelly. And Jax. We need all hands on deck with this one."

"Okay. What's the plan?" Trina asked.

"How do you feel about hosting an impromptu war room at your place? And before you say you've got showings, you should know I already called Jax and had them double-check that you were free."

Trina laughed. "Well, in that case, I guess I'm okay with it."

"Awesome. You're the best. Everyone will be over there by eleven. So that gives you, like, two hours for celebratory *Yay, we're moving in together!* sex and a shower."

"That's not enough time for either," Trina complained.

"We could just combine the two," Kendall said, and Lauren heard what sounded like kissing.

"Focus, ladies!"

Trina sighed. "Well, since you've invited an entourage to my house to eat the rest of my ice cream and brainstorm about saving your girlfriend's farm, that means my end of the deal is filled, right?"

"Not by a long shot. I need your Rolodex. And I'm going to leverage your name. You okay with that?"

Trina laughed again. "I learned a long time ago not to fight that beautiful, quirky brain of yours, Lau. I'm all in. Whatever you need."

Lauren's heart swelled. She could do this. With her friends' help, she knew she could. She could save this farm and make good on her promise to Thea. But her time was running out and every minute counted.

❖

Thea rolled over at the sound of the door opening.

"You're back," she said, rubbing her eyes. "Where'd you go?"

Lauren held up a coffee and bag that contained breakfast sandwiches. "I foraged for caffeine and protein. My hunt was successful."

"You're too good to me." Thea sat up, and the blanket slipped off her chest, revealing her nakedness from last night. Thea had the best chest. And the sexiest collarbones. And Lauren swore that since she'd been up here on the farm full-time, her shoulders were stronger and sexier than ever.

"Well, with a body like that, I'd be a fool not to be."

Thea blushed and pointed to her discarded shirt on the floor. "If you'd be so kind."

Lauren handed it to her, but not before stealing a quick kiss. "Fine, ruin all my fun."

Thea yawned and took a sip of her coffee before placing it on the bedside table. "You can ogle my nakedness later, I promise. But I've overslept and still have to get back to the house to change. And if you keep leering at my tits, I'm going to invite you back into bed to do more than just look at them."

Lauren smiled at the challenge. "You make it sound like that's a bad thing. I know what you like, and I know what turns you on. I can be quick."

"I know you can," Thea said as she licked her lips. "But I prefer when you aren't."

Lauren resisted the urge to climb onto the bed. There was far too much to do, and if she did, she knew she'd be naked with Thea in no time at all. "I'll remember that for later."

"Please do," Thea said, sipping her coffee again. "This is good."

"It's from the café downstairs. Guess whose milk they use?"

Thea gave her a sad smile. "Ours. My mother worked hard to make sure when we went to a more commercial market that Casterville got first dibs before we expanded. Nearly every meal or beverage in this town that uses milk uses Boudreaux farm's milk. Including those pastries you tried last night from Out of the Oven."

"That strawberry rhubarb tart was insultingly good. Like, I was offended. My tastebuds died from excitement. I'll never taste anything again," Lauren joked, trying to brighten her mood.

Thea laughed. "I love those guys. Did you know they've been together for thirty-five years? When they legalized gay marriage, the whole town showed up for them. I love this place," Thea said, her contemplative look returning.

Lauren watched as Thea climbed out of bed and dressed in silence. She could tell she was warring with her emotions about the farm and Casterville being in her rearview shortly. Lauren wanted to tell her she had a plan, but she didn't want to get her hopes up. At least, not yet anyway.

Thea caught Lauren watching her and gave her a brave smile, but Lauren knew she had to force it. "Any interest on giving me a lift back to the farm so I can put on fresh clothes?"

"I'm very fond of these," Lauren said, tugging at the hem of Thea's shirt. "But sure, I suppose that's a fair request."

"Thanks," Thea said.

"I have to get some work stuff done today, so I won't get to the festival until later," she said as she reached for her messenger bag.

"Are you staying another night?" Thea asked, hopeful.

"I am."

"Here?"

Lauren had only booked the night, unsure of what to expect when she arrived. "My reservation was only for last night."

Thea looked pleased by this information. "So you can come home with me, then."

"If you'll have me," Lauren said.

"Any way I can," Thea said. She'd walked right into that one.

"You know that means we can't be nearly as loud as last night, though, right?" She paused, panicking. "Do we have to sleep in separate rooms?"

"I'm aware, and we didn't last time, remember?"

"Don't remind me. I'm still not over the fact that your mom basically told us to get a room last night. I really need to not be doing nasty things to you when she's around. It's going to ruin her opinion of me."

"I doubt that. But we'll be more careful, I promise." Thea slipped on her boots as she said, "I'm glad you'll be back at the farm tonight."

"Oh? Why's that?" she asked as she started putting her things into her suitcase.

"Because the farm is home. But my time there is going to come to an end soon, and I'd like to soak up as much of you and it together as possible. I think it'll help that we have shared memories there. That way if I'm having a hard time once the sale is final, we can reminisce together. It means a lot to me to be able to share that with you. Because as much as the farm is home, I've come to realize I feel that same way about you, too." Thea looked at her with such sincerity that Lauren nearly cried.

I'm going to try to save it for you. I'll do everything I can. "Thank you for sharing your life with me."

"Always," Thea said, and something about the way she said it made Lauren believe it.

CHAPTER THIRTY-ONE

Faith gave her a hug. "I have to say, I was surprised to get your call this morning."

"Yeah. I was surprised to make it."

"You know that there's a time limit on those offers, right? I only have so much wiggle and negotiation room before the offers expire. And if Kathleen wants any bargaining power, she really needs two offers to pit against each other."

"I know," Lauren said. "Which is exactly why I'm working overtime to map this plan out and make sure it's airtight. You know, in like twenty-four hours."

Faith raised an eyebrow in her direction. "Okay, so run it by me once more."

Lauren had been on the phone and videoconferencing with her war room team since midmorning. Jax and Shelly had been able to get all the online research she needed with ease. And Claire was already working on a pitch using the dairy products Trina had as inspiration. Trina had relinquished her contact list without resistance and was making sure everyone was fed and hydrated. All Lauren had to do was get Faith on board, and she could pull the trigger on the final piece.

She pulled out the blueprints she'd gotten from Kathleen's office and spread them out on the large countertop in front of them. She had pulled Kathleen aside before she left for the festival to tell her that she might have another buyer interested in the farm, and that she wanted to give them a tour if that was okay. Kathleen had easily agreed to grant her access to the property in their absence. Thea and the rest of them were at the festival, so Lauren knew she'd have the place to herself for the rest of the day. Which was perfect, considering how many balls she was juggling at the moment.

"So you're familiar with the property lines, but I wanted to get your insight on mixing things up a bit." She started marking off sections with household objects. "The twenty-two acres of natural woods are beautiful, but in regard to function, they are underused."

"That's the space marked with the orange, right?" Faith asked as she familiarized herself with the blueprints.

"Right."

"But that's because making them level and functional would be costly," Faith added.

"Well, that depends on what their reason for buying the land is," Lauren said. This was where the numbers dream came in. "What if someone wants to buy the land as is and leave it untouched?"

"Why would anyone want to do that? The point is to make the land profitable. If it's level, it can be built on. But that's going to be expensive, which is why that acreage isn't selling for as much as it could."

"Okay, look…" Lauren shifted the kitchen scissors with the orange and used the spatula to designate the main road, while the hen and rooster shaped salt and pepper shakers marked the end of the Boudreaux property line along the lake. "What if instead of selling the land in bulk to a developer or a dairy hating newbie fitness giant—what if we sell it to someone who is already in the community? What if we sell it to someone who will directly benefit from keeping the land a part of the Casterville heritage?"

"Okay. Who?"

Lauren pointed to the hen and rooster. "The people who own the property immediately along the demolition line. People who might not like the idea of losing their lakefront quiet to a year of major construction and a lifetime of outsiders and onlookers. People who value their privacy above all else."

Faith looked at the name Lauren had scribbled along the forest area beyond the Boudreauxs' gorgeous lakefront back pasture. "The Carpenters?"

"The Carpenters or, more specifically, Hayley Carpenter and her wife, superstar actress Emerson Sterling."

Faith looked at her, unsure. "But the sale of the land alone won't save the Boudreauxs. We've gone over this every which way."

"I know," Lauren said, more grateful than ever for Jax's and Shelly's combined research brilliance and Shelly's numbers skills. "But my team tells me that if we market the woods for what it could be—

land rented out for the bustling film industry that has arrived in New England—to the new owner of Sterling Productions, Emerson Sterling, then maybe, just maybe we can break up the remaining plots to keep community as community.

"If we sell the woods to Hayley and Emerson with the pitch of permanent privacy for their cabin or use for film production without the traffic or distractions of Boston, then she'll be able to make a profit off the land by renting it out to other film companies that might want to use it." She pulled up Jax's information about zoning and licensing issues. "Since Hayley is already a resident here at least part of the year now that she and Emerson live on this coast almost full-time, she'll have next to no trouble getting all the paperwork in order. And they could leave most of the land untouched, to keep that *Twilight* vampirey Hollywood feel. It's like a diamond in the very rough, but it's in their backyard. Or they could do nothing with it but sleep well knowing that it would never be developed. Either way, they have options, and my team is writing up pitches for both avenues."

"All right, I think this sounds insane, but I'll give you the benefit of the doubt for now. What about the other plots? What's this about community staying as community?"

This was the part of Lauren's idea that felt the most like a gamble. She knew that even if she couldn't get Emerson and Hayley on board for the land sale, she had the two backup offers on the table. But this move would cancel those out. "The Boudreauxs keep the farmhouse and Hector's place as well as the barn and the dairy processing and aging center. But the milking parlor and the back pastures go."

"Oh, I have to hear this," Faith said, looking amused.

"Community farming," Lauren said. It was an idea that Thea had brought up early on and one that the Newbridge project in Boston helped bring clarity to. "I'm working on developing a building in Boston that has a community garden behind it. The idea is that the owners of the units will have a stake in the land and bring beauty and function to this gorgeous but previously neglected garden space. By adding a pond and bringing water and electricity to the area, we're making a safe, sustainable space for the people that live there. It's a way to bring the community together. I think we can do the same things here by involving the community to utilize the land.

"Kathleen can't keep up with the demands of the farm and the cows, but she can manage and has a love for the products made here. So let's get rid of the hassle. Let's have them use community farming to get milk from elsewhere, like from, say, Killinger's dairy farm. That will allow them to keep making the Boudreaux products commercially sold and loved in every surrounding town without having to do the work of dairy collection.

"The unused milking parlor and the land surrounding it can be used for community farming as well." Lauren looked at her. "I talked to those farmers at the festival last night. They all had the same complaint—it was hard to manage the land they had and still put out the products that generate their income. Everyone is getting older, and the younger generations aren't tied to the land in the way that they used to be. Community farming lets the community remain on the land and profit from it. Let's take those plots of pasture that the Boudreauxs will no longer need, and let's market them as ripe for community ownership."

"But you'd have to find farmers willing to rent the land," Faith said. "In twenty-four hours, I might add."

"Or I just find a really creative and wealthy individual who has a strong sense of community who would want to give back, as well as keep the economy around here prospering."

"I think I see where you're going now. You think Emerson and Hayley will jump at that."

"If they buy the whole spread of land, they'll get production space, community farming with rental income, and potential state tax cuts because of it. They can give back to the community with jobs for movie production and for farming *and* still keep developers out of their backyard. They get privacy and ownership."

"You're really banking on this approach, aren't you? What makes you think they'll go for it?" Faith seemed unconvinced.

"Because they love Casterville and the escape from celebrity it offers them. And since they took over the Carpenter cabin and spend at least a third of their time here, it's worth the gamble."

"This is the gutsiest move I have ever heard," Faith said. "What makes you think Emerson and Hayley will agree to the price tag without the full lot space Edmund wanted? They won't be getting the houses or the barn," she noted.

"Houses can be built and demolished, but land sales are harder to come by. Sometimes only happening once in a lifetime."

Faith seemed to consider this.

"I have an amazing team finishing up the marketing pitch now. All I have to do is convince Hayley and Emerson to get on board, and we've done it. We'll have saved the farm and dug the Boudreauxs out of debt while making sure they still maintain their livelihood."

"And if it doesn't work?" Faith asked.

"Then they sell the land as previously planned and everything is terrible." Lauren wasn't ready to accept that yet. "But I know I can do this. This is a good plan."

Faith laughed. "You're really sure about this, huh?"

"I'm willing to bet the farm on it. Yeah." Lauren's phone pinged, and she smiled. Claire had finished her marketing draft. Now all Lauren had to do was perfect her pitch.

"Have you even gotten in touch with Emerson or Hayley? When will you have the chance to talk to them?" Faith asked.

"Now," Lauren said as she heard a car pull up outside the farmhouse. She saw them exit the vehicle and gave them a wave from the front porch.

"You already scheduled a walk-through with them?" Faith looked impressed. "You aren't messing around, are you?"

"You said yourself, we're racing the clock." She extended her hand to Faith as she asked, "Now, are you on board with my crazy plan? The sale is all yours still, but this way the Boudreauxs have a fighting chance."

Faith shook her hand. "I'm in. If this works out, Ellison owes me dinner for a month."

"I'm sure I can help convince her of that," Lauren said. "C'mon. Let's sell the farm to the celebrity couple that lives next door."

CHAPTER THIRTY-TWO

Thea was bone-tired, but when her cell phone started to vibrate she felt a rush of adrenaline. Lauren must be calling. It had been all day, and she'd missed her desperately.

She stepped away from the sales table to find Avni FaceTiming her. Only, when she accepted the call, it became clear that this was an accidental, not intentional dial.

"Avni," she said, unable to unsee the visual before her. "*Teagan?*"

In her view from the floor of Avni's apartment, she could see Avni and Teagan—the bartender from The Mirage—in a heated make-out session on Avni's couch.

Avni pulled back, looking freaked-out. "Thea?"

"You're shacking up with Teagan?" Thea was so excited for her best friend she almost forgave her for blinding her with all the near-naked kissing.

"Where are you?" Avni was looking left and right in search of her voice.

"On the floor," Thea said, and Teagan looked down first. "Hey, Teagan."

"Hey," she said with that signature half smile. "What's good?"

"Oh my God." Avni's hand went to cover her bra-clad chest as she scrambled out of sight of the camera lens. "Well, this was not how I intended you to find out."

"I mean, I'm pretty pumped for you. And I could use the distraction of good news. Congrats," Thea said as Avni's head slowly reentered the frame. "How long has this been going on?"

"Well, our first formal date was at your place—" Teagan was cut off by Avni's hand on her mouth.

"My place? I went to Maine to help save my family farm, and you used my place to pursue your secret crush?" Thea couldn't believe it.

"Are you mad?" Avni looked mortified.

"Nah, I'm just sad I missed the incredibly awkward come-on you must have used at the bar to get her to date you," Thea teased.

"Well, that's the thing," Avni said, now draped in a blanket. "We sort of connected outside of the bar."

"Tell me everything," Thea said as she plopped down on a folding chair at the back of the tent.

"Well, you know my neighbor, Mrs. Jenks?"

"Of course, she was our eyes in the field," Thea replied, recalling how she played spy for Avni once she'd broken up with Raj to make sure he vacated the property as agreed upon.

"Well, she's my buddy, and we've always been close. And I was going back to the apartment to assess what the place looked like after Raj left, and Teagan was there."

"At your apartment?" Thea wasn't following.

"At her grandma's place. Mrs. Jenks is her grandma."

Thea's jaw dropped. "You're related to Mrs. Jenks?" she asked Teagan, who seemed to be enjoying herself.

"I am. And my grandma had been telling me about her favorite neighbors for the last two years, and I never realized we sort of knew each other. Until that day."

"And then you fell into bed together?" Thea asked.

"Well, I needed help moving back in," Avni said with a shrug. "And you kept telling me to embrace the moment and just admit I liked her. So after she helped me move a few big heavy boxes—when her hands were too full to run away—I just told her I had a crush on her."

"And I told her I'd always thought she was cute," Teagan said with a shrug.

"Oh, man. Wow." Thea ran her hand through her hair. "This is great. I'm so happy for you guys."

"Thanks," Avni said while looking at Teagan affectionately. It made Thea miss Lauren that much more. Where was she anyway?

Just then she heard Lauren's voice from the front of the tent.

"Oh, I have to run. Get back to what you were doing. You seemed busy," she said with a wink.

"Sorry," Avni said, looking embarrassed again.

"No worries. Congrats again. I'll text you later," Thea said. "Oh, and maybe lock your phone screen so next time I don't get a full-on porn call."

Teagan laughed and Avni hid under the blanket before the line disconnected.

"Hey," Lauren said, standing nearby with a teasing smile on her face as she asked, "Who's showing you porn?"

"Avni. She's dating Teagan from The Mirage, and they accidentally video-called me while hooking up."

"Avni's gay now?" Lauren asked, looking as surprised as Thea had felt.

"I guess? I don't know that she's put a label on anything, but they seem happy."

Lauren pulled her out of her chair, and Thea loved the way she possessively wrapped her arms around her waist. "Happy like we are?"

"So happy," Thea said as she kissed the woman she loved more than anything. "I missed you today."

Lauren looked up at her with a small smile. "It was a long day without you."

"Did you accomplish everything you wanted to?"

Lauren seemed to consider this. "I sure did my best."

"Then that's all you can do," Thea said. Her father used to say that to her when she was younger. She'd always found peace with that statement.

Lauren yawned. "We'll find out in the next day or two if my best was enough. I'm choosing to be optimistic."

Lauren looked exhausted. And Thea could relate.

"We're just about done here," Thea said. "Why don't we pack up and head right out?"

Lauren yawned again. "You don't want to stay and enjoy the atmosphere?"

Thea looked back at her mom. Today had seemed to be a harder day for her emotionally. She had seen the toll it was taking as more and more people started asking if they were reserving a spot at the festival for next year.

"I think we all need to pack up and get some rest. Last night was exactly how I want to remember my last Berry Festival," Thea said as she looked back at Lauren. "Because it was with you."

"Take me home, then," Lauren said against her collarbone, and Thea's heart soared and ached at the same time. Because Lauren considered the farm to be home, but that home wasn't going to be hers for much longer.

Lauren held her hand the entire drive back to the farm. Thea loved being able to just reach out and touch her all the time. She hoped that they could bottle this magic between them and keep it alive when they were back in Boston. Back in real life and not on borrowed farm time.

They had dinner as a family, and Carl and her mom regaled Lauren with stories of the things she'd missed that day. It was a perfectly normal summer night at the Boudreaux house, almost as if nothing was about to change. Lauren dried dishes as Thea washed them, and Carl double-checked on the animals and the barn before turning in for an early bedtime. She'd been surprised when Carl came right home after the festival and didn't go out with Annie. But she had a feeling it had to do with their mom and how hard today seemed to be for her. It was hard on all of them, even if they'd mostly avoided the topic.

"You ready for bed?" Lauren asked as she approached Thea from behind.

"Does this mean I get to be the little spoon tonight?" Thea asked, leaning back slightly.

"Oh no. I'm just being affectionate and letting you know I am about to fall asleep standing up. But in no way am I relinquishing little spoon status."

Thea laughed, turning to face her. "I'm kidding. I wouldn't do that to you. You'd get too cold."

"This is a fact. You're a furnace, and that means you are always the big spoon." Lauren ran her hands up and down Thea's shoulders. "Plus you're all muscly and strong. And you give the best hugs. I would hate to take that from you."

Lauren stifled another yawn, and Thea took pity on her. "Come on, let's get you to bed."

Thea walked her upstairs to the guest bedroom she'd dropped Lauren's things off in earlier. They washed up, and before climbing into bed, Lauren checked her phone again. She'd checked it a few times after dinner and made a brief call to her boss in hushed tones on the front porch. Thea couldn't help but wonder what was up. She was worried maybe the Newbridge project needed her attention and her being here was problematic. She'd felt better knowing that

Lauren hadn't missed her championship softball game, but work was as important. She knew Lauren had made sacrifices to be here this weekend, and she wanted her to know she appreciated that.

"I'm really glad you made it up here this weekend," Thea said as Lauren rolled to her side to face her. "I know there were probably a million other things you had to get to. But I'm really glad you're here."

"You're worth it," Lauren said as she leaned forward for an all too brief kiss. She settled back on her pillow, closing her eyes as she said, "Plus I would never miss the festival. It's too important. You all are."

"I love you," Thea said, but Lauren was already softly snoring. She cuddled next to her and wrapped her arm around her, happy to be the big spoon once again.

CHAPTER THIRTY-THREE

Lauren could easily say that the last few days had been some of the best of her life. She had dozens of memories to hold dear to her heart, and though she was still waiting on Emerson and Hayley's decision, she knew she'd done everything she could. And for the first time since this all began, she felt a little closure. There was nothing more she could do. What was done was done.

They'd only been home an hour or so after the final day of the festival when Ellison's Maserati kicked up dust along the Boudreauxs' driveway. Lauren immediately checked her phone for any missed messages, but she found none. What was Ellison doing here?

She walked out of the farmhouse and onto the porch to greet her when she saw another surprising sight—Faith was getting out of the passenger seat, and she had a smile a mile wide.

She watched them chat unobserved, their familiarity with each other obvious. Ellison said something Faith found funny, and her laugh was unbridled and raw. When Ellison got to her side of the car, Faith touched her arm affectionately. Lauren saw Ellison briefly take her hand before looking up and catching her watching.

"Spying, Lauren?" Ellison asked as she dropped her hand from Faith's.

"Just observing two old friends being friendly," she teased as she leaned against the railing of the wraparound porch she loved so much.

Faith shot Ellison a look, and Ellison shrugged.

"I told you—she's brilliant," Ellison said, motioning toward Lauren. "Don't count Lauren out."

"I've learned that from the source," Faith said, looking up at her now. "How are you?"

"Oh, you know, anxiously awaiting news. Any news. Preferably good news." Lauren rocked side to side. "Tell me you drove all the way up from Boston to deliver me good news. And not fire me."

Ellison climbed the stairs of the porch and opened her arms to give Lauren a hug. "Why do you always assume I'm going to fire you?"

Lauren stepped into her embrace and shrugged. "As much as I love you, I'm also sort of terrified of you. I think that's why this whole dynamic works."

Faith laughed. "She has no idea you're a big pushover, huh?"

Ellison shushed her. "Don't give away my secrets."

Lauren stepped back, looking between them. "So? Do you have news?"

Faith's smile faded. "We do. But maybe it's best if we sit down as a group and talk about our options."

Lauren's heart dropped like a stone. Fuck. Her Hail Mary hadn't worked. Ellison was here to break the news and soften the blow. She had history here after all. Maybe it would hurt less coming from her.

"I'm so sorry," Lauren said, feeling like a failure. "I really thought I'd solved it."

Ellison touched her forearm before pulling back. "Let's find Kathleen."

Lauren nodded. It was better to pull the Band-Aid off all at once, she guessed.

Thea, Carl, and Kathleen were all in the kitchen when they walked in. Carl was wiping down the Berry Festival trophy the town of Casterville had awarded them for Best Dairy Farm. From what Thea had said, they'd won every year since they'd been a part of the festival, and it was sort of a participation award. But they'd all seemed to be touched by it. Kathleen had planned to gift it to Hector after the weekend was over—she wanted him to have something to remember the farm by.

"Ellie?" Kathleen said as she stood to greet them. "What are you doing here?"

"Hi, Kath," Ellison said as she gave her a hug. "Long time no see."

"I'll say," Kathleen said, giving her a once-over. "You are not the flannel and overall wearing girl I remember."

"I grew up a bit," Ellison said with a laugh. "But I'm still the same girl, I promise."

"Good." Kathleen looked pleased. She glanced between the three of them and asked, "So what's going on here?"

Faith spoke first. "We wanted to meet with you to talk about the farm. There've been some developments." She looked at Lauren, and Lauren wanted to shrink on the spot. "But we know you want transparency with Thea and Carl, so we thought you'd like to hear this as a group."

"All right." Kathleen motioned for Carl to pull out the table. Thea reappeared from the other room with a spare chair, and Lauren took the closest seat to Thea available. She was dreading what was coming next, but she figured being near her might help. Or make it worse. She wasn't quite sure.

Ellison looked at Faith before starting. "I know you've had a long few months, and we did our best to help you find the best alternative to selling the farm, but we weren't able to."

Thea took Lauren's hand under the table, and Lauren hazarded a glance in her direction. Thea looked as nervous as Lauren felt, but her hand was comforting nonetheless.

"But luckily for you, where we failed, Lauren succeeded," Faith said with a smile.

"Lauren did what now?" Lauren asked.

Ellison pulled a folder out of the bag by her feet. "Your pitch worked, Lauren. Emerson and Hayley made a cash offer on the farm early this morning."

"They did?" Lauren was in shock.

"They did," Ellison said, looking elated.

"Fuck yes!" Lauren jumped out of her seat with a cheer. She did a celebratory dance before realizing that all eyes were on her. "Oh, I mean, *woo*." She did a tiny raise the roof signal.

Ellison and Faith lost it. Their laughter was contagious, and soon Lauren was wiping her eyes as tears streamed down her face. Happy tears. Relieved tears. All the tears.

"Does anyone want to tell us what's going on here?" Kathleen asked, looking amused.

"You're not losing the house. Or the farm. Well, not all of it. You can still make that awesome cheese and live by the lake, and things will be a little different, but you'll still have your home. And Hector's, too," Lauren said before thinking better of it. She looked at Ellison and Faith for confirmation. "Right?"

"Right," Faith said, and before Lauren knew it she was out of her chair and being spun around, first by Thea and then by Carl. And then by them both.

"Is this really happening? Is this true?" Thea asked, and Lauren kissed her because she could.

"Wait, wait. What's going on? What do you mean?" Kathleen asked with tears in her eyes.

"Lauren had the bright idea to try another avenue after she ran into Hayley Carpenter at the festival the other night. She realized that if you sold the farm, the land that was abutting the Carpenter property would likely be leveled and turned into a development or a yoga retreat or something that would generate foot traffic that neither she nor Emerson wanted. They value their privacy, so Lauren made them an offer—match what was being offered and get the back pastures, the woods, and the milking parlor as a permanent privacy divider to be used in any way that they pleased." Ellison brought out a map of the property circling what was left. "You'll keep ownership of the kitchen and dairy production facilities, the barn, your house, and Hector's as well as the storage sheds and whatever this is."

"The sketchy-ass canoe garage," Lauren said, and Thea laughed as she caressed her cheek.

"But how? I thought the land alone wasn't going to be enough to save us. How if we are selling less land than we'd agreed upon are we still able to keep the house?" Kathleen asked.

Faith looked at Lauren. "Do you want to tell them?"

Lauren nodded, taking Thea's hand as she addressed the room. "To Emerson and Hayley, privacy is priceless. But they're locals at heart, too. And Hayley, in particular, didn't want to lose the tradition and community of Casterville. The Boudreaux farm is an institution around here. I was honest with them—we needed to accept the best offer for the good of your family, and they'd have to match the offer that was on the table, even with less acreage, in order to ensure that their privacy remained intact. And it seems like they didn't hesitate."

Ellison added, "They didn't. And that was in large part due to the work your team did, Lauren." She pulled out screenshots of Claire's proposal. "They loved the idea of using the back pastures as community farming land. They thought the idea was innovative while also giving them a lucrative business option. Save the farms, pay off the land through renting back to the community. They're willing to take on the larger cost to ensure Casterville stays afloat. With one caveat, that is."

"Which is?" Kathleen asked, wiping her eyes.

"Boudreaux farm stays open for as long as you're willing to run it.

And if and when you decide to sell, you offer it to them first," Ellison said.

Kathleen was full-on happy crying now. And so was Carl. Which of course made Lauren start to cry.

Ellison placed another packet on the table as she continued, "Lauren's team drafted a few ideas of how to expand your dairy empire. Claire Moseley at Clear View sampled some of your products, and our colleague Jax, with the help of Claire's partner Shelly, helped formulate a step-by-step outline and timeline as to how that would be possible if you decided to go that route."

"So you could fulfill that dream you and CJ had," Lauren said, "and make Boudreaux a household name outside of just the Casterville area without the hassle of keeping cattle. I'm sure we could get Mr. Killinger to agree to sell his milk directly to you, and you could still work your cheesy magic here."

Kathleen said nothing, but the sobbing hadn't stopped, so Lauren was hopeful that was a good thing.

"Is that a yes? Should I draw up the paperwork?" Faith asked.

"Yes," Kathleen said, and Lauren felt herself being lifted up again.

"You did it," Thea said, her eyes wet, and her cheeks tear-streaked. "You beautiful, perfect creature. You saved the farm."

Lauren wrapped her arms around Thea's neck, still not quite believing it herself. "You're not mad that I kept you out of the loop of my crazy but extraordinarily effective sales approach?"

"Not in the least," Thea said, and nothing else mattered in that moment because Thea was looking at her like she was the most important person in the world.

"So you still love me, then?" Lauren asked, unable to stop smiling.

"You feta believe I do," Thea said, and Lauren fell in love with her all over again.

EPILOGUE

Six months later

"Are you ready?" Thea asked from the bedroom door.

Lauren turned. "How do I look?"

Thea licked her bottom lip as she looked her up and down. "Delicious."

"I was going for sexy yet professional," Lauren replied.

"I mean, you've got the sexy part down," Thea said as she leaned against the doorframe.

"Don't start with that look," Lauren said, wagging her finger at her.

"What look?" Thea feigned innocence.

"The look that says, *We totally have time for a quickie, Lau,*" Lauren said, mimicking her voice.

Thea said with her hand over her heart, "I sound nothing like that."

"You totally do," Lauren argued.

"Agree to disagree," Thea said as she walked toward her.

"Mm-hmm." Lauren didn't believe her for one second. "Then what *was* that look trying to convey?"

Thea stepped in front of her, placing her hands on Lauren's hips. "I was merely thinking that you seemed to go through a lot of trouble to get into this dress. And if perhaps it's not the most appropriate attire for your celebration gala tonight for the opening of Newbridge on the Gardens, then I would be more than happy to help you out of it." Thea's hand found the zipper along Lauren's side. "You know, in the interest of saving time."

Lauren ran her hands along Thea's abdomen and over her chest before looping them behind her neck. "You're going to help me out of my dress to *save* time? Is that what we're going with?"

"It's the least I can do," Thea reasoned as she started to ease down the zipper, one agonizingly slow tooth at a time. She brought her lips to Lauren's neck, sucking on the skin over her pulse point as she said, "I'm trying to be helpful."

Lauren slid her hands into Thea's hair, holding her mouth against her neck as her dress dropped to the floor.

Thea's hands found her naked breasts, and within moments, her nipples were hard and being teased relentlessly.

"We don't have time for this," she said, doing nothing to stop it.

Thea's mouth moved to her earlobe, and Lauren's knees nearly buckled when she sucked and nibbled on it. "You sure?"

Thea dropped a hand to the waistband of her panties while the other moved to cup her ass, holding her flush against her.

"I can make it quick," Thea said as she nuzzled Lauren's jaw before placing a searing kiss to her lips.

"And if I don't want it to be quick?" Lauren asked, panting for breath.

"What would you prefer?" Thea asked against her lips.

"Long, slow, memorable," she said, contradicting herself as she brought her sex closer to Thea's hand.

"I can make it quick *and* memorable. In the interest of time." She slipped her hand into Lauren's panties, causing her to gasp. "Seems like you're ready for both."

Lauren clutched at Thea's hair as she moved her hips against Thea's teasing affections. "You're wearing too many clothes," she managed between kisses.

"Then help me out of them," Thea said, stepping back and leaving Lauren aching for friction.

Lauren pulled off Thea's tank top and unbuckled her belt. She helped her out of her jeans and underwear, pushing her back on the bed as she crawled up onto her lap.

Thea ran her hands up and down the front of Lauren's thighs. "Is this better?"

"Much," Lauren said, though any further banter was cut short when Thea cupped her breasts, palming them possessively.

"Agreed," Thea said, and Lauren closed her eyes, enjoying the sensation of Thea's touch. Her breath caught when she felt Thea's lips and tongue close around one of her nipples. She reached out and ran her fingers through Thea's hair, holding her mouth against her. Lauren rolled her hips, seeking friction, and Thea moaned beneath her.

"I love when you're on top," she said, and Lauren cursed. She wasn't sure she had the self-control to resist Thea's seductions and her touch even if they had somewhere to be soonish.

She pulled back on Thea's hair, breaking the contact between Thea's mouth and her breast, and hating herself for it. "We're going to be really late."

Thea looked up at her with a glint in her eye. "You keep doubting me. I promised you quick and memorable. Let me show you."

"Show me." Lauren rose off Thea's hips just long enough to shimmy out of her panties.

"Come here," Thea said, and Lauren let herself be guided back into her prior position, straddling Thea. "Now kiss me."

Lauren leaned down until she could feel the heat of Thea's naked chest against hers. Thea's mouth pressed against hers, and she moaned at the feeling of Thea's tongue against hers. She opened her mouth to deepen the kiss as Thea's hands settled on her hips, encouraging her to grind.

"Oh God." Lauren was already plenty turned-on from all the earlobe sucking and nipple play, and this verbal foreplay and grinding and kissing were making her sex throb and her clit ache. When Thea's hand shifted off her hip, and her thumb grazed her clit, Lauren cried out, "Yes."

Thea continued to rub against her, while encouraging her to grind over and over again, and Lauren felt herself starting to get too excited too fast. Thea's tongue massaged against hers, and Lauren started to pant.

"There is nothing I prefer more than the sound of your moans and the feeling of your wetness on my skin," Thea said between mind-melting kisses. "Except maybe the taste of your sex on my tongue."

Lauren struggled to control the warning tremors that had begun to course through her. There was something about Thea talking dirty to her that made her sex clench tighter than it ever had before.

Thea kissed away from her lips to nip at her earlobe again as she whispered, "Sit on my face."

Lauren nearly came on the spot. "Fuck."

Thea lifted her up and slid down the bed, and before Lauren knew it, she was on her knees looking down at Thea about to lose all control.

"Good girl," Thea said before lifting her head and connecting her mouth to Lauren's flushed and swollen lips.

Lauren had to bite the inside of her cheek to keep from climaxing at the first well-placed lick. She reached behind herself to find Thea stroking her clit as she pleasured Lauren. Lauren rocked her hips against Thea's mouth as she guided Thea's hand away from herself. "Let me touch you," Lauren panted, arching back to make good on her promise.

Thea moaned, and Lauren loved the wetness she found as she stroked and teased Thea's clit, but soon Thea's mouth was making her see stars. She didn't have time to indulge the way she'd like—she was going to come hard and fast. And she wanted Thea to follow.

She moved her hand away from Thea's clit to grab her wrist and bring her fingers back. "Fuck yourself while I rub your clit and ride your face. Come with me. But hurry." Lauren was half begging.

Thea slipped into herself, and the visual alone made Lauren crash over the precipice and come undone, but Thea's mouth kept her there, suspended in a blissful, erotic agony of tremors and spasms until Thea followed her to orgasm shortly after.

Lauren collapsed forward, bracing herself on the headboard before falling back on the bed next to Thea, out of breath and dizzy with lust. "Jesus Christ, you're good at that."

Thea laughed next to her, her breathing still labored as she said, "And you're my favorite."

Lauren closed her eyes while her breathing returned to normal. Thea wrapped an arm around her waist, rolling to face her. Her touch was warm and comforting. She opened her eyes to find Thea watching her.

"Hi."

"Hi," Thea said.

"So, that happened, huh?"

"Seems so, yup."

Lauren covered her face with her forearm. "You were supposed to help me finish getting dressed."

"And yet here we both are, naked and sated," Thea said as she kissed Lauren's arm. "I'm okay with that if you are."

Lauren put her arm down and smiled at her. "You're sort of super irresistible."

"I learned from the best." Thea gave her a quick kiss before slipping off the bed and pulling her up with her. "Now, as much as

I'd love to lie next to you and start that all over again, we do have a building launch to get to."

"Are Carl and your mom still coming?"

Thea nodded as she kissed her temple. "They're meeting us at the hotel after the ribbon cutting."

"Who's manning the plants?" Lauren asked as she pulled a fresh pair of panties out of her dresser.

"Hector," Thea called out from Lauren's en suite as she freshened up. After Kathleen had agreed to the sale, Emerson and Hayley started converting the land right away. They made good on their promise and set up community farming opportunities for the locals, but in a surprising turn of events, Emerson had taken Lauren's half-serious suggestion that they grow marijuana in what used to be the milking parlor very seriously. So seriously, in fact, that once the permits and papers were filed with the state, they were suddenly in the marijuana business. And with Carl's successful venture into specialized grass growing with their old agriculture teacher Mr. Fuller and the publication of that study in *Journal of Agriculture*, Emerson asked him to help manage the plants. With Hector back on his feet in a new but somewhat limited capacity, he was the perfect assistant to Carl. And now the pot business was booming.

"That's great," Lauren said as she joined her in the bathroom, touching up her smeared lipstick and redoing her hair.

"Who else will be there tonight?" Thea asked as she began brushing her teeth with the toothbrush she kept at Lauren's place.

"All of Gamble and Associates will be in attendance. Avni is bringing Teagan, and Claire and Shelly will be there, but they'll be a little late—they're finalizing their engagement party plans with Courtney over at The Mirage." Lauren puckered her lips in the mirror to make sure she'd applied her makeup evenly. "Oh, and don't forget, my mother gets here tomorrow morning."

Thea spit, rinsing her mouth as she looked up at Lauren in the mirror's reflection before them. She looked a little nervous, which Lauren found adorable.

"Relax. She's going to love you," she reassured her.

"Even though you spent Christmas and New Year's with me?"

"Even though," Lauren said, leaving a lipstick heavy kiss on the side of Thea's temple.

Thea gave her a look as she rubbed it off. "And she's bringing Greg and Lainey, too, right?"

"Yup. The whole threesome family is getting together with your mom and brother, meeting for the first time over brunch tomorrow morning." Lauren squeezed Thea's ass as she walked back into the bedroom. "What could go wrong, right?"

"Right," Thea said, and Lauren loved how much she wanted to make a good impression on her family.

"Don't be nervous. They'll love you as much as I do," she said as she retrieved the discarded dress from the floor and slipped it back on. She hoped that Thea would be thinking about their tryst all night while she wore it. She knew she certainly would be.

"Would you bet the farm on that?" Thea asked, leering as Lauren adjusted the snug fabric over her chest.

"Most definitely."

About the Author

Fiona Riley was born and raised in New England, where she is a medical professional and part-time professor when she isn't bonding with her laptop over words. She went to college in Boston and never left, starting a small business that takes up all of her free time, much to the dismay of her ever patient and lovely wife. When she pulls herself away from her work, she likes to catch up on the contents of her ever-growing DVR or spend time by the ocean with her favorite people.

Fiona's love for writing started at a young age and blossomed after she was published in a poetry competition at the ripe old age of twelve. She wrote lots of short stories and poetry for many years until it was time for college and a "real job." Fiona found herself with a bachelor's, a doctorate, and a day job, but felt like she had stopped nurturing the one relationship that had always made her feel the most complete: artist, dreamer, writer.

A series of bizarre events afforded her with some unexpected extra time, and she found herself reaching for her favorite blue notebook to write, never looking back.

Contact Fiona and check for updates on all her new adventures at:

Twitter: @fionarileyfic
Facebook: "Fiona Riley Fiction"
Website: http://www.fionarileyfiction.com/
Email: fionarileyfiction@gmail.com

Books Available From Bold Strokes Books

A Woman to Treasure by Ali Vali. An ancient scroll isn't the only treasure Levi Montbard finds as she starts her hunt for the truth—all she has to do is prove to Yasmine Hassani that there's more to her than an adventurous soul. (978-1-63555-890-6)

Before. After. Always. by Morgan Lee Miller. Still reeling from her tragic past, Eliza Walsh has sworn off taking risks, until Blake Navarro turns her world right-side up, making her question if falling in love again is worth it. (978-1-63555-845-6)

Bet the Farm by Fiona Riley. Lauren Calloway's luxury real estate sale of the century comes to a screeching halt when dairy farm heiress, and one-night stand, Thea Boudreaux calls her bluff. (978-1-63555-731-2)

Cowgirl by Nance Sparks. The last thing Aren expects is to fall for Carol. Sharing her home is one thing, but sharing her heart means sharing the demons in her past and risking everything to keep Carol safe. (978-1-63555-877-7)

Give In to Me by Elle Spencer. Gabriela Talbot never expected to sleep with her favorite author—certainly not after the scathing review she'd given Whitney Ainsworth's latest book. (978-1-63555-910-1)

Hidden Dreams by Shelley Thrasher. A lethal virus and its resulting vision send Texan Barbara Allan and her lovely guide, Dara, on a journey up Cambodia's Mekong River in search of Barbara's mother's mystifying past. (978-1-63555-856-2)

In the Spotlight by Lesley Davis. For actresses Cole Calder and Eris Whyte, their chance at love runs out fast when a fan's adoration turns to obsession. (978-1-63555-926-2)

Origins by Jen Jensen. Jamis Bachman is pulled into a dangerous mystery that becomes personal when she learns the truth of her origins as a ghost hunter. (978-1-63555-837-1)

Unrivaled by Radclyffe. Zoey Cohen will never accept second place in matters of the heart, even when her rival is a career, and Declan Black has nothing left to give of herself or her heart. (978-1-63679-013-8)

A Fae Tale by Genevieve McCluer. Dovana comes to terms with her changing feelings for her lifelong best friend and fae, Roze. (978-1-63555-918-7)

Accidental Desperados by Lee Lynch. Life is clobbering Berry, Jaudon, and their long romance. The arrival of directionless baby dyke MJ doesn't help. Can they find their passion again—and keep it? (978-1-63555-482-3)

Always Believe by Aimée. Greyson Walsden is pursuing ordination as an Anglican priest. Angela Arlingham doesn't believe in God. Do they follow their vocation or their hearts? (978-1-63555-912-5)

Courage by Jesse J. Thoma. No matter how often Natasha Parsons and Tommy Finch clash on the job, an undeniable attraction simmers just beneath the surface. Can they find the courage to change so love has room to grow? (978-1-63555-802-9)

I Am Chris by R Kent. There's one saving grace to losing everything and moving away. Nobody knows her as Chrissy Taylor. Now Chris can live who he truly is. (978-1-63555-904-0)

The Princess and the Odium by Sam Ledel. Jastyn and Princess Aurelia return to Venostes and join their families in a battle against the dark force to take back their homeland for a chance at a better tomorrow. (978-1-63555-894-4)

The Queen Has a Cold by Jane Kolven. What happens when the heir to the throne isn't a prince or a princess? (978-1-63555-878-4)

The Secret Poet by Georgia Beers. Agreeing to help her brother woo Zoe Blake seemed like a good idea to Morgan Thompson at first…until she realizes she's actually wooing Zoe for herself… (978-1-63555-858-6)

You Again by Aurora Rey. For high school sweethearts Kate Cormier and Sutton Guidry, the second chance might be the only one that matters. (978-1-63555-791-6)

Love's Falling Star by B.D. Grayson. For country music megastar Lochlan Paige, can love conquer her fear of losing the one thing she's worked so hard to protect? (978-1-63555-873-9)

Love's Truth by C.A. Popovich. Can Lynette and Barb make love work when unhealed wounds of betrayed trust and a secret could change everything? (978-1-63555-755-8)

Next Exit Home by Dena Blake. Home may be where the heart is, but for Harper Sims and Addison Foster, is the journey back worth the pain? (978-1-63555-727-5)

Not Broken by Lyn Hemphill. Falling in love is hard enough—even more so for Rose, who's carrying her ex's baby. (978-1-63555-869-2)

The Noble and the Nightingale by Barbara Ann Wright. Two women on opposite sides of empires at war risk all for a chance at love. (978-1-63555-812-8)

What a Tangled Web by Melissa Brayden. Clementine Monroe has the chance to buy the café she's managed for years, but Madison LeGrange swoops in and buys it first. Now Clementine is forced to work for the enemy and ignore her former crush. (978-1-63555-749-7)

A Far Better Thing by JD Wilburn. When needs of her family and wants of her heart clash, Cass Halliburton is faced with the ultimate sacrifice. (978-1-63555-834-0)

Body Language by Renee Roman. When Mika offers to provide Jen erotic tutoring, will sex drive them into a deeper relationship or tear them apart? (978-1-63555-800-5)

Carrie and Hope by Joy Argento. For Carrie and Hope, loss brings them together but secrets and fear may tear them apart. (978-1-63555-827-2)

Detour to Love by Amanda Radley. Celia Scott and Lily Andersen are seatmates on a flight to Tokyo and by turns annoy and fascinate each other. But they're about to realize there's more than one path to love. (978-1-63555-958-3)